"ASIMOV IS ONE OF OUR NATURAL WONDERS AND NATIONAL RESOURCES."

—*St. Louis Post-Dispatch*

TODAY AND TOMORROW AND . . .

No one has done more to explain the mysterious workings of our Universe than Isaac Asimov. No one has done so with greater clarity, charm, and wit. All of these qualities are in ample evidence as the master tackles such questions as:

- What are those mountains doing flying around in space?
- How will the Universe end?
- Can anything move faster than light?
- What are the hidden benefits of space exploration?
- Why may women make the best astronauts?
- Is today's science fiction tomorrow's reality?
- . . . and much, much more in this stunning, entertaining collection of essays that opens the door to . . .

TODAY AND TOMORROW AND . . .

ISAAC ASIMOV IS "OUR MOST AWESOME LIVING WRITING MACHINE. . . . WE SHOULD BE GRATEFUL THAT A PERSON WITH SUCH A GIFT FOR ORGANIZING KNOWLEDGE ALSO POSSESSES SUCH A DRIVE TO SHARE IT!"

—*Dallas Morning News*

TODAY AND TOMORROW AND...

Isaac Asimov

A DELL BOOK

Published by
Dell Publishing Co., Inc.
1 Dag Hammarskjold Plaza
New York, New York 10017

ISBN: 0-440-15933-4

Reprinted by arrangement with
Doubleday & Company, Inc.
Printed in the United States of America
One Previous Dell Edition
New Dell Edition
First printing—December 1983

Grateful acknowledgment is made to the following for permission to reprint the articles included in this book:

"Prediction as a Side Effect," July 1972 issue of the *Boston Review of Arts*. Reprinted by permission.

"The Scientists' Responsibility," reprinted from *Chemical and Engineering News*, Vol. 49, April 19, 1971, pp. 3–7. Copyright © 1971 by the American Chemical Society. Reprinted by permission of the copyright owner.

"The Romance of Mars" by Isaac Asimov, copyright © 1971 by Doubleday & Company, Inc. from the book *Mars, We Love You* by Jane Hipolito and Willis E. McNelly. Reprinted by permission of the publisher.

"Beyond the Ultimate," as "Speed Limit 186,300 M.P.S.," July 1969 issue of *Holiday*. Copyright © 1969 by The Curtis Publishing Company. Reprinted by permission of *Holiday* Magazine.

"The Flying Mountains," July 1972 and "A Literature of Ideas," as "When Aristotle Fails, Try Science Fiction," December 1971 issues of *Intellectual Digest*.

"What Do You Call a Platypus?," March–April 1972 issue of *International Wildlife*. Copyright © 1972 by the National Wildlife Federation. Reprinted by permission.

"No Space For Women?," March 1971 issue of *The Ladies' Home*

To *Michele Tempesta*
the small package
good things come in

CONTENTS

TWO AND TOMORROW

1 • In Space

2 • On Earth

3 • In Science Fiction

THREE AND . . .

INTRODUCTION

I suppose it is almost inevitable that there will be some who will wonder why I bother to collect articles that have already appeared in various magazines. Have they not seen print? Is it just that I am anxious to milk them of every last penny I can collect from readers?

There is no point in denying that income is welcome. I make my living by my pen (my personal pen being an imposing electrical machine) and am pleased to have a book that may earn something for me.

But it goes beyond that. A specific issue of a magazine is short-lived. It struts and frets its hour upon the stage, and then is heard no more.* People have to hunt through the dusty confines of a second-hand bookstore if, for any reason, they want an old magazine.

And if they find it, and if it is an article of mine they are looking for, they will find it surrounded by other items and, in the case of some magazines, interrupted by copious advertisements.

But if I take all my articles and put them together in a book (supposing they are worth preserving, which I carelessly assume to be so in my own case) I have something which is more long-lived and which is concentrated me, without dilution or intrusion. The reader who wants and enjoys my articles is therefore bound to be pleased.

This about exhausts the reasons why I collect my monthly articles from *The Magazine of Fantasy and Science Fiction*. It does not, however, exhaust the reasons why I have prepared *this* book, which contains articles from magazines other than that one.

In *F&SF*, my articles appear exactly as I write them, except for corrections of typos. My titles are invariably kept exactly as I make them up, too. Not so in the case of

* Hey, that's a good sentence. I'm glad I made it up.

other magazines. In other magazines, where space is a problem, hasty surgery may be performed on my article to make room for an advertisement of some sort.

Furthermore, whereas in *F&SF*, the editor knows the readers know me and are willing to follow me through all my quirks and vagaries, the editors of other magazines have no such security. There is a certain mistrust of my articles by those other editors, a suspicion that the reader will not read it unless grabbed by the throat and made to.

Consequently, an editor sometimes searches through the article for the single most dramatic sentence and starts with that, making whatever other changes are required to hide the dislocation (and calling on me to do it in detail).

There is also the matter of style. I tend to be informal, chatty, colloquial. Partly it is a matter of taste; partly it is a mistrust of the literary. This tends to make editors nervous. If I quote from Shakespeare's *Macbeth* without acknowledgment and then insert a footnote in which I actually seem to take credit for it (as I did earlier in this introduction), they will surely cut out the "Hey" as too colloquial and very probably cut out the entire footnote, afraid that the reader will not get the joke.

Finally, there is the matter of the title. I sometimes tend to the realistic. If my article is written shortly before the first landing on the Moon and deals with this lunar landing, I call it, in all honesty, "The Lunar Landing." The editor, seeking punch, changes that to "The Moon Could Answer the Riddle of Life"—which lures the reader on to read the article. But since it causes him to wade through a mess of stuff on the lunar landing before he gets to the short bit I devote to the matter of the riddle of life, he is apt to feel cheated.

Or sometimes *I* decide to be dramatic. If I discuss the possibility of speeds greater than that of light, I entitle the article "Beyond the Ultimate," giving it a fine flavor of paradox. The editor, however, fearing that the reader will not get the meaning and will therefore not look at the article, entitles it "Speed Limit, 186,300 M.P.S." which lacks drama altogether.

Don't get me wrong, now. I understand and sympathize with the difficulties of editors. I understand that they can't make space where there isn't any. I understand that they must catch the attention of a heterogeneous mass of readers. Therefore I very rarely quibble. I make the changes they ask of me. I cut. I slash, I alter. And I never complain about the titles they choose to put upon the articles.

In fact, sometimes they actually improve on me. I'll admit that, too.

I wrote an article on my reasons for believing there should be women astronauts. I entitled it, prosaically, "Ladies in Space." The editor changed that title to "No Space for Women?" and, in my opinion, improved it out of all recognition.

Sometimes, too, I am caught in errors. In preparing my essay "The Flying Mountains" I read my references as saying that Mare Imbrium had been formed 700 million years ago. I therefore said so in the article, building a chain of argument upon it. At the last minute, the cute little girl in charge of checking factual statements (they're always girls, somehow) came to my office in a panic because she read the reference as saying that Mare Imbrium had been formed 700 million years after the formation of the Moon—which means nearly 4,000 million years ago.

I was stupefied when I went over the reference and found she was right. With my ears red-hot, I quickly revised the article. What a disaster that would have been if they had not back-stopped me so efficiently.

So I am grateful to one and all. Honest!

Just the same, I want my articles in this book, not only because I want them all in one readily available place with no extraneous intrusions; but because I want my own titles back on them, and my own order of exposition, and my own style—except that I insist on the right to retain improvements.

One word of warning, though. The articles have been written at different times for different audiences. There is, therefore, some overlapping here and there. Encouraged by the Erudite Copyreader, I have removed some particularly egregious examples, but others remain. Forgive me.

ISAAC ASIMOV

New York, N.Y.
September 1972

ONE

TODAY

1 · IN BIOLOGY

WHAT DO YOU CALL A PLATYPUS?

In 1800, a stuffed animal arrived in England from the newly discovered continent of Australia.

The continent had already been the source of plants and animals never seen before—but this one was ridiculous. It was nearly two feet long, and had a dense coating of hair. It also had a flat rubbery bill, webbed feet, a broad flat tail, and a spur on each hind ankle that was clearly intended to secrete poison. What's more, under the tail was a single opening.

Zoologists stared at the thing in disbelief. Hair like a mammal! Bill and feet like an aquatic bird! Poison spurs like a snake! A single opening in the rear as though it laid eggs!

There was an explosion of anger. The thing was a hoax. Some unfunny jokester in Australia, taking advantage of the distance and strangeness of the continent, had stitched together parts of widely different creatures and was intent on making fools of innocent zoologists in England.

Yet the skin seemed to hang together. There were no signs of artificial joining. Was it or was it not a hoax? And if it wasn't a hoax, was it a mammal with reptilian characteristics, or a reptile with mammalian characteristics, or was it partly bird, or *what?*

The discussion went on heatedly for decades. Even the name emphasized the ways in which it didn't seem like a mammal despite its hair. One early name was *Platypus anatinus* which is Graeco-Latin for "Flat-foot, ducklike." Unfortunately, the term, platypus, had already been applied to a type of beetle and there must be no duplications in scientific names. It therefore received another name, *Ornithorhynchus paradoxus*, which means "Bird-beak, paradoxical."

Slowly, however, zoologists had to fall into line and admit that the creature was real and not a hoax, however upsetting it might be to zoological notions. For one thing, there were increasingly reliable reports from people in Australia who caught glimpses of the creature alive. The *paradoxus* was dropped and the scientific name is now *Ornithorhynchus anatinus.*

To the general public, however, it is the "duckbill platypus," or even just the duckbill, the queerest mammal (assuming it is a mammal) in the world.

When specimens were received in such condition as to make it possible to study the internal organs, it appeared that the heart was just like those of mammals and not at all like those of reptiles. The egg-forming machinery in the female, however, was not at all like those of mammals, but like those of birds or reptiles. It seemed really and truly to be an egg-layer.

It wasn't till 1884, however, that the actual eggs laid by a creature with hair were found. Such creatures included not only the platypus, but another Australian species, the spiny anteater. That was worth an excited announcement. A group of British scientists were meeting in Montreal at the time, and the egg-discoverer, W. H. Caldwell, sent them a cable to announce the finding.

It wasn't till the twentieth century that the intimate life of the duckbill came to be known. It is an aquatic animal, living in Australian fresh water at a wide variety of temperatures—from tropical streams at sea level to cold lakes at an elevation of a mile.

The duckbill is well adapted to its aquatic life, with its dense fur, its flat tail, and its webbed feet. Its bill has nothing really in common with that of the duck, however. The nostrils are differently located and the platypus bill is different in structure, rubbery rather than duckishly horny. It serves the same function as the duck's bill, however, so it has been shaped similarly by the pressures of natural selection.

The water in which the duckbill lives is invariably muddy at the bottom and it is in this mud that the duckbill roots for its food supply. The bill, ridged with horny plates, is used as a sieve, dredging about sensitively in the mud, filtering out the shrimps, earthworms, tadpoles and other small creatures that serve it as food.

When the time comes for the female platypus to produce young, she builds a special burrow, which she lines with grass and carefully plugs. She then lays two eggs, each about three quarters of an inch in diameter and surrounded by a translucent, horny shell.

These the mother platypus places between her tail and abdomen and curls up about them. It takes two weeks for the young to hatch out. The new-born duckbills have teeth and very short bills, so that they are much less "birdlike" than the adults. They feed on milk. The mother has no nipples, but milk oozes out of pore openings in the abdomen and the young lick the area and are nourished in this way. As they grow, the bills become larger and the teeth fall out.

Yet despite everything zoologists learned about the duckbills, they never seemed entirely certain as to where to place them in the table of animal classification. On the whole, the decision was made because of hair and milk. In all the world, only mammals have true hair and only mammals produce true milk. The duckbill and spiny anteater have hair and produce milk, so they have been classified as mammals.

Just the same, they are placed in a very special position. All the mammals are divided into two subclasses. In one of these subclasses ("Prototheria" or "first-beasts") are the duckbill and five species of the spiny anteater. In the other ("Theria" or just "beasts") are all the other 4,231 known living species of mammals.

But all this is the result of judging only living species of mammals. Suppose we could study extinct species as well. Would that help us decide on the place of the platypus? Would it cause us to confirm our decision—or change it?

Fossil remnants exist of mammals and reptiles of the far past, but these remnants are almost entirely of bones and teeth. Bones and teeth give us interesting information but they can't tell us everything.

For instance, is there any way of telling, from bones and teeth alone, whether an extinct creature is a reptile or a mammal?

Well, all living reptiles have their legs splayed out so that the upper part above the knee is horizontal (assuming they have legs at all). All mammals, on the other hand, have legs that are vertical all the way down. Again, reptiles have teeth that all look more or less alike, while mammals have teeth that have different shapes, with sharp incisors in front, flat molars in back, and conical incisors and premolars in between.

As it happens, there are certain extinct creatures, to which have been given the name "therapsids," which have their leg bones vertical and their teeth differentiated just as in the case of mammals. —And yet they are considered reptiles and not mammals. Why? Because there is another bony difference to be considered.

In living mammals, the lower jaw contains a single bone; in reptiles, it is made up of a number of bones. The therapsid lower jaw is made up of seven bones and because of that those creatures are classified as reptiles. And yet in the therapsid lower jaw, the one bone making up the central portion of the lower jaw is by far the largest. The other six bones, three on each side, are crowded into the rear angle of the jaw.

There seems no question, then, that if the therapsids are reptiles they are nevertheless well along the pathway toward mammals.

But how far along the pathway are they? For instance, did they have hair? It might seem that it would be impossible to tell whether an extinct animal had hair or not just from the bones, but let's see—

Hair is an insulating device. It keeps body heat from being lost too rapidly. Reptiles keep their body temperature at about that of the outside environment. They don't have to be concerned over loss of heat and hair would be of no use to them.

Mammals, however, maintain their internal temperature at nearly 100° F. regardless of the outside temperature; they are "warm-blooded." This gives them the great advantage of remaining agile and active in cold weather, when the chilled reptile is sluggish. But then the mammal must prevent heat loss by means of a hairy covering. (Birds, which also are warm-blooded, use feathers as an insulating device.)

With that in mind, let's consider the bones. In reptiles, the nostrils open into the mouth just behind the teeth. This means that reptiles can only breathe with their mouths empty. When they are biting or chewing, breathing must stop. This doesn't bother a reptile much, for it can suspend its need for oxygen for considerable periods.

Mammals, however, must use oxygen in their tissues constantly, in order to keep the chemical reactions going that serve to keep their body temperature high. The oxygen supply must not be cut off for more than very short intervals. Consequently mammals have developed a bony palate, a roof to the mouth. When they breathe, air is led above the mouth to the throat. This means they can continue breathing while they bite and chew. It is only when they are actually in the act of swallowing that the breath is cut off and this is only a matter of a couple of seconds at a time.

The later therapsid species had, as it happened, a palate. If they had a palate, it seems a fair deduction that they needed an uninterrupted supply of oxygen that makes it look as though they were warm-blooded. And if they were warm-blooded, then very likely they had hair, too.

The conclusion, drawn from the bones alone, would seem to be that some of the later therapsids had hair, even though, judging by their jawbones, they were still reptiles.

The thought of hairy reptiles is astonishing. But that is only because the accident of evolution seems to have wiped out the intermediate forms. The only therapsids alive seem to be those that have developed *all* the mammalian characteristics, so that we call them mammals. The only reptiles alive are those that developed *none* of the mammalian characteristics.

Those therapsids that developed some but not others, seem to be extinct.

Only the duckbill and the spiny anteater remain near the border line. They have developed the hair and the milk and the single-boned lower jaw and the four-chambered heart, but not the nipples or the ability to bring forth live young.

For all we know, some of the extinct therapsids, while still having their many-boned lower jaw (which is why we call them reptiles instead of mammals), may have developed even beyond the duckbill in other ways. Perhaps some late therapsids had nipples and brought forth living young. We can't tell from the bones alone.

If we had a complete record of the therapsids, flesh and blood, as well as teeth and bone, we might decide that the duckbill was on the therapsid side of the line and not on the mammalian side. —Or are there any other pieces of evidence that can be brought into play?

An American zoologist, Giles T. MacIntyre, of Queens College, has taken up the matter of the trigeminal nerve, which leads from the jaw muscles to the brain.

In all reptiles, without exception, the trigeminal nerve passes through the skull at a point that lies between two of the bones making up the skull. In all mammals that bring forth living young, without exception, the nerve actually passes *through* a particular skull bone.

Suppose we ignore all the matter of hair and milk and eggs, and just consider the trigeminal nerve. In the duckbill, does the nerve pass through a bone, or between two bones? It has seemed in the past that the nerve passed through a bone and that put the duckbill on the mammalian side of the dividing line.

Not so, says MacIntyre. The study of the trigeminal nerve was made in adult duckbills, where the skull bones are fused together and the boundaries are hard to make out. In young duckbills, the skull bones are more clearly separated and in them it can be seen, MacIntyre says, that the trigeminal nerve goes between two bones.

In that case, there is a new respect in which the duckbill falls on the reptilian side of the line and MacIntyre thinks it ought not to be considered a mammal, but as a surviving species of the otherwise long-extinct therapsid line.

And so, a hundred seventy years after zoologists began to puzzle out the queer mixture of characteristics that go to make up the duckbill platypus—there is still argument as to what to call it.

Is the duckbill platypus a mammal? A reptile? Or just a duckbill platypus?

THE RHYTHM OF DAY AND NIGHT

Sherlock Holmes looked at the objects placed before him and then turned his glance keenly on the photographs.

Inspector Lestrade said, "These are the clues, Holmes. He died at one-fifteen P.M., struck from behind by a blunt instrument, while he was taking color photographs in the garden. He died at once. And the only person with a motive for that death has a cast-iron alibi for one-fifteen P.M."

"And how do you know the victim died at one-fifteen P.M.?"

"His wristwatch was broken by one of the blows and its hands are jammed at that point."

"I see," said Holmes. "And these photographs were taken at the time of the murder?"

"The camera was found under the crumpled body. We had the pictures developed, hoping it would reveal the murderer, but as you see"—and the little inspector grimaced in disgust—"they show only the garden."

"On the contrary," said Holmes, "they show much more than that. They show that the time of death was after two P.M. The murderer, having killed his victim, undoubtedly turned the wristwatch back an hour and then smashed it. Your suspect's alibi is worthless."

Inspector Lestrade smiled. "Come, now, Mr. Holmes. You have made lucky guesses in the past but surely you can't tell time from a garden."

"It is quite simple to do so, Lestrade. This garden is an accurate clock. You will note, inspector, that the scarlet pimpernels are closed but that the hawkbits are open. That places the time quite accurately between two and three

SOURCE: "The Rhythm of Day and Night" appeared in *National Wildlife* as "Hidden Rhythms That Make Nature's Clock Tick" December–January 1972.

P.M. I assure you that you can rely on your flowers. Whatever the wristwatch says, the victim was alive at two P.M."

No, you needn't look through your collected tales of Sherlock Holmes. You won't find the above passage because I just made it up, but it is accurate enough. That indefatigable botanist Carl Linnaeus made a list, over two centuries ago, of the times of opening and closing of flowers. Here it is:

6 A.M.	Spotted Cat's Ear opens
7 A.M.	African Marigold opens
8 A.M.	Mouse Ear Hawkweed opens
9 A.M.	Prickly Sowthistle closes
10 A.M.	Common Nipple Wort closes
11 A.M.	Star of Bethlehem opens
12 N.	Passion Flower opens
1 P.M.	Childing Pink closes
2 P.M.	Scarlet Pimpernel closes
3 P.M.	Hawkbit closes
4 P.M.	Small Bindweed closes
5 P.M.	White Water Lily closes
6 P.M.	Evening Primrose opens

It is quite possible to plant a garden in the shape of the face of a clock with appropriate flowers planted at the site of the twelve numbers, and in nineteenth-century Europe this was sometimes done. On a sunny day, by merely noting which flowers were open and which closed, the time could be told, at a glance, to within half an hour.

But how do flowers know what time it is?

Ah, if we but knew the answer, we'd know a great deal, for all living things know what time it is. We do ourselves, even in the absence of all mechanical aids, whether we realize it or not, for we live by the rhythms of nature, as do all other species.

We can't help but be aware of the rhythms. The rhythm of spring and autumn, sowing and harvest, has been life and death to mankind for thousands of years. We know the rhythm of our stomachs which tell us when it is mealtime without need for a clock.

Yet of all the rhythms in nature, surely the most pronounced and noticeable is the steady alternation of day and night. Plants and animals have had to adapt to it over the eons. Leaves must open to the sun if plants are to live and might as well furl or droop at night. Animals benefit by rest and lowered activity at night, if they hunt or forage by day; or by day, if they prowl by night.

The daily rhythm is not entirely expressed in the crude alternation of rest and activity, but is reflected in much more subtle changes. Plant leaves rise and fall in a slow rhythm that repeats itself day after day; the rate of cell division in various microorganisms rises and falls in a twenty-four-hour rhythm; the rate of egg hatching among moths does the same as does the rate of cortical hormone secretion in rats. In human beings, temperature rises and falls a degree or two in a daily cycle; as does blood pressure, hormone and enzyme activity, and many another factor.

Is this because creatures simply follow the waxing and waning of light? Is it just a matter of convenience to sleep at night or wake by day? Could they establish any other rhythm if they cared to make the effort?

If that were so, it might be that if we lived somewhere where there was neither day nor night, and in isolation, so that there was no social pressure, we could do precisely as we chose and establish whatever rhythm we wished.

To test this men and women have lived for months at a time in the darkness of caves. During this time, they had no idea whether it was night or day outside and, since they had no clocks, soon lost all track of time. Indeed, they ate and slept rather erratically. However, they also noted their temperature, pulse, blood pressure, brain waves and sent these and other measurements to the surface, where observers kept track of them in connection with time. It turned out that however confused the cave-dwellers were, their body rhythm was not. The rhythm remained stubbornly at a period of about a day through all the stay in the cave.

Actually, in the absence of the physical guideline of day–night alternation, the rhythm was a bit longer than a day —24½ hours. Perhaps that makes sense. Before any organism could become a land animal it had to have ancestors who for ages lived in the tidal region between sea and land. For millions of years, two rhythms counted. In addition to the light-dark alternation, the two together making 24 hours, there was the rise and fall of the tides, which depended on the rotation of the Earth, and also on the motion of the Moon during that rotation. The latter effect lengthened the rhythm slightly so that there were two high tides and two low tides every 25 hours.

By establishing a basic rhythm of 24½ hours, some aspects of life might be adjusted to the 24-hour cycle of light and dark, and others to the 25-hour cycle of the tides. Land organisms have gone over wholly to the light-dark cycle but in its absence, the older life in the tidal region seems to reassert itself.

Thus the leaves of plants rise and fall in a day-long rhythm to match the coming and going of the sun. This is made apparent by time-lapse photography. Seedlings grown in darkness showed no such cycle, but the potentiality was there. One exposure to light—one only—was enough to convert that potentiality into actuality. The rhythm then began, and continued even if the light were cut off again. From plant to plant the exact period of rhythm varied—anywhere from 24 to 26 hours in the absence of light—but 24 hours with the help of the regulating effect of the Sun.

A 20-hour cycle could be established if artificial light were used on a 10-hour-on and 10-hour-off cycle. The leaves would rise and fall with the light, but as soon as the light were turned off altogether, the about-24-hour-rhythm re-established itself.

This daily rhythm, even in the absence of outside hints, permeates all life and Dr. Franz Halberg of the University of Minnesota named it "circulation rhythm" from the Latin *circa dies*, meaning "about a day." The circadian rhythm is the chief component of what we might call the "biological clock."

The biological clock is not absolutely inflexible. It does not start at the same moment for everybody. There are "morning persons" who rise cheerfully with the lark and grow sleepy in the evening; and "night persons" who drag out of bed late in the morning, but who are lively and bright at midnight. Their chemistry differs, not merely their habits. The body temperature that begins to rise at dawn in the morning person, may not rise till 10 A.M. in the night person. (And trouble really arises when a morning person marries a night person.)

The biological clock can be adjusted. The man with the night job, who must be active all night and sleep all day, has trouble to begin with. Still, if he sticks it out for a while, his rhythm alters. His temperature is rising and his hormones are flooding just when the temperature of other people is falling and the hormones ebbing.

There is a limit to how far one can tamper with the biological clock, however. This is shown in experiments with rat mothers, which are actively involved with their litters during a 12-hour light period and neglect them during the 12-hour period of darkness. Even if the light is kept on perpetually, the rats maintain their 24-hour circadian rhythm.

If the rhythm is made 12-hour in nature, with the lights on for 6 hours and off for 6 hours, the rats try to follow the guidance of light and dark for a while, but can't maintain that for long. They fall back on the circadian rhythm, nurturing their litters in alternate light periods.

If the rhythm is 16-hours, with light for 8 hours and darkness for 8 hours, that rhythm cannot be so easily fitted into the circadian period. The rat mothers grow disorganized. Their body clocks do not adjust.

Even when adjustments are possible, they seem to involve a price. Suppose, for instance, you take a group of mice and allow them all to live on a schedule of 12 hours light and 12 hours darkness. This fits in with their circadian rhythm and they get along famously. But suppose that at a certain time, you allow either the light cycle or the dark cycle to continue 24 hours and then start alternating again. The circadian rhythm continues, but now it is night when the rat's biological clock says it is day, and day when it says it is night. With time, the mouse makes the adjustment. The rhythm in blood pressure, temperature, hormone secretion all shifts and then continues normally. If you make another inversion, the mice adjust again.

Suppose, next, you take two groups of mice and allow one group to live in a steady circadian rhythm without shifts, while the second group, after doing so for a while, begin to experience shifts—one a week.

It turned out in such an experiment that the mice that experienced no shifts lived an average of 94.5 weeks, but that the mice that experienced weekly shifts lived an average of 88.6 weeks. It would seem that the effort of adjusting the biological clock was sufficiently debilitating to decrease the life-span by 6 per cent.

This is by no means a purely theoretical matter. In nature, the Earth's rotation remains steady and the alternation of day and night remains constant and beyond human interference—but only if you remain in the same spot on Earth, or only shift north and south.

If you travel east or west for long distances and quite rapidly, however, you change the time of day. If you travel to Japan by speedy jet, you might land at a time when all the Japanese were eating lunch but when your own biological clock was announcing it was time to be in bed. After all, when it is 10 P.M. in New York, it is noon in Tokyo. The jet-age traveler will have difficulty matching his activity to that of the at-home people surrounding him. If he forces himself to do so, he will be tired and inefficient; he will suffer from "jet fatigue."

But what about jet pilots who are forever switching across the time zones. Does this continual interference with their circadian rhythms affect their efficiency? Their health? Their life-span eventually, perhaps? Recommendations are being made now to allow pilots rest time between flights; the length of rest being determined by the number of time zones crossed after a particular flight.

Even when the circadian rhythm is allowed to run undisturbed, a creature is not the same at different points in the rhythm. As the chemical changes pulse up and down, so does sensitivity to stimuli, whether physical or chemical. When a rat is at a point in its rhythm where it is naturally somnolent, it is dull-sensed and less reactive to noise. A loud noise will affect it little. At the point in its rhythm when it is active and on the alert, its hearing is sharper and its reaction intensity more extreme. In this latter case, the same loud noise which scarcely bothered it before, may throw it into a frenzy that can lead to convulsions and death.

Similarly, a rat's sensitivity to X-ray treatment varies with the circadian rhythm, and a dose that would merely make it sick at one time will kill it at another. A dose of amphetamine that will kill 78 per cent of the test animals at one time of day will kill only 8 per cent at another.

Clearly, this has important applications to medicine. It may well be advisable to plot in considerable detail the circadian rhythm of every human being who requires medication. By applying the medication at an appropriate time by the biological clock, a smaller dose might be required and side effects might be rendered less dangerous.

What keeps the biological clock so well regulated? The alternation of light and dark is surely of prime importance; but is the clock regulated by way of the eyes alone? Rats blinded at birth maintain their circadian rhythms just as accurately as do normal rats. Could it be that the alternation of light and dark somehow influences some portion of the brain directly.

Suspicion in this respect falls upon the pineal gland, a small structure in the brain. In some reptiles the pineal gland is particularly well developed and seems to be similar in structure to the eye. It is most developed in the tuatara, the last surviving species of the reptilian order, Rhynchocephalia. This lizardlike reptile (but *not* a lizard) survives only on some small islands off New Zealand, where it is now rigorously protected. The "pineal eye," a skin-covered patch on top of its skull, is particularly prominent for about six months after birth, and is definitely sensitive to light.

The pineal gland does not "see" in the ordinary sense of the word, but it may produce some chemical in rising and falling rhythm in response to the coming and going of light, and thus may regulate the biological clock.

But then how does the pineal gland work in mammals where it is no longer located just under the skin at the top of the head but is buried deep in the center of the brain? Can light somehow still stimulate it? Or is it something else?

After all, circadian rhythms, once established, continue correctly even in continuous light or in continuous darkness. Is there something other than light, which has a similar rhythm?

There are speculations that cosmic rays might be the answer, or rather the radiation within the atmosphere produced by cosmic ray impingement. Cosmic rays approach Earth from all directions evenly and at all times of day and night evenly, but they don't quite reach us evenly. They are affected by Earth's magnetic field, which is, in turn, affected by the streams of particles reaching Earth from the Sun (the "solar wind"). This means that cosmic radiation tends to rise and fall in a circadian rhythm of its own. Could this be the regulator, where the pineal gland is far within the brain, shielded from light but not from the penetrating cosmic radiation?

There is another question, too. Granted that the biological clock is regulated by something (light, cosmic rays, something else) through some organ (the pineal gland, the pituitary gland, something else)—is the biological clock itself something that can be identified? Is there some chemical reaction in the body which rises and falls in a circadian rhythm and which controls all the other rhythms of temperature, blood pressure, hormone secretion and everything else? Is there some "master reaction" which we can tab as *the* biological clock?

If so, it has not yet been found.

All we can say is that the biological clock exists and is of key importance in all organisms. —But what it is, where it is, how it is set in motion, how it is regulated—we still don't know.

2 · *IN ASTRONOMY*

THE SUN VANISHES

On Saturday, March 7, 1970, Americans by the millions, in happy excitement, flocked to see a sight that was once the most fearful phenomenon in Nature—for there was a time when men thought it signified the possible end of all life. So fearful was the sight that no one prior to modern times bothered to record the fact that it was also by all odds the most beautiful vision the sky could ever afford us.

The phenomenon is the eclipse of the Sun, the slow vanishing of that body from its post in the sky, the coming of night when no night should be.

Primitive (and not so primitive) men would come howling into the streets and fields in times gone by, wildly beating pans or drums, shooting arrows into the sky, doing anything that might serve to frighten the monster that seemed to be devouring the Sun. Only when the monster left and the Sun reappeared, apparently unharmed, could men relax once more.

Of course it was necessary to be ever prepared, for who could tell when an eclipse might come. A Chinese legend reports that in very ancient times, an eclipse came to the capital without warning because the royal astronomers, Hsi and Ho, preferred to be drunk rather than at work. After the emperor had gotten over his imperial fright at the unexpected event, the suddenly sober astronomers were led off to execution, and all agreed it was richly deserved.

Farther west, in ancient times, the Sun's disc was encroached upon by darkness, little by little, over a field of battle in Asia Minor. The armies of Lydia on the west and Media on the east stopped fighting and peered at the vanishing Sun. The few minutes of eclipse-night came, and when it passed, the opposing generals could do only one thing. They signed a treaty of peace and went home. Lydia and Media never fought again, for they knew the anger of the gods when they saw it.

As it happens, modern astronomers can calculate the date of the eclipse of the Sun that took place in Asia Minor at about the time in question. It was on May 28, 585 B.C., so that the battle which came to a premature and permanent end is the earliest earthly event in all history that can be pinned down to an exact day.

The "monster" that devours the Sun is, of course, the Moon. In its pathway across the sky, the Moon occasionally moves in front of the Sun and obscures its light. In doing so, it displays the effect of an extraordinary coincidence. The Sun is just 400 times as wide as the Moon is, and it is also just 400 times as distant from us as the moon is. The result is that size and distance cancel each other and both bodies appear to be almost exactly the same size in our sky.

Therefore, when the Moon moves squarely in front of the Sun, it neatly covers it. From no other planet can any satellite be seen to fit so perfectly over the Sun. On Earth itself, the Moon was closer millions of years ago and seemed larger; while millions of years from now it will be farther and seem smaller.

There is no astronomical reason why distance and size should match so as to give us the chance of a perfect eclipse, just in the place and time of man's existence. It is pure chance, but a very lucky chance too, for it is the perfect fit that makes the eclipse the gorgeous spectacle it is.

It seems a shame to carp, but chance might have served us even better. If the Moon and Sun followed the same path across the sky, then the Moon would move in front of the Sun once each month. There would be at least twelve, and sometimes thirteen, eclipses of the Sun each year.

Unfortunately, the two paths are tilted, one to the other. The Moon usually passes the Sun sufficiently higher in the sky, or sufficiently lower, to miss it altogether as viewed from the Earth. Only when the Moon passes the Sun near the point of path-intersection is there an eclipse.

This means there can only be five eclipses of the Sun,

at most, in any given year. In some years, there are only two. What's more, most of these eclipses aren't total—the Moon doesn't pass squarely in front of the Sun. We will find an actual total eclipse somewhere on earth only once every eighteen months, on the average.

The Moon, intercepting sunlight, casts a shadow, as anything else would. Passing between the Sun and the Earth, the Moon casts that shadow upon our planet. People standing on Earth's surface and finding themselves in the Moon's shadow, experience the total eclipse and the coming of a brief period of night.

But the Moon's shadow narrows with distance and by the time it reaches Earth's surface, it is shrunken nearly to a point. The shadow, which is 2,100 miles across in the neighborhood of the Moon, is down to 150 miles across, at best, at the surface of the Earth. That means only a tiny part of the Earth can experience a total eclipse at any one time.

Suppose you were on Earth's surface someplace where the Moon was squarely over the Sun so that you were standing in a total eclipse. Someone else standing a couple of hundred miles away would see past one edge of the Moon and catch a sliver of Sun. He would be seeing only a "partial eclipse." The farther away an observer was, the farther he'd see around the edge of the Moon and the more Sun would be visible. If he were a few thousand miles away, he wouldn't see the Moon's disc cover any part of the Sun and there would be no eclipse at all for him.

What counts, then, is not just the fact that there is an eclipse, but where along the Earth's surface the Moon's narrow shadow traces out a line. This can be almost anywhere, but fortunately astronomers can calculate where that line will fall, and will travel to the ends of the earth to be at those spots where totality will occur. (Scientists have gained much knowledge from their laborious studies of eclipses. Most spectacularly a French astronomer Pierre Janssen studying an eclipse in India in 1868 discovered a new element, helium, which was only discovered on Earth thirty years later.)

For non-travelers, the wait can be long—much longer than a lifetime, alas. A particular spot on Earth must wait 360 years (on the average) between total eclipses.

Since fully 70 per cent of the Earth's surface is ocean, and since most of its land surface is desert, mountain, or jungle; most eclipses trace their paths over trackless wastes and are seen by few. Not so the eclipse of March 7, 1970, which moved over areas where it was conveniently reached by up to sixty million Americans.

The path of totality started in the mid-Pacific, moved eastward, then veered north to cross Mexico at its narrowest point. It then moved across northern Florida, missing Tallahassee by a couple of miles, and next crossed the coastal Southeast, moving over Savannah, Charleston, and Norfolk. It was just offshore in more northerly regions, but passed across Nantucket Island, then along the length of Nova Scotia and across eastern Newfoundland.

During a period of several hours there was a total eclipse over one part or another of the path traced by the shadow. In any one place, however, the shadow came and went in the space of a few minutes. Seven minutes is about the record length for any total eclipse, but in Savannah, Georgia, for instance, this eclipse lasted only 2.9 minutes from a little before 1:23 P.M. to a little after 1:25 P.M.

While it is the time of totality that is the real period of awe and beauty, the excitement begins when the Moon's disc first encroaches upon the shining circle of the Sun. Those who intend to watch an eclipse had better be in place, then, about an hour before the time of totality.

Since ordinarily (barring clouds and other obstructions) we see the Sun as an invariably perfect circle of blazing light, there is a certain wonder in seeing a small black "bite" being taken out of it on one side. That "bite" is the only visible portion of the Moon. It is the edge of the Moon that shows up black against the brightness of the Sun, while the rest of the Moon is invisible against the scattered blue light of the sky.

Little by little, as the Moon moves across the face of the Sun, more of its blackness grows visible and more of the Sun is covered.

There is a natural desire to watch this happen, but resist the impulse to do so without extreme caution. To look at the Sun directly for even a short period of time is to risk serious damage to the eye.

One can dim the brightness of the Sun by using smoked glass or exposed film. Brief looks at the Sun through such objects are not overly dangerous. However, it is almost impossible to resist the temptation of continuing to look and if you do that, then the protection of smoked glass is insufficient. There is a particular temptation to use crossed strips of Polaroid film from dark glasses. These so darken the Sun and seem so "modern" that the user is lulled into a feeling of security. However, the Polaroid does not block out much of the infrared radiation and that can do damage.

By all means, then, use an indirect means of viewing the Sun. That can be arranged easily enough. All you need are two pieces of cardboard. In one of the pieces punch a small hole about an eighth of an inch across. That will serve as a "pinhole camera." Let the Sun shine through that hole and place the second cardboard under it. An image of the Sun will appear on the white cardboard with a piece bitten out of it, that piece corresponding to the encroachment of the Moon's disc.

By increasing the distance of the second piece of cardboard from the first, you will make the Sun's image larger and dimmer. Keep it fairly dim and you will be able to watch the growing eclipse in full detail and comfort and without the slightest scrap of danger.

In fact, if you are at a place and at a time of the year where trees in full leaf are about, they would offer a more interesting sight than that of any artificial viewer. The interstices between the leaves act as numerous pinhole cameras and the sunlight on the ground is made up of a series of overlapping, shifting circles, each an image of the Sun. During the progress of the eclipse, each circle is bitten off at one side. The bite grows larger and eventually there are shifting, wavering crescents on the ground. Place a piece of white cardboard there and you'll see it beautifully.

As the eclipse progresses, there comes a stage where it is the landscape, not the sun, that you want to watch. Until the Sun is half covered, no great diminution in its light is to be noticed. After that, you will become aware of dimming. By the time that four fifths of the Sun is covered and only a thin crescent remains, we are getting light from only the edge of the Sun and it is distinctly redder than we are accustomed to.

The ruddy paleness of the fading light now seems to

affect the animal world. All the voluntary noises of life come to a halt. Birds that have been singing fall mute and prepare to roost. Hens gather their chicks under their wings. Uneasy dogs cower at their master's legs. A kind of unreality hovers over a strange world.

And toward the end, the light fades so rapidly that one can almost sense the Moon's gigantic shadow swooping softly down.

Just before the point of totality there comes a sight you will not want to miss. When the crescent is down to hair-line thickness, look up at the Sun through your dark film. As the Moon's surface crosses in front of the last bit of Sun, the thin line of the visible Sun breaks up. You get one last fugitive look at the disappearing Sun as it shines through the valleys between the Moon's craters and mountains. The Sun shining through those valleys produces a string of bright splinters of light. These are "Baily's beads," named after the astronomer who, in 1836, first described the phenomenon. In a few seconds, they are gone.

But when Baily's beads vanish, the moment of totality has come and that is what you were waiting for. Nothing short of totality will do. Only with the last sliver of sunlight gone, do you really see the true beauty of an eclipse. All that has gone before is as nothing in comparison.

All around the Sun is its thin atmosphere, or "corona," stretching out for millions of miles. It is lost in the Sun's glare, even when the Sun is reduced to a thin crescent. Only when the Sun's light is utterly gone, only when the moment of totality arrives, does the corona flash out.

If the Moon were a bit smaller than it is, there would never be totality, never a corona. If the Moon were a bit larger, we would never see the whole corona at once. It is the perfect fit that makes the ultimate vision possible.

At totality, look without anything darkening your vision. The light of the corona is like the light of the full Moon and you can look at it with the bare eye.

Look, and you will see immediately around the black disc of the Moon a pinkish rim. That is the Sun's lower atmosphere. It will contain spikes and streamers in graceful arching curves. With distance from the Sun they will fade and grow more delicate until there is the pearly whiteness of the true corona stretching out unevenly from the blackness of the covered Sun to a distance of several times the Sun's diameter.

If you can look away for a moment, notice that the brighter stars have emerged from daylight hiding. (It was by studying the position of such stars during an eclipse in 1919 that astronomers were able to test Einstein's General Theory of Relativity for the first time.)

Then, too, the temperature will drop noticeably and that will be accompanied by the sudden rise of a cool wind.

But look quickly, for in a few minutes the Moon will have moved enough for the Sun to begin to emerge at the side opposite from that where its last bit had disappeared. Baily's beads will suddenly appear and with that the corona will fade.

Look away now, for the first blinding crescent edge of the Sun is about to appear. Totality is over, the light will brighten, normality will gradually return and you will be left with a sight you may never see again but which, once seen, will surely never be forgotten.

AFTERWORD

This article is especially dear to me because never in my life have I seen a total eclipse, and the editor didn't guess. (The description is accurate, just the same.)

THE FLYING MOUNTAINS

There are mountains out there, flying around loose. Out there in space, I mean. Every once in a while one of them is spotted, more or less by accident, as it skims by past Earth.

One of them was discovered in 1964 by Samuel Herrick of the University of California. It is called Toro, it is perhaps three miles across, and it can come as close to the Earth as 9,300,000 miles.

That doesn't seem very close, however. After all, even when it does its best, Toro never approaches Earth closer than thirty-seven times the distance of the Moon.

That wouldn't bother us if it would just come that close and then leave and go about its business for a good long time. It doesn't, though; its motions are locked in with those of the Earth. It moves out, receding farther from the Sun than we ever are, and then moves in, coming closer to the Sun than we. In doing so, it follows a complicated pattern that never allows it to get entirely away from us. It moves around the Sun five times every eight times we move around the Sun because on the average it remains in the aphelion position of its orbit longer than in the perihelion position.

It is as though Earth and Moon are engaged in a close-held waltz in the center of the ballroom, while far at one end, a third person is engaged in an intricate minuet of its own, one that carefully stalks, from a distance, the waltzing couple. Hans Alfven, of the University of California, calls Toro a "quasi-moon" of Earth.

Toro would pose no threat to our peace of mind if it

SOURCE: "The Flying Mountains" appeared in *Intellectual Digest*, July 1972.

kept to its orbit forever, shuffling through its dance without change. If it did, then it would have a stable orbit which we could work out in every detail as is true of our other, larger, and much more familiar Moon, which is not "quasi" at all. And if the Moon, so much huger and so much closer, doesn't bother us, why should tiny Toro?

Well, there are complications.

Among these are the other planets in the solar system. Each one has a gravitational pull. Considering the distance of those planets, the pull is tiny indeed, and exerts only the most trifling effect on Earth, or on the Moon, which each respond to the other's much stronger gravitational pull. The effect of these minor gravitational pulls of distant planets on the orbits of Earth and Moon can be detected by only the most delicate astronomical measurements. They are called "perturbations" and are of no practical importance.

Toro is so far from the Earth, however, that Earth's gravitational hold is small and doesn't serve to hold it in place with any efficiency at all. The pull of distant planets is then a respectable fraction of Earth's pull upon Toro. So as the distant planets pass and re-pass in a complicated pattern, what are they doing to Toro's orbit?

Alfven and his associates have computerized the orbit of Toro a couple of centuries into the past and into the future, including not only the effect of the gravitational pull of the Earth and the Moon, but also of the perturbations of Venus, Mars, Jupiter, and Saturn as well. Over the period for which they made their calculations, Toro did not shift significantly out of its orbit.

But beyond that in either direction?

At some time in the past, perhaps even only a few thousand years ago, Toro may have been an independent asteroid. Then once, at some close approach to Earth, planetary perturbations were such as to shift it just enough to cause it to fall into lock step with Earth. And some time in the future, another perturbation might free it again.

Then, if it someday took up an independent life again, could it happen to move into an orbit so drawn that it would intersect Earth's orbit? And if so, would the two objects happen to pass through the intersection simultaneously, so that there would be a collision?

The chances are excessively small, of course, because space, as a whole, is a perfectly enormous target and the Earth, in comparison, is a microscopic bull's-eye. The chances are, however, not zero.

And remember, Toro is not our only close neighbor in space. It is the first "lock step" neighbor we have detected (always excepting the Moon itself) but in addition there are flying mountains with independent orbits of their own, that occasionally brush by us.

This fact became known to us as long ago as 1898, when the German astronomer Gustav Witt discovered a new asteroid of a most unusual type. Hundreds of asteroids had been discovered in the preceding century, but all the others, every one of them, had orbits that lay entirely between those of Mars and Jupiter. Even the nearest was never closer to us than 50 million miles.

Witt's asteroid, however, penetrated inside the orbit of Mars. At one point, its orbit came within 13 million miles of Earth's orbit. If both objects were at just the right place in their respective orbits, the separation would be only half that between Earth and our nearest planetary neighbor, Venus.

Witt named the new asteroid Eros, giving it a masculine name where all other asteroids had honored the fair sex. Ever since then, asteroids with unusual orbits have been masculine in name.

And ever since then, asteroids that have been found to have orbits that made it possible for them to approach Earth more closely than Venus does, have been called "Earth-grazers." This is a most uncomfortable name indeed, for they are no tiny meteorites.

Eros is brick-shaped and is fifteen miles across its longest dimension. If it ever made a head-on collision with us, both bodies moving at eighteen miles a second or so, it might be just a pinprick for Earth but it would be an unbelievably huge catastrophe for man.

To be sure, the odds against Eros ever shifting from "Earth-grazer" to "Earth-crasher" are astronomically high. No one worries about it. —Besides, Eros turned out to have its uses.

The combination of small size and close approach meant

that it could be detected as a sharp point with a large shift against the background of the stars ("parallax") when simultaneously viewed from two widely separated observatories. The large parallax made it possible to determine its distance with unprecedented accuracy and from that, one could determine all other planetary distances in the solar system.

Astronomers had to wait for a close approach. After all, it is only once in a long while that both bodies are in those particular portions of their orbits that allow "grazing" to take place. In 1931, Eros passed within 16 million miles of us and that was close enough. Nothing closer would take place for many years.

A huge program was prepared for 1931. Fourteen observatories in nine countries took part. Three thousand photographs of Eros were taken over a period of seven months, and ten years (non-computer ones) were then spent on every variety of calculation before the job was completely done.

By that time, another Earth-grazer had been found, too. Albert, first detected in 1911, was three miles across and could pass (every once in a long while) as closely as 20 million miles to Earth.

Then, in the years following the great Eros project, four more Earth-grazers were detected, with orbits that could carry them considerably closer to Earth than even Eros ever managed.

The climax came with the detection of the asteroid Hermes, in 1937. It was only one mile across, but preliminary calculations of its orbit showed that when everything was exactly right, when it and the Earth were at just the right spots in their respective orbits, the separation would be only 200,000 miles! Hermes would then be closer to us than the Moon was!

To be sure, the calculations were rough and astronomers weren't positive. If they could see it again, note positions, and make additional calculations, that would be very helpful. The trouble is that Hermes was seen that once in 1937 and was never seen again. All that can be said is that somewhere in space there is a flying mountain a mile across, with its orbit so poorly calculated that we can't spot it again except by accident, but with a good chance that

that orbit might, every once in a long while, carry it uncomfortably close to us.

In 1949, the asteroid Icarus was discovered. That wasn't as bad as Hermes. It never comes closer than 4 million miles to us, but it comes fascinatingly close to the Sun. It approaches within 17 million miles of the Sun at each of its revolutions. This is only half the distance of Mercury, otherwise the closest object to the Sun (except for a very occasional comet). If we could place instruments on Icarus, what fascinating details concerning the Sun it could tell us.

But all these Earth-grazers put together are no real source of worry. They do not represent near and urgent dangers. Toro doesn't come really close; and if some of the other "Earth-grazers" come closer on occasion, those occasions are not at all frequent.

And yet the large bodies of the solar system *have* been hit by these flying mountains. Most of these strikes took place in the youth of the solar system, to be sure, when the debris left over by its formation was still thickly distributed through space. The Moon picked up thousands of sizable chunks of matter and the marks left are the craters that are still clearly visible on it. Mars has similar encounter-scars, and so, undoubtedly, has Mercury.

And the Earth? How has it managed to escape?

It hasn't!

The scars, however, don't show on Earth, because Earth has something that none of the other inner worlds has: a large ocean and a rampant surge of planetary life. Undoubtedly, Earth, in its early history, absorbed its share of large strikes. Some of these splashed into the ocean, perhaps, and left no marks. Others scarred the land, but those scars were slowly eroded away by wind and weather—and life.

We might comfort ourselves, then, that those bad old days have passed. The flying mountains that were close enough to be dangerous have been swept up during the first billion years of the solar system's existence, leaving their gigantic splash marks in some cases.

The Apollo 14 astronauts have, for instance, brought back some rocks from the neighborhood of Mare Imbrium which may be the remnants of the object that struck the Moon 700 million years after its formation and created that mare by smashing the Moon flat for a distance of hundreds of miles in every direction. (There is a possibility that the Imbrium body was a member of the Earth-Moon system, as Toro is today, and that its orbit was altered into a collision course.)

Such a collision on Earth would gouge out an American state or a European nation, and spread destruction over a continent. If it struck the ocean it would create a splash that would drench every plain on Earth.

But they are gone, those flying mountains; or at least most of them are and the few that are left are far enough away to be safe under any but the most unlikely concatenation of circumstances.

Still, if planet-shaking collisions are no longer likely, city-shaking collisions may still be possible. There are always more small objects of a particular sort than large ones; and if the flying mountains are down to a dozen or so in numbers, what about "flying hills"? There may be thousands of flying hills, too small to be seen through even the best telescopes, that may be littering the spaceways.

It is not surprising, then, that there should still be strikes in quite recent times, even during Man's brief stay on this planet. Such strikes should be fewer and smaller on the whole, than those giant smash-ups that formed huge craters, dozens to hundreds of miles across. Even so, the strikes are damaging enough, at least potentially.

There is the famous Barringer Crater in Arizona, which must have been formed not more than 50,000 years ago. Desert conditions have preserved it fairly well. It is four fifths of a mile across and looks like a small Moon crater.

There are signs of earlier and larger craters on Earth, too, partially filled with water and masked by vegetation, but still seen as circular marks on the landscape when viewed from an airplane. Chubb Crater in northern Quebec, for instance, is three miles across.

That is still child's play on a planetary scale but it is the sort of strike that can utterly destroy a large city.

Some have speculated that even now Earth is being struck by two "city-busters" per century, on the average. In 1908, for instance, an apparent meteorite struck central

Siberia with enough force to gouge out craters up to 150 feet in diameter and to knock down trees for twenty miles around. Amazingly, it hit one of the few places on land where it could do its damage and not kill, as far as is known, a single human being.

If it had come along five hours later, Earth would have turned enough in its orbit to allow a direct hit on St. Petersburg (now Leningrad). Surely, not a building would have been left standing; not a human being left alive.

The second city-buster of this century struck in 1947; in eastern Siberia this time, and again, in an uninhabited area.

This century has been a lucky one, but it is possible to argue that at this rate, the chances are even that in the next 30,000 years or so, some good-sized city somewhere on Earth will sustain a reasonably direct hit and be nearly or entirely wiped out. The chance is perhaps one in a thousand that this will happen before A.D. 2100. The chance of its happening within the next year is tiny—but not zero.

And if it should happen in any of several particularly critical areas, an angered or panicky government leader may assume a nuclear strike to have taken place and could press the button for retaliation before the word comes through that there was no sign of suspicious radioactivity.

The most agonizing point is that as things stand now, there is no warning possible. A flying boulder might be aimed right at Earth at this moment, with a dead strike on Moscow, Peking, London, or New York, within the hour and, barring a chance sighting of reflected light from the Sun as it approaches the atmosphere, we wouldn't know. —Not until time zero.

And because of that there is one possible justification for the space program that may be most practical of all for Earth's teeming population, and one I have not yet seen advanced.

The men in the space stations of the future, the men who work in the lunar observatories, may find themselves, among other things, the big-game hunters of space.

Without an interfering atmosphere, they will have a better chance to sight the Earth-grazers. They can watch more accurately and plot more closely the orbits of those sizable bodies, those Toros and Hermes that we can see from Earth's surface. More important, they can watch for those smaller and perhaps closer bodies we cannot see and which, through their greater numbers, are the more dangerous.

Without an interfering atmosphere, the men in space will be able to detect better than we can, and chart more efficiently, the dangers of Earth's near-space. They will note the shoals and reefs of the space-sea; they will be the new iceberg watch of the vast vacuum; they will locate every whirling rock and lump of metal of dangerous size and keep an eye on them all, insofar as that is possible, seeing to it that their orbits are calculated and recalculated and that every change is carefully noted.

Then perhaps a hundred years from now, or a thousand, some space-astronomer will look up from his computer to say, "Collision orbit!"

And a counterattack, kept in waiting for this necessary moment for decades, or centuries, would be set in motion. The dangerous rock would be stalked and, at a convenient, precalculated position in space, some powerful device would be shot into its path, designed to trigger off on collision.

The rock would glow and vaporize and change from a boulder to a conglomeration of pebbles. Earth would avoid the damage and be treated instead to a set of spectacular shooting-star effects.

And, sooner or later, mankind may decide on a grimmer task. Why waste time checking on orbits? Why not clear space altogether? Anything that approaches Earth more closely than 25 million miles at any time would be suspect and marked for destruction.

Perhaps if it were distant enough to be reasonably safe, or interesting enough to have scientific value, it might be spared. Eros would be spared, certainly, if only because it would surely come under the purview of the "Landmark Preservation Commission" for its usefulness to mankind in 1931. Icarus would be preserved because its close approach to the Sun makes it a unique astronomical laboratory.

But nothing else might be spared. Every other rock that could be detected in the space between the orbits of Venus and of Mars would be relentlessly stalked. Each would be examined closely for whatever of scientific interest could be extracted from it, or, possibly, for the chance of actual capture and a safe haul to the space station, the Moon, or Earth. And when examination was done and capture proven impractical, it would be destroyed.

And if, as a result, one city is left undestroyed, one massive tidal wave is left unconsummated, one particular crater on Earth is left unformed—

Then would not all the investment in space exploration have turned out to be worthwhile for that reason alone?

THE ROMANCE OF MARS

The romance of Mars began a hundred years ago with Virginio Schiaparelli.

With Schiaparelli's description of the "*canali*" just about a century ago, came the picture of an old and sophisticated, but slowly dying civilization on our sister planet—with its great canals, its jeweled cities, its lovely princesses, its spindly scholars, its savage aggressors (which author do you read?).

In science fiction, the romance has never died. Mars is still the special planet of Ray Bradbury, and Heinlein can still make it a plausible place of alien culture.

Nor was it just science-fictional imagination at work. The romance seemed quite plausible. After all, Mars had ice caps and it had an atmosphere. Surely the ice caps meant water and the atmosphere meant oxygen and the two together meant life. The air and water might be drifting away, else why the need for the vast irrigation project of the canals, but surely those very canals meant that life survived. And, if canals, surely *intelligent* life!

At the turn of the century, H. G. Wells could, with entire justice, assume an oxygen atmosphere on Mars, and an advanced civilization that could be driven by growing need into an invasion of Earth.

But then the intelligences of Mars dimmed. Year by year, they retreated—in science, if not in science fiction. The American astronomer Percival Lowell reported he could see the canals clearly and he mapped them in detail. No other astronomer, however, could really duplicate

SOURCE: "The Romance of Mars" appeared as an introduction to the anthology *Mars, We Love You* by Jane Hipolito and Willis E. McNelly, Doubleday, 1971.

Lowell's vision of the Martian canals. Despite occasional glimpses, more and more began to view them as optical illusions and more and more raised their voices to say that the emperor's new clothes did not exist after all.

The closer the investigation of the Martian atmosphere, the thinner it proved, and the less likely it seemed to be terrestrial in character. If intelligent Martians existed at all, it began to seem more and more likely that they were living now only under extreme difficulty, if at all. Did they live in domed cities or underground? Was it not more likely they had died out millions of years ago?

Was it not most likely, in fact, that they had never existed at all?

This, of course, did not mean that life did not exist, for intelligence is only an accidental concomitant of life and perhaps not even a very useful one. On Earth, life existed and flourished ebulliently for three billion years without anything we would call an even faint intelligence.

Then how about life-minus-intelligence on Mars? There were still the ice caps, still the atmosphere—and there was a surface that showed dark markings as well as ruddy ones. If the ruddy ones were stretches of desert, might not the dark ones be vegetation? With the change in seasons, the ice caps melted in alternation, and the dark areas spread through that hemisphere in which spring had come. And if there was vegetation, ought there not to be animal life, too?

Yet successively improved studies of Mars continued to make clearer the harshness of its environment. The vision of pseudo-trees and pseudo-rodents gave way to something less ambitious. How about lichens? Surely there could be lichens.

So biologists took lichens and other plants that flourished in the high Himalayas and Pamirs and exposed them to what they thought the Martian environment was like—and they grew. The chance of life on Mars, at least simple life, seemed to become great indeed.

Then came the crucial year of 1965 and Mariner 4 skimmed past Mars and took photographs and sent them back to Earth. For the first time, the surface was seen better than by the best telescope.

There were no canals, but there were craters. The

rugged terrain resembled that of the Moon. The lack of erosion indicated that the lack of air and water was not a new situation on Mars but extended backward through geological eons. Closer studies of the Martian atmosphere showed that it was even thinner than had been thought and that the temperature was colder. There was no oxygen at all in the atmosphere and hardly any water anywhere. The ice caps might be frozen carbon dioxide.

No intelligent life. No higher plants and lower animals. Perhaps not even lower plants or bacteria. Perhaps no life at all.

Perhaps Mars is another dead world like the Moon.

Yet can this be? Mars's gravity is 2.4 times that of the Moon. It does have a thin atmosphere. Surely there must be some water somewhere; even if the ice caps are solid carbon dioxide, there ought to be solid water mixed with it.

And if there is water, even in small quantities, might there not be life of some sort?

Hope dies hard and that part of Martian glamour will not give up the ghost. Though every step in the study of Mars has made the planet seem more unlikely as an abode of life, the hope will not entirely vanish.

Even as I write, Mariner 9 has just taken off for Mars and will go into orbit around it (we hope) mapping the surface as it has never been mapped before.* Its maps will not answer the question of life on Mars, but eventually, an instrument package may make a soft landing and perhaps it will provide an answer. —And if not, there is the manned landing that must someday take place.

But why bother? Of what use is life of the primitive sort that is all that can possibly exist on Mars? Who cares about germs or viruses or bare organic remnants halfway to life but never making it?

Astronomers and biologists do!

The fact of life on another world would be the greatest and most exciting discovery in either astronomy or biology to date—no matter how simple that life might be.

All life on Earth, however various it may seem, is one. It is all related biochemically, making use of nucleic acids

* *Added in proof:* Mariner 9 succeeded magnificently, showing volcanoes, canyons, and even markings that look like ancient river beds.

and proteins of the same basic sort, making use of the same vitamins, the same sets of reactions, the same scheme of metabolism. In short, the trillions of organisms on Earth make up exactly *one* ecology. And though Martian life might be so sparse in numbers and variety as to be beneath contempt from the standpoint of our own lush planet, it would form a different ecology, and the number of ecologies we could study would be exactly doubled.

The fact that life existed at all would tell us something, even if we knew not one solitary detail about that life. We can fairly make the assumption that life can exist only through molecules sufficiently complex to be capable of great versatility and flexibility of reaction; and if so we would know that the Martian environment encouraged the development of such complex molecules as soon as we knew life existed.

We know this could happen on Earth (it *did* happen) and we explain it in terms of Earth's primordial environment, but how *inevitable* was the development of life? The Martian environment will scarcely allow the development we have imagined on Earth. The temperature is so low, the radiation of the Sun so feeble, the air so thin, the water so lacking, that the chances of life-type molecules forming is only a tiny fraction of what it was on Earth.

If, nevertheless, life of any sort, however simple, formed on Mars, then the physico-chemical pressures forcing it must be so strong that we can rest assured that life exists on any planet that is even approximately Earth-type in character.

If life exists—of any sort and however simple—then the next step is to discover its biochemical basis. The possibilities are two in number. The macromolecules that make it up are either proteins and/or nucleic acids, as on Earth, or (the second possibility) they are not.

If the macromolecular basis of Martian life is fundamentally different from that of Earth, then joy must surely be unconfined. Not only would we have a second ecology, but one that would be utterly new to us. It is impossible to speculate on how important this may turn out to be or what new insights into life we would gain if we could find a completely new variety of it.

If, on the other hand, Martian life were protein/nucleic

acid in basis, there might still be a very good chance that there would be variations on the theme that would be extremely interesting. There might be alternate metabolic pathways never observed on Earth; roles played by individual atoms or atom groupings unduplicated on Earth; biochemical adaptations undreamed of on Earth.

Consider one example—

All protein molecules on Earth are built up of some twenty amino acids, of which all but one are capable of either a left-handed or right-handed orientation—one the mirror image of the other. Under all conditions not involving life, the two types, labeled D and L, are equally stable and equally capable of being synthesized. If an amino acid is synthesized under conditions not involving life, half the molecules are L and half are D.

In terrestrial proteins, however, with only the most insignificant and rare exceptions, all the amino acids are L. A uniform L-ness makes it possible for amino acid chains to be built more neatly and stack more snugly, but a uniform D-ness would have done just as well.

Why, then, is terrestrial life all L? Why not all D? Or why not some life forms L and others D?

We can't be sure. Did it just happen that the first protein formed was all L? Or were L and D both formed and the L happened to win out by sheer chance? Or is there some basic asymmetry in nature that makes the L form inevitable?

Well, then, would Martian proteins be L or D? Either way it might prove something about earthly life. If it were a mixture of both, one way or another, that might prove even more fascinating.

But suppose that Martian life existed and that it was biochemically precisely like that on Earth. Does that mean that there would be no interest in it at all? That it would be a trivial discovery—just more of the same?

Not at all.

For one thing, it would indicate that perhaps our biochemical basis was the only one that could support life, at least under conditions even faintly like that of Earth. Two cases would be far better evidence for this than one is. Secondly, if Martian life were precisely like earthly life, but were much simpler (as surely it must be), it might be possible to discover something about the primitive basis of life that the complex life forms on Earth obscure.

In that case, Mars would be a laboratory in which we could observe the proto-life that once existed on Earth and even experiment with it—as on Earth we could do only with a time machine.

Indeed, even if life did not exist on Mars, but if in its soil were half-formed molecules manifestly on their way to life in earthly fashion, that might be helpful. It might indicate the nature of the path once taken on Earth and we would have a laboratory for pre-biotic chemical evolution—with possibly incalculable consequences in the way of new knowledge of direct application to earthly biology.

So there it is. The fictional romance of Mars continues, but the true romance is (albeit, as yet, problematically) in the future. It will come, along with results beyond what fiction may yet have imagined, when the first microscopic fragment of anything indubitably living, or even nearly living, is detected in the cold red soil of Mars.

KNOWLEDGE IS ANYWHERE

Charity, they say, begins at home, and the bluebird of happiness is to be found in one's own backyard. So it may be, but knowledge is indivisible and can be found anywhere.

It has no boundaries. It may be that information concerning the Moon can arise out of a careful consideration of a cliffside just outside of town—or information concerning your body out of a careful analysis of radio waves arriving from dust clouds light-years away in space.

In fact, let us hope that space science *will* enlighten our biological investigations, for living cells are infuriatingly complex. They are so complex that some scientists now fear that the techniques of physics and chemistry will be forever inadequate to penetrate their intimate workings.

Yet unless and until we tease out the details of those intimate workings, we may never truly understand such diseases as cerebral palsy or cancer; we may never be able to handle genes in such a way as to improve and elevate the human machinery; worst of all, we may never be able to comprehend the workings of the brain in either its normal or abnormal aspect.

It wouldn't be so bad if we had something simple to work with as a start. That is what we do in the case of the many problems in which physics and chemistry have been successful. Simplified situations are studied in the laboratory and from these studies general rules are evolved. With the understanding of those rules fixed clearly in the mind, more and more details can be added, until we find ourselves working with quite complicated systems.

Newton's laws of motion were based on Galileo's experi-

SOURCE: "Knowledge Is Anywhere" was distributed to various newspapers by Publishers-Hall Syndicate, Spring 1971.

ments with balls sliding down slanting grooves; they ended up sending rockets to the Moon. Dalton's atomic theory began with simple experiments involving atom combinations ("molecules") made up of merely two or three atoms each; it ended up helping chemists analyze the exact structure of protein molecules made up of thousands of atoms, and put together brand new molecules that had never existed in nature before.

Put it this way— What we deal with when we look at the universe is a vast panoramic picture of enormous detail. If we try to study it directly, we are lost in complications and can make nothing of it. But suppose we find, or can construct, the artist's initial concept; the few basic lines and curves on which he built the panorama. That can give us our foundation and if we add to it, little by little, additional items here and there, we can end up understanding large sections of the picture in detail.

In biology, we can't seem to do that. We are stuck with the complexity. There seems no way we can tackle the living cell by starting with something simple. We might move down to creatures simpler than a man, even much simpler —but they only seem simpler because they have fewer cells, less intricately arranged. The cell itself, even the single cell of a tiny bacterium, is always complicated; as complicated as that of a man.

Long ago, billions of years ago, before the first modern cell developed, there must have been sub-cells in existence; forms of life far simpler than the simplest we know today. If we had those forms to work with we might have something like the "basic concept" of life to which we could add, little by little, until we finally understood the modern cell. —Unfortunately, those sub-cells are long gone. No trace remains.

Of course, we can take modern cells apart, but as soon as we do, they are no longer alive. We can study the nonliving parts, but even these are enormously complicated and how to go from the parts to the whole, as far as the intimate nature of all are concerned, is as yet beyond us. We might study viruses, which are far smaller than cells, but they only do their work after they have invaded cells, and once within a cell, they are lost to our view.

But if nature will not supply us with the basic concepts of life and show us the artist's original guidelines, so to speak, then perhaps we can construct our own. Astronomers have worked out the possible chemical structure of the ocean and the atmosphere of the Earth as it may have been billions of years ago before there was any life on our planet.

The simple atoms and molecules of the beginning, in the presence of the energy of sunlight, ought to come together to form more complicated molecules. Perhaps this can be tested in the laboratory.

Back in the middle 1950s, chemists began to try to duplicate what must once have happened on the earth. A mixture of common small molecules was exposed to energy in the form of ultraviolet light or electric sparks. After a week or so, the material was analyzed and small amounts of new and more complicated molecules were found.

The next step was to begin with a mixture of the small molecules and to add to them considerable quantities of one or more of the more complicated molecules that had been formed. After a while, still larger molecules were formed.

When the process was repeated over and over, chemists ended up with amino acids, which are the building blocks of proteins; nucleotides, the building blocks of genes; rings of atoms related to the coloring matter in plants and in blood.

In fifteen years of trying to duplicate the conditions of the early Earth, chemists haven't gotten anywhere near actual living things, but at least all the substances they form in this way point in the direction of life. The more complicated the molecules they form, the more closely connected they are with the giant molecules of living tissue.

It would look as though chemists are on the right track. They seem to be repeating the process that actually took place on the sterile Earth billions of years ago, the process that ended by filling the planet with life. If they continue long enough, will they build a picture of the basic guidelines of life and guide us to an understanding of the biological problems that seem beyond us now?

Or are the chemists kidding themselves?

Do they *really* know what the Earth was like four billion years ago? Are they *really* duplicating the original conditions? Perhaps, knowing what they want to end with, they are unconsciously designing the conditions of the experiment in such a way as to end there. If only there were some way of checking the chemists' deductions about the conditions on the very early Earth.

Suppose we look out in space and find matter before it has formed planets. Maybe the composition of that matter can tell us something about what the Earth was like when it first came into being.

All through our Galaxy of over a hundred billion stars there are clouds of dust and gas with some sort of chemical makeup. There are reasons for thinking that these clouds consist chiefly of a few different elements such as hydrogen, oxygen, carbon, and nitrogen. The gas is so thinly spread out, however, that chemists and astronomers both guessed it would consist entirely of single atoms.

Occasionally, of course, two atoms might come together and cling. In the 1930s, astronomers were able to tell from the type of light arriving from those clouds that there were carbon-hydrogen combinations (CH) and carbon-nitrogen combinations (CN) present. But nothing further was discovered. The light radiations couldn't be analyzed in enough detail.

Since then, however, astronomers have learned to receive and analyze radio waves from space. Radio waves can be studied in far greater detail than light waves can. Every atom and every molecule puts its mark on those radio waves and can be identified by its "fingerprint" so to speak.

In 1963, radio waves from certain dust clouds were analyzed by radio astronomers of M.I.T. and were found to indicate the presence of combinations of oxygen and hydrogen atoms (OH). It would not have been detected through ordinary light waves.

Astronomers were not very surprised by these two-atom combinations but to them it seemed quite unlikely that more than two atoms would come together in one place and stick there; not with the atoms originally being so far apart.

Wrong! Beginning in late 1968 at the University of California, the radio wave "prints" of a number of more-than-two-atom molecules were discovered. The first was ammonia, with molecules made up of one nitrogen atom and three hydrogen atoms (NH_3). Then there was water (H_2O), and hydrogen cyanide (HCN).

In March 1969 came a real surprise. Using the radio telescope at Green Bank, West Virginia, astronomers located signs of formaldehyde in the gas and dust of outer space. Formaldehyde molecules are made up of a carbon atom, two hydrogen atoms, and an oxygen atom (CH_2O). No one had expected that. Then came cyanoacetylene (C_3HN), formic acid (CH_2O_2) and methyl alcohol (CH_4O). The molecule of methyl alcohol is made up of six atoms.

Astonished astronomers found they had a new science on their hands, "astrochemistry," the chemistry of the thin matter of outer space. What's more, the molecules they were detecting might also be on the highroad to life. They were beginning to point in the same direction as that shown by the chemists working with their made-up primitive mixtures in the laboratory.

It looked as though the chemists might *not* be kidding themselves.

Did that mean that if we looked harder and in more detail we might find such important compounds as amino acids, the building blocks of proteins?

In December 1970, a team of American scientists under Cyril Ponnamperuma analyzed a meteorite which fell in Australia on September 28, 1969, and found it to contain traces of five amino acids—each one of which is common to all proteins.

There is a chance, then, that the guidelines to an understanding of life may exist after all—if we can only study those gas clouds of outer space closely enough. If they are not the guidelines themselves, they may well give us enough information to enable scientists to build those guidelines with confidence.

How can we make our studies of the gas clouds more detailed? For one thing, we have to get out from under our atmosphere, which obscures so much. We must get away from Earth's distracting radio noise.

If we could build an observatory on the Moon; or place one on a space station circling the Earth; or even just launch a telescope in orbit (two attempts to do the last have failed); we might be able to get enormously sharper and clearer pictures of the radio waves coming from those clouds.

And it is just possible that if we increase our knowledge

of those distant gas clouds, we *may* end up with a cure for cancer, or an understanding of the nature of genius. (It would be like going from Galileo's timing of rolling balls, to rockets reaching the Moon.)

Knowledge, you see, is wherever we find it, and it would be foolish to inhibit the search for knowledge in any direction.

The *use* we make of knowledge is another thing. One or another particular application of new knowledge may seem useless, wasteful, or even downright harmful. People may rightly regret the building of hydrogen bombs, the collecting of bacterial toxins, the indiscriminate use of insecticides and detergents. To avoid such evils, it would be wise to agree to use our knowledge with greater care and discrimination—but it would certainly be criminally foolish to deprive ourselves of knowledge altogether, lest we *might* use it wrongly.

We may use a knife to prepare a meal or to kill a man. To avoid killing, must we abolish all knives—or cut off all the hands that might hold knives?

And what about the expense of gaining knowledge? Space exploration is expensive and there is no guarantee that it will show an immediate profit. Still, it gathers knowledge and no amount of expense in gaining knowledge is equal to the expense of not gaining it.

As short a time as two and a half years ago, not one astronomer would have dreamed his science was on the threshold of the development of an exciting field of deep-space chemistry. Amino acids in meteorites had been reported before but they were dismissed as contamination; now with the knowledge of what is going on in clouds they are taken seriously. Chemists building their way toward life chemicals in the laboratory were working in a vacuum, wondering if it all meant anything; now radio waves from light-years away are backing them up.

Even if men were willing to give up the excitement of science, the sheer adventure of following on the track of knowledge wherever that might take us, would anyone be willing to give up the great good it will surely bring all of us—if only man can somehow gain the wisdom to match his knowledge?

3 · *IN CHEMISTRY*

EARTH

The tradition of modern science is usually traced back to the Greek philosopher Thales (640–546 B.C.). There were scientific thinkers before him certainly, for Babylonian mathematics and astronomy were painfully built up during a two-thousand-year period before Thales, and the Egyptians certainly built their pyramids (also two thousand years before) by some method other than the haphazard heaping of stone.

Thales, however, is the first person whom we know by name and as an individual, who advanced questions concerning the Universe which he then tried to answer by observation and reason and without calling on the gods. And one of the questions he asked was: What is the Universe made of?

It is a question any inquisitive child might ask and, then, looking about him, answer: Of a vast number of things!

But Thales went further. He ignored the massive and obvious heterogeneity of the world about him and strove to penetrate to the subtle core. His question was, in essence: Is the Universe made of some one substance of which all the different objects we see are merely variations?

If the answer is "No," then we are left with a Universe built up of numerous substances associated in even more numerous relationships. The Universe might then easily be too complex for the human mind ever to grasp and man might be curious to no purpose. It is tempting to reject the answer "No" then, if only for the sake of human dignity, unless and until it is quite clear that no other alternative exists.

On the other hand, if the answer is "Yes," then that

would be evidence of an austere simplicity to the Universe, even though that simplicity is not at once apparent. It would make more likely the notion that the Universe is guided by certain rules of behavior, certain "laws of nature" that are simple enough to be comprehended by the human mind.

So Thales answered, "Yes."

But if there was indeed a basic substance of which the Universe is composed, what might that substance be? To Thales, living in a coastal city oriented very largely toward seafaring, that substance would have to be water.

A basic substance of the Universe was called in later-century Latin *elementum* (a word of unknown derivation) and this has become "element" to us. To Thales, then, water was the element of the Universe.

Thales' conviction in this matter was not utterly convincing to others. Water was unfixed in shape and formless compared to the solid things about us. Water might therefore represent a primitive kind of matter out of which more advanced kinds could be molded—but then air was even less fixed in shape than water was, and even more formless. Anaximenes (c. 570–c. 525 B.C.) felt air might more logically be viewed as the element of the Universe.

Heraclitus (c. 540–c. 475 B.C.) carried this line of thought to an even more logical conclusion. Still less fixed and more formless than air was fire. Moreover, if the element of the Universe existed in countless variations it must have an inborn capacity for infinite change and surely anyone watching a fire would agree that the flame was constantly in the process of changing.

The opposing views on the nature of the element of the Universe might persist forever without a decision on whether any one of them, or none, was correct. Wearying, perhaps, of the profitless conflict, Empedocles (c. 490–c. 430 B.C.) offered a compromise. He suggested that there was more than one element of the Universe. To those suggested earlier, all of which he accepted, he himself added earth, and in that way arose the doctrine of "the four elements."

Aristotle (384–322 B.C.), the great synthesizer of Greek science, accepted that doctrine and this acceptance made it official for over two thousand years to come. In his orderly fashion, Aristotle pointed out that each element had its natural place in the Universe, each occupying its own sphere about the center of the Universe (which was at the center of the Earth).

Of the four elements, earth, the most compact, was closest to the center and made up the solid sphere of the Earth itself. Surrounding the earth and covering it almost entirely was a spherical shell of water, and surrounding that was a spherical shell of air. So much was clear to the most cursory observation. Fire was more difficult. If the reasoning were followed, it should exist in a spherical shell beyond the air. And occasionally, to be sure, during storms, the shell of air would be rent and the fire beyond would then be seen momentarily in the stroke of lightning.

Each element would strive to find its place. Things of earth would fall downward; water would bubble up from below; air and fire would move upward even more eagerly.

Beyond the sphere of fire lay the heavens. These must, in Aristotle's view, be of an utterly different element because the properties of things heavenly were in such sharp contrast to the properties of things earthly. On the Earth, everything changed and decayed; in the heavens, the bodies were changeless and eternal. On the Earth, natural motions were up or down; in the heavens, the natural motions were great, endless circles. The heavens therefore were of a fifth element, which Aristotle called "ether" (from a word meaning "to glow," since the heavenly bodies all glowed).

From the hindsight of modern science, it is easy to dismiss all this as a kind of primitive guessing game. The choice of earth as an element seems particularly foolish. How could the solid matter that is neither water, air, nor fire, all be lumped together as a single element? After all, the most casual inspection showed that the properties of the earthy bodies varied radically from spot to spot. There were minerals that were transparent, others that glittered, others that were dully opaque; there were dense rocks, hard rocks, crumbly rocks; blue rocks, yellow rocks, red rocks; metals; living things—

How, then, find in all this a single element?

But the very point of an element is that it could appear

in different varieties while being basically the same. In its purest, primal form, it might not even exist anywhere. The element "earth," which ought to be put in quotation marks to distinguish it from ordinary earth, could be an ideal substance, which did not exist as such but only in the various impure varieties with which we were acquainted.

And surely all the infinite varieties of "earth" about us, did share one property in common. They were all solid.

Suppose, then, that instead of giving the elements ordinary names, they had been named by their most characteristic property. Suppose the Greeks had named three of their elements, not earth, water, and air, but "solidness," "liquidness," and "gaseousness." We would then recognize the Greeks to have classified matter into its three "states," something we still do today. As for "fire," which is not matter at all, if the Greeks had said "energy" instead, we would have marveled at their insight—yet the difference would be only semantic and not substantive.

Even Aristotle's guess as to the fifth element in the heavens is not so far wrong. The most important heavenly bodies are the stars and these are made up in part of what we now call "plasma" and in part "degenerate matter" and these might well be called fourth and fifth states of matter. Aristotle's mistake was not so much in postulating a fifth element, as in not having postulated a sixth as well.

The lay interest in the elements would seem to increase as one approached the center of the Universe. The ether might fascinate the philosopher, but it was forever beyond the grasp of the practical man. Fire could be placed before his eyes, but it could not be handled. And although air could be made contact with safely, there was very little one could do with it.

Water was still more easily handled and it could be made to undergo interesting changes. If sufficiently heated, it could be made to boil and change into vapor; if sufficiently chilled, it could freeze into ice. (If the ancients wrote chemical equations, they might have written: earth + fire → water; water + → air.)

The element earth was clearly the most interesting indeed. It was what the practical man dealt with all the time. Some varieties were valuable indeed; gold, most of all.

Gold was a fascinating variety of earth. It had a beautiful yellow luster; it was easily worked into charming shapes; it did not change, dull, or decay. And it was very rare.

This combination of properties made gold coveted; for it was ideal as a medium of exchange. Small quantities of the so-rare gold could represent large quantities of anything else, and the transfer of gold could therefore conveniently mark the transfer (in the opposite direction) of anything else.

The fact that it was the "anything else" that represented wealth and that gold only kept track of the shifts of that wealth (like chips in a poker game) was lost on most people. To them, gold was, in itself, wealth, and the theoretical speculations concerning the elements of the Universe were of interest chiefly in so far as they might make it possible to increase the supply of gold.

Practice was, of course, ahead of theory. The first smelting of metal may have taken place about 4000 B.C., millennia before Thales began to speculate. Metallurgists learned their trade by the hard and slow method of trial and error, but once they had learned, they were skillful enough. Nor was it only metal that technicians worked with; there was the making of glass, the baking of brick, the fermenting of fruit juice, and so on.

What it all came down to was the ability to bring about change, usually through the agency of heat. Dull rock could turn to shiny metal; and two metals (copper and tin) could be blended to form a new one (bronze) better in some respects than either parent.

There was no question, then, but that the Universe exhibited change and that this change could be directed by the techniques worked out by man. What was uncertain were the *limits* of change. Since so many changes *could* take place, were there any changes that could *not?*

It is much harder to decide what can't be done, than what can, and it is not surprising that the technicians of ancient times, with the evidence of directed change all about them, felt that gold could be manufactured. In some way, two or more relatively common substances could be put together under appropriate conditions to form gold. It would have been foolish of them, and completely against such evidence as they had, to suppose that gold could *not* somehow be formed.

Until the heyday of Greek science, however, any attempts to form gold had been directed purely by hit-and-miss and nothing had succeeded. With the elaboration of the theory of the four elements, new hope arose. Perhaps a consideration of those elements might guide the technician in the proper direction toward forming gold.

Perhaps all real substances were made up of different proportions of the four earthly elements. It might then be a matter of changing those proportions—increasing the air, decreasing the earth—to change lead into gold, for instance.

In the centuries after Aristotle, the study of methods of changing one substance into another came to be called *khymeia* in Greek. A common theory for the origin of this name is that since there were important practitioners of the science in Alexandria, Egypt (the intellectual center of the Greek world in the centuries after Aristotle), the word comes from "Khem" which was the native word for Egypt. A more likely, if less romantic, possibility is that it comes from the Greek word *khyma*, meaning to fuse or cast a metal.

The *khymeists* worked in many fields, sometimes quite productively, but it was the conversion of non-gold to gold ("transmutation," meaning "to change across") that most fascinated them. What's more, it was transmutation that most fascinated the laymen who patronized the *khymeists* and thought that through their art, instant and fantastic wealth would lie at hand. (Actually, this was not so. Had any *khymeist* succeeded in easily forming gold from lead, or from wood, and had the knowledge of the process become widespread, then gold would merely have dropped in value to that of lead, or that of wood.)

Greek science faded during the centuries of, first, pagan Roman and, then, Christian Roman domination. It was not until the Arab conquests in Asia and Africa that the old speculations of the Greeks struck new fire. In the eighth century, brilliant Arabic scholars began to consider *khymea*. They thought of it with their definite article *al*. It became *al khymea* (the *khymea*) and in Latin spelling this became *alchemia* or, in English, "alchemy."

One of the earliest and best of the Arabic alchemists was Jabir ibn-Hayyan (c. 760–c. 815), known to Europeans in later centuries as Geber. He was a careful experimentalist. He described ammonium chloride and showed how to prepare white lead. He distilled vinegar to obtain strong acetic acid and prepared weak nitric acid.

In addition, though, he and the Arabic alchemists who followed him were inevitably interested in transmutation. They delved deeper into the matter, and took up certain Aristotelian notions in greater detail. There was enough variety in the earthy substances, for instance, to indicate that "earth" might involve more than one principle ("subelements," so to speak).

For instance, there were seven different metals known and they had to have something, "a metallic principle," in common. Of the seven metals, one that was unique was mercury, for it was the only liquid metal. It was perhaps the closest approach to the ideal metallic principle, containing the least admixture of the non-metallic aspects of earth that made up all the solid varieties, including the six solid metals.

In addition, since metals were smelted out of ore by the use of fire and great heat, metals had to contain a "combustible principle," too. Sulfur was, again, very unusual (if not quite unique) among minerals, in that it was capable of burning. Sulfur might then be the closest approach to the "combustible principle."

It might seem, then, that metals were composed of intimate mixtures of mercury and sulfur, with gold representing the best and most perfect mixture. Other solid metals were a kind of imperfect gold and it remained only to find some way of adjusting the proportions, adding either mercury or sulfur in some appropriate way.

Undoubtedly, mercury, or sulfur, or both, were added to the various metals in every conceivable combination without forming gold, and the feeling arose that the proper combination would take place only in the presence of some intermediary. (In modern parlance, we would say that a "catalyst" was needed.)

Speculations of this sort dated back to the Greeks, who

conceived the catalyst to be a dry material. They called it *xerion* from their word for "dry." The Arabs converted this to *al-iksir* and we to "elixir." It might also be called the "philosopher's stone"; "stone" because it was dry and hard, and "philosopher" because this was the name given to those who studied the Universe. (Other fanciful properties were granted the philosopher's stone, including that of curing all disease and prolonging human life, so that we find frequent references to "the elixir of life.")

For a thousand years, alchemists searched for the philosopher's stone. It was the case of the overgrowth of a single problem strangling a science. The glamour of creating gold and the greed for the wealth such a secret process would bring (and might, in the very unlikely case that it were really kept secret, and were used very sparingly) was too much to resist. It was as though all medical progress were sacrificed in a single-minded search for a cancer cure; or if all astronomical research were stopped except for a single-minded attempt to work out the nature of the quasars.

It was worse, for a cancer cure is conceivable and the nature of the quasars ought to be penetrable, but transmutation (if the alchemists but knew) was impossible—at least under the conditions the alchemists could use.

This meant that alchemy became the happy hunting ground for frauds and fakers, and a heartbreaking affair for those legitimate few who seriously sought the process. The great Isaac Newton, nine centuries after Jabir, wasted untold time and effort in a futile effort to work out a method of transmutation.

With the coming of the seventeenth century (Newton's), however, a new mood of experimentalism entered science. Those investigating the Universe were increasingly reluctant to make large decisions on the basis of deduction from observation and first principles. There was rather the drive to design experiments intended specifically to guide the making of those decisions. Instead of *telling* the Universe of what it was composed, the greater humility of *asking* it seemed more and more appropriate.

An important turning point came in 1661, when the Irish chemist Robert Boyle (1627–91) published a book in which even the title marked a watershed. So foul had alchemy become under the distorting effect of its overriding problem that its very name had fallen into disrepute. So Boyle dropped the Arabic first syllable and returned closer to the original Greek (but using the Latin *ch* in place of the Greek letter we usually symbolize as *kh.*) He called his book *The Sceptical Chymist.* From that point on, alchemists became "chemists" (with the further change of the *y*) and alchemy became "chemistry."

Boyle was "sceptical" because he was no longer willing to accept, blindly, the decisions on the nature of the elements, which the Greeks had arrived at through sheer speculation. Instead, he preferred to define elements in a practical and entirely empirical manner.

A substance was an element if, in actual practice, it could not be broken up into two or more apparently simpler substances, and if, in actual practice, it could not be built up from two or more apparently simpler substances.

Since bronze could be manufactured out of the proper mixture of copper and tin, bronze was not an element. Since the mineral malachite could be broken down to yield copper and other substances, malachite was not an element. However, since copper could *not* (for all chemists could do at the time) be broken down, or built up out of, simpler substances, copper *was* an element.

This sort of definition removed the "element" from the realm of the ideal and absolute, and made it a pragmatic term that was entirely dependent upon the state of the art. By Boyle's definition and in Boyle's time, the real substances water, air, and fire, were still elements. Only earth had ceased to be an element.

Of the simpler components of the earth that made up the solid structure of our planet, one could still maintain, with perfect justice, in Boyle's time, that the minerals quartz and lime were elements. Neither could be broken down into simpler substances, *then.* Eventually, each was, and then they ceased to be elements by Boyle's definition.

In fact, there was no reason to suppose that any substance which was considered an element might not turn out to be no element at all. Something which seemed an element because the state of the art was at one time inadequate to break it down, might be broken down at a later time in a more advanced state of the art. Boyle himself might, quite reasonably, have argued that the seven known metals were certainly elements as of 1661, but might *not* be as of 1662.

As it happens, Boyle felt exactly that. His new empirical approach to the question of the elements gave him no reason to suspect that the alchemical goal of transmutation was impossible. In 1689, he urged the British Government to repeal the law against the alchemical manufacture of gold (instituted by the government because they feared the effect on the economy of a flood of synthetic gold) since he felt the law hampered chemical research.

Through the eighteenth century, chemists discovered more and more substances which were elements by Boyle's definition. By 1803, some thirty-three of those substances which are still considered elements even today were known —but even so, the definition of elements was still empirical and provisional.

In 1803, the English chemist John Dalton (1766–1844) first formally advanced the "atomic theory," something which was in line with the thinking of Boyle and even with that of some of the Greek philosophers over two thousand years before. All matter, Dalton held, is made up of atoms and each element is made up of atoms of a characteristic type.

If atoms are the simplest substances capable of existing, then indeed the elements are the elements forever; none can possibly be broken up into simpler substances. Furthermore, if one atom cannot be changed into an atom of another type, then one element cannot be changed into another, and if gold is an element, then transmutation is forever impossible.

Nineteenth-century chemists quickly came to accept this new view, but their belief still rested on the assumptions that atoms were the simplest substances capable of existing and that one atom could not be changed into another of a different kind. Nor was it possible to decide whether a substance consisted of only one kind of atom (and was therefore an element) except by the empirical method of trying to break it down into simpler substances, and failing. So the definition of an element still depended on the state of the art, despite the atomic theory.

In 1869, the Russian chemist Dmitri I. Mendeleev (1834–1907) devised the modern periodic table, in which the elements were arranged according to their various properties. The periodic table made such sense and was so useful (even guiding chemists to the discovery of new elements) that it was strong evidence in favor of believing that the substances thought to be elements were, indeed, actually elements. Yet even so, this was merely circumstantial evidence, heightening the probability, but not yet allowing a satisfactory definition independent of the state of the art.

In the final decade of the nineteenth century, however, came the discovery of the electron and of radioactivity. It turned out, rather to the astonishment of scientists, that the atom was not the simplest possible object after all but was a rather complex structure built up of still simpler objects.

In 1913, The English physicist Henry Gwyn-Jeffreys Moseley (1887–1915), finally—*finally*—advanced a competely rigorous definition of an element. An element, it turned out through Moseley's researches, was any substance made up of atoms all of which contained a characteristic number of protons in their nuclei. This number of protons (the "atomic number") could be accurately determined. It was 1 for hydrogen, 8 for oxygen, 26 for iron, 79 for gold, and so on.

Now, 105 different elements are known, with atomic numbers from 1 to 105 inclusive.

And now transmutation is possible again, for there are methods whereby the number of protons in the nuclei of particular atoms can be altered. Indeed, many of the more complicated atoms spontaneously break down into atoms with different proton numbers. These are "radioactive changes" which are usually accompanied by relatively large energy releases. The nuclear bombs are examples of sizable transmutations. The Sun and other stars radiate energy as a result of unbelievably vast transmutations.

Does this mean that the alchemists "were right after all"? —Only in the sense that an ultimate goal they pursued was after all realizable, *though not by any methods available to them.*

After all, you might believe firmly that you could reach

the Moon by jumping, and might spend your whole life jumping with all your might, yet not reach it. If, then, Neil Armstrong and company reached the Moon by rocket, with all the backup of modern technology involved, would that mean that you (who, after all, *did* think the Moon could be reached) "were right after all"?

From Thales to the nuclear bomb!

There *are* basic substances making up the Universe, but none Thales could have conceived of in his time. —And for all we know there are yet still more basic basics of which we do not conceive today. The pursuit of knowledge has no end—for which we can all be grateful.

AIR

It was rather clever of the Greeks to consider air to be an element. It was rather clever of them to consider it at all, for the general population, even we ourselves with all our modern sophistication, ignore it completely. The tendency is to look into a container full of air and say, "This is empty; there's nothing in it."

Of all the Greek elements, only air is invisible. Earth and water are all about us and can be felt as well as seen. Fire is visible, and even the ether that Aristotle thought made up the heavens can be seen in the form of the glowing Sun, Moon, planets and stars.

Only air of the five elements is used as a synonym for nothing. In Shakespeare's *The Tempest*, Prospero produces a gorgeous entertainment through magic, then lets it all vanish and says:

> These our actors,
> As I foretold you, were all spirits and
> Are melted into air, into thin air

That is, into nothingness.

Yet air is not nothing and when it is in motion, though we may still not see it, we can feel it easily enough. When the motion is great enough, we feel it all too intensely. No one who has lived through a hurricane or a tornado can deny that *something* invisible exists all about us. Yet when the wind stops, it will have "melted into air, into thin air" literally, and in its place there will remain (it would seem) nothing.

The Greek engineer Hero, who lived some time in the first century A.D., made a special effort to refute the com-

SOURCE: "Air" appeared in *Smithsonian*, July 1971.

mon misconception in his startlingly modern-sounding book *Pneumatics*. He says:

> Vessels which seem to most men empty are not empty, as they suppose, but full of air . . . composed of particles minute and light, and for the most part invisible. . . . If then, we pour water into an apparently empty vessel, air will leave the vessel proportional in quantity to the water which enters it . . . Hence it must be assumed that air is matter. The air when set in motion becomes wind (for wind is nothing else but air in motion) and if, when the bottom of the vessel has been pierced and the water is entering, we place the hand over the hole, we shall feel the wind escaping from the vessel, and this is nothing but the air which is being driven out . . .

Quite right, and it couldn't be better expressed today.

Nevertheless, though air is matter and, in the Greek view, an element of the Universe, it was different in important properties from all other matter. It had, after all, no form, no shape. A piece of earth, such as a rock, had a definite shape which persisted for all time if left to itself. A quantity of water had no permanent shape, but if confined would take on the shape of the container, and retain that shape indefinitely. Fire had a shape that perpetually changed, but it was a definite shape of some sort at each instant of time. Ether had the shape of the heavenly bodies. Only air had no shape at all.

In Greek mythology, the Universe originally consisted of a random mixture of elements, without shape or form. The creation of the Universe as we know it, then, was not the creation of matter out of nothing, but was the imposition of form on unformed matter already existing.

To the Greeks, the original mass of unformed and unshaped matter was "chaos"; while ordered, formed, and shaped matter was "cosmos." To many thinkers, it seemed that air, unformed and unshaped, was a remnant of the original chaos. Indeed, the Swiss alchemist Paracelsus (1493–1541) sometimes referred to air as "chaos."

Something else that impressed the early chemists was the fact that air seemed to remain permanently air. Water did not remain permanently water—if it were heated it readily changed into something that seemed to have the properties of air. Indeed, water slowly changed into a kind of air and disappeared if it were merely allowed to remain in an open container.

Air itself, however, could not be changed into any kind of water. If water were heated and the "air" formed from it were mixed with ordinary air, then that part of the air that had once been water could be turned back to water by cooling the mixture. The air itself, the air that had always been air, remained air.

The Flemish chemist Jan Baptista van Helmont (1579–1644) took note of this about 1620. He termed those varieties of air which could be formed from water or from other substances as "vapors." For air itself, he reserved the Paracelsian term "chaos." He pronounced the word, however, in Flemish fashion and spelled it as he pronounced it—"gas."

The word did not catch on at once. For a long time vapors of all sorts were spoken of as "airs." When the term did come into general use, however, two centuries after it was invented, it was used not for air alone, but for all airlike substances. Thus we can now say that water vapor is a gas.

Van Helmont discovered that some vapors differed from air not only in their ability to be returned to liquid form, but in other properties as well—and not only from air but from each other. He discovered a heavy vapor, which he called *gas sylvestre* ("gas from wood"), because he obtained it by burning charcoal. He obtained another which he called *gas pingue* ("gas from fat") by heating organic matter.

Gas sylvestre (which we now call carbon dioxide) would put out a candle flame, which ordinary air would not. *Gas pingue* (a mixture of what we today call hydrocarbons) would burn, as air would not.

Van Helmont's different vapors went unstudied in detail by him and by others largely because of technical difficulties. The vapors were difficult to isolate, for as soon as they formed, they expanded outward, mixing with the vast quantities of air all about, and were gone.

Despite Van Helmont's observations, then, it remained

easier to believe that air was a single substance (though trivial variations might be imposed upon it).

In the seventeenth century, to be sure, scientists had learned how to pump most of the air out of a closed container to form a vacuum—a container that was really empty (or almost empty) and not just air-filled. The Irish chemist Robert Boyle (1627–91), a leader in the early research into vacuums, also studied the manner in which air could be compressed and made denser. His accurate studies in this respect helped show that air consisted of tiny particles (as Hero had maintained) that were widely separated, with vacuum between, and this was an important step toward the establishment of the atomic theory.

However, whether the air were pumped out or squeezed together, it remained air—thinner or denser, but air.

As the eighteenth century opened, air gained a new kind of interest, for scientists were beginning to wonder about combustion. For the first time since Hero had experimented with steam, ingenious men were beginning to use heat to boil water and to force the expanding steam they produced to do work. Primitive steam engines were in existence by 1700 and it was clear they would work only as long as a fire was burning under the boiler. Interest in what it was that made some substances burn, and not others, therefore increased sharply.

About 1700, a German chemist, Georg Ernst Stahl (1660–1734), advanced an explanation of the process of combustion. He said that substances were capable of burning because they contained something he called "phlogiston" (from a Greek word meaning "to set on fire").

As such a substance burnt, it lost its phlogiston, and it was the rapid passage of the phlogiston out of the substance that was visible as fire. Thus wood was rich in phlogiston, but the ash left behind after the wood had burned was naturally phlogiston-free and would therefore no longer burn.

As a result of the phlogiston theory, air gained a new and important role. It was a receptacle for phlogiston. When a pile of wood burned, it was the surface pieces that burned first because they were near the air that would accept the phlogiston. The inner pieces, not near the air, would not burn. They might give off vapors and char, but because air was not available, they would lose little if any phlogiston. Indeed, the "charcoal" that was formed in this way, which was lighter than the original wood, would possess a greater concentration of phlogiston and would burn with a hotter fire than ordinary wood would.

Stahl's most important and enduring contribution was his recognition that the rusting of metals was somehow analogous to the burning of wood. Iron, for instance, was full of phlogiston according to his theory. As it rusted, phlogiston poured slowly out of it, too slowly to cause a visible flame, and the iron rust (or "calx," as metallic rusts were called at the time) that formed was utterly lacking in phlogiston.

Any decent theory, in explaining observations and systematizing facts, naturally raises new questions.

It would seem, for instance, that although air readily accepted phlogiston, it would only accept so much and no more. Thus, if a piece of wood were burned in a limited supply of air—in a small, closed container, for instance—it would eventually stop burning. The air about it would have gained all the phlogiston it could hold, apparently, and might be called "phlogisticated air." The partly burned wood still had the capacity for burning, of course, and would burn vigorously if put into a fresh supply of air.

If that be the case, then, how does "phlogisticated air" differ from ordinary air? Are there any differences in properties other than the failure of the former to support combustion?

Such questions would be difficult to answer as long as chemists had no convenient method for isolating and studying gases other than ordinary air. Fortunately, the necessary technique was developed by 1727 by the English botanist Stephen Hales (1677–1761). It occurred to him to form vapors in a closed container so that they could not mix freely with unlimited quantities of air. Instead, the vapors were led from the container through a tube under water and into a second container, which was upended with its surface below the water. The vapor bubbled up into the container, driving out the water. A glass cover could then be slipped under the open mouth of the container, which would then be upended and would be full of vapor mixed with very little air.

Hales produced several different vapors in this fashion but persisted in thinking of them all as trivial varieties of air and did not study them thoroughly. Fortunately, his younger contemporary the Scottish chemist Joseph Black (1728–99) did better in this respect.

In 1756, Black strongly heated the mineral limestone, and found that it decomposed, giving off a gas and leaving behind lime. If the lime were allowed to cool and were then exposed to the gas that had been given off, it would combine with the gas once more and form limestone again. This was the first demonstration of the manner in which a gas could take part in a chemical reaction.

Because the gas could be "fixed," that is, made to combine with and become part of a solid substance, Black called it "fixed air." (Black's "fixed air," like Van Helmont's *gas sylvestre*, is what we today call carbon dioxide.)

"Fixed air" did not support combustion. What's more, when wood burned, "fixed air" was formed. Could it be, then, that "fixed air" was actually "phlogisticated air"? Certainly it seemed possible.

Black made another observation that seemed to favor this possibility. He allowed lime to stand in fresh air in which nothing had been burned. Very slowly, the lime changed over to limestone. From this, it could be seen that ordinary air contained a small quantity of "fixed air." If "fixed air" were "phlogisticated air" this would not be surprising. One might deduce that even the freshest air contained a little bit of phlogiston, perhaps from all the fires that had poured phlogiston into the atmosphere through all of history.

And yet if "phlogisticated air" were "fixed air," then the former could not merely be ordinary air plus phlogiston. "Fixed air" was distinctly different from ordinary air in ways other than merely not supporting combustion. It was distinctly denser, it dissolved somewhat in water, it combined with lime, and so on.

This suggested another experiment, which Black's student the Scottish chemist Daniel Rutherford (1749–1819) carried through in 1772. Suppose a candle were burned in a closed container until it would burn no more. A burning candle formed "fixed air" and also "phlogisticated air." The "fixed air" could easily be removed by being bubbled through a solution of lime. If it were also "phlogisticated air," then any gas that survived passage through the lime solution would be free of phlogiston and in it a candle could burn once more.

Rutherford carried through the experiment. He formed the "fixed air" and removed it, finding that after its removal most of the volume of the original air remained. What's more, the air that survived passage through the lime solution seemed to possess all the properties of ordinary air. It was no denser than air, would not dissolve in water, would not combine with lime, and so on. And yet *it would not support combustion.*

It was this new gas which seemed to be "phlogisticated air" and that was what Rutherford called it.

Rutherford's "phlogisticated air" fit the phlogiston theory much better than Black's "fixed air" did, but it left behind one small crack in the common notion of air as a single substance. After all, there were small quantities of "fixed air" present in air, and now it turned out that "fixed air" was not merely air plus phlogiston, but was a distinct substance altogether. It remained true, however, that "fixed air," though present, was present in very small quantities and so it was generally ignored.

An even more startling discovery was made by the English chemist Joseph Priestley, one that came about through a series of coincidental events. He was a Unitarian minister, who practiced chemistry as a hobby. Since he lived next door to a brewery, the fermenting grain gave him ample supplies of "fixed air" to experiment with. He took note of the manner in which it dissolved in water (and indeed it was Priestley who first formed "soda water" or "seltzer"—a solution of "fixed air" in water—and gave it to the world).

In order to avoid losing vapors to water, however, he began to collect vapors by passing them through mercury rather than water. In this way, he was able to collect and study, for the first time, the water-soluble vapors known today as ammonia, sulfur dioxide, and hydrogen chloride. —But this turned his attention to mercury.

When mercury is heated in air, it will form a brick-red

"calx." By the phlogiston theory, mercury contained phlogiston which, under the influence of heat, escaped into the air, leaving the phlogiston-free calx behind.

In 1774, Priestley put some of this mercury calx in a test tube and heated it with a lens that concentrated sunlight upon it. The calx broke down to mercury again, for the metal appeared as shining globules in the upper portion of the test tube. In addition, the calx gave off a gas as it broke down and this gas seemed to be very much like air in all its properties but one.

When Priestley thrust a smoldering splinter of wood into the test tube containing the new gas, that splinter burst into brilliant flame. Apparently, phlogiston tended to pour into the new gas more readily than into ordinary air. Priestley decided this was because the new gas had smaller quantities of phlogiston in it than ordinary air did. After all, had it not been formed from the mercury calx, which contained no phlogiston, and under the influence of heat, which would tend to allow any phlogiston which might be present to escape?

Because it contained so little phlogiston, perhaps none at all, the new gas accepted phlogiston with particular avidity, and a piece of wood that barely smoldered in ordinary air, would naturally burst into flame in it. Priestley therefore called the new gas "dephlogisticated air."

Priestley's "dephlogisticated air" did, indeed, seem to be the opposite of Rutherford's "phlogisticated air." Mice died in the latter, but were particularly active and frisky in the former. Priestley tried breathing some "dephlogisticated air" and found himself feeling "light and easy."

Yet in 1774, just as the phlogiston theory seemed to be at the height of its success, it was nevertheless about to disappear forever under the hammer blows of a French chemist, Antoine Laurent Lavoisier (1743–94).

Lavoisier recognized the importance of accurate measurement. In this he was not alone, of course. Joseph Black had made careful measurements in connection with his experiments and so had others. Lavoisier had gone about it more systematically, however, and had used quantitative experiments to test theories. It was not enough, for instance, to show that under certain conditions wood would turn to ash. The question was: From a given quantity of wood, how much ash would form?

Such questions put the phlogiston theory to a hard test almost at once. It was obvious, for instance, that when wood burned, the ash left behind weighed less than the original wood. This posed no mystery, for burning wood lost vapor and phlogiston, so naturally the ash would weigh less. How much of the loss, however, was vapor, and how much phlogiston?

There was one way of answering. The rusting of metals involved the loss of phlogiston, but not the loss of vapors. Hence, any deficiency in the weight of calx was due entirely to the loss of phlogiston. —But here came a shocker. It was easy to determine that when a metal rusted, it *gained* weight. A calx was invariably heavier than the original metal from which it formed. The loss of phlogiston alone seemed invariably to result in a gain of weight.

From this, many phlogistonists concluded that phlogiston had negative weight. Since nothing else was known to have this peculiar property, the conclusion was an uncomfortable one.

Lavoisier decided to test the matter in a new way. He heated metals such as tin and lead in closed containers, with a limited supply of air. Both metals formed a calx on the surface up to a certain point and then rusted no farther. But Lavoisier did something else. He carefully weighed the container to begin with and he then carefully weighed the container after the calx had formed. *There was no change in weight.*

Since it was well known that the calxes were heavier than the metals from which they formed, that gain in weight must have been balanced by an exactly equivalent loss of weight in something else within the container. The only other substance within the container was air. Could it be then that the calx had formed not because the metal had lost phlogiston to the air, but *because it had gained something from the air?* If so, there should be less air in the container now than before it had been heated, and the container should hold a partial vacuum.

To test this, Lavoisier opened the stopcock to the vessel and air rushed in. There had indeed been a partial vacuum within. When Lavoisier then weighed the container, it had gained weight in the amount expected from the formation of calx.

To Lavoisier, and indeed to all chemists eventually, this was a fatal blow to the phlogiston theory. All combustion and all rusting were the result of the combination of air with the substance that burned or rusted. Phlogiston did not exist or, at any rate, all the facts about combustion could be explained without any reference to it.

Yet Lavoisier remained dissatisfied. In the course of rusting or combustion, not all the air would combine. Only about one fifth of it would, and thereafter nothing could make combustion continue farther. So casually did he accept the two-thousand-year-old Greek assumption that air was a single substance that for a time he failed to see why one fifth of it should act differently from the other four fifths.

In 1774, however, Priestley visited Paris and, in a conversation with Lavoisier, described his recent experiments with "dephlogisticated air."

In a blinding flash, apparently, Lavoisier saw the truth of the matter. Ordinary air was one fifth Priestley's "dephlogisticated air" and four fifths Rutherford's "phlogisticated air" and only the former was involved in combustion. The difference between these two "airs" could not lie in the content of phlogiston, since Lavoisier had demonstrated to his own satisfaction that there was no necessity to assume the existence of phlogiston.

What he decided instead, was that the two "airs" were utterly different substances; different elements; and that the Greeks and everyone following them were wrong in assuming air to be a single substance. To emphasize this, Lavoisier gave the two "airs" different names. The "dephlogisticated air" he called "*oxygène*" from Greek words meaning "producer of sourness" since he was of the opinion that it was an essential constituent of acids. In this he was wrong, but the name has been kept ever since, and in English it is "oxygen."

As for Rutherford's "phlogisticated air," Lavoisier renamed it "*azote*" from Greek words meaning "no animal life" since animals died if placed in it. This name, however, did not survive. Since the substance formed a constituent part of the common mineral niter, it came to be called "nitrogen" ("producer of niter"). Yet there are nitrogen-containing organic substances which still incorporate the letters *azo* in their name in memory of Lavoisier's name.

To emphasize the fact that air was not an element, but was mainly a mixture of two elements (plus small quantities of still other elements not recognized for an additional century) Lavoisier would no longer use the term "air" for vapors. He went back to Van Helmont's "gas" as the general term for all airlike substances, and established its use among chemists.

Rutherford retains the credit for the discovery of nitrogen and Priestley for that of oxygen, but Lavoisier was greater than either. He served chemistry in many ways: through his emphasis on measurement, his devising of the modern system for naming chemicals, his declaration of the important principle of the conservation of mass, his writing of the first modern chemistry textbook, and so on.

Nevertheless, his insight into the nature of combustion was sufficient, all by itself, to place chemists on the right track in their study of the makeup of the Universe, a track from which they never deviated thereafter. It is with full justice, then, that Lavoisier is known as the "Father of Modern Chemistry."

And he accomplished the task by a close study of air, which, to most people even today, is simply nothing.

WATER

The Greeks thought of the elements (earth, air, water, and fire) as the fundamental components of the Universe, but not necessarily as independent substances. There seemed ample evidence that one could be converted to another.

The Greek philosopher Plato (427–347 B.C.) says so, specifically, in his dialog *Timaeus:* ". . . water . . . when melted and dispersed, passes into vapor and air. Air again, when inflamed, becomes fire: and again fire, when condensed and extinguished, passes once more into the form of air; and once more, air, when collected and condensed, produces cloud and mist, and from these, when still more compressed, comes flowing water, and from water comes earth and stones once more . . ."

Examples of such interconversions are known to all. If water is allowed to stand in an open vessel, it slowly disappears, and it can be argued that it has been converted to air. The reverse process seems to happen, as clearly and unmistakably, when first clouds and then rain appear from thin air. Many earthy substances, if added to water, seem to disappear, and how better to interpret that than to suppose they had turned to water? And if seawater is allowed to evaporate, a crust remains behind as though some of the water had turned to earth.

A volcanic eruption produces not only cinders, but vapors, and flame—air and fire being produced from earth. A thunderstorm can produce rain, hail, and lightning, so that water, earth, and fire are produced from air. (This old view of matter still persists among us today, by the way, whenever we speak of a bad storm as "the raging of the elements.")

But if the elements were interconvertible, was one of

SOURCE: "Water" appeared in *Smithsonian*, September 1971.

them more important than the rest; were three of them only varieties of the fundamental fourth? Or was there some still more basic substance, some super-element, of which all four elements were only varieties?

Greek philosophers could argue indefinitely over such matters but as long as they were content only to observe and reason, and never to experiment, they could come to no conclusion. The first to attempt to put the matter to an actual and elaborate test, was a Flemish alchemist, Jan Baptista van Helmont (1579–1644).

About 1620, he began by transplanting the shoot of a young willow tree into a large bucket of soil. He weighed the willow tree and the soil separately, and carefully kept the soil covered so that no materials could fall into the bucket and confuse the manner in which changes of weight took place. You see, if the growing plant did indeed obtain its substance from the soil it grew in (as seemed reasonable at first blush), it would follow that the soil ought to lose weight as the plant gained.

Naturally, Van Helmont had to water the willow; it wouldn't grow otherwise. For five years, he watered this tree with rainwater. It grew and flourished and at the end of the time, he carefully removed it from the bucket, knocked the soil from its roots, and weighed it. In five years of growing, the willow tree had added 164 pounds to its weight. The soil, on the other hand, had lost only two ounces.

Van Helmont deduced that the willow tree had obtained its substance from the water since that was all he added to the plant-soil system. It seemed proof—experimental proof—that water could turn into the earthy substance of plant tissue and Van Helmont was convinced thereby that water was the basic element and the primal substance of the Universe.

(Actually, Van Helmont made the mistake of underestimating the importance of the fact that air also touched the growing plant. We now know that a major part of the plant substance was derived from the carbon dioxide of the atmosphere. It was just about this period, too, that carbon dioxide was discovered and studied. By whom? As it happened, by Jan Baptista van Helmont.)

Van Helmont was, however, at the end of an era.

Within a generation of his death, new notions of elements were rising. Beginning with the Irish chemist Robert Boyle (1627–91), the attitude developed that an element was identified not through deduction but through experiment. Something that could not be further simplified in the laboratory was an element. From that standpoint, earth was not an element but a mixture of elements (see the earlier chapter, *Earth*).

The statement that water could be turned into earth had a new kind of meaning in the new chemistry. Into which elements of earth could it be turned? And which was the simpler, and therefore *the* element, the water, or the particular earthy element into which it had turned?

Nevertheless, many chemists clung to the old views, comfortable with the sonorous opinions of the great ancients, opinions that were so complete, so final. They were naturally uneasy with the new ways that involved eternal experimentation and constant changes in point of view.

As late as 1770, when seventeen different solid materials were already recognized as so many different elements, and when different gases were on the point of being recognized as elements—some still held to the old notions and maintained, in archaic fashion, that water could be converted into earth.

They conformed, however, to this extent. They pointed to experimental evidence. It had been observed many times that if water were boiled for a long time in a glass vessel, at least some of the water hardened and coalesced into solid particles which could be seen plainly and whose presence could not be disputed.

In 1770, however, a new man was on the scene. The French chemist Antoine Laurent Lavoisier (1743–94) regarded the science with fresh and vigorous eyes. To him, experimentation had to be *quantitative*; it had to involve the exact determination of "How much?" There had been others before Lavoisier who had experimented quantitatively; Van Helmont and Boyle, to name two. It was Lavoisier, however, who went about it so systematically and demonstrated the importance of measurement in chemistry so unmistakably as to make it an integral part of the science forever.

Why not, then, use measurement as an aid in the interpretation of the experiment in which water boiled itself, at least partly, into earth?

Lavoisier began with a large, clean glass vessel which he weighed carefully. He added water and heated it till the air within the vessel was driven out and replaced by steam. He then sealed the vessel and weighed it with the water content. Subtracting the weight of the empty vessel gave him the weight of the water itself.

He then heated the water for over three months, during which time it boiled gently and continuously. The steam condensed at the top of the vessel and rolled down to the bottom to be boiled again. In that period of time, distinct grains of solid appeared in the flask.

After 101 days, he stopped the fire and let the vessel cool. He weighed it again, with its water content, and the total weight of vessel plus water had not changed measurably. Filtering out the solid material, he found the weight of the water itself was also unchanged. The weight of the empty dried glass container, however, had *decreased* by a thirtieth of an ounce.

It was clear now what had happened. Through prolonged exposure to hot water, some of the substance of the glass vessel had eroded away. The solid flecks were from the glass and not from the water, and water had not been turned into earth. This was the final defeat of the old Greek notions of the elements.

Through the decade of the 1770s, the new view of elements received further confirmation. Different gaseous elements were discovered and, in 1774, Lavoisier presented strong evidence that air was no more an element than earth was (see the earlier chapter, *Air*). Air, he maintained, was a mixture of two elements which he named oxygen and azote (though the name nitrogen is now used for the latter).

With earth and air gone from the list of elements, what about water? Was water an element in the new-fashioned meaning of the word? Could water be broken down to simpler substances? Could it be built up from simpler substances?

This question arose at a time when many chemists, especially in England, held to the phlogiston theory, then three quarters of a century old. They felt that combustion involved the transfer of a subtle, weightless fluid, phlogiston, from one substance to another.

Ordinary air would accept phlogiston from a fuel, such as wood or oil, and would thus support combustion. When it had accepted all the phlogiston it could hold, it would take no more and would no longer support combustion. Such "phlogisticated air," as it was called, was actually prepared, and isolated in pure form. On the other hand, if air lost what little phlogiston it had under ordinary circumstances, the "dephlogisticated air" that was formed would support combustion with particular vigor. It, too, was prepared and isolated.

Lavoisier's reasoning pointed to the conclusion that "phlogisticated air" and "dephlogisticated air" were really the two different gaseous elements, nitrogen and oxygen, respectively, but the English chemists would not, for a while, accept that.

One of these stubborn English phlogistonists was the chemist Henry Cavendish (1731–1810). In 1766, he had treated certain metals with acid and had noted that a gas was given off which was extremely inflammable. He called it "inflammable air." Actually, this gas had been noted earlier by several chemists, including Boyle, but Cavendish was the first to describe it carefully and to work with it, so he is usually considered its discoverer.

Cavendish was fascinated by the unusual properties of "inflammable air." For one thing, it was extremely light, much lighter than air. Secondly, it burned so easily, even explosively.

By the phlogiston theory, combustible substances contained phlogiston. It was the loss of phlogiston to the air that was marked by flame. Suppose one could isolate phlogiston itself and transfer it to air without the interference of any accompanying inert material of wood or oil? Would not the result be a particularly ready and even explosive combustion? Might the light, combustible "inflammable air" really be phlogiston?

When "inflammable air" burned, whether it was pure phlogiston or merely a gas with an abnormally high phlogiston content, the end product ought to be "phlogisticated air."

Some chemists had observed the burning of "inflammable air" but had come to no conclusion as to the product. For one thing, they worked with small quantities and any product formed was present only in traces. Some reports had spoken of droplets of liquid forming after "inflammable air" had burned, but there was no clear identification of that liquid.

Cavendish had tried such experiments also and received no clear-cut answers. He puzzled over the early results and held his council till he had straightened the matter out to his own satisfaction.

Finally, in 1784. he felt on sufficiently firm ground to describe what he had done. He began with a large quantity of "inflammable air" and plenty of ordinary air. When all the "inflammable air" had been burned under conditions designed to retain the product, he found about a quarter of an ounce of liquid at the bottom of the vessel. That was enough to analyze, and the results were rather startling—he had formed water.

Cavendish sought to explain this in terms of the phlogiston theory.

Suppose that water, in its normal state, possessed a certain amount of phlogiston; not enough to make water combustible, but some.

Suppose, next, that more phlogiston could somehow be pumped into it; a great deal. Possessing a great deal of phlogiston, water would have a strong tendency to lose the excess easily and that would make it combustible. Indeed, water with an abnormally high content of phlogiston would be "inflammable air."

On the other hand, suppose that in some way, water were forced to give up the phlogiston it ordinarily carried. It would then have a strong tendency to absorb phlogiston again. Things would burn in this "dephlogisticated water." Indeed, "dephlogisticated water" might well be identical to what was then being called "dephlogisticated air."

Instead of "inflammable air," then, let us write "water + ph" (where "ph" stands for phlogiston) and for "dephlogisticated air" let us write "water − ph." When "inflammable air" burned to form water, then what happened, according to Cavendish's speculation was:

$$(\text{water} + \text{ph}) + (\text{water} - \text{ph}) \rightarrow \text{water}$$

Mathematically, we see that "+ph" and "−ph" cancel. Chemically, we see that the excess phlogiston in the "inflammable air" transfers to the phlogiston-deficient "dephlogisticated air," leaving water, with its moderate phlogiston content. —And, of course, water remains an element, modified only by varying phlogiston content.

This sounds awfully neat but, actually, if allowed to stand, it would let loose a wilderness of confusion. If "dephlogisticated air" and "dephlogisticated water" were one and the same, then when phlogiston was added, was air or water produced? If "inflammable air" burned, it became water, certainly, but if charcoal burned, the "dephlogisticated air" absorbed all the phlogiston it could take, without forming a trace of water at any time.

Lavoisier heard of Cavendish's experiments almost at once, but he did not interpret them according to the phlogiston theory. He was quite convinced that no such thing as phlogiston existed. Air was composed of nitrogen and oxygen, and combustion consisted of the combination of the burning substance with oxygen.

He repeated Cavendish's experiment, confirmed the production of water, and interpreted this as signifying that "inflammable air" combined with oxygen to form water. He renamed "inflammable air" at once, calling it "hydrogen" from Greek words meaning "water-former" and that has been used ever since.

By Lavoisier's system, the burning of hydrogen took on a new and much greater importance. It meant that water was not an element, but was a combination of two simpler substances, the elements hydrogen and oxygen.

To maintain that water was a compound substance and not an element was something that needed all the evidence one could gather. Having argued that hydrogen and oxygen could be combined to form water, Lavoisier next wished to demonstrate that water could be pulled apart again to form hydrogen and oxygen.

This he could do, but only in part. He passed steam through a heated gun barrel and the hot iron pulled the oxygen out of the steam. That this had happened was proved, indirectly, by the rapid development of rust along the inner surface of the barrel, for rust, by Lavoisier's chemistry, was a compound of iron and oxygen.

To be sure, the oxygen was not isolated as a gas and its formation demonstrated directly, but at the other end of the barrel, what was left of the water after the oxygen had been subtracted appeared: a stream of hydrogen.

The final nail in the coffin of water-as-an-element came in 1800, six years after Lavoisier's tragic and unjustified death on the guillotine during the French Revolution. In 1800, the Italian physicist Alessandro Volta (1745–1827) developed the first electric battery, a device which served to produce a usable current of electricity. The news reached England on March 20 and by May 2 an English chemist, William Nicholson (1753–1815), and his colleague, an English surgeon, Anthony Carlisle (1768–1840), had constructed a battery of their own.

Nicholson and Carlisle used the battery to pass a current through water and found bubbles of gas being given off. Investigation soon showed these to consist of hydrogen and oxygen and it was not at all difficult to collect them separately. Water had been "electrolyzed" and Lavoisier's contention had been proved beyond dispute.

This was scarcely needed, however. Lavoisier's work had carried conviction. Some of the older chemists went their way stubbornly, but the new generation was Lavoisier's. When Cavendish died in 1810, he was the last of the phlogistonists.

Lavoisier's discovery of the compound nature of water (made possible by his prior discovery of the true nature of air) proved of vital importance in two ways.

Lavoisier had noticed that when chemical reactions took place in a closed system, the mass (considered a measure of the quantity of matter present) never changed, whatever the reaction. Was this universal, or did it apply only to the simple mineral substances that chemists worked with?

When coal burned, oxygen was consumed and carbon dioxide was produced. When animals (including man) breathed, oxygen was consumed and carbon dioxide was produced. Must it not be, then, reasoned Lavoisier, that respiration was a form of combustion taking place in living tissue, and was the quantity of matter maintained unchanged (that is, was matter "conserved") in the body also?

Between 1782 and 1784, Lavoisier and a co-worker,

Pierre Simon de Laplace (1749–1827)—far better known in later years as a great astronomer—had carefully measured the oxygen consumed and carbon dioxide produced by a guinea pig and matched the heat developed by it with that developed by burning ordinary carbon under conditions that consumed an equal quantity of oxygen.

The results were puzzling. Some of the oxygen consumed by the guinea pig did not show up as carbon dioxide. Had some of the oxygen disappeared? What's more the guinea pig produced more heat for the oxygen it consumed than the coal did. Did living tissue produce heat out of nothing?

As soon as the compound nature of water was worked out, Lavoisier had the answer to the puzzle. It was not merely the carbon of living tissue that combined with oxygen, but the hydrogen also. It was not merely carbon dioxide that was being produced, but water, too. Once the water content of the expired breath was measured, that accounted for the missing oxygen. The greater amount of heat formed by combining hydrogen (rather than carbon) with oxygen, explained why the guinea pig produced more heat than expected.

Lavoisier was convinced, then, that the quantity of matter remained constant even in the complicated and mysterious reactions that went on in living tissue. He announced his "law of conservation of matter" and that has been a cornerstone of experimental chemistry (despite its slight modification by Einstein's theory of relativity) ever since.

The discovery of the compound nature of water led onward, after Lavoisier's death, to something that was even more revolutionary. Lavoisier's stress on the importance of measuring had wide influence and meant that chemists were not content with noting that hydrogen and oxygen combined to form water. The question now became: How much hydrogen combined with how much oxygen to form how much water?

Cavendish reported in 1784 that a particular volume of hydrogen required two and a half times its own volume of air for complete burning. Since one fifth of the air was oxygen, this meant that a particular volume of hydrogen combined with half its own volume of oxygen.

In 1786, the French mathematician Gaspard Monge (1746–1818) reported his work in this area. He weighed the oxygen and hydrogen that combined and the water that was produced. He found, first, that the water produced had exactly the mass of the hydrogen and oxygen (together) with which he had started, thus upholding the law of conservation of matter. Second, he found that a given weight of hydrogen combined with eight times its own weight of oxygen. (The oxygen might have a smaller volume than the hydrogen it combined with, but even that smaller volume was considerably heavier than the very light hydrogen.)

Similar measurements of the relative weights of different elements that combined to form a particular compound were carried out by others, particularly by the French chemist Joseph Louis Proust (1754–1826). By 1799, Proust was able to maintain that all compounds consisted of combinations of definite proportions of elements by weight, and that these proportions did not and could not vary. The case of hydrogen and oxygen combining in a 1-to-8 weight-ratio remained the most spectacular and easily cited case.

Proust's "law of definite proportions" gave an enormous impetus to the development of an atomic theory. Many of those who had pondered on the nature of the Universe had come to the conclusion that matter must be made up of tiny indivisible units, even back in Greek times. So far, though, it had only been a matter of speculation.

Beginning in 1803, however, the English chemist John Dalton (1766–1844) went a crucial step farther. Not only did he postulate the existence of atoms, as many before him had done, but for the first time in human history he began to work out what their properties might be, from experimental data.

Suppose both hydrogen and oxygen are made up of atoms, and that in forming water one atom of hydrogen combines with one atom of oxygen. If so, the most direct way of accounting for the 1-to-8 ratio of combination by weight is to suppose that the single oxygen atom is eight times as heavy as the single hydrogen atom. The actual weight of the two atoms could not be determined by Dalton, but he could state them in relative terms. If the weight of the hydrogen atom were set at 1, then the weight of the oxygen atom would have to be 8. He determined the weight of other types of atoms on this same basis, by using the law of definite proportions, and thus devised the first table of "atomic weights."

It was that which converted the atom from the vague speculation of the philosopher to a concept that was useful, and even indispensable, to the chemist.

To be sure, Dalton was incorrect in some details. It was not long before it was pointed out that since, in terms of volume, two parts of hydrogen combined with one part of oxygen, it followed that two atoms of hydrogen combined with one of oxygen to form water. (The terms of the argument were more complicated and convincing than the mere statement would make it seem.) In that case, the single oxygen atom was not eight times heavier than a single hydrogen atom; it was eight times heavier than *two* hydrogen atoms and therefore sixteen times heavier than one. If the atomic weight of hydrogen is set at 1, then the atomic weight of oxygen is 16.

Despite such correction, and many others, and despite considerable elaboration and increased sophistication, Dalton's structure, stemming in large part from the manner of combination of hydrogen and oxygen, remains the framework of modern chemistry.

And what of Lavoisier?

It is often considered ironic that in Lavoisier's lifetime, important elements were discovered by lesser men, while Lavoisier himself, the greatest of all chemists in history, never discovered one.

Hydrogen and oxygen bear the names that Lavoisier gave them, for instance, but the credit for their discovery goes elsewhere.

Yet Lavoisier must not be downgraded for this. In the case of air and water, he had *un*discovered two elements, and this proved of greater importance, ultimately, than all the element discoveries of the period put together.

FIRE

Of all the substances viewed as elements by the Greeks, certainly fire was the most dramatic. It alone blazed with light. It leaped and danced, and changed its shape at every moment. It seemed the very embodiment of impermanence.

In the sixth century B.C. there lived a Greek thinker known as Heraclitus (c. 540–c. 475 B.C.). He lived in Ephesus on what is now the Aegean coast of Turkey and was known to the later Greeks as the "weeping philosopher" because of his pessimistic view of life. To him, nothing was eternal, nothing stable. All was evanescent, everything changed, everything came into being and was eventually destroyed.

To him, fire was the symbol of change and destruction and it was fire (or some ideal version of fire) which he therefore accepted as the basic substance of the Universe. Only through fire could the impermanence of the Universe be explained. Paradoxically, Heraclitus maintained that the only thing that was unchanging was change and that only fire, then, was eternal and basic.

In the course of the next two centuries, Heraclitus' concept was tamed and made less radical. Fire came to be accepted as merely one of the four elements that made up the Earth and its works, the other three being earth, air, and water.

Aristotle (384–322 B.C.) gave fire its place in his picture of the organization of the Universe. It was placed in the highest regions appertaining to the Earth; lying above the air. Ordinarily invisible, it appeared briefly as lightning when the air was rent by the fury of storms. Fire, when formed in the lower regions, tended to burst upward in an effort to reach its natural place on high. Thus fire shot up out of volcanoes, and even the small flames set by man strove upward.

Through ancient and medieval times, fire, as a substance, resisted investigation. It could not be handled easily, as earth and water could. Nor could it be trapped and studied as air could.

It could be used, however. It was used everywhere, in forming glass from sand, pottery from clay, metal from ores.

In all the various ways in which fire might be used, it produced, invariably, light and heat. Indeed, it was often used by man for no purpose other than to provide light and heat, to turn night at least a little into day, and winter at least a little into summer.

Light and heat were not alike as aspects of fire, however. Light existed only as long as the fire lived. When the fire died, the light was gone. Heat on the other hand persisted. Long after the fire died down, the kettle and its contents remained hot.

Could it be, then, that heat was the essential element to be considered? Were light and flame, the most visible and striking attributes of fire, merely a temporary accompaniment of heat rushing out and mixing with air?

The Dutch physician Hermann Boerhaave (1668–1738) was the first to distinguish between fire-as-heat and fire-as-flame and after his time, scientists began to think of heat and of flame separately. Gradually, heat began to seem the more fundamental.

The first to study heat in the modern sense was the Scottish chemist Joseph Black (1728–99).

If a kettle of water were placed over a fire, its temperature started to rise. Heat poured into the water, raising its temperature.

If, however, the kettle contained a mixture of ice and water, the temperature did *not* rise when it was placed over a fire. Instead, the ice melted, gradually. Only after the ice had all melted, did the temperature rise. The same thing happened when water was brought to a boil. The temperature rose until the boiling point was reached. After that, more and more of the water boiled away but the temperature rose no higher no matter how fiercely the fire beneath roared.

Black tried to explain this in terms of a kind of heat-fluid which gradually filled the ice, melting it (or, at higher temperatures, filled the water, boiling it). It was not until the ice was saturated with the heat-fluid so that it had all melted, that there was finally heat-fluid available for the water. Only after the ice had melted, then, did the temperature of the water begin going up.

The French chemist Antoine Laurent Lavoisier (1743–94) accepted Black's thinking on the heat-fluid. In 1789, when Lavoisier published the first modern textbook of chemistry, he included heat among his list of elements. He named the weightless heat-fluid "caloric," from the Latin word for heat.

The theory of heat-as-fluid rather conveniently explained certain observations. For instance, substances almost invariably expand when they are heated, and it is easy to suppose that caloric takes up room. Why not? When it pours into the substance being heated, it naturally elbows the particles aside to make room for itself and the substance expands.

On the whole, the theory of heat-as-fluid satisfied the chemists, but it left the physicists with a gap in *their* theories.

Ever since the Italian scientist Galileo Galilei (1564–1642) had first studied motion quantitatively in the 1590s, physicists had been making more and more elaborate measurements. They had been particularly interested in those aspects of motion which did not change when the conditions of a particular group of bodies altered.

In 1668, for instance, the English mathematician John Wallis (1616–1703), dealt with the "momentum" of moving bodies, that is, with the product of their mass and velocity. He showed that he could successfully analyze the results of collisions between moving bodies by supposing that momentum could be transferred from one body to another, but could not be either created or destroyed.

This is called "the law of conservation of momentum." It is the first-discovered member of a group of conservation laws which, taken all together, set the ground rules, so to speak, for all the changes that go on in the Universe.

Another type of conservation can be demonstrated by a

ball thrown in the air. It moves more and more slowly as it rises, until at some point in midair, it comes to a halt.

But what we now call the "energy" of a body (its capacity to do work) depends in part on its motion. A moving ball will break a window or knock over a tenpin, but a stationary ball will do neither even if in contact with window or tenpin. Furthermore, the more rapidly the ball is moving the more spectacularly it produces its results on collision.

In the case of the ball rising into the air, the energy of motion ("kinetic energy") gradually diminishes and, when it is at a halt, the kinetic energy is zero.

But, high in the air, the ball has a certain energy by virtue of its position. If it were held there, it could do nothing, but once it is free to move, it falls at once and begins to gain kinetic energy. The higher in the air it is, the more kinetic energy it gains by the time it strikes the ground. The energy content by virtue of position is called "potential energy."

It would seem, then, that as the ball rises in the air, kinetic energy gradually turns to potential energy, and as it falls again the potential energy turns back to kinetic energy again. It is easy to show that the potential energy at the moment when the ball is motionless in the air is equal to the kinetic energy at the moment the ball begins to rise upward and also to the kinetic energy at the moment the ball completes its fall downward.

As the ball rises and falls, its kinetic energy is converted to potential energy and then back to kinetic energy without loss. What's more, at every point in its rise and fall, the kinetic energy *plus* the potential energy (together they are called "mechanical energy") remains constant.

Ideally, the ball, if it were perfectly elastic, would strike, bounce, rise to a height, fall, strike, bounce, rise to the same height again, and so on indefinitely, changing back and forth between kinetic energy and potential energy forever.

The effect is shown more elegantly by a pendulum, where the bob has its maximum kinetic energy at the bottom of the swing. If it is then heading leftward, it will rise more and more slowly, coming to a halt at a point where all the kinetic energy is turned to potential energy, drop back to the bottom faster and faster, swing to the right, come to a halt again at a point where all the kinetic energy is turned to potential energy—and so on, over and over and over.

The notion of the conservation of mechanical energy gradually emerged in the course of the late seventeenth century, though most of the actual terminology (even the word "energy" itself) didn't come till the nineteenth century.

One of the difficulties with the law of conservation of mechanical energy was that it was imperfect. It could only hold under ideal conditions that could never be attained in actual practice. A bouncing ball reaches a lower height with each bounce and finally comes to rest. A pendulum's swing very slowly contracts and it finally comes to rest. More or less slowly, the mechanical energy disappears and, in the end, an object has neither energy of motion nor energy of position.

The villain in the case is friction: friction with the ground, friction with the air, friction with anything the moving object touches.

Could it be that the mechanical energy is somehow transferred to the ground or air or whatever? At first thought, this doesn't seem likely. After all, the matter accounting for the friction does not visibly gain either kinetic energy or potential energy. It neither moves nor changes position as a result of friction.

But is it necessary for the object supplying the friction to move as a whole or to change position as a whole? Suppose that apparently solid matter (or liquid, or gaseous) were actually made up of tiny particles far too small to be seen, and suppose that these tiny particles moved every which way in a kind of blur that was not visible to the unaided eye.

After all, objects could be warmed by friction. Perhaps, the invisible motion of the invisible particles of matter was what we called heat; and the faster the motion, the greater the heat. The loss of mechanical energy in visibly moving objects might then result from the transfer of that energy to the tiny particles of matter, which would gain a corresponding amount of mechanical energy. Another way of putting it is that friction converts mechanical energy into heat.

As early as about 1700, the English philosopher John

Locke (1632–1704) was suggesting the idea of heat-as-motion (kinetic theory), which was eventually opposed to heat-as-fluid (caloric theory).

If heat were accepted as a form of motion, then the law of conservation of mechanical energy might be extended to include heat and it might then become less imperfect; or not imperfect at all.

The chief trouble with the suggestion was the notion of tiny particles too small to see, engaged in motions too subtle to detect. Scientists, generally, were not ready to accept so apparently mystical a concept and the law of conservation of mechanical energy remained as it was—imperfect.

Yet before the end of the eighteenth century, some strong blows were struck in favor of the kinetic theory of heat.

The first of these involved one of the more colorful characters in the history of science. He was Benjamin Thompson (1753–1814), who was born in Massachusetts. During the Revolutionary War, he was a Tory serving the British authorities as a spy. Naturally, when the British left Boston, Thompson found it safer to leave with them. He never returned to the United States.

In 1783, he left Great Britain for the Continent, and eventually entered the service of the Elector of Bavaria, who was pleased enough with the American's services to give him a title of nobility. Thompson chose to be titled after the town near which he had owned some land and became Count Rumford. It is by this name that he is usually known.

One of Rumford's tasks, in 1798, was to supervise the boring of cannon for the Bavarian army. The way this was done was to have a horse work a treadmill, the turning of which supplied the power that kept a borer turning. This borer forced its way into a solid block of brass, slowly forming a cylindrical hole of the required size.

As the borer worked, brass shavings were gouged out and these, together with the block itself, grew so hot that the metal had to be constantly cooled with water.

Rumford couldn't help but wonder where the heat all came from. According to the caloric theory, the breaking up of the solid brass into shavings released some of the caloric content of the brass into the air, where it was more evident.

To Rumford, however, this seemed nonsense. After all, how much caloric could be liberated in such a way? Certainly not more than the metal contained in the first place. Yet he calculated that if all the caloric released in the process of boring were put back into the metal, the entire block would melt.

He tried something else. He began with a partly excavated cannon and then began operations with a borer so blunt that it could not gouge out any further brass. The brass was now not breaking up and no caloric ought to be released. Yet heat was developed in even greater quantities than when a sharp borer was used.

Rumford pointed out that heat was produced without fire, without light, without chemical combustion. It came just out of motion, out of the turning of the borer and the treadmill, out of the motion of the horse. He maintained that heat was a form of motion and that heat would be formed endlessly as long as horse, treadmill, and borer moved.

Then in 1799, the young English chemist Humphry Davy (1778–1829) also tackled the problem. He worked out some interesting demonstrations with friction. He used clockwork to make a metal wheel turn against a metal plate. Though he kept the entire system below freezing, enough heat was developed to melt the wax with which he had coated the plate.

In the same series of experiments, he rubbed two pieces of ice together by a mechanical setup and, though the temperature was again kept below freezing, the ice melted.

The point was clear. If there was insufficient caloric in the entire system to raise the temperature above freezing, how could the release of only some of that insufficient quantity produce enough heat to melt ice and wax?

Again the conclusions seem to be that there was no such thing as caloric and that heat was kinetic in nature, a form of motion.

The calorists defended their position vigorously, of course. When, however, in 1803, less than five years after the experiments of Rumford and Davy, the English chemist John Dalton (1766–1844) began to advance his atomic theory, it might have seemed that the calorists had received their deathblow. After all, Dalton's reasoning in favor of atoms was so strong that many chemists began to accept it at once and here was the refutation of the strongest point against the kinetic theory of heat. Matter *was* composed of particles so tiny as to be invisible and surely these particles might be invisibly in motion.

As it happened, though, the early atomists were also calorists. Dalton himself used the caloric theory to explain the existence of gases.

According to the atomic theory, atoms were in contact in liquids and solids; but in gases, the atoms had to be far apart from one another. Only by so much wide separation could it be explained why gases were so much lighter than were equal volumes of liquids and solids, and why gases could so easily be compressed, whereas liquids and solids could not be.

But what kept the atoms of gases so far apart? Since gases are formed when liquids are heated, Dalton suggested that gases had gained so much caloric that all the atoms were surrounded by it. They were atomic islands embedded in weightless caloric seas.

Thus the caloric theory survived the coming of the atoms and competing kinetic theory of heat made no headway. The latter was not, however, forgotten. Stubbornly, some physicists kept returning to it.

It was clear that if, indeed, a certain amount of mechanical energy (whether kinetic, potential, or a combination) could be turned into heat, then, if energy was to be conserved, the mechanical energy had to be turned into a *fixed* amount of heat. How much energy meant how much heat? What, in other words, was the "mechanical equivalent of heat"?

Rumford had made a rough estimate to the effect that (using modern units) 5.55 joules of work was equivalent to 1 calorie of heat. In 1842, a German physicist, Julius Robert von Mayer (1814–78)—he was born in the year Rumford died—offered a new figure on the basis of a single experiment in which a horse-powered device stirred paper pulp in a caldron. This was 3.90 joules per calorie, which was much closer than Rumford's value to that which is now accepted.

Mayer also advanced a startling insight. He claimed that energy was perfectly conserved *if all its manifestations were included*. One had to take into account not only mechanical energy and heat, but light as well, and electrical energy, magnetic energy, and so on. Even the energy of living things must be included.

Energy might change its form in a dozen different ways but when, within a particular "closed system" (one which did not lose energy to, or gain energy from, the outside world), all the energy was added up, the sum remained constant always, no matter what changes took place within the system.

However, Mayer's enunciation of the "law of conservation of energy" went utterly unnoticed. It was too daring an idea, too far in advance of experimental data.

Even as Mayer worked, however, the insufficiency of data was being corrected.

An English physicist, James Prescott Joule (1818–89), who was unaware of Mayer's work, was tackling the problem of the mechanical equivalent of heat. For years he worked to determine this value in a score of different ways, using every form of energy he could handle. He heated water and mercury by churning them with paddles. He passed water through small holes to heat it by friction. He expanded and contracted gases. He used electricity to heat water. Even on his honeymoon, he made use of a special thermometer to take the temperature at the top and the bottom of a waterfall.

In the end he found that a given amount of energy *of whatever form* always yielded the same amount of heat, and he set the mechanical equivalent of heat at 4.18 joules per calorie. (He didn't use the unit "joule," of course, nor is the similarity between that and his name a coincidence. The joule was invented later, set equal to 10,000,000 ergs, an older unit, and named in his honor.)

Joule found it difficult to get his results published in a learned journal. He lacked a professorial appointment, for one thing, and that made him seem an amateur. For another, he was presenting results which depended on tiny temperature differences; differences which most physicists at the time felt were too small to determine with the necessary precision.

Joule was therefore forced to present his views in a public lecture in Manchester, England, in 1847. Having done that, he managed to persuade a reluctant Manchester newspaper to print the lecture in full. In this way, he at least managed to assure himself of credit for his findings.

A few months later, he finally had a chance to present it before a scientific gathering. The audience was unsympathetic and when he was finished, they sat in stony silence, until a young Scotsman, William Thomson (1824–1907), who was in later life to become Lord Kelvin, rose to ask a question. Thomson's shrewd questioning and Joule's clear answers began a lifelong friendship between the two and their enthusiasm at this time infected the audience. Joule was taken seriously at last.

In that same year, 1847, a young German physiologist, Hermann von Helmholtz (1821–94), presented a paper that maintained the conservation of energy in precisely the same terms that Mayer had done five years before (though Helmholtz had not heard of Mayer's work any more than Joule had).

For a time, Helmholtz could not get his paper published, but under the hammer strokes of Joule's experimental labors, more and more physicists were rallying to the kinetic theory of heat, so the notion of a law of conservation of *all* energy had to be accepted. The notion of caloric tottered to its fall.

Helmholtz was given the credit for the discovery of the law of conservation of energy at the time. Mayer's claims to priority were rejected and he was treated as a plagiarizing crackpot—to the point where frustration drove him to mental collapse and attempted suicide. He survived to receive his due credit in the last decade of his sad life, however.

Nowadays, the credit for the law of conservation of energy, sometimes considered the greatest and most fundamental of all the laws of nature, is shared among Mayer, Joule and Helmholtz.

Two others might be added, though. Ahead of all of them was a French physicist, Nicolas Léonard Sadi Carnot (1796–1832), whose studies of the steam engine cycle in 1824 showed the relationship between mechanical energy and heat. Carnot, however, died prematurely of cholera and his single publication went unnoticed until the 1840s. There was also a Danish physicist, Ludwig August Colding (1815–88), who in the 1840s independently advanced notions of a mechanical equivalent of heat and of the conservation of energy.

The relationship of the motion of atoms to temperature and heat was placed on a firm theoretical basis about 1860 by the labors of the Scottish mathematician and physicist, James Clerk Maxwell (1831–79). The work was further extended by the Austrian physicist Ludwig Eduard Boltzmann (1844–1906), who made Maxwell's mathematics more rigorous.

In this way, the kinetic theory was completely established on the basis of random motions of atoms and molecules, and caloric was killed forever.

The tragic fate of those involved with kinetic theory continued, however. Maxwell died prematurely of cancer. Boltzmann's situation was even worse. He was subject to fits of depression, aggravated by last-ditch opposition to kineticism on the part of some scientific conservatives, and in the end Boltzmann committed suicide.

But we can see now that the Greeks' choice of fire as one of the elements of the Universe was a tribute to their insight. If we consider fire as the most obvious and dramatic form of energy available to ancient man, we can appreciate the insight better.

It is of energy in all its forms (and even matter is but a form of energy) that the Universe is constructed. What's more, energy is eternal, can neither be created nor destroyed, and every change in the Universe from the explosion of a galaxy to the motion of an electron is an aspect of energy change.

So it follows that the old sage Heraclitus was quite right after all. Fire is (in a subtle way) the fundamental substance of the Universe and the basic unchanging factor in a changing Universe.

AFTERWORD

When *Smithsonian* asked me to write the preceding four articles on the four Greek elements, I'm not sure what they had in mind, but it occurred to me to use them as the base for a quick overview of the history of chemistry.

By the end of the fourth article, however, I had only reached the latter end of the nineteenth century. It occurred to me that the Greeks had a fifth element, "ether," one suggested by Aristotle. I could write a fifth article based on ether that would carry me well into the twentieth century. I suggested it to *Smithsonian*, which, however, had had enough.

So—anyone else want it?

4 · IN PHYSICS

SPACE

Space is what makes possible differences in position. We become aware of differences of position, and therefore of an extension within which those differences can exist, as a result of muscular effort. We must turn our heads, or at least our eyes, to see first one thing and then another. We must reach out our arms this way, then that, this far, then that, in order to make our fingertips coincide with this object or that. Or we must move bodily here, then there, to reach first this, then that.

The notion of space begins with the concept of "here, not there," or "there, not here." As soon as one can localize a particular object as being in one particular place, the idea of a limitless extension of potential place within which all objects are located becomes possible.

Naturally, the idea of extension does not have to be specifically formulated in the mind to be made use of. We can be reasonably sure that no species other than man has a clear idea of space in the abstract, yet all organisms that move seem to utilize the concept. The tigress that springs makes some obscure judgment, however mechanical and non-conscious, concerning the effort required to change her position from a starting point in space to another which will coincide with the position of her prey. The chameleon launching its tongue at an insect does the same for its tongue-tip. Even the growing tendrils of a plant climbing upward to the Sun, or the probing rootlets aiming at water are changing position in a manner designed to keep the plant alive and the organism thus makes a surely unconscious, but surely advantageous, use of the concept of space.

How, then, does man's attitude toward space differ from

that of all other organisms? Of course, he can communicate his thoughts about it through carefully modulated sounds. Two or more human beings can sharpen their abstract concepts by mutual mental friction. Still, for all we know, other species of organisms do the same in some way. It seems entirely improbable that this can be so, but we can never be certain what concepts exist in the brains of species other than our own, and how these may be communicated, unless we can learn to share in their communications thoroughly and they in ours.

What we can judge by, however, is deeds, not thoughts. We can take the attitude that it doesn't matter what an organism thinks or understands about a particular concept, for that we might never know. What counts is what an organism *does* about a particular concept.

The tigress and the chameleon judge distance, but they do so intuitively, guiding muscular effort by the subtle adjustments of the focusing mechanisms of their eye. (We do that, too, every time we pick up a pencil, or do almost anything else.) The beaver in building a dam, or the bird in building a nest, makes use of logs and twigs that are more or less of the right size for the purpose, but there is at best a hit-and-miss quality to the process, and the final decision is the attempt at a direct fit, which either succeeds or fails.

Here, though, mankind's approach to space is unique. Alone among the species, he goes beyond simple trial and error in comparing two or more sets of differences in position. In other words, man *measures* distance (the separation of position) in a mechanical way and thus reduces the notion of extension in space to a form that makes possible accurate comparisons without superimposition.

He might begin by placing a log across an opening until he finds one that is sufficiently long to stretch across without falling in (if he wishes to construct a barrier across a cave opening). The log that fits can then be used as a reference log against which other logs are measured so that no effort is wasted bringing back logs that are too short. It is simpler, though, to use a handspan and count, and that is the truly crucial addition—the use of counting.

There are so many handspans across the log that fits; therefore you need find other logs that are as many handspans across. You might even learn to break a too long log to leave one of the proper length. You don't need a reference log in that case; you need only carry your hand —provided you possess also the ability to count and remember the count.

There are a variety of parts of the body that can be used to make measurements of various sizes, and their imprint leaves a mark on common measures today. The foot is exactly what its name implies, the length of a foot. The height of horses is measured in hands, and the "mile" is from the Latin *milia passuum* or "a thousand paces."

As long as measurements are private, the advance over the situation in other species is small. The human would be more efficient than the beaver at finding logs of the right size, but not very much more so, if each man worked alone. But to communicate your measuring system to others, and thus establish a community of labor, produces problems since the foot or pace of one person is not the same size as that of another.

To suit a number of different people there must be developed the notion of a "standard measure." Everyone will use the chief's foot as a way of measuring the length of logs; and since the chief would not be available for everyone's measuring (nor wish to be) it would occur to some genius to produce logs measuring exactly the length of the chief's foot and distribute them to those who need to have measures in common. It would be the "standard log" once again, but the same for all, and adaptable to all purposes, particularly if it is neatly subdivided into still smaller units.

When did the notion of a standard measure arise? Surely it could not have come much later than the development of agriculture, about 8000 B.C. or so, It is very likely men could not cultivate their farms in peace unless there were some agreement (by measurements according to some accepted standards) as to how wide a piece of land belonged to each. The simple use of boundary stones invited surreptitious shiftings.

By the time civilization developed to the point of the invention of writing, elaborate systems of measurement were in use, and it was considered an important part of the governmental apparatus to maintain the integrity of the standard measure. That integrity was even made part of the divine command. Thus, as part of the pronouncements of God upon Mt. Sinai (according to the biblical story) we have, in the words of the modern translation, the New English Bible: "You shall not pervert justice in measurement of length, weight, or quantity. You shall have true scales, true weights, true measures dry and liquid. I am the Lord your God who brought you out of Egypt." (Leviticus 19:35–37.)

The next important step in the understanding of space came with the development of geometry, the study of interconnected measures. By understanding the relationship of one part of a figure to another, it became possible to measure the length, let us say, of one part and from that deduce the length of a second part *without* actually measuring it.

For instance, it is quite impractical to measure the height of the Great Pyramid directly, since one cannot stand at the apex, bore a hole to the ground through its rocky structure, drop a plumb line through the hole and then measure the length of line needed to reach the ground. However, one can measure along the slope of the pyramid from ground to apex (if one wants to climb it and drag a cord behind him). From that, and a knowledge of the angle the slope makes with the ground, one can *calculate* the height of the pyramid.

Even this is an arduous task, requiring much muscular effort, and a line that is about 615 feet long. The next step is to be able to relate the measurements of one figure to that of a second figure which is easier to handle. A small triangle, for instance, would have the same measurement relationships as would another, much larger triangle of the same shape, so why not work with the convenient former rather than with the inconvenient (perhaps impossible) latter?

There is a story that the Greek philosopher Thales, about 570 B.C., measured the height of the Great Pyramid without ever climbing a foot. He noted that when the Sun was in a certain position in the sky, his shadow was the same length he was. (He and his shadow formed the two legs, we would now say, of an isosceles right triangle. He presumed this was true for all objects at this time. He therefore measured the distance from the edge of the base of the pyramid to the shadow of its apex on the ground (something much easier to do than measuring the slope by climbing it) and added to it the distance from the edge of the base to the center of the large square on which the pyramid stood (an easy calculation).

All such measurements of objects not directly accessible, can be reduced to the manipulation of triangles of similar shapes and that branch of mathematics is "trigonometry."

The climax reached by trigonometry, as far as our planet was concerned came in 240 B.C., when a Greek philosopher, Eratosthenes, working in Alexandria, Egypt, measured the size of the entire Earth (and accurately) without ever leaving home, and certainly without wrapping a measuring tape about its fat girth.

Travelers had told Eratosthenes that in the city of Syene (the modern Aswan) in southern Egypt, the noonday sun was directly overhead at the summer solstice so that every object stood on its own shadow. On that same day, however, Eratosthenes could tell that the noonday sun in Alexandria was seven degrees south of the zenith—by measuring the length of the shadow as compared with the length of the object casting the shadow.

This difference, Eratosthenes realized, was due to the curvature of the spherical Earth. The Sun looked down (so to speak) directly on one part, but looked at the surface somewhat to the north of that part at a slant because the surface curved away. There are 360° to a circle and the distance from Syene to Alexandria represented 7°. The entire circle of the Earth was therefore about 360/7 or some fifty times that between the two cities. The north–south distance between Syene and Alexandria was 500 miles, so the circumference of the Earth was 25,000 miles. —And so it was.

Until the time of the Greeks, there was no way of making measurements of distance anywhere but at or very near the surface of the Earth. No one could rise up through the atmosphere, trailing a measuring cord. Nor did there seem any way to compare distances in the sky and get any but the most primitive notions. It was clear, for instance, that the Moon passed in front of the Sun during solar eclipses, so the Moon was closer to the Earth than the Sun was.

Less obvious reasoning gave rise to the notion that both Moon and Sun, together with five bright stars that constantly changed position against the background of the other "fixed" stars, were closer to the Earth than those fixed stars were. From the rapidity of motion of these "planets" (from a Greek word meaning "wanderer") the Greeks decided their order of distance away from the Earth was the Moon, Mercury, Venus, the Sun, Mars, Jupiter, and Saturn.

This order is not exactly correct and the Greeks could determine nothing else. And without a real notion of heavenly distances, there could be no true understanding of the size of the heavenly bodies and the nature of the structure of the Universe. Mankind was forced to suppose that the heavenly bodies were, in actuality, exactly what they seemed to be. The stars were small specks of light, fixed to a solid sky that was blue in the day and black at night. The planets were fixed to other, closer spheres, that were perfectly transparent and therefore perfectly invisible. (For all anyone could tell, each sphere touched the one beyond.) And the Moon and Sun were spheres of light which were as small as they looked to be.

The Greek philosopher Anaxagoras, living in Athens, suspected that things were *not* as they seemed. The Sun might be a great distance off and, if so, though it looked small it might be a large glowing rock a hundred miles across. He said so about 435 B.C. and created a furor. He was forced into exile.

The first person to try to transfer to space the mathematical methods that worked on Earth was the Greek astronomer Aristarchus. The Earth's shadow falls on the Moon during a lunar eclipse, and from the size of the shadow, Aristarchus argued, about 280 B.C., that the Moon was much larger than anything even Anaxagoras had suspected and presented the mathematics to prove it. At least one Greek philosopher, Cleanthes, believed he ought to be brought to trial, but Aristarchus weathered the storm better than Anaxagoras had.

About 150 B.C., the Greek astronomer Hipparchus (the greatest astronomer of ancient times) made use of trigonometry. He recorded the position of the Moon against the stars from two widely separated positions on Earth at the same time (naturally, two observers were required). This enabled him to draw an imaginary triangle from the Moon to two points on the Earth. He could measure the angle at the apex at the Moon in this way, and the length of the base of the triangle on the Earth. From this he could calculate the altitude of the triangle (which represented the distance of the Moon from the Earth) by comparing it with a small triangle of the same shape.

Hipparchus could show, then, that the Moon was at a distance equal to thirty times the diameter of the Earth, or 240,000 miles, if Eratosthenes' earlier figure of the size of the Earth was accepted. It meant the Moon was a body about 2,100 miles across.

In theory, the distance of any other heavenly body could be determined in the same way, but for all other bodies but the Moon, the size of the angle at the apex was so small that it was impossible to measure with the unaided eye. All Hipparchus could say was that all other heavenly bodies were much farther than the Moon.

But Greek science was steadily losing its vigor in Hipparchus' time. The vast distance of even the nearest heavenly body made little impact on a world turning away from scholarly probing of the Universe.

It was not until the seventeenth century that man's concept of space beyond the surface of the Earth was really altered radically and then it was not through any measurement in heaven, oddly enough. It involved something very Earthbound.

It had long been known that it was impossible to pump water higher than thirty-three feet above its natural level. An Italian physicist, Evangelista Torricelli, wondered, in 1643, if a water pump worked by allowing the weight of air to push the water upward. In that case, when a water column reached a height of thirty-three feet, its weight per unit area was perhaps equal to that of air. Air, exerting its maximum force under those conditions could then hold up no more.

If this were so, then a liquid less dense than water could be pumped higher, one that was more dense than water, not as high. It would be convenient to experiment with short columns, so what about mercury, which was thirteen and a half times denser than water? Air should hold up a correspondingly shorter column of mercury, one only about thirty inches tall.

Torricelli filled a four-foot length of glass tubing (closed at one end) with mercury, stoppered the opening and upended it into a large dish of mercury. When he unstoppered the opening, the mercury began to empty out of the tube as one might expect, but it did not do so altogether. Thirty inches of mercury remained in the tube, supported by the weight of the air pressing down on the mercury in the dish.

Torricelli had invented the barometer, had proved that air had weight, had demonstrated that it was air pressure that made a water pump work. In addition, he had produced the first good vacuum that mankind had ever seen. When the mercury began to pour out of the tube, the space between the top of the mercury level and the closed end of the tube contained *nothing*, except for a vanishingly small trace of mercury vapor.

And he had done still more than that; much more.

The ancient Greeks had had the concept of a vacuum but didn't believe it could really exist. "Nature abhors a vacuum," said Aristotle, who felt the entire Universe was filled with matter of one sort or another.

But Torricelli had not only demonstrated a small piece of vacuum, but had indicated the whereabouts of an infinitely larger piece. If air had only enough weight to support a column of mercury thirty inches high, and if it had the same density everywhere that it had near the surface of the earth, then the air was only five miles high. Even if air spread out and grew thinner as one traveled higher (as soon appeared to be the case) it would still be only a few dozen miles high before thinning out to such an extent that it might as well be considered vacuum. —And the Moon was 240,000 miles high!

Torricelli's experiment meant that, for the first time, mankind had to face the notion that the air made up only an exceedingly shallow shell of gas immediately surrounding the Earth and that beyond it lay mile upon limitless mile of *nothing*—of vacuum—broken only occasionally by some heavenly body.

It was with Torricelli that there arose the notion of "outer space" as a special entity of limitless nothingness.

Then in 1672, the Italian-French astronomer Giovanni Domenico Cassini worked out the distance of Mars by trigonometry. (He had a telescope, which Hipparchus had not, and could measure tinier angles.) By that time the true structure of the solar system was known, thanks to the Polish astronomer Nicolaus Copernicus and the German astronomer Johann Kepler, so from Mars's distance, all other planetary distances could be calculated. As the measurement was refined, it turned out that the Sun was over 90 million miles from the Earth and Saturn was nearly 900 million miles away. Other planets, still more distant, were discovered, and their distances measured.

The vast distances of empty space were dumbfounding, and yet man was only at the beginning. The position of certain stars were determined at two times, six months apart, when the Earth was at opposite ends of its orbit about the Sun. With a base line over 185 million miles across, a triangle could be measured with its apex at a star called 61 Cygni, for instance.

In 1838, the German astronomer Friedrich Wilhelm Bessel announced the distance of that star to be 35 million million miles away. It was already known that light traveled at the unheard-of speed of a little over 186,000 miles per second, but even at that speed, it took light six years to reach 61 Cygni (or to reach us from 61 Cygni), so that the star was said to be 6 light-years away.

The closest star, Alpha Centauri, is 4⅓ light-years away, but astronomers probed ever outward, ever outward, with ever newer and more subtle techniques and they can now detect heavenly bodies which are 9 billion light-years away from Earth.

Space is much vaster than anyone would dream, just looking at the sky, and by developing the act of measuring a handspan to the point of being able to measure a trillion trillion handspans, something indescribable in dimension could be dimly grasped.

And even so, not entirely. It is not by measuring space alone that we can learn about space. There is the question of time, a concept perhaps even more elusive than that of space, which began as something altogether distinct from space and ended—

However, let us continue that part of the story next article.

TIME

From the first, time seemed to be something completely different from space. The concept of space involved the sense of sight and touch, to begin with. Something is *here*, not *there*.

Time is much more subtle, involving an inner sense of duration. First it is day, then it is night; first one eats and then one is hungry again. The concept of *first* and *then* implies the passage of time.

Learning to measure duration and getting a quantitative sense of time was more difficult than learning to measure distance and getting a quantitative sense of space. It was easy to pace off distance; not so easy to pace off duration. The sense of duration was all the more difficult to measure in that it was so subjective. A night in which you stand in a cold rain on sentry duty seems interminable; one spent with a sweetheart seems to pass in a twinkling. The same period of time may seem long to one person and short to another, depending on circumstances.

In order to come to some agreement, men had to use some external phenomenon that was periodic; that is, that was judged to be repeating its actions over and over at fixed intervals of time. The earliest periodic phenomena used for the purpose were the motions of the heavenly bodies. Thus spring came at yearly intervals, the new moon at monthly intervals, and sunrise at daily intervals.

It was not until the seventeenth century that a man-made periodic motion was found superior. The swinging pendulum made the modern clock possible and for the first time in history man could measure time by the minutes and seconds. This was followed by the vibrating spring and finally, in the twentieth century, by the vibrating atom. Modern time-telling devices can split the second into a million parts easily, and time can be measured with greater facility and greater precision than space can.

But are space and time truly independent? Subjectively our concept of space is intertwined with our concept of time. We could get no sensation of separation in space without a separation in time, too. We have to turn our head to look first at one thing, then another, and this would have no meaning unless we looked *first* at one thing, *then* another.

If, in pacing off a distance, we find that one is twice as many paces long as a second, we also find that it takes us twice as long to pace off the first as the second. Even today, someone buying a house, for instance, has to consider its distance from a school or from his place of business—with the automatic thought that this will affect travel time. Space and time melt together.

To be sure, the melting isn't perfect. There are ways of measuring distance that are less direct than pacing off and are not so immediately dependent on time. A long distance can be measured by triangulation, for instance, in about the same time as a short distance. Again, it is easily possible to travel a hundred miles by superhighway more quickly and easily than ten miles through crowded city traffic.

Then, too, advances in transportation have altered the relationship of space and time for mankind generally. First the railroad, then the airplane, and then the jet plane, have associated the sensation of a given distance with a radically smaller sensation of duration. In colonial days, it was barely possible to breakfast in New York and lunch in Poughkeepsie; nowadays it is easily possible to breakfast in Paris and lunch in New York.

But the reaction to this? Invariably it is: "The world is getting smaller." The lessening of time is interpreted as a lessening of space.

Truly, though, all this is subjective and you can argue that a distance as a physical separation of two points possesses some quality that is not affected by any change in the time it takes to go from one to another.

Let's consider *objective* connections between space and time.

Real objects in the universe can only be located if at

least three measurements are taken. Suppose you have a glass cube with an air bubble in it sitting on a table top, and with its sides facing due north, south, east, and west. To locate that air bubble, you must measure how far it is above the table top, how far from the north side, and how far from the east side. This gives the exact position in the up–down direction, the north–south, and the east–west. Only one point in the cube can correspond to all three measurements.

You can pick some other system of making measurements, but it will always be necessary to make at least three of them to pinpoint a particular spot. Hence, space is said to be "three-dimensional," where dimension comes from a Latin word meaning "to measure out."

But suppose that instead of a gas bubble in a glass cube, you are considering a fly in an empty cubical room. You could locate the fly by giving three measurements and if you looked at the point indicated by those measurements, you would find the fly wasn't there after all. It is flying and has changed its position since the measurements were made. Not only must the spatial distances be defined then, but also the time, so that you can describe not only exactly where the fly was, but exactly when it was there.

Three dimensions are sufficient only for a motionless, unchanging universe. As soon as any motion is introduced, any change, then the measurement of time is also required to locate any object. The Universe as we know it, then, is not three-dimensional at all, but four-dimensional.

And yet the four dimensions are not equivalent. We can take a cube and twist it so that what was east–west becomes north–south and vice versa. Or we can twist it so that east–west becomes up–down and vice versa. All three dimensions that seem to involve space only (the three "spatial dimensions") are completely equivalent, in other words, and which is which depends only on the orientation of the observer.

Time, however (the "temporal dimension") is not equivalent to the others in this fashion. There would seem to be no way in which a cube can be twisted so that what was first in the up–down direction is placed in the yesterday–tomorrow direction and vice versa.

Then, too, there is free progression in either direction in all three spatial dimensions. One can move right, then left, and return to the starting place; or forward, then backward; or up, then down. One can move quickly or slowly, at will, in any of these directions.

In the temporal dimension there seems no question of varying direction or speed at will. You and I and the whole Universe seem to be progressing forward along the temporal dimension in one direction and one direction only—from yesterday toward tomorrow—without any chance of reversing. What's more, the progression seems to be at one constant, unalterable speed.

Science fiction writers have dreamed of finding some device that would make travel along the temporal dimension to be as easily controlled as along any of the three spatial dimensions. First to do so was H. G. Wells in 1895 in his novel *The Time Machine*. Many (including myself) have used time machines since, but such a device is not practical and, as far as science now knows, will never be. Time travel, in the sense of moving freely backward and forward, at will, along the temporal dimension, is impossible.

And yet, if we can move only forward in time, it seems that it doesn't always have to be at a fixed unalterable rate after all—

In 1905, Albert Einstein advanced his "Special Theory of Relativity." Its view of the universe seemed bizarre at first but physicists have checked it a number of times and in a number of ways and it has met all tests without exception, and so triumphantly that no physicist now doubts its validity.

Among other things, the Special Theory pointed out that the measurement of distance depended upon the relative motion between the object being measured and the device doing the measuring.

Imagine two spaceships, A and B, each 360 feet long, passing each other in space in opposite directions, with each able to measure the length of the other instantaneously as it passes. If they pass each other at the kind of velocities we are used to, then each would be measured as 360 feet long by the other. Actually, the length would be a bit less than 360 feet long, but such a trifling tiny bit less as to be unnoticeable.

The shortening would become more noticeable as the

velocities grew greater. Suppose they passed at a velocity of 1,000 miles per second, relative to each other. A would then measure B's length as 359 feet and B would measure A's length as 359 feet. This would grow more extreme as the velocity relative to each other continued to increase. If they passed each other at 162,000 miles per second, each would measure the length of the other as 180 feet, only half its "rest-length." And at 186,282 miles per second (the velocity of light in a vacuum) each would measure the length of the other as 0 feet.

At all velocities, A and B would each appear normal to itself, with its full length of 360 feet. The people on board A would maintain they were motionless and normal, while it was B, flashing by at high speed, that was shortened. The people on board B would say the same thing in reverse.

And both are correct!

To see why, consider that an American considers a Russian to be speaking a foreign language and a Russian considers an American to be speaking a foreign language. And both are correct. The quality of foreignness depends on who is doing the judging—and the quality of length depends on who is doing the measuring.

As it happens, the Special Theory of Relativity requires that the same thing happen to time.

Suppose that men on each ship have methods for testing the rate at which a clock on the other ship is going. As A and B flash by each other, it will seem to men on A that the clock on B has slowed down. Indeed, to the men on A, all motions on B, even atomic vibrations, will have appeared to slow down by an equivalent amount. In other words, it will seem to men on A that the progress of time itself has slowed on B. On the other hand, to men on B, it will seem that the progress of time has slowed on A.

If they flash by each other at a velocity, relative to each other, of 162,000 miles per second, each will measure the progress of time on the other to be just half normal. If the speed relative to each other is 186,282 miles per second, each will measure the progress of time on the other to be 0. To the men on A, it will seem that time is standing still on B; and to the men on B, that it is standing still on A.

Can we still say that both are correct? Perhaps not, in this case. To see why, let's go back to length.

Suppose we wondered whether one of the two ships might really have shortened its length during the flash-by. One way to decide that would be to have one of the ships slow down, turn around and catch up with the other. When they are side by side, the lengths can be compared and we can see if one is shorter than the other.

Once side by side, however, the two ships are at rest relative to each other and each measures the other as normal in length. Neither is shortened.

Of course, one may have been shorter than the other while they were moving relative to each other, but that leaves no marks. There is no way of telling, by looking at a body at rest, that it was once shortened while it was moving.

Does the same thing hold for time? Not quite. When the two ships come together again, the rate at which time is progressing is the same on both, and both ships will agree to that, for now each is at rest relative to the other. However, past difference in rate of time passage does indeed leave a mark.

Suppose the two ships had started their flight with a clock marking exactly 1 P.M. on board each. If the time rate on B was actually slower than that on A at any time, the clock on B would now be behind the clock on A. The situation would be the same (in reverse) if it had been A that had been experiencing the slower time rate.

The men on A have observed time to be moving more slowly than normal on B. Therefore when B pulls up to A, the men on A expect the clocks on B to be behind clocks on A. But the men on B have observed time to be moving more slowly than normal on A; and it is the clocks on A that they expect to be behind.

Well, which is it? Is neither clock behind? Do they record the same time? In that case, when did one catch up with the other? If B was observed by A to be running on slow-time, it would have had to catch up in order for the clocks to be equal; it would have had to race ahead to make up for lost time, and that seems impossible. There is nothing in relativity that would allow any clock ever, under any circumstances, to move at faster than normal time-rate, so B could never catch up to A. But the men on B would argue, by precisely the same reasoning, that the clock on A could never catch up to the clock on B.

Well, then, what happens when the ships come together that will supply the answer to this "clock paradox"?

Actually, the Special Theory of Relativity is inadequate to deal with the situation. It applies only to objects moving at constant velocity; that is, at the same speed and in the same direction forever. This means that A and B, having flashed by each other, must continue to separate forever if the Special Theory of Relativity is to be invoked. They can never come together again to match clocks, so there is no paradox.

In 1916, however, Einstein broadened his concept to include objects that accelerate—that is, change their speed or direction of travel, or both. To do this he produced his "General Theory of Relativity."

As long as two ships are moving at constant velocity with respect to each other, there is no way of choosing one over the other as the one whose measurements are more valid than the other. As soon as one ship begins to slow down, turn about, and catch up, it is accelerating. The situation with regard to the two ships is no longer identical, for one is moving at constant velocity and one is not.

The General Theory of Relativity shows that it is the ship that undergoes acceleration which experiences a real change in rate of time. The ship that undergoes acceleration will end with its clock behind when the two ships approach and compare.

But was it B that accelerated? The men on B could argue that to themselves it seemed that they were at rest and that it was A that accelerated in such a way as to effect a meeting. After all, each ship seems motionless to the men on board, no matter how matters seem to an observer outside the ship.

One argument against this is that B had to use its rocket engines, or some sort of energy, to slow up (relative to A), change its course, and approach A. No matter how the men on B might argue that they were at rest and that it was A that accelerated, the fact would remain (and the men on B would have to agree) that it was B that used its rocket engines and not A.

An even stronger argument rests on the fact that when B used its engines to accelerate, it did so not only with respect to A but with respect to the Sun, the planets, and all the stars and galaxies in the Universe. This involves an enormous asymmetry. You can see that B had to observe not only A accelerating its motion relative to B but the entire Universe accelerating its motion relative to B in a corresponding fashion. A, on the other hand, observed only B accelerating; the rest of the Universe remained in place.

The slowing of time is real, then, and it holds for the object that is undergoing accelerated motion relative to the Universe, generally.

In fact, under the General Theory of Relativity, motion through time becomes so intimately related to motion through space that it is impossible to consider space and time separately. Instead, one has to speak of "space-time" and the equations of General Relativity include all four dimensions, though time is treated with some mathematical difference.

Imagine next a space traveler heading for a distant star and accelerating to a high speed in order to get there as soon as possible. If he reaches a speed of 162,000 miles a second heading away from us, and if we can measure the rate at which time is passing on his ship, it will seem to us that time is going at half speed for him. To himself, the space traveler will feel time to be progressing at its usual rate, but if he could view Earth (which is receding from him at 162,000 miles a second) and measure its time rate it will seem to him that it was everything on Earth that was moving at half speed.

It is, however, the space traveler who had accelerated with respect to the rest of the Universe to reach his velocity with respect to Earth. Earth did not have to accelerate with respect to the rest of the Universe to reach its velocity with respect to the space traveler.

It is therefore the space traveler who is *really* experiencing a slowdown in the rate of his progression along the temporal dimension.

Suppose a space traveler is moving at the velocity of 186,200 miles per second. For every hour that passes for him, thirty hours pass on Earth. If he travels for a year in this fashion (having accelerated instantaneously) and then turns around and comes back at this speed (having turned around instantaneously), he will find that while he has seemed to himself to have traveled two years, the men on Earth would claim he had been absent for thirty years.

Suppose the space traveler had left at the age of thirty, leaving behind a twin brother also aged thirty. When he returned he would be thirty-two, but his stay-at-home twin brother would be sixty. (That is why the "clock paradox" is sometimes called the "twin paradox.")

Of course it takes quite a long while to accelerate to a high speed, and a long while to make a turn and head back again, so conditions aren't quite as clear-cut as just described.

Still, suppose a space traveler could somehow travel at 186,282 miles per second, exactly the speed of light. Time would slow down to zero for him. It would seem to him, no matter how far he went, that no time at all had elapsed. Then, when he returned to Earth (assuming again it would take him no time to reverse his direction), he might be surprised to find that men on Earth were under the impression he had been away for a hundred years, a thousand, a million—depending on how far he had gone at light-speed.

So time travel *is* possible, in a way. By moving through space fast enough, you can move forward through time as well. But only forward; it is time travel *one-way*. Once our space traveler has moved thirty years or a million years into the future, he can never move back again.

But what, you might ask, if he went *faster* than the velocity of light? Wouldn't the time rate become less than zero? Wouldn't it become negative, in other words? And wouldn't he then move back in time?

Alas, no. The firmest rule in the Theory of Relativity, Special or General, is that any object that moves more slowly than the velocity of light in a vacuum can never, merely by accelerating, come to move faster than the velocity of light in a vacuum.

Time, therefore, can do no more than stand still. No one can ever go back in time by any method that as yet seems to fit in with the structure of the Universe.

MASS

It seems very natural to think of space as something that doesn't exist, but merely contains. We can think of it as just a vast emptiness which holds matter—and not very much matter at that.

It is possible that there may be as many as ten thousand billion billion stars in the Universe. If each star were as voluminous as our Sun, all these stars, put together, would nevertheless make up a volume that is only about a millionth of a trillionth of a trillionth of the volume of the Universe that contains them.

What's more, the stars themselves are for the most part empty space, in a manner of speaking. That is, they are made up of atoms, which are, in turn, made up of particles far smaller than themselves. If all the subatomic particles (the real matter of the Universe) in all the stars were packed together, each star would be, on the average, eight miles across. The matter in the Universe would then take up only a trillionth of the room that all the loosely packed stars now do.

Perhaps we can get an idea of what this means by tackling something closer to home. Imagine the huge Earth we live on to be hollow; a vast, hollow, spherical cavity eight thousand miles across. Imagine next an influenza virus, too small to be seen in an ordinary microscope, but large enough to be made out in an electron microscope.

Take this influenza virus and place it inside the hollow Earth; place nothing else inside at all. The volume of the hollow Earth would then be to the volume of the single virus molecule floating inside as is the volume of the

Universe to the total volume of subatomic particles which it contains.

If the hollow Earth contained nothing but a single virus, we would certainly feel justified in considering it empty. The single virus would, as content, be totally insignificant. Might we not feel justified in thinking of the Universe as empty then? Of what importance can the incredibly small smattering of matter be to it?

But suppose we imagine an empty Universe, a really empty Universe, a completely empty Universe. And suppose there were some way in which we could observe it without being part of it. What conclusions could we come to concerning it?

None, really. In order to deal with the concept of distance within a Universe, we must begin by locating two points within it and using the separation between those two points as a unit of distance. In order to deal with the concept of duration, we would have to sense changes in that separation and accept some convenient segment of change as a unit of duration.

But if a Universe is completely empty, there is no way of locating two points within it; no way of noting separation or change, distance or duration. In short, there is no way of indicating the existence of either space or time. It is fair to say then that it is meaningless to speak of space and time in the absence of things contained in space and time. The container only exists and endures by virtue of the contents, regardless of how insignificantly small the contents might be in comparison.

Suppose, next, we imagine a Universe with a single piece of matter in it; a single featureless sphere. Imagine, further, that we can sense the rest of the Universe from a position at the center of the sphere. Now what can we tell about the Universe?

To begin with, we might suppose the single piece of matter is moving. There is something called the "first law of motion" which states that if any object in the Universe is left entirely to itself and is completely unaffected by anything else in the Universe, then, if it is moving at some speed, it will continue moving at that speed constantly and forever in the same straight-line direction. In the special case that its speed is zero, it would be "at rest" to begin with and it would stay "at rest" forever.

This law was worked out, nearly four centuries ago, from observations made in our own Universe with its trillions of trillions of pieces of matter, but it does not seem to depend on the number of pieces of matter present in the Universe. If, one by one, those pieces disappeared, there seems no obvious reason why the first law of motion should cease to hold.

Consequently, you might suppose that the first law of motion ought to apply to a piece of matter that was alone in the Universe. In fact, you might even argue that it should *particularly* apply to that single piece. After all that one piece can't possibly be affected by anything else in the Universe, since there isn't anything else in the Universe. It ought to obey the first law of motion exactly; if it is at rest, it will stay at rest forever; if it is moving, it will move at the same speed in the same straight-line direction forever.

But how can we check that? All one can observe from the center of that lonely piece of matter is nothingness all around. Whenever we make the observation, there is nothing. The nothingness would be precisely the same if the piece of matter were at rest. It would also be precisely the same if the piece of matter were moving at any constant speed in any given direction. From all we can sense, then, we would have no way of deciding whether the single piece was at rest or was moving; and if it was moving, we could not decide how fast it was moving or in what direction.

A Universe with one featureless piece of matter in it would be as blank and as immeasurable as one with no matter in it at all.

Let us pass on, then, to a Universe with two featureless pieces of matter in it. We can suppose the two pieces of matter are relatively close to each other; close enough so that one can be sensed from the other. (If they were so far apart that one could not be sensed from the other in any way, we might as well say that there were two Universes, each with one piece of matter.)

In fact, let us suppose that the two pieces have the relative positions of the Earth and the Moon, and that a picture can be taken of one piece from the center of the other. (We can imagine that each piece glows with light or can, in some other way, be detected.)

If we study the successive images of Piece A from the

vantage point of Piece B's center, we will notice that Piece A gets brighter and dimmer, brighter and dimmer; or perhaps (if it shows a visible disc) that it gets larger and smaller, larger and smaller. We might suppose that it is really brightening and dimming periodically, or expanding and shrinking. Or we might suppose that its brightness and size remain unchanged really, but that Piece A is approaching Piece B and receding, approaching and receding. As it approaches it seems brighter and larger; as it recedes it seems dimmer and smaller.

Whatever the reason for it, there is a periodic change and therefore the concept of time becomes possible. If the change is assumed to be one of distance, then the concept of space becomes possible.

Now, though, we must ask how the situation would change if we were observing Piece B from the center of Piece A, instead of Piece A from the center of Piece B?

It would not change at all. From either piece, the other would approach and recede, approach and recede.

Then which one is *really* approaching and receding?

The only answer we can make is: There is no way of telling. We can, with equal justice, assume that either piece is at rest and find the other to be shifting position.

What's more, no matter how many other pieces of matter are added to the Universe, there is no way of telling whether any one of them is at rest while the others are moving. We can *assume* that some particular body is at rest and determine the positions and motions of all other bodies according to the distances and direction we measured from the place of assumed rest. But then we can equally well assume that some other particular body is at rest and determine a new set of positions and motions of all other bodies.

It may be more *convenient* to choose one body rather than another to be at rest, but never more *right*. No matter which body we assume to be at rest, the basic laws of nature we deduce from the behavior of the bodies of the Universe will remain the same. (Which is fortunate, for the Universe would be chaotic otherwise and impossible to understand.)

What this means is that there is no such thing as "absolute rest," no body that is *really* at rest. Nor is there "absolute motion," determined by comparing positions of a moving body with that of something that is *really* at rest. Nor is there "absolute space" or "absolute time," determined by noting the progressive changes in position of a moving body compared to something that is *really* at rest.

All we can measure is motion, space, and time relative to some object it is *convenient* to *pretend* is at rest. This gives you "relative motion," "relative space," and "relative time." It is because Einstein worked with these to build his sytem of the Universe that we refer to his "Theory of Relativity."

Another thing we can deduce from the behavior of the two pieces of matter is that something is wrong with the first law of motion. If both pieces were following the first law of motion, then Piece A would behave in one of a certain limited number of ways as observed from Piece B. It might remain motionless, neither approaching nor receding. It might recede forever according to some simple mathematical relationship that can be worked out. It might approach, reach some minimum distance (which would be zero if there were a collision), and then, if there were not a collision, recede forever.

One thing that would *not* happen under any circumstances, if the first law of motion were in operation, would be the periodic approach and recession, approach and recession.

Can it be that only one of the pieces is disobeying the first law of motion? No! From either piece, the other one will appear to show the periodic approach and recession. Since it cannot possibly be decided that the periodic motion belongs to Piece A only or to Piece B, it can only be concluded that *neither* piece is obeying the first law of motion.

But remember—the first law of motion states that a body will travel at a constant speed and in the same straight-line direction, *if* it is left to itself and is unaffected by any other body. The fact that the two pieces of matter are not following the first law means that each is being affected by something else. Since there are only two pieces of matter in the Universe we are imagining, we must conclude that Piece A is somehow affecting Piece B, and Piece B is somehow affecting Piece A.

What is the nature of the effect? Can we be sure that all that is happening is the approach and recession? Can it be that Piece A is also moving sidewise relative to Piece B?

Perhaps, but how can we tell? If we see consecutive images of Piece A as seen from Piece B, we could only tell if there were sidewise movement by considering its position relative to other objects in the sky—but there are no other objects.

Well then, suppose we add a third object to the Universe, much farther away from Piece A and Piece B than those two are from each other. (We can imagine the third piece of matter to be where the Sun is with reference to the Earth and the Moon.)

Now we can use the third object, Piece C, as a background against which to measure the position of Piece A as seen from Piece B (or Piece B as seen from Piece A). The distance between Piece A and Piece C will progressively increase so that sidewise motion can be measured.

It will then be possible to decide that Piece A and Piece B are both moving in ellipses about a point located somewhere between their centers.* In the case of the Earth and the Moon, the point happens to be located only 3,000 miles from Earth's center, which is still 1,000 miles below Earth's surface, so at a casual inspection it would seem that the Moon was moving in an ellipse about an unresponsive Earth—but close attention will show the Earth is moving about the "center of gravity" of the Earth-Moon system just as truly as the Moon is.

What's more, if we add a fourth object very far away, say at the position of the star Sirius, we can use that as a background and discover that Pieces A and B, even as they circle each other, are together moving in a grand sweep about Piece C (assuming that Piece C is much larger than Pieces A and B, as the Sun is much larger than the Earth and Moon).

The more pieces added to the Universe the more the

* It is because they are moving in ellipses, flattened curves, that the distance between them changes periodically. If they had happened to be moving in exact circles about that point (as is possible but extremely unlikely) then the distance would have remained constant and if the Universe had contained only those two pieces of matter and nothing else, it would have seemed that each was following the first law of motion.

effects of piece upon piece multiply and the more complicated things might be. Fortunately, the complications do not go beyond the capacity of the human mind to unravel, because the pieces of matter are usually so arranged that one piece or another is large enough, or close enough, to have by far the dominating influence over others in its neighborhood. By concentrating on the dominating influence in some particular group of pieces of matter, the nature of that influence can be puzzled out.

Three hundred years ago, Isaac Newton was able to show that the motions of the heavenly bodies could be satisfactorily explained by assuming that each body affected all the other bodies in accordance with a rather simple rule.

Any particular body in the Universe, he decided, attracted any other particular body by an amount that was proportional to the product of the masses of the two bodies and was inversely proportional to the square of the distance between their centers. In other words, the attraction between two bodies grew stronger when their masses were increased, and weaker when the distance between them increased. The attraction is called "gravitation" and Newton's rule represents the "law of universal gravitation."

But what is this "mass" that is suddenly being mentioned?

Actually, no one really knows. Mass is whatever it is about matter that produces a gravitational attraction and reacts to it. When the gravitational attraction exists between two bodies, the conclusion is that both bodies possess mass. From the size of the gravitational attraction it is possible to come to certain conclusions concerning the amount of mass in either body or in both. On the other hand, if there is no gravitational attraction between two bodies, then one or the other (or both) does not possess mass.

It is usually considered that anything which has mass is "matter." By this criterion* a rock or a human being is matter, but a beam of light is not.

By Newton's rule, if Earth and Moon suddenly doubled

* Einstein qualified this by speaking of "mass at rest" or "rest-mass"; that is, the mass of a body which is at rest relative to the observer; but that is another story.

their distance from each other, the attraction would be 2×2, or four times weaker than it was before. If they tripled their distance, the attraction would be 3×3, or nine times weaker. If, on the other hand, the distance were decreased, the attraction would become correspondingly stronger.

Again, if the distance between Earth and Moon were unchanged, but the mass of the Earth suddenly doubled (or halved) the gravitational attraction between Earth and Moon would be doubled (or halved). The same would be true if the mass of the Moon suddenly doubled (or halved.) If *both* masses doubled (or if *both* were halved), the gravitational attraction would be quadrupled (or quartered).

But let's get back to Earth. Suppose we are dealing with the Earth and some small object on its surface, such as yourself. We can assume your distance from the Earth's center will always be the same as long as you remain on one spot on the Earth's surface; and that the mass of the Earth always stays the same, too. The only thing we can't be sure of is the exact quantity of *your* mass, and the gravitational attraction between you and the Earth will be greater or less according to whether your mass is greater or less.

It is the gravitational attraction between yourself and the Earth that you measure when you weigh yourself on an ordinary bathroom scale. You determine your "weight" in this fashion and this is often accepted as being equivalent to your mass.

Weight, however, is *not* identical to mass. If you weighed yourself on a mountaintop, you would be farther from the Earth's center than when you were at sea level. The gravitational attraction between yourself and the Earth would be slightly weaker and you would weigh slightly less—but not because you had less mass, only because there was greater distance. If you weighed yourself on the Moon, you would be closer to the Moon's center than ever you were to the Earth's, and you would be standing on a body with considerably less mass than the Earth. The result of the combination of factors would be that your weight on the Moon would be one sixth what it is on the Earth—but not because *your* mass had changed.

It is more accurate, then, to weigh not only yourself, but also other objects which have a known mass, and compare the gravitational attraction on yourself and on them. Then changes in distance or in the mass of the body you are standing on cancel out and you get a truer notion of your own mass. This is what we do on the kind of scale in which we shove weights along a lever, or when we weigh objects in a balance with the unknown in one pan and standard weights in the other.

The question arises, now, how one body can affect another body across space? There is a quarter of a million miles separating Earth and Moon, and 93 million miles separating the Earth-Moon system and the Sun. What is it that can reach across that distance and produce gravitational attraction?

One way of looking at it is to suppose that the presence of mass distorts the fabric of the Universe.

To see what is meant by that, consider a two-dimensional analogy— Imagine a perfectly smooth, frictionless surface, extending in every direction for some distance above the surface of the Earth, with Earth's gravitational attraction pulling down at right angles to the surface.

If the surface were hard and rigid, a body would slide along it in a perfectly straight line and at a constant speed, something like a hockey puck speeding along smooth ice. It would obey the first law of motion.

Suppose, however, that the smooth surface is actually a very thin, rubbery material, which gives under the pull of the Earth upon the mass of a body resting upon it. Each piece of matter on the rubbery surface would sink down, pulling the surface with it. The more massive the body, or the more the mass is concentrated into a small volume, the farther down it sinks. The entire surface is distorted in this fashion: greatly so in the neighborhood of the massive body, less so, farther away. The distortion is never quite zero, though, however far we go from the body.

Now imagine two such bodies on the surface, each in motion. Imagine that the fabric rises behind them and sinks in front of them without friction and without impeding the movement. As the less massive body approaches the more massive one, it slides down the sharp declivity produced by the latter. It moves faster and faster and may strike the body; or, if it passes by, it may slide partway down, whirl around, and go shooting up and out of the declivity on the other side. Seen from above it will have followed a curve called a hyperbola. If it made a particularly close near-miss, it would circle the declivity round and round in what would seem, from above, to be an ellipse, accompanying the larger body wherever it goes and unable to shoot out of the pit into which it has tumbled.

If you imagine an endlessly large elastic fabric of this sort with a vast and even gravitational attraction pulling downward, and place trillions of bodies here and there on it, you will have a bumpy and uneven surface. No part of it will be quite level, except where two or more slants will just happen to cancel each other out very temporarily. Every part of it will slope at a continually changing angle according to the movement of the various bodies and all motions will be affected by the slope.

If the fabric were invisible and were viewed from above, we would very likely conclude that there were mysterious attractions between all the various bodies and work out a law of attraction that would be like Newton's.

In a three-dimensional way, the picture outlined above is what Einstein visualizes the Universe to be. There is a subtle fabric of space which is distorted by mass and every piece of matter is sliding up and down gravitational slopes, so to speak, and moving in closed ellipses or open hyperbolas, large or small; speeding up; slowing down; all in accordance with the immensely complicated and ever changing nature of the local distortions.

In that case, we might logically maintain that the Universe contains not just the actual matter in countless trillions of pieces but contains also the sum of the distortions each piece produces. Since the distortions are everywhere, the Universe is not nearly-empty after all. Quite the contrary: it is *full* and would be full even if there were only two subatomic masses in the Universe and nothing more.

AFTERWORD

The preceding set of three articles (like the set of four that went before it) is incomplete.

Electronic Age asked me to do a series of articles on "big concepts" in science. I thought a while and suggested six topics: space, time, mass, energy, life, and intelligence; to be done in that order because I thought I could make a connected story out of it in a way.

They agreed and I did the first three and was just starting on the fourth—so help me, the first sheet of paper was in the typewriter—when the phone rang and the news reached me that *Electronic Age* had suspended publication.

There are three more left to do, then, but meanwhile the succeeding article will talk about energy, even though it is not quite the article I would have written for the aborted series.

YOU CAN'T EVEN BREAK EVEN

What a pleasure it is to be young, and hopeful, and unsophisticated. All things are possible and we are ready, in our heart of hearts, to believe that a fairy godmother might just come and wave her wand and turn our rags into a lavish costume and our hovel into a mansion. Why shouldn't an enchanted ring exist somewhere which will, at a rub, load our pockets with gold and jewels? Or why should not a jinn, slave to our commands, build a castle for us in the twinkling of an eye and fill it with dancing girls?

If this has not happened, we might wistfully imagine, it is because we just haven't been lucky enough to find the fairy godmother, or the enchanted ring, or the jinn. All we need is that incredible stroke of luck and we will have something for nothing.

But never mind fairies, rings, and jinn; in the real world it is energy that is the prime mover of all.

We can define energy as anything that makes it possible to do work; anything capable of bringing about movement against resistance. In that case, we see at once that there must be various forms of energy.

Heat will make a thread of mercury rise against the pull of gravity; light will turn the vanes of a radiometer against the slowing effect of friction; electricity will turn a motor; magnetism raise a pin; a moving bat hurl a baseball over the fence; exploding dynamite lift a boulder; a hydrogen bomb in action heave a mountain.

Heat, light, electricity, magnetism, motion, sound, chemical bonds, nuclear forces—all represent forms of

SOURCE: "You Can't Even Break Even" appeared in *Smithsonian* as "In the Game of Energy and Thermodynamics You Can't Even Break Even", August 1970.

energy, and all are different forms of essentially the same thing, for one form can be freely turned into another.

Electricity moving through a wire can produce light, and a paddle rotating rapidly in water can produce heat. Magnetism can be turned into electricity; chemical explosions into motion; nuclear reactions into sound; and so on.

We have now sharpened the problem of getting something for nothing, and can consider it realistically. Whatever we want costs us energy, for it is only energy (by definition) that will allow work to be done. To be sure, we may need other things as well, for to build a palace we need not only the energy to lift materials but also a certain architectural knowledge—but we need energy *at least*. Without energy, all the architectural knowledge in the world won't budge one grain of sand.

To get something for nothing, then, is just another way of saying that we want to create energy.

But alas, this apparently can't be done. In the 1840s, as a result of careful experimentation and measuring, several physicists came more or less simultaneously to the conclusion that energy cannot be created (see the earlier article, *Fire*). One form of energy can be converted into another, or transported from one place to another, but that is as far as it can go.

But wait, that isn't all. If energy cannot be created, neither can it be destroyed. When energy is used, it doesn't disappear; it merely goes elsewhere or is changed into another form. The light that streams out of a candle does not vanish; it heats up the air and surroundings about itself. The hot water in a kettle may cool down but the heat does not disappear; it is transferred to the outside world.

To express all this, we can say: "Energy can be transferred from one place to another, or transformed from one form to another, but it can neither be created nor destroyed."

Or we can put it another way: "The total quantity of energy in the Universe is constant."

When the total quantity of something does not change, we say that it is conserved. The two statements given above, then, are two ways of expressing "the law of conservation of energy." This law is sometimes considered the most powerful and the most fundamental generalization about the Universe that scientists have ever been able to make.

No one knows *why* energy is conserved and no one can be completely sure it is truly conserved everywhere in the Universe and under all conditions. All that anyone can say is that in over a century and a quarter of careful measurement, scientists have never been able to point to a definite violation of energy conservation either in the familiar everyday surroundings about us, or in the heavens above, or in the atoms within.

The study of changes of energy from one form to another, or the transport of energy from one place to another, is called "thermodynamics" (from Greek words meaning "heat-motion") because the earliest studies of the sort were made on the manner in which heat flowed from one part of a system to another.

For that reason the law of conservation of energy is sometimes called the "First Law of Thermodynamics." It is first because it is the starting point for all else in the study. Before you can come to any useful conclusions in thermodynamics you must accept the fact that energy can neither be created nor destroyed.

Once that is accepted, we might decide that even so we have not entirely lost. In the great game of the Universe, maybe we can still win. If we can't get something for nothing, maybe the First Law will allow us to get something for *almost* nothing.

For instance, heat is a form of energy and we can make it do work. Suppose we take a quantity of heat and change it into work. In doing so, we haven't destroyed the heat, we have only transferred it to another place or perhaps changed it into another energy form. Why can't we then simply gather it up wherever it is and in whatever form, and use it again, and then again, and then still again?

If that is so, then even if we can't create energy out of nothing, we can at least start with just a little energy and make it do any amount of work. By using the energy of a burning candle over and over we could move the world; and it would be a greedy man indeed who wouldn't be satisfied with that or who would complain he wasn't really getting something for nothing.

Alas, it sounds good, but it can't be done. The trouble is that once energy is used, it still exists, yes, but it is spread out thinner. The heat of the burning candle spreads out into the air all about and into all the things the warmed air comes into contact with.

To put that heat back to work again, it has to be collected from the surroundings and concentrated again so that the candle flame is re-created. Heat *can* be concentrated, energy *can* be collected—but it takes energy to do so, invariably more energy than the energy you are concentrating and collecting.

What is the sense in using fresh energy to collect dissipated old energy, and using more to get less? You might as well use the fresh to begin with. It would be more economical.

In short, in your attempt to use the same old energy over and over again, you would be using up more energy than if you made up your mind to use each bit of energy just once.

You can't get round it. What the First Law of Thermodynamics really means is that in the great game of the Universe, *you can't win!* You can't get something for nothing, or even for nearly nothing.

This is a hard thing to accept and the indomitable human spirit is bound to fall back to the next line of defense. If it is true that you can't win, then perhaps you can at least break even. In other words, given a certain supply of energy, perhaps you can at least turn it *all* into work.

This problem came up when the steam engine was first developed in the eighteenth century. To begin with, the early engines were extremely inefficient. Great quantities of fuel were burned but most of the energy was wasted in heating up the world generally; very little ended in such useful work as pumping water.

Naturally, one assumes that if one could only cut down on friction, prevent the flow of heat in unwanted directions, make the general design more efficient, one could eventually build a machine that would turn all the energy into work.

The first person to point out that this was not so, that even a *perfect* steam engine could not turn all energy into work, was a French physicist named Nicolas Léonard Sadi Carnot.

He demonstrated, in 1824, that the steam engine did work because part of its system was quite hot (the part that consisted of steam) and part was quite cold (the part that consisted of the cold water that condensed the steam). The heat energy present was, in other words, in greater-than-average concentration in one place and in less-than-average concentration in another. We can quite easily measure the heat-concentration, which we usually call "temperature." The fraction of the energy that can be turned into work by a steam engine depends, then, upon the *difference* in temperature between the hot part of the system and the cold part.

The greater the difference in temperature between two parts of the same system, the greater the fraction of the heat energy we can turn into work. This difference in temperature becomes a maximum when *all* the heat in the system is concentrated in one part and *none* is concentrated in another.

The trouble is that physicists have shown it is impossible to concentrate *all* the heat in a system in one particular part of it. Even to approach total concentration takes an enormous effort.

If a steam engine uses ordinary steam for its hot part and ice water for its cold, the difference in heat concentration or temperature is such that only 27 per cent of the total heat energy can be converted into work, even if the steam engine were perfect in every other respect: if it lost no heat to the outside world, if there were no friction, and so on.

This is true for any system which uses energy of any kind. To make any system useful, to allow it to turn energy into work, there must always be a difference in energy concentration in different parts of the system. There must be a high energy concentration here and a low energy concentration there, and the work to be gotten out of the system depends not on the total energy, but on the difference in energy concentration within the system.

We can say: "No device can deliver work unless there is a difference in energy concentration within the system, no matter how much total energy is used."

That is one way of stating what is called the Second Law of Thermodynamics.

Since there is never any way of reaching an ultimate difference in energy concentration, never any way of putting *all* the energy into one part of the system, and *none* into another, we can never turn every bit of the energy of a system into work. Some of the energy always manages to get away from us without being turned into work.

What the Second Law tells us, then, is that in the great game of the Universe, we not only cannot win, *we cannot even break even!*

Given energy at two different levels of concentration, we will note as part of the common experience of mankind that there is always a spontaneous transfer of energy from the place of higher concentration to the place of lower concentration; and never vice versa.

For instance, heat will flow, of itself, from a hot body into a cold body, but not vice versa. Water will spontaneously flow from hilltop to hill bottom, but not vice versa.

We can say: "Energy will always flow spontaneously from a point of high concentration to one of low concentration."

Physicists can show that it is because this statement is true that devices will convert energy into work when there is a difference in energy concentration within the system. It is the spontaneous energy flow from high to low that produces the work.

The statement about spontaneous energy-flow is therefore another way of expressing the Second Law.

But work is never done instantaneously. It invariably occupies time. What happens during that time?

Suppose we consider a steam engine with a portion of itself that is at high heat-concentration and another portion that is at low heat-concentration. By the Second Law, the heat flows from high to low and that heat flow is turned into work. If the heat flow happened all at once and was converted into work in zero time, then we would at least get all the work out of the energy flow that we could.

But it takes time, and as time passes, some of the heat in the high-concentration portion is pouring out into other parts of the Universe. Meanwhile heat from other parts of the Universe is pouring into the low-concentration portion. In other words, the hot part of the steam engine is cooling faster than you would expect just from its transfer of heat to the cold portion. The cold portion, on the other hand, is warming faster than you would think just from its receipt of heat from the hot portion.

The *difference* in temperature is dropping faster than you would expect from the work done.

Since the amount of work you can get out of any device depends upon the difference in temperature, it would seem that the quantity of energy capable of conversion into work decreases with time. The quantity of energy *not* capable of conversion into work increases with time.

A German physicist, Rudolf Clausius, pointed this out in 1865. He invented a quantity consisting of the change in heat with time, divided by temperature, and called it "entropy." He showed that entropy was a measure of the quantity of energy *not* capable of conversion into work.

In any physical change that takes place by itself the entropy always increases.

In the case of the steam engine this comes about because there is heat flow to and from the Universe. If a boulder rolls down the mountainside there is increase of entropy because of friction and air resistance. An electric current flowing from one pole of a battery to another encounters resistance from whatever it passes through and hence experiences increase in entropy.

To be sure, we can imagine ideal cases. A hot and cold area might be perfectly insulated so that heat flows only from one to the other; a rock may fall through a perfect vacuum; an electric current may flow through a perfect conductor. In all cases, there is no entropy increase.

Approximations to such ideals (a planet moving through outer space; an electric current moving through a superconducting metal) are highly special. If we consider the ordinary systems we work with, we can say: "In any energy transfer, there is an increase in entropy."

This, too, is a way of expressing the Second Law.

In fact, a good brief way of stating the First and Second Laws of Thermodynamics is: "The total energy content of the Universe is constant and the total entropy is continually increasing."

This means that although the Universe never loses any energy, less and less of that energy can be converted into work as time goes on.

The Second Law can be interpreted in terms of atomic theory, and the Scottish mathematician and physicist, James Clerk Maxwell did so in the 1860s.

Heat can be viewed, for instance, as being represented by the random movements of the separate particles (either atoms or molecules) making up some body of matter. The greater the *average* velocity of particle motion, the higher the temperature.

When two particles collide, they bounce apart and some momentum (mass multiplied by velocity) is transferred from one to the other. The transfer can take place in any fashion, but the most likely result is that the particle with more momentum will lose, and the particle with less momentum will gain. If all the particles are the same size, we can say that the faster particle will slow down after collision, the slower particle speed up. It is possible, of course, that the fast particle may just happen to bounce off faster, and the slow one slower, but it is unlikely.

(If a rich man and a poor man put all their money in a single pile and each grabbed what he could, the chances are the rich man would end up with less money than he started and the poor man with more.)

Where more and more particles are involved, it becomes less and less likely that a large proportion of the fast particles will all bounce off slow particles and end by moving still faster.

Let us suppose there is a one-in-ten chance that a fast particle will bounce off a slow particle and become faster in the process. The chance of six fast particles *all* bouncing off faster from six slow particles will be one in ten times ten times ten times ten times ten times ten, or one in a million. The chance of ninety-six fast particles all bouncing off faster at the same time from ninety-six slow particles would be only one in a trillion-trillion-trillion-trillion-trillion-trillion-trillion-trillion.

Suppose you took a kettle of water containing uncounted trillions of particles and put it over a fire. It might be that more than half the hot, very fast-moving particles in the hot gases of the fire might strike the kettle and bounce off still faster-moving. In that case, the water in the kettle would get cooler while the fire would get hotter. This is possible, but the chance of its happening is so small that there is no way of writing it in ordinary figures. If you tried to write: one chance in such-and-such a number, the surface of the earth wouldn't be large enough to hold all the zeros you would have to write down for "such-and-such a number."

That is why the entropy of the Universe constantly increases—because the collisions of atoms and molecules tend always to chop off energy extremes. Wherever energy is more concentrated than usual, that concentration drops; where it is less concentrated than usual, that concentration rises.

It is also possible to think of entropy in terms of "order" and "disorder." Something is orderly when its individual parts are arranged according to some simple rule we can quickly grasp. We can then predict from each part something about the next part. The simpler the rule, the easier the prediction, and the greater the order.

Consider a deck of cards. You might have it arranged as follows: ace of spades, two of spades, three of spades, and so on, followed by hearts, clubs, and diamonds, each suit arranged from ace to king. That is very orderly, for if you show me any card (the seven of clubs, for instance), I will instantly tell you the next card (the eight of clubs).

Or you might arrange the suits in another order; or each suit might run from king down to ace; or you might have the four aces in a certain order of suits, then the four twos, then the four threes, and so on. These all represent order.

We might also arrange the cards so that they are alternately red and black without any consideration for numbers or suits. We can then still make some prediction. If I am shown the seven of clubs, I know the next card must be a red one. That is some information, but not much, so that the red and black in alternation still represents some order, but not much.

It should be obvious, though, that if you consider all the possible arrangements of the cards in a deck, the number of arrangements that allow you to make predictions about each card from the one before is a very small, a *very* small, portion of the whole.

Suppose you shuffle a deck in such a way that it can take on *any* arrangement. The chances that the arrangement will be one of the few that will allow even a small amount of prediction and will therefore have at least a small amount of order is not great. There are so many utterly disorderly arrangements possible that one of those is just about sure to be obtained.

That is why, when you shuffle cards thoroughly, you would be most astonished to find, when you were through, that the cards have ended up arranged ace of spades, two of spades, three of spades, and so on—or even red-black-red-black-red-black and so on.

Let us take another example from the world of life. When a platoon of soldiers marches by four abreast and in perfect step, that represents a high degree of order. When we see one group of four soldiers move by, we can predict exactly when the next group will pass by, how many will be in the group, whether they will be moving their right foot or left at the moment of passing, and so on.

Other examples of order would have soldiers moving two abreast; or in single file; or one row marching and the next skipping, in alternation; and so on.

But suppose you considered all the different possible ways in which the individual soldiers of a platoon could pass by if each consulted his own tastes only and paid no attention to the others. Some might be strolling, some walking, some running, some hopping perhaps, some in this direction, some in that. The number of ways of passing *without* any perceptible order is much, much higher than the number of ways *with* order.

Consequently, if you told the soldiers of a platoon to move from one point to another at will, you would be utterly surprised if, when each did exactly as he pleased, they just all happened to move four abreast and in step. In fact, if they were already moving four abreast and in step and were suddenly told to do as they pleased, you would expect the entire platoon to break formation and become disorderly.

In short, in every possible situation you can think of, the number of ways of being disorderly is much, much, much, much greater than the number of ways of being orderly.

This is exactly comparable to the fact that the number of ways in which extremes get chopped off in the random collisions of particles is much, much, much, much greater than the number of ways in which extremes get more extreme.

Another way of stating Second Law, then, is: "The Universe is constantly getting more disorderly."

Viewed that way, we can see Second Law all about us. We have to work hard to straighten a room, but left to itself, it becomes a mess again very quickly and very easily. Even if we never enter it, it becomes dusty and musty. How difficult to maintain houses, and machinery, and our own bodies in perfect working order; how easy to let them deteriorate.

In fact, all we have to do is nothing, and everything deteriorates, collapses, breaks down, wears out, all by itself—and that is what Second Law is all about.

You can argue, of course, that the phenomenon of life may be an exception. Life on earth has steadily grown more complex, more versatile, more elaborate, more orderly, over the billions of years of the planet's existence. From no life at all, living molecules were developed, then living cells, then living conglomerates of cells, then worms, vertebrates, mammals, finally man. And in man is a three-pound brain which, as far as we know, is the most complex and orderly arrangement of matter in the Universe. How could the human brain develop out of the primeval slime? How could that vast increase in order (and therefore that vast decrease in entropy) have taken place?

The answer is it could *not* have taken place without a tremendous source of energy constantly bathing the Earth, for it is on that energy that life subsists. Remove the Sun and the human brain would not have developed —or the primeval slime, either. And in the billions of years that it took for the human brain to develop, the increase in entropy that took place in the Sun was far greater—far, *far* greater—than the decrease represented by the evolution of the brain.

But where did it all start? If the Universe is running down into utter disorder, what made it orderly to begin with? Where did the order come from that it is steadily losing? What set up the extremes that are steadily being chipped away?

Scientists are still arguing the point. Some think the Universe originally had its matter and energy all smashed together into one huge "cosmic egg"—a situation something like a tremendous deck of cards all arranged in order. The cosmic egg exploded and ever since, for billions of years, the Universe has been running down; the deck of cards is being shuffled and shuffled and shuffled.

Others think that there are some processes in the Universe that spontaneously decrease entropy; some natural process which unshuffles and re-orders the cards. We don't know what it can be, perhaps because it takes place under conditions we cannot observe and cannot duplicate in the laboratory—say, in the center of exploding galaxies. Perhaps, in that case, as some parts of the Universe run down, others build up.

Then again, it may be that once the Universe runs down, the random collisions of particles may—after umpty-ump years—just happen to bring about an at least partial unshuffling. After all, if you shuffle cards and shuffle cards and shuffle cards ceaselessly for a trillion years, you may end up with an arrangement possessing at least *some* order, just by the laws of chance.

Once that happens, the Universe begins to run down again at once. Perhaps, then, we live in a Universe that was partially unshuffled after a quadrillion years of having been run-down. We are now running down again and after the Universe is all run-down, another quadrillion years or another quadrillion quadrillion years may see a section of it unshuffled once more.

Stars and galaxies will then re-form, and life may be established here and there, and finally some science writer will sit down and begin to wonder again where it all came from and where it will all end.

THE SECRET OF THE SQUID

For thousands of years, man has envied the birds their independence of the ground, their ability to soar into the sky. Yet the bird's locomotion was essentially like ours—it was the result of a push against something else.

If we walk or run, our feet push against the ground. So do the legs of a running horse, and the wheels of a moving locomotive or automobile. On the seas, the paddle or ship's propeller pushes against the water. And in the air, the wing of the bird, or the propeller of the airplane, pushes against the air.

But the air is a thin layer of gas a few miles thick, clinging to Earth's surface. What if we want to travel beyond the air, where there is *nothing* to push against. Birds and airplanes would be as helpless in space, as a fish would be.

Yet there is a way out, and millions of years ago the squid discovered it. When the squid wants to dart through the water, it squirts a jet of water out behind and that makes it move forward. It is, literally, jet-propelled.

So is the jet plane, of course. The jet plane sends a stream of heated gases backward and the plane proper moves forward.

It may seem that the squid's jet pushes against water and that the jet plane exhaust pushes against air, but that is not the essential part of the workings. The system of jet-in-one-direction-and-move-in-the-other would work in a vacuum, too.

We *know* it does because that's how space vehicles maneuver, but let's see *why* it does.

Imagine an object suspended in the vacuum of outer

space. If there's nothing to move it, it must stay in the same place forever.

But suppose that an explosion inside the object sends part of it flying off in one direction. There is only one way to keep the *average* position of the object in place. The rest of the object must move in the opposite direction. As the two parts of the object continue to fly apart, the *average* position stays the same.

The faster one part is hurled in one direction, the faster the rest moves in the opposite direction. A jet plane burns fuel and sends the blazing hot exhaust gases through a narrow nozzle. Those gases must move at great velocities through the nozzle if they are to escape as quickly as they are formed; hence the plane builds up a very rapid speed, too—in the opposite direction.

Could a jet plane zoom out of the atmosphere altogether in this way? Not quite. It carries fuel only, and picks up its oxygen from the surrounding air. As the air gets thinner with height, the fuel eventually stops burning and there is no exhaust. The jet plane can gain no more speed and, as it coasts, gravitational pull brings it down into the thicker air again.

If a vehicle carried not only fuel, but also something to mix with it and make it burn (like liquid oxygen, for instance), then we would have a rocket. The rocket could keep its jet going even in outer space because it carried its own air along with itself, so to speak.

As long as the rocket jet was maintained, the vehicle would keep moving faster and faster. As soon as the jet ceased, the vehicle would coast and begin to respond to the Earth's gravitational pull (since there would now be no jet effect to counter that pull.)

Like the jet plane, the rocket would proceed to drop downward and, eventually, fall to Earth. It is possible, however, for a rocket vehicle to fall without ever hitting the ground, if it is pointed in the right direction and is moving quickly enough.

Suppose a rocket vehicle is a hundred miles up and is coasting parallel to the Earth's surface. It is constantly falling, but the Earth is round and the surface of the planet is constantly curving away from the vehicle. The falling vehicle and the curving surface can move "in step" so that although the vehicle is falling, falling, falling, it always remains a hundred miles above the curving, curving, curving surface. The vehicle is "in orbit."

In order to be in orbit, the vehicle must travel at least five miles per second. Otherwise, it doesn't move far enough, while falling, to allow the ground to curve sufficiently, and it eventually strikes the ground.

What's more, the vehicle can only do this outside the atmosphere. Inside the atmosphere, a five-mile-per-second speed would burn it up because of friction with the air.

Suppose a vehicle in orbit turns on its engines and sends out a jet of exhaust. It speeds up. After the jet is shut off, the vehicle is coasting more rapidly than it had been before. It moves farther while it falls a given amount and therefore moves away from the Earth's surface.

Now it is, in effect, climbing away from the Earth, and the Earth's gravitational pull gradually slows it. Eventually, it begins to fall back toward the Earth, speeding up as it does so.

If the vehicle continues to circle the Earth without further use of its engine, it repeats its new orbit over and over, climbing up and away from the earth, then sinking toward it again. The orbit has become a flattened curve called an ellipse.

By using the rocket engine at the proper moment and for the proper length of time, a vehicle can be put into an ellipse about the Earth that is as flat and as elongated as we wish. One side of the ellipse can stretch far out, as far as the Moon, while the other side continues to hug the Earth.

By choosing the right orbit (and allowing for the fact that the Moon is itself moving and has a gravitational pull of its own) a vehicle can coast to the Moon. If the orbit turns out to be not quite perfect, an additional touch of rocket firing at the right time and for the right duration will make a mid-course adjustment that will alter the orbit and place the vehicle on target.

Actually, once it becomes possible to place a vehicle into orbit, it doesn't take much more power to reach the Moon.

The strength of the Earth's gravitational pull weakens as the distance from the Earth increases. The greater the height a vehicle attains, the less power it takes to pull it higher still.

Suppose a vehicle is moving 7 miles per second to begin with. Earth's gravitational pull will eventually slow it to 3.5 miles per second but by that time the vehicle will have gained such a height that Earth's gravitational pull has been cut to half its original force. Now the gravitational pull can only slow the vehicle's speed at half the original rate. It takes the vehicle as long to drop down to 1.75 miles per second as it had taken to drop down to 3.5 miles per second originally.

After every equal unit of time the vehicle's speed is cut in half (1, ½, ¼, ⅛, 1/16, 1/32, and so on), so it is never cut entirely to zero. If the vehicle leaves with a speed of 7 miles per second it need never return to earth. That speed is "escape velocity" from the Earth's surface. This means that though 5 miles per second is required just to put a vehicle into orbit, only 2 additional miles per second is needed to carry it to the Moon.

Of course, the vehicle is still in the Sun's gravitational field. If it moves past the Moon, it will therefore continue in an orbit about the Sun and become a man-made planet.

The Sun-circling vehicle might use its retro-rockets. These send out a jet of exhaust ahead of the vehicle, giving it a push in the opposite direction (i.e., backward). Naturally, the vehicle slows down and begins to fall closer toward the Sun. The orbit is a new ellipse with one end hugging the Sun, and if it is correctly chosen, the vehicle will pass close to Venus.

Or else the vehicle may make use of its rear engines to increase its speed. It will then lift away from the Sun and move into an elliptical orbit that will carry it farther from the Sun than the Earth's own orbit ever does. Along this new ellipse, the vehicle may pass close to Mars.

Suppose a vehicle in space manages to attain a speed of 26 miles per second. This is the escape velocity with respect to the Sun (at least at Earth's distance from the Sun). The vehicle can then move away from the Sun at such a speed that the Sun's gravitational field will weaken with distance too quickly to bring it back.

The vehicle can then move out of the solar system altogether and coast toward the stars.

There is only one catch. Even the nearest star is a hundred million times as far as the Moon, and with a starting speed of 26 miles a second, it would take many thousand years to reach it even if that speed could be maintained.

Even if we took off with the speed of light—186,282 miles per second—it would take 4.3 years to reach the nearest star. And faster than the speed of light nothing can go.

So reaching the stars will prove a hard problem indeed. For a while, perhaps, we had better be satisfied with the Moon.

HOW MANY INCHES IN A MILE?

How many inches are there in a mile? Quickly now.

You don't know? Of course not. Who does, except for some joker who has deliberately decided to figure it out? There are 5,280 feet in a mile (you're lucky if you remember *that*) and, of course, 12 inches to each foot. The number of inches to the mile is therefore 5,280 × 12, or 63,360.

You might wonder, though, why anyone would want to know how many inches there are in a mile. What's the difference?

None, most of the time, but this sort of difficulty comes up in problems of more immediate importance. Suppose you have a rectangular living room that is 12 feet 6 inches in one direction and 18 feet 4 inches in the other. You are going to carpet that room side to side and fore to aft, and would like to get some sort of an idea of what it will cost. The carpeting is sold at a price which is so much per square yard. Therefore, you have to know the area of the room in square yards.

You are welcome to work this out for yourself right now. The necessary information you may need is that there are 12 inches to the foot and 3 feet to the yard. It may also be useful to know that there are 144 square inches to the square foot and 9 square feet to the square yard. Or perhaps you prefer to make use of the fact that there are 36 inches to the yard and 1,296 square inches to the square yard.

If you try to work out the problem three times and find three different answers at the end of the arithmetic, don't be too surprised. I worked it out in two different ways. I tried the first way twice before getting the right answer; and the second way four times! (Actually, the area of the room is almost 25½ square yards: 25.46 to be a little more exact.)

Heaven only knows how many hours your children sit hunched over their homework trying to solve problems like this! I do know, however, how many of them can still answer such problems after they have been out of school for one year. None of them!

But why is it so hard to do such a problem? After all, to work out the area of a rectangle we need only multiply the lengths of adjacent sides. A rectangle that is 12 feet by 18 feet is 12 × 18 or 216 square feet in area.

The trouble seems to be that what is easy where only feet are involved becomes difficult when inches and yards are dragged in as well, because one unit goes into another an inconvenient number of times. Why are there 3 feet to the yard? Why not 2, or 4? Why 12 inches to the foot? Why 5,280 feet to the mile?

The answer is that each measure arose independently in the dim, dim past, each being based on the only handy measuring system available to all human beings, however primitive—the human body itself.

The end joint of the adult thumb is about an inch long and can be used to measure off the width of a sheet of paper. The length of the foot is about a foot (of course!) and can be used to mark off, heel to toe, the length of a room. The distance from the tip of the fingers of an arm, outstretched sideways, to the tip of the nose is about a yard, and this can be used to measure off lengths of cloth from a bolt.

This is convenient, but each person's measurement is slightly different from that of the next. To get a bargain you would have to buy cloth from a merchant with a long arm—and he will send out a short-armed assistant to do the measuring.

For that reason, standard measures are adopted; a yard rule or a foot rule is constructed that is to be the same everywhere. It is convenient to have such a rule divided into smaller measures; so that a yard rule is divided into feet and inches. Naturally, the different units don't fit quite evenly to begin with, but they can be made even. There are about twelve thumb end lengths in the length of a foot, and about three foot lengths in the length from fingertip to nose. Make it exact for convenience and you end with 12 inches to the foot and 3 feet to the yard.

The Romans based a longer unit on the marching of their legions. They measured distances as so many thousands of the paces stepped off by the swinging strides of the Roman soldiers. They called a thousand paces "milia passuum" and in English, this became "mile."

The Roman thousand-paced mile is a little over 5,000 foot lengths. Why not make it 5,000 feet to the mile? The English, however, had a smaller unit called the "furlong," which was the length of a conveniently sized furrow ("furrow-long") formed in plowing. The furlong is 220 yards. A 5,000-foot mile would be roughly 7½ furlongs long, and it seemed more convenient to make the mile just 8 furlongs long, or 5,280 feet, or 1,760 yards.

The same sort of hit-and-miss jamming together of different units was done in the case of other kinds of measures.

In measuring the volume of liquids such as water, wine, or milk, there are 4 fluid ounces to the gill; 4 gills to the liquid pint; 2 liquid pints to the liquid quart, and 4 liquid quarts to the gallon. (There are also 9 gallons to the firkin and 7 firkins to the hogshead.) I wonder if anyone ever remembers for sure whether it is 4 pints to the quart and 2 quarts to the gallon, or 2 pints to the quart and 4 quarts to the gallon?

Of course, if you are measuring non-liquid materials, such as grain, flour, or vegetables, there are 2 dry pints to the dry quart, 8 dry quarts to the peck, and 4 pecks to the bushel.

Are you curious as to why I specify liquid pints and dry pints? Well, they're different. A dry pint is about 1⅙ liquid pints, so that 6 pints of flour is equal in quantity to 7 pints of milk. The same discrepancy holds for liquid quarts and dry quarts.

At least that is the way the Americans do it. The British make use of the same pints and quarts for both liquid and solid. Their pints and quarts, however, are different from both our varieties. The British "Imperial Gallon" is 1⅕

American gallons, as you will find when you buy gasoline in Canada.

As far as weight is concerned, there are 16 ounces to the pound and 2,000 pounds to the ton (or 2,240 pounds to the "long ton"). To this, the British add 14 pounds to the stone and are always saying that someone weighs 12 stone when they mean 168 pounds.

Of course, this is "avoirdupois weight," which you use most of the time. In measuring gold, gems, or drugs, you use "Troy weight," in which there are only 12 ounces to the pound—and the Troy ounce is not the same as the avoirdupois ounce. The Troy ounce is equal to about 1-1/10 avoirdupois ounces.

It is possible to go on and on and talk about acres and carats and cubic feet and drams—but surely you get the point. The interrelationship of the common units of measure is a jungle through which no one can possibly find his way.

Is there any way of switching to sanity? Yes! All the rest of the world has made that switch. In almost every other nation in the world, schoolchildren can learn all they have to know about units of measurement in a day, and they can remember it for the rest of their lives.

Sanity is the metric system!

The metric system was devised in France in 1795. At that time, France had a system of measures as insanely complex as did England and the baby nation of the United States. —So did every other nation on Earth; no two alike, save in their utter lack of logic. Often measures varied from section to section within a nation.

In 1795, however, France was in the midst of revolution and a new start seemed advisable. They decided to invent a system of measurements with simply and logically related units.

They did so, beginning with a "meter," a unit that, originally, represented a ten millionth of the distance from the Equator to the North Pole and that comes out to be equal to just a little over a yard in our common units. The French then divided the meter into ten smaller units, each smaller unit into ten still smaller ones, and so on. They also built up the meter into larger units by tens. To summarize in table form:

1 kilometer = 10 hectometers
1 hectometer = 10 dekameters
1 dekameter = 10 meters
1 meter = 10 decimeters
1 decimeter = 10 centimeters
1 centimeter = 10 millimeters

The names may seem strange at first, but once they are memorized in the correct order, our work is almost done.

Converting one into another is simple. How many centimeters are there in a kilometer? 100,000. How many meters in a hectometer? 100. Once you have memorized the order, its just a matter of multiplying tens.

In fact, it's even easier than that. Since the decimal system is based on tens also, the metric system can be manipulated by shifting decimal points. A length equal to 27 decimeters is also equal to 2.7 meters, to 270 centimeters, and to 0.27 dekameters.

Suppose, for instance, you have a rectangular room which is 32 decimeters 4 centimeters long and 49 decimeters 6 centimeters wide, and you want to carpet it completely at a price of so much a square meter. That sounds like our earlier problem in yards, feet, and inches, but—

Anyone using the metric system sees at once that 32 decimeters 4 centimeters is equal to 32.4 decimeters or 3.24 meters; and that 49 decimeters 6 centimeters is equal to 49.6 decimeters or 4.96 meters. The area is 3.24 × 4.96, or just about 16.07 square meters. You have that one nasty multiplication to make and no divisions. All the rest is taking care of the decimal point.

Furthermore, other types of measurements are tied in with the meter. Consider a cubic decimeter; that is, a cube with each side one decimeter long. Such a cube, if empty, will hold one "liter" of material. The liter is the basic unit of volume in the metric system. It can be divided and multiplied by tens just as the meter is and *with the same prefixes.* Since a millimeter is a tenth of a centimeter and a thousandth of a meter, you can be sure that a milliliter is a tenth of a centiliter and a thousandth of a liter. Again all switches can be made by shifting decimal points.

Next, a milliliter of water weighs one "gram." That is the unit of weight in the metric system. A kilogram is 1,000 grams and a milligram is 1/1000 gram. You already know that, and can work out all the rest yourself with no further information from me.

In actual practice, things are still simpler. In units of length, one rarely runs into the hectometer, dekameter, or decimeter. About nine tenths of the time, it is sufficient to remember that 1 kilometer = 1,000 meters; 1 meter = 100 centimeters; 1 centimeter = 10 millimeters.

In volume, liter and milliliter are the only units commonly encountered, so 1 liter = 1,000 milliliters is almost all you need to know. As for weight: 1 kilogram = 1,000 grams; and 1 gram = 1,000 milligrams. That gives you the story.

There's more to it, of course, but with what I have told you, it would be possible to make use of the metric system for almost every run-of-the-mill purpose. A child can learn in a day and memorize for life more about the metric system than you or I have been able to learn and retain about our common system in a lifetime.

The usefulness of the metric system is such that it spread over all the world quite rapidly. Nation after nation adopted the new French system. Only the English-speaking nations held out into the mid-twentieth century. Now even they are falling into line and the only holdout of any consequence among all the nations of the world is the United States of America. The next largest nation that still resists the metric system is, I believe, the African nation of Liberia.

What does this mean?

For one thing, *only* American children will waste incredible numbers of hours trying to ram into their heads an unlearnable system, when they might be learning something useful instead. Only American children will have this additional reason for learning to hate school. All other schoolchildren, including Russians and Chinese, dismiss the measurement system in a day of explanation and a week of practice.

What else? All scientists everywhere, *even in the United*

States, use the metric system *exclusively* in their scientific labors. Everywhere else, scientists use the metric system in daily life and learn it as children. In the United States, scientists learn the metric system only late in life and have to keep on using the common system also. It means that American scientists are never quite as much at home with their basic language of measurement as are all other scientists.

What else? Only American industry makes use of the inches and pounds. The rest of the world is on the metric system. A double standard must therefore be used in international trade, with ourselves inevitably on the losing side.

The United States *must* accept the metric system sooner or later, then. It is not too late now. Would that it had been done long ago in the infancy of the republic, but better now than later.

Of course, the in-between generation, the one which must abandon the common units and adopt the metric ones, will be a little uncomfortable, but that can't be helped. And it can be lived with—

A mile is equal to 1⅗ kilometers. A yard is equal to 9/10 of a meter. An inch is equal to 2½ centimeters. Those equivalences aren't exact, but they are sufficient for everyday purposes and it is not so brutal to memorize them. If you travel 2½ miles to get to work, that becomes 4 kilometers. If your speedometer reads 60 miles an hour, that is a thrilling 96 kilometers an hour. If you are 6 feet tall (72 inches) that is the same as 180 centimeters of height or 1.8 meters. If your girl's measurements are a lovely 34, 24, 34 in inches, they become an astounding 85, 60, 85 in centimeters.

As for the liter, that is equal to 1-1/20 liquid quarts. A liter of milk will seem just the same size as a quart of milk. You'll hardly notice the difference.

The kilogram is equal to about 2⅕ pounds. Put it another way—a pound is equal to about 450 grams and 3 ounces is equal to about 85 grams. If you weigh 170 pounds, that is about 76,500 grams or (move the decimal point three places to the left since there are 1,000 grams in a kilogram) 76.5 kilograms. Your 16-pound turkey will weigh 7.2 kilograms, and your quarter pound of butter will be a little over 110 grams.

This is an inconvenience, perhaps, but you will get used to it; butter will begin to be sold in even 100-gram lots soon enough; you will forget feet and pounds after a while and use meters and grams instead without having to translate in your mind.

And even if you remain annoyed, your children will be less annoyed and your grandchildren will bless you (as you would be blessing your grandparents if they had had the gumption to abandon insanity and go through a little trouble for *your* sake).

Nor will everything change, you understand. Working in the kitchen will scarcely be affected. Half a cup of sugar will remain half a cup though metric systems come and common systems go, and while you have your fingers, a pinch of salt will remain a pinch of salt and nothing else.

Oh, and by the way, before I sign off: How many inches were there in a mile? No, don't look back. Forgotten again, have you? Well, how many centimeters in a kilometer?

AFTERWORD

This article is especially dear to me because I was supposed to be taking it easy for two weeks and when nobody was looking, I cheated and wrote it.

BEYOND THE ULTIMATE

Until less than two hundred years ago, man could go on land no faster than a racing horse; and on sea no faster than the wind could push a ship. Through the air, he could not go at all; that was for birds and dreams.

Then came the age of vapors. Hydrogen, lightest of the gases, lifted balloons into the air and men were soon floating mountain-high. Steam, boiling forcibly out of water, turned mighty wheels and sent ships racing upwind and upstream, and locomotives speeding over steel rails. Gasoline vapors, combining with air in tiny explosions within engines, made possible the automobile and the airplane. Finally, gaseous exhausts, blowing furiously downward, lifted enormous rocket ships majestically through all the miles of atmosphere and out into space itself.

In less than two centuries, man reached the ultimate; the very limit of earthly speed. An astronaut circling the earth in ninety minutes is traveling at nearly five miles a second and that is as fast as he can profitably go. At this speed, Earth's gravitational pull inward is just balanced by the centrifugal effect pushing him outward and he remains at a fairly constant height above the Earth's surface.

Were an astronaut to insist on increasing his speed by firing his rear rockets, the centrifugal effect would strengthen and overpower the gravitational pull. The rocket ship would move away from Earth just as an automobile would go skidding off the road if it took a corner too quickly.

Of course, an astronaut might not only fire his rear rockets but might also fire auxiliary side rockets to push him downward toward the Earth. He would then take the corner, so to speak, at an unusually high speed while a mighty rocket-powered force pushed inward and kept him from "skidding off the road."

In doing this, however, the energy expended would far outweigh the time gained. Moreover, the astronaut would feel an outward-directed force upon himself that would mount rapidly as speed increased and would quickly become unendurable.

No, if we are to insist on traveling at more than this "ultimate" speed of five miles a second, there's only one place to go and that is away from Earth altogether.

This departure from Earth has already been accomplished. By 1969, manned spaceships had reached the Moon; unmanned spaceships had reached the vicinity of Mars and Venus.

Actually, once we attain a speed of more than seven miles a second, we can move on indefinitely against the pull of Earth's gravity (which, after all, gets weaker and weaker as we move farther away). At such speeds, we can coast as far as we like, without the expenditure of further fuel and (provided we avoid being trapped in the gravitational field of any astronomical object in between) we can reach any point in the Universe *given sufficient time.*

But that "sufficient time" is long indeed. Planetary distances beyond our immediate neighbor-worlds are huge and even seven miles a second is slow. It would take us over a year to move into Jupiter's orbit at such a speed and over a decade to move into Pluto's orbit.

If we accelerate to a more rapid speed before moving into the coasting stage, the time of journey is cut down, but there is a limit to what we can do in that direction. Acceleration costs fuel, tremendous quantities of it, and if we expect to accelerate to really high velocities with chemical rockets of the types used today to reach the Moon, the quantity of fuel required would make a spaceship prohibitively large.

The chemical rocket is not the last word, of course. Controlled nuclear explosions would drive exhaust gases backward at far greater velocities than is the case with ordinary chemical combustion. The greater energy of the exhaust would allow longer accelerations and greater final velocities per mass of fuel. A nuclear-powered spaceship could be reasonably compact and yet carry enough fuel to reach the outer solar system.

Even with nuclear power the time of journey could not be cut indefinitely. Acceleration must be held below a certain limit for the human body could not tolerate more, and in a journey of a certain length, only a certain velocity can be attained. It is probable that as long as we depend on any reaction motor, whether chemical or nuclear, exploration of the outer solar system will involve voyages that will endure for years.

A voyage of several years is perhaps within human achievement if the prize is large enough, but even such voyages will carry men only through our own solar system. What about the regions that lie beyond?

Outside our solar system is a whole Galaxy of stars, 135 *billion* of them, most of them, perhaps, with planetary systems of their own. Can we reach these other stars and their possibly attendant families of planets?

Unfortunately, even the nearest star is 25 trillion miles away, and such a distance is a most effective insulator. Coasting along at seven miles a second, it would take a spaceship one hundred thousand years to reach the nearest star. It would take two billion years for it to reach the other end of our Galaxy and forty billion years to reach the next large galaxy.

The solar system is a tiny island in an unimaginably large and unimaginably empty ocean of space. To cross the gap between one tiny planetary system and another is a proposition altogether different from travel within the solar system itself.

We might, of course, simply accept the time element.

Suppose we used efficient nuclear rockets and carried enough fuel to build up a speed of 700 miles a second. It would still take a thousand years or so to reach the nearest star and another thousand years to return.

To handle that, we might build a ship large enough to serve as a miniature world: a ship that would recycle its water and air, supply its own energy from fusion reactors, grow its own food, provide comfort for its own people. On that ship, generations of men would, each in its turn, be born, live, and die.

Eventually, the thirtieth generation would reach the

vicinity of the nearest star, with (who knows?) Earth forgotten, the original purpose of the ship a dim and legendary memory. Even if records had been maintained, the thirtieth generation might have no interest in Earth any longer but would continue in the only life they knew and cared for, journeying on forever in the private little Universe that was their home.

For that matter, would the people of Earth be able to build up enthusiasm for the outfitting of ship-Universes to be launched in various directions at various target stars with no return possible for millennia? They have engaged in long-range projects, yes (the medieval cathedrals, for instance), but only when progress, however slow, was at least visible.

Alternatively, it might be possible to freeze the ship's crew for indefinite periods, with automated machinery designed to thaw and rouse them when the destination is near at hand. (No method is now known that will serve to freeze human beings into true suspended animation with all physiological functions entirely unimpaired, but we may suppose that someday a method for doing this will be discovered.)

Through freezing, the *original* crew might reach the destination even though thousands of years had passed. They would remember their purpose and, presumably, be highly motivated to return to Earth. But on Earth, those thousands of years would still have passed and the lack of enthusiasm for a project in which neither end nor progress was visible in one's own lifetime would still be a factor.

Great time lapses must be eliminated, then. Higher speeds must be attained; much higher speeds.

One way in which this can be done is by using an ion drive. Instead of making use of gases, heated by either chemical or nuclear reactions, and emerging from the rear in huge masses at several miles a second, we can send individual ions (that is, electrically charged atom fragments) out the rear. These ions would have very little mass but they could be made to move at speeds of several tens of thousands of miles per second.

An ion drive would produce very small accelerations thanks to the tiny masses involved, but precisely because so little mass is used up, there would be enough fuel to continue that acceleration for years if necessary. Speeds would build up to a hundred thousand miles per second or more. Now the nearer stars can be reached in a single man's *unfrozen* lifetime; and, what's more, they could be reached in the lifetime of men on Earth. Dozens of stars might be reached in fifty years or less.

But these stars are only those in our immediate neighborhood. What about more distant stars? The many billions of them?

Well, if one goes faster and faster (according to Einstein's Special Theory of Relativity) the passage of time proceeds more and more slowly for the speeder. For speeds over 160,000 miles per second, this slowing of time is considerable and for speeds over 180,000 miles per second, it is enormous (see the earlier article, *Time*).

Astronauts moving through space at better than 180,000 miles per second might, in what seems to them to be merely twenty-five years, reach the other end of the Galaxy. (That is, in their *slowed* time. On Earth, with time moving at its usual velocity, the time lapse would seem much, much greater.)

There is, in fact, an ultimate speed—186,282 miles per second. This is the speed of light in a vacuum. At that speed, time slows to an utter halt.

And this raises a thought. Is it absolutely necessary to transfer a massive object itself through space? Can we perhaps merely transfer the description of the mass. As a familiar analogy, we need not send a document across a continent; we merely reduce it to a succession of light and dark dots that adequately characterize the document. These are converted into a fluctuating electric current, and this current sends its message, *at the speed of light*, across the continent, to be reassembled at the receiving point into a facsimile document.

Is it possible to reduce matter to a fluctuating beam of photons (the tiny "particles" that make up light and other forms of radiant energy) that would completely describe that sample of matter? This beam could then be sent across space for reconversion to a duplicate of that matter at some receiving point.

Could a photon beam of this sort be made to represent a

human body, or a complete spaceship with its cargo of human bodies? I would hate to predict that it could, for it would be an accomplishment of unimaginable complexity—but I would have said this in 1800 concerning a flight to the Moon.

If "mass-transference" becomes possible, then an astronaut could conceivably be transported *anywhere* in the Universe at the speed of light. To that astronaut, *no time at all* would seem to have elapsed from conversion to reconversion.

However, though an astronaut might travel at nearly the speed of light and experience little time lapse, or actually at the speed of light and experience no time lapse at all, time would still proceed in its ordinary fashion on Earth. The photon beam that is an astronaut would still take 4.3 years, Earth time, to reach the nearest star and 100,000 years to traverse the Galaxy from end to end.

Nothing so far described would make it possible to do more than reach our neighborhood stars, the fifty closest perhaps, within the lifetime of a stay-at-home on Earth; and it would be only these neighborhood journeys that Earth might be willing to support.

Well then, could a spaceship travel at speeds greater than that of light? Until recently, the answer would have been a flat negative. The speed of light in a vacuum is an ultimate velocity according to Einstein's Special Theory of Relativity and no one today doubts the validity of that theory.

But in the 1960s, a vision that stretched beyond the ultimate was presented. It was pointed out that if the speed of light was viewed as an impenetrable limiting wall, it might be argued that a wall has two sides. On the other side of the wall might exist a whole universe of particles that could only move *faster* than the speed of light and could never slow down below that speed and yet fulfill all the requirements of Einstein's theory.

These super-fast particles are called "tachyons" from a Greek word meaning "swift."

Such tachyons would have odd properties indeed, and the one that concerns us at the moment is this: The *more energy* you pump into a tachyon the *slower* it would go, until at very large energies it would slow down almost to the speed of light. The *less energy* present in a tachyon the *faster* it would go until at very low energies it would travel millions of light-years per second.

Tachyons would not interact with ordinary particles and could not be detected through collisions. Since they move so rapidly, they are in our vicinity and, therefore, capable of being detected, for only a tiny fraction of a second. Nevertheless, theory requires a passing tachyon to produce a tiny, but perhaps detectable, flash of light as it passes. Physicists have tried to detect those flashes and so far, they have failed.

That, however, doesn't really matter. Even if tachyons aren't actually detected, they may nevertheless exist, and perhaps that means that though none are to be found at the moment, some can be created—if we only knew how.

Well, we have already imagined the conversion of matter (and whole men-packed spaceships) into a stream of photons that would carry all the information of the matter precisely, and that could be reconverted into an exact duplicate of the original at a far distant point.

Having gone that hog-wild, why not go one more step and suppose that matter could be turned into a stream of tachyons, rather than photons?

Such a beam of tachyons, if sufficiently low in energy, would move so rapidly that it might reach the vicinity of the nearest star, say, in five seconds. That five-second time lapse would hold not only for the astronauts themselves but also for the stay-at-home Earthmen. The Galaxy might be spanned in a minute, the most distant outer galaxies reached in a week.

To such a beam of tachyons, the whole enormous Universe would be but an insignificant speck.

It might also be possible to use modulated beams of tachyons to carry messages from one far distant star to another. In this way, both transportation and communication might become possible over all distances, however great, and, what's more, with virtually no time lapse.

This means that it is no longer utterly inconceivable that the day (a far distant one, perhaps) might come when the ultimate is surpassed and all the vast Universe becomes man's neighborhood.

TWO

AND TOMORROW

1 · IN SPACE

THE LUNAR LANDING

The most wonderful thing about the Moon is that it is there.

It is a large and handy world, over two thousand miles across, and only a quarter of a million miles away. It hangs in the sky, large, gleaming, and incredibly inviting, so that men have dreamed of going there long before our own planet was thoroughly explored.

Suppose the Moon didn't exist—

After all, it might not have existed. None of our immediate neighbors among the planets has anything like it. Mercury and Venus have no satellites at all as far as we can tell. Mars has two satellites, which, however, are so contemptibly small (less than a dozen miles across, each) that they can be dismissed.

Without our Moon, the objects visible in Earth's night sky would all be nothing but points of light. There would be nothing to stimulate the pre-telescopic imagination into dreaming of the existence of other worlds. Points of light would scarcely have the effect on us that a visible disc would; especially a disc like the Moon, with splotches and shadows apparent to the unaided eye.

And even after the invention of the telescope, when some of the points of light would be revealed to be sizable globes, the nearest would still never approach closer than 25 million miles, fully a hundred times the distance of our Moon.

With the first step made more difficult by a hundred times, would we have the courage to dream of venturing into space?

SOURCE: "The Lunar Landing" appeared in *The New York Times Magazine* as "The Moon Could Answer the Riddle of Life", July 13, 1969.

Fortunately the Moon *is* there, a super-convenient stepping-stone into space—and the queerest part of it is that it would seem to have no business being there. There is something about it that is radically different from all other satellites in the solar system.

There are 32 known satellites in the solar system, distributed among 6 of the known planets (Earth 1, Mars 2, Jupiter 12, Saturn 10, Uranus 5, and Neptune 2) and of these, 25 are small worlds ranging from a few miles to a few hundred miles across.

That leaves 7 satellites that are sizable. Jupiter has 4 of them: Io, Europa, Ganymede, and Callisto. Then Saturn and Neptune have one apiece: Titan and Triton, respectively. And, of course, Earth has the Moon.

In terms of sheer size, the Moon is next to last among these large satellites. Only Europa is smaller.

What, then, makes the Moon so unusual?

It's not size alone that counts, but the size of the satellite in comparison to the planet it circles. Jupiter's largest satellite is Ganymede, with a diameter of about 3,200 miles. Jupiter itself, however, has a diameter of 86,000 miles. The diameter of Ganymede is only about 3.7 per cent that of Jupiter.

Compared to giant Jupiter, Ganymede and all the other Jovian satellites, large and small, are only scraps. We can imagine a huge cloud of dust and gas swirling about in primordial times and slowly condensing to form Jupiter. Tiny sub-swirls on the outskirts would form the satellites. Even those swirls which produced quite sizable satellites on the earthly scale would be tiny compared to Jupiter—which has eleven times Earth's diameter.

The same is true for the other planets. Saturn's large satellite, Titan, is only 4.3 per cent the diameter of Saturn itself. Neptune's large satellite, Triton, does a little better—8.5 per cent.

But now compare this with the Moon. Its diameter of 2,160 miles (considerably less than that of Ganymede, Titan, or Triton) is, nevertheless, fully 27.5 per cent the diameter of the Earth. Earth has a satellite that is over a quarter as wide as itself. No other planet can make such a claim or anything like it. The Moon is so large compared to Earth that, seen from a distance, the two might almost be said to make up a double planet.

Why should the Moon's size be so lopsided? When the swirling cloud of dust and gas condensed to form the Earth, why should so large a proportion of it have formed a comparatively large satellite on the outskirts, when nothing like that happened in the case of any other planet?

It's easy to say, "Well, it just did, that's all," but there may be a reason and astronomers would love to know it. So far, they haven't the vaguest notion of any explanation.

Perhaps the Moon formed in a different manner and did not take shape by way of a sub-swirl of dust and gas.

Here is one alternate explanation—

As the Moon circles the Earth, it drags the ocean water with it, giving rise to the tides. In the shallow parts of the ocean, the friction of the moving water against the sea bottom acts as a brake on the Earth's rotation. This means that the length of the day is very slowly increasing. It can also be shown from the principles of physics that it means the Moon is very slowly increasing its distance from Earth.

Hundreds of millions of years ago, Earth must therefore have been rotating much more quickly and the Moon must have been much closer to it. A couple of billion years ago, the Earth must have been rotating very rapidly and the Moon must have been practically touching it.

Can it be that when the Earth was first formed, it lacked a satellite, as is true of Venus? Can it be that as it spun rapidly, a piece of it (now the Moon) broke away? Can the Moon be as large as it is because it did not form from the cloud of dust and gas as the Earth itself did, but because it was born by a different route, breaking away from an already formed Earth?

There are serious difficulties with this theory, however.

Think of the spinning Earth. As the planet turns, the Earth's surface makes only a small circle at places near the poles; larger circles farther from the pole. It is at the equator that the surface makes the largest sweep, a full 25,000 miles, and at the equator that the surface is moving most quickly. (The surface moves at 1,040 miles an hour at the equator but only 650 miles an hour at the latitude of New York.)

If we imagine the Earth spinning so rapidly as to begin throwing off air, water, and chunks of solid land into space, it would be from the equatorial regions these would come, for those regions would be moving fastest. The thrown-off material, as it formed the Moon and traveled farther from the Earth, would continue to circle the Earth in line with the Equator. It would still be doing that today.

This would also be true if the Moon formed on the outskirts of the whirling cloud of dust and gas that was forming the Earth. As that cloud whirled, movement would be fastest in the equatorial regions and it would be there that the Moon material would cluster.

We see examples of this in the solar system. Jupiter's four large satellites all circle their planet directly above the line of its equator. This is also the case of most of the satellites of the other planets. As for the planets themselves, almost all revolve about the Sun more or less in the line of the Sun's equator, for they apparently formed at the equatorial outskirts of the huge whirling cloud that condensed to form the Sun.

The Moon is a notable exception. It does not move about the Earth in the line of Earth's equator. It revolves about the Earth (and, along with the Earth, about the Sun) more nearly in the line of the Sun's equator. In this respect, the Moon acts like a planet in its own right, and not like a satellite.

Can it be that the Moon *was* an independent planet originally? One which somehow wandered into the vicinity of the Earth and was captured by Earth's gravitational pull?

If so, where could the Moon have come from?

One interesting suggestion as to the place of the Moon's origin involves the asteroid belt. Between the orbits of Mars and Jupiter are many thousands of tiny bodies (asteroids), of which the largest is less than 500 miles across. It is often suggested that these asteroids are the remains of an exploded planet. However, even if all the known asteroids are lumped together, they make up a very small planet indeed.

Can part of the original planet between Mars and Jupiter be missing? Can it have been driven by the explosion closer to the Sun? Can it, in fact, be the Moon?

If it is, we might next ask when the capture was effected. There are geologists who argue that some billion years ago or less there are signs, in the rocks, of a large catastrophe that could easily have been the result of huge tides that swept the continents clean. These might have resulted by the sudden capture of a then nearby Moon.

Can it be, then, that the Moon was captured by Earth less than a billion years ago? In that case, through most of Earth's 5 billion year history, it existed as a lonely world, like Venus, and it is only recently that the Moon joined it.

Of course, there are catches to this suggestion, too. When astronomers try to work out the actual mechanics that would be involved in driving the Moon from the asteroid belt to the vicinity of the Earth and then having it captured by the Earth, matters become entirely too complicated for easy credibility.

In short, there is no really plausible way of explaining why the Moon exists where it does and why it should be the size it is.

But it *is* there and it *is* extraordinarily large and the lunar landing may supply us with an answer to that immense puzzle. And with other answers, too—

There are many ways in which the Moon can be useful to us and there are many ways in which lunar landings can ultimately be expected to yield us a profit. The key word, however, is "ultimately." In most directions there will be an unavoidable wait, perhaps a long one, before those profits can be realized.

It is easy, for instance, to argue that the Moon offers an ideal spot for an astronomic observatory. Without an atmosphere, seeing will be unrivaled; the Sun can be studied through all its range of radiation, and there will be an unparalleled opportunity to study the Earth itself as a whole.

Yet certainly the initial landing on the Moon won't succeed in establishing an observatory then and there. It will undoubtedly require many landings on the Moon and much in the way of tremendously complex preparations to set up an observatory.

The same can be said for almost any other practical aspect of lunar exploration. The possibilities are wonderful, but *when*—

Well the vacuum that covers every part of the lunar surface is more free of gas than any vacuum that can be produced on Earth, and there are millions of square miles of it. Materials could be manufactured with unprecedented purity, for they would lack the gas film that is almost universal on Earth. Without the gas film they would have different properties from those which we are used to and the techniques of welding would be utterly changed, while metallic films could be layered onto other substances with unprecedented thinness.

At the low temperatures of the two-week lunar night, it would be much easier to refrigerate objects the rest of the way down to near absolute zero, than it would be on the much warmer Earth. Devices such as computers and large magnets, which make use of unusual properties that only exist near absolute zero, could be more easily constructed and more easily studied.

Complicated chemicals that are difficult or impossible to handle (such as many of those found in living tissue) might be put together in mass quantities at the Moon's low temperatures and then purified by distillation in its excellent vacuum. Thanks to that vacuum, the distillation could take place at temperatures so low that the fragile molecules would not be damaged.

The energetic radiation of the Sun in the far ultraviolet and beyond is stopped by Earth's atmosphere, but on the Moon, it reaches the surface. Such radiation could be used to initiate novel chemical reactions. The effect of radiation on the cause or cure of cancer, on mutation, on cell damage, could be studied.

Solar batteries can be used more profitably on the Moon than on Earth, thanks to the Moon's blaze of a two-week cloudless day. Research in the construction and use of all sorts of devices involving solar power can be greatly advanced, to Earth's own ultimate profit.

But when, when, when can elaborate factories and laboratories be built to take advantage of all these opportunities?

An independent colony on the Moon might be of great use to Earthmen psychologically, offering us the stimulating vision of a renewed frontier and the profitable example of a closed society making rational use of its limited resources.

But when can such an independent colony be established?

It is only natural, then, to dismiss these long-range possibilities rather impatiently and to ask whether the early lunar landings, even the very first perhaps, can be of use to us in any way. After all, we would surely like to have the first landing on the Moon something more than an extremely expensive exercise in one-upmanship over the Soviet Union.

Well, it is quite conceivable that even the first landing can earn its keep and that it can gain us enormous information.

The first astronauts to land on the Moon plan to gather up samples of the Moon's crust and bring them back to Earth for detailed study.

Those few pounds of dirt may help decide the question of the place of origin of the Moon. If the Moon were once part of the Earth or were part of the dust cloud out of which the Earth had also been formed, then the Moon's crust should be very much like the Earth's in a large variety of chemical ways.

What, though, if the Moon had originally been part of a planet in the asteroid belt, out beyond Mars?

The dust cloud out there, two or three times as distant from the Sun as we are, might well have been significantly different in chemical composition from our own much closer-to-the-Sun cloud. The planet that formed out there, taking shape under different conditions of temperature and radiation, might have assumed interesting differences in the nature of its crust.

If, then, the dirt from the Moon is markedly un-Earth-like in important respects, that would be a strong indication that the Moon did not originate in the neighborhood of the Earth; that the Moon is an accidental and perhaps recent acquisition of our planet.

In that case, the first lunar landing would have handed us the kind of bonus we would not really have had the right to expect. It would have given us an opportunity to travel 237 thousand miles in order to explore a portion of the solar system that ought by rights to have been perhaps 237 million miles away—a thousand times as far as the Moon.

If, on the other hand, analysis of lunar material shows that in all likelihood, the Moon had always existed in the vicinity of the Earth, we need not feel disappointment. There could still be much to learn about the Moon. There are the newly discovered mascons, regions of higher-than-average density centered about the lunar seas. What and why is this? The astronauts report softer outlines on the mountains on the far side of the Moon? Could there have been more erosion on that side? If so, why?

Even though the Moon's crust, formed in Earth's vicinity, might have been very like the Earth's crust to begin with, the subsequent history of the two worlds has been radically different.

Over billions of years, the Earth's crust has been enormously affected by the action of wind, water, and living things. The result is that virtually no traces remain in being in the Earth's crust that can give us information as to what the situation was like more than, say, half a billion years ago.

On the Moon, however, the action of wind, water, and living things has been minimal. To be sure the Moon's crust has been affected by temperature differences, by solar radiation, and by meteor bombardment, but the resulting effects have been small compared to those on the Earth.

It follows, then, that the Moon's crust will be much more informative concerning the Moon's early history (and, therefore, the early history of the Earth as well) than Earth's crust is. Between what the astronauts see, photograph, and instrumentally detect, and the analysis of what they bring back, it is quite conceivable we may learn a great deal about conditions on *Earth* 2 to 4 billion years ago.

There is, in addition, very likely to be more in the Moon's crust than the minerals and crystals we expect to find in it.

If the Moon had its origin in the neighborhood of the

Earth, it ought to have had its share of the common elements and molecules that go into the makeup of Earth's atmosphere and ocean. (If it was once actually part of the Earth, it might have brought some air and water with it when it broke away.)

To be sure, the smaller gravitational pull on the Moon's surface (only one sixth that on the Earth's surface) would have been ineffective in holding any ocean and atmosphere in the long run.

But what is "the long run"? For some millions of years, the Moon may have retained a shrinking supply of surface water and a gradually thinning atmosphere. Some surprising evidence in favor of that thought arises from recent studies of the Moon's surface by way of satellite photography. Meandering marks have been found on the Moon's crust that look so like dried-up riverbeds in so many details that it is hard to think of anything else they could possibly represent.

Then, too, astronauts circling the Moon have detected browns and tans among the stark black and white of the Moon's surface. Such colors usually imply the existence of iron oxide. Does this mean there was once a little free oxygen on the Moon?

If the Moon had its ocean and atmosphere once, the simple molecules in that ocean and atmosphere might have undergone changes similar to those undergone on Earth, since both worlds were exposed to the energetic radiation of the same Sun at the same distance.

The changes undergone by these simple molecules are of particular importance because they ended in the development of the enormously complex molecules of living tissue. Biochemists have been trying to duplicate the course of these changes in the laboratory, setting up small-scale analogs of what they imagine primordial conditions to have been like.

Naturally, it is difficult to tell to what extent the laboratory conditions are really like the situation on the primordial Earth and how far, therefore, laboratory results are to be trusted. On the Moon, however, we have a worldwide "experiment," perhaps, in which the changes began and then came to a halt at some midway point when the ocean and atmosphere finally disappeared.

In the samples of crust brought back from the Moon, then, biologists may find organic molecules representing a point partway toward life. Perhaps the molecules may even have reached a Moon-born life far more primitive than anything on Earth, but superlatively interesting for that very reason.

(And if the Moon had once been part of Earth, these organic traces might have been formed from actual Earth-developed chemicals. We would, in that case, have a view of phases of early terrestrial evolution long since blotted out completely on Earth itself.)

In any case, the study of the organic molecules in the Moon's crust might advance our knowledge of the formation of life by decades when compared with the laborious advance that would have been possible by Earth-based experiments only. (Of course, one bag of rocks won't tell us all, either. We will want samples from various sections of the Moon, samples which have been parts of different environments. Our researchers will want many lunar landings—a permanent lunar base, if possible.)

Nor need we think that the question of the chemical evolution of life is something that merely exercises the theoretical speculations of ivory-tower biologists. It is quite conceivable that the ramifications of such research could be amazingly useful to humanity on an immediate medical level.

With all the biological advances made in recent decades, we still remain pitifully ignorant of the fine detail of what goes on inside cells. For instance, we know that we can alleviate the symptoms of diabetes with injections of insulin, or that we can cure scurvy by adding ascorbic acid (vitamin C) to the diet. We do not know, however, even today, exactly what it is that either insulin or vitamin C does in the body. In fact, we don't know the actual fine workings of any hormone.

That we can engage in successful hormone therapy at all is due to the fact that we imitate the action of the body. We don't know what it is doing, but if we keep exact step with it, we may get results. The fact that we don't know what it is doing, however, means that we have no way of predicting undesirable side effects until they display themselves in what is sometimes a most unwelcome fashion.

In the case of hormones, we can at least determine what the body is doing in a rough sort of way by depriving experimental animals of those hormones. What do we do when we have no such easy key? What about cancer, for instance?

Not all the research lavished on cancer in the twentieth century has told anyone exactly what goes wrong in a cancer cell. Something is wrong, obviously. The cell is not normal; it keeps growing and reproducing when it shouldn't. But *what* is wrong? What chemical reaction or reactions has or have taken the wrong turning?

We don't know, and until we find out, we may not have much of a chance of working out a satisfactory way of preventing or curing the disease.

The reason why it is so hard to find out exactly what is happening inside a cell, is that so *much* is happening. There are many thousands of chemical reactions and physical changes all taking place simultaneously and all affecting each other in the most delicate fashion. It is like trying to unravel a fine cord which has been worked into an intricate, intertwining, three-dimensional ball a foot across.

But suppose an analysis of the Moon's crust tells us what the chemistry of organic molecules is like, partway to life, or shows us the chemistry of a sub-life far more primitive than Earth's most primitive cells.

We may then get visible clues to the workings of the cell; clues that are obscured in Earth-cells themselves by the piling up of towering complications.

Once we get the basics in this fashion, it is possible that we may get some notion as to what may have gone wrong in a cancer cell. With that knowledge in hand, biologists can then turn to Earth-cells and, knowing exactly what they are looking for, find the biochemical cause of cancer at last.

This, therefore, is the answer (or, anyway, *an* answer) to those who ask why we are spending billions on reaching the Moon, when it is so much more important to solve the cancer mystery here on Earth.

All science is one. If we push back the boundaries of darkness in any direction, the added light illuminates all places and not merely the immediate area uncovered.

It is just conceivable, in other words, that by taking the

long trip to the Moon, we will be taking the shortest route to unmasking the riddle of cancer.

AFTERWORD (1972)

This article appeared in 1969, just before the first Moon landing, and a number of other such landings have taken place since. A considerable quantity of Moon rocks has been brought back on each occasion and some rocks have been brought back by unmanned Soviet rockets.

So far, so good, but unfortunately the optimistic attitude of the article has proven unwarranted, so far. The rocks have not clearly answered the problem of the Moon's early history, but have posed new puzzles.

The rocks show no evidence of water or perceptible quantities of organic matter, and the markings that seemed to be the evidence of one-time flowing water are much more likely the result of one-time flowing lava.

Undoubtedly the lack of really sensational discoveries has contributed to the loss of public interest in the Moon landings.

Nevertheless, who knows what tomorrow brings? If there is water on the Moon at all, it would not be at the surface, which has been exposed to solar radiation for billions of years, but several feet under the surface.

So far we have only scratched a few isolated patches on the Moon's surface. I hope we continue to look.

AFTER APOLLO, WHAT?

The assumption is that we (and the Russians, too) will reach the Moon within a very few years. Even the tragic accidents that cost the lives of three Apollo astronauts and a Soviet cosmonaut do not alter that assumption. NASA has already scheduled the first Apollo flight for very early in 1968 and still looks to a Moon landing before 1970.

But it takes a few years to plan an advanced program of space exploration beyond that already existing, so we must now begin to think beyond Apollo. If we do not begin our preparations *now*, we face a halt of perhaps several years after we do reach the Moon. And with that halt might come a loss of interest in the space program generally, a loss of psychological momentum that would stretch those years of delay into decades.

The trouble, perhaps, is that the motivation behind our space program was childish to begin with. Too many Americans have aimed to "get to the Moon first," not because they wanted to get to the Moon at all, but only because they wanted to get back at the Soviets for putting up the first satellite in 1957 and humiliating us. As a result, we kept on pumping increasing billions into the program because every once in a while the Soviets would score another "first."

But the Soviets have sent up only one manned flight in two years, and that ended in disaster. We are clearly ahead of them in virtually every phase of the program (far ahead in some). That settles it, many people believe. We showed them and sputnik is avenged. The interest in spending billions on space already is fading. We'll reach the Moon because we're committed to the goal (and because the Soviets might make a last-minute spurt) but after that, there are no definite plans.

Lately, there has been talk of going on to make more elaborate manned or unmanned shots to Venus, Mars, or to some comet flashing by. But is that all the Moon means to us? Is it just a relay station on the way to somewhere else, so that the space race can continue in all its expense and competitive folly?

We and the Soviets need a new motive, one that places a value on something other than scoring "firsts" and one-upping each other. Merely reaching the moon is no end in itself. Having reached it, cannot we and the Soviets and any other nation that cares to join the venture combine to explore it, develop it, and make it a home for man?

To some, of course, the question isn't "After Apollo, what?" but "After Apollo, why?"

And just as there are those who questioned the project of reaching the moon in the first place, many more will ask, "Why colonize it?"

Presumably there were also those who asked "Why?" in 1492. Once Columbus had discovered America and brought Spain great prestige, was it really necessary to go beyond that immediate gain and invest large sums of money to explore and colonize those far-distant savage wildernesses?

That old "Why?" was easily answered with material reasons: gold and silver and new and unheard-of products—maize, potatoes, tobacco, quinine—to bring back to a wondering Europe. No doubt, if the Moon had obvious resources that men valued, many would see the purpose of colonizing the Moon at once.

Yet the greatest gift of the New World to the Old was not gold or tobacco or any material resources. It was the gift of an intangible—the gift of a second chance, a new start. Later, men came to America looking for freedom as well as for precious metals and for relief from oppressive traditions as well as from poverty.

One result of that search for intangibles was the establishment of the United States of America on an equalitarian basis that was impossible for the caked society of eighteenth-century Europe to initiate, or even imitate, without vast blood and turmoil. Moreover, our size and our century-long isolation enabled us to develop a technology which the rest of the world eagerly attempts to duplicate—and which our enemies accept even more avidly than our friends.

We are now faced with a still newer New World and the opportunity arises for a segment of mankind to make still another fresh start.

To be sure, the original New World was only 3,000 miles from Europe, while the Moon is 240,000 miles from Earth. Yet such distances must be viewed in their technological contexts. The wooden hulls that pushed off from Spain more than four centuries ago faced a voyage much longer in time than the one that separates us from the Moon. The ocean voyagers were frightened men, not knowing where they were going, ill fed, poorly cared for, completely isolated from home. Our astronauts are superbly trained and cared for, highly motivated and at all times in contact with home. The advantage is all with the first men to the Moon over the first men to America.

But once the New World was reached, one might argue, men could live in it. It contained trackless wilderness, hostile natives, wild animals, but it had air and water, edible plants and animals. Men could make friends with the natives (or enslave them), hunt the animals, clear forests, and plant crops.

What can the Moon offer in comparison? It is a dead and useless world, without air and water. Its surface is exposed to the ceaseless rain of micrometeorites, ultraviolet radiation from the Sun and X-rays and cosmic rays from space. Temperatures drop to 200 below zero Fahrenheit during a two-week night and rise to 200 above zero Fahrenheit during a two-week day. Man could not live for five minutes on the Moon without artificial protection.

But what is wrong with artificial protection? The Pilgrims could not have survived their first winter in New England if they had not built some sort of shelters. On the Moon, too, it will be necessary to build shelters against the harshness of the environment. At our level of technology, it would be as easy to burrow into the Moon and carve out airtight caverns as it was for the first New World colonists to hack down trees and build houses.

The airtight caverns would provide marvelous protection. Even just a few feet of rock overhead would bar the harsh sunlight and all unfriendly radiation except for a few cosmic rays which, after all, reach us here on Earth. Micrometeorites would be warded off, and extremes of heat and cold would disappear. Underground, temperatures would remain equable at all times.

Of course, there would remain the question of water and air, indisputably a serious drawback.

At first, astronauts will have to bring their air and water with them. This might entail the prior construction of two space supply stations, one orbiting the Earth and one orbiting the Moon, like mountain camps established on the slopes of a Himalayan peak. The dependence of pioneer Moon colonists on periodic supplies from Earth is not without parallel. Three years after Jamestown was founded, the English colonists were famished and ready to abandon the project or die when they were saved only by the last-minute appearance of Lord De la Warr's flotilla with new men and supplies.

As long as Moon colonists would have to depend on an umbilical cord stretching a quarter of a million miles to Earth, the colony would be an expensive venture indeed. Yet might not the umbilical cord be dispensed with eventually? Might not the colony grow independent?

When we say the Moon has no water, we really mean it has no water lying freely on its surface. It has no oceans, lakes, or rivers, or even swamps or marshes. But it may have water just the same. Water is so common a substance all over the universe (as far as we know) that it seems reasonable to hope that the Moon will have retained at least a moderate quantity.

Moon water might consist of layers of frost in recesses of craters into which the Sun never shines. Underground, perhaps seams of ice could be mined as we mine coal. Failing those sources, we could utilize water molecules which almost certainly are tied loosely to the mineral substances that make up the Moon's crust. The water supply would not be large enough to support a population of billions who are accustomed on Earth to consuming and polluting water as though it existed in infinite supply. It could, however, support a space colony of thousands who made shrewd and chary use of the available amount.

Such water, obtained from the Moon itself, could easily be separated by the process known as electrolysis to yield hydrogen and oxygen. The oxygen then could be used to supply the underground caverns with an atmosphere.

Minerals, too, could be locally obtained. Astronomers have long thought the Moon's crust to be essentially similar to the Earth's and everything we have learned from satellites orbiting the Moon and making soft landings confirms the belief. From the Moon's minerals, metals and ceramics could be derived, and nitrogen and carbon dioxide, too. Appropriate minerals, plus water and carbon dixoide, could be used to grow plants under artificial light. Eventually, perhaps, animals could also be fed and used as a meat supply.

Everything would have to be recycled, of course; that is, used over and over again. Men would consume oxygen, water, and food, breathe out carbon dioxide and eliminate wastes; the carbon dioxide, water, and wastes would be used by the plants to reform oxygen and food. The process is not completely efficient, but any slow leakage could be overcome by increasing the water supply from the Moon's crust and using additional minerals. Then more oxygen and carbon dioxide could be made.

This sort of tight recycling is by no means fantasy. Such systems are being developed right now since they are essential for any spaceship undertaking a journey longer than a trip to the Moon. A spaceship carrying men to Mars, for example, can scarcely count on a round trip much shorter than two years. Carrying a supply of food, water, and air—without recycling—would be quite impractical.

Recycling presents psychological difficulties. The thought of producing drinking water by evaporating urine, for instance, seems unpleasant but that is precisely what happens on Earth. At least some of the fresh water we drink was in urine once and in substances even more unpalatable. On the Moon, the cycle would be tighter and more obvious, but it would be no different in principle.

It would also demand a continuing and reliable source of energy, since it takes energy to mine the Moon, electrolyze water into oxygen, irradiate algae with light and make plants grow.

It would be impractical to carry coal or oil to the Moon as the source of energy; those materials are too bulky for their energy content. Undoubtedly an early project for any Moon colony would be to transport and assemble a nuclear fission plant like those which exist today.

But the Moon has its own source of energy, solar energy, which man on Earth is already using directly. Solar batteries that convert sunlight directly into electric currents, for instance, power a number of our satellites. Sunlight on the Moon pours down for two weeks at a time, without interference from clouds or fog. It is a tremendous and absolutely reliable energy source and one can imagine batteries eventually covering the Moon's surface by the square mile, supplying enough energy in the daylight period for immediate use and for storing and later use during the two-week night.

Then, if we learn how to control nuclear fusion, heavy hydrogen could become a far more compact energy source than solar batteries. Heavy hydrogen from Moon water might be all the colonists would need. If not, the supplementary supply could easily be brought from Earth, so compact is it as an energy source.

It seems that Moon colonists would have to depend on the perfect functioning of an intricate technology for survival. What if something goes wrong? Suppose they had to face something like the Great Northeast Blackout of 1965? Suppose a meteorite punctures a cavern or a Moonquake cracks one and the air escapes in a rush? How can men be expected to live under such imminent threats of instant death?

Men live with danger on Earth, too. They farm on the slopes of volcanoes, live on vast plains where tornadoes are common, swarm along the sea coasts where hurricanes bring floods. They mass in rabbit-warren cities where fires rage daily, and teem on highways where auto accidents kill thousands. Add it up.

Admit the possibility of technical failures on the Moon, but admit the existence of backup systems as well. Admit the puncturing of caverns, but admit also the existence of alarms, of partitioned subcaverns to limit air loss, of space suits for all personnel in emergencies. Then note the absence of blizzards, hurricanes, tornadoes, tidal waves, biting frosts, or scorching heat. Add it up.

It would not be hard to argue that, on the whole, the Moon would offer a much safer environment than the earth ever did.

But consider the unique psychological difficulties of establishing a Moon colony. Could men live out long periods, or even entire lifetimes, in crowded caverns? Could men give up the limitless freedom of the Earth, the open air, the wind and flowing water, the green below and blue above?

Not every man, perhaps, but a great many could.

Don't underestimate the adaptability of the human spirit. Men by the millions have spent their youth in some pleasant village and then hurled themselves without preparation into the maelstrom of a New York City slum. Most of them survived the vast change and a surprising number actually flourished.

The canyons of New York streets and the crowded caverns of megalithic New York office buildings closely approach likely habitats in a Moon society. Those who live in New York or any other large city are already so far from nature, so unaware of green below and blue above, so unacquainted with open air and flowing water, that the shift to the Moon will seem like a mere detail.

Yes, Moon caverns would be claustrophobic, but not every man suffers from claustrophobia. Enough men are found to crew our submarines or spend weeks in our space capsules—and enough men will be found to fill the caverns of the Moon.

As for those who eventually will be born on the Moon, they will know no other life. For them, the possibility of finding themselves suddenly on the openness of the Earth's hot-cold surface would be the true terror.

But, come to think of it, could a Moon colonist return to Earth to face that terror once he was well established on the Moon? This is a serious question for it brings up the matter of gravity—the one difference between Moon and Earth that cannot be neutralized or minimized by technology and which will require an enormous acclimation. Moreover, it seems unlikely that science can do anything at all about gravity in the foreseeable future.

The Moon is a smaller world than the Earth and its surface gravity is just one sixth the Earth's. To a man landing on the Moon for the first time, the mere act of walking will require careful adjustment, for since he will press less heavily upon the surface he will experience less friction. The Moon will seem much more slippery than the equivalent surface on Earth.

If he jumps, he will rise higher and stay in the air longer; but he mustn't be fooled, since he will come down just as hard as he did on Earth. Things will be much lighter but will contain as much inertia as always. Learning a new set of facts of life for the instant guidance of his muscles may be a matter of survival or death.

Beyond the mechanical problems of gravity, there remain unexplored physiological mysteries. How, for example, will the low gravity affect a Moonman's heart, kidneys, chemical balance? There is no easy way to answer such questions except by living through the experience. We can float a person in water, which is not quite the same thing, or subject him to zero gravity in orbiting satellites for limited periods, which is also not quite the same thing.

Though the need to endure prolonged low gravity is a gamble the first colonists must face, at least there is no reason—so far—to expect unavoidably serious consequences. Indeed, based on what we know, there is a decent chance that the gamble would succeed.

Granted, then, that men can completely acclimate themselves to low gravity—but won't that very acclimation make a return to Earth difficult or even impossible? The sudden change from low gravity to high could be much more dangerous than that from high to low.

Perhaps the Moon colonists will adhere to a regimen of periodic exercise, designed to keep bones and muscles in preparatory trim for a return to full gravity. Or it might turn out that the colonists will see no point in returning to Earth. They may get to like the Moon and feel no urge to leave. For those born on the Moon, that would almost certainly be true.

Imagine, then, that the Moon colony is established as a going, prosperous, secure, and reasonably happy concern. What then? What's in it for us back here on Earth?

One thing is sure: the Moon will be of no use as a dumping ground for excess population. In the next fifty years, by the most optimistic estimate, we can place several thousand people on the moon. But in the next fifty years, Earth's population (if the present birth rate and death rate continue) will increase by several billion. So cross off the Moon as the solution to Earth's population explosion.

Neither is the Moon a probable source of raw materials for Earth. Nothing on the Moon is likely to be present in greater quantities than on Earth, and if an unexpected resource were discovered it would have to be valuable indeed to be worth the cost of transportation here.

Why bother with the Moon, then? Well, how about immaterial reasons?

The Moon will export knowledge. It will be a haven for astronomers, who will be able to aim their telescopes without an atmosphere to dim their view, without clouds and fog to blot it out or city lights to blur it.

Based on the side of the Moon that faces away from the Earth, astronomers will not hear Earth's rising radio wave clamor and can probe distant depths unreachable from here. And by analyzing the Moon's ancient structure, scientists will trace the early history of the solar system and learn much about the Earth that they could not determine from Earth itself.

Is all this academic, ivory-tower research? Don't you believe it. Don't commit the fallacy of the "practical man" who thinks that because he sees no immediate use for a piece of knowledge, it has no use. All past history assures us that new knowledge, however rarefied it may seem, cannot avoid being helpful to mankind in the long run—and usually in the short run.

Nor is all Moon-knowledge and Moon-technique so very rarefied in the metaphorical sense. Some of it is clearly useful and rarefied in the literal sense.

The Moon's surface is covered with millions of square miles of a vacuum no Earth laboratory can match. Numerous technological processes can make use of so enormous and so effective a vacuum, employing devices which can easily be manufactured on the Moon but which could not possibly be duplicated on Earth.

Pure metals could be prepared without contamination by surface gases. Tiny microcircuits, built of ultrathin metallic film, could be formed with greater precision. Welding could be carried on at lower temperatures. The possibility of large-scale molecular distillation in the vacuum could permit chemical syntheses which are impractical on Earth.

The deep cold of the Moon's surface at night might make research in cryogenics (the behavior of matter at extremely low temperatures) much simpler than on Earth. Techniques for freezing living tissue could be developed, and low-temperature surgery might open new medical horizons.

An entire technology might arise on the Moon that could show us its heels. We would be reduced to stumbling after it, borrowing what we could.

And what about the space effort itself? We talk of sending men to Mars but can men endure the tight quarters of a space cabin for a one-way journey of millions of miles that will last for many months? Is it not possible that Earthmen can only reach out so far—withstand the depths of space only so long—and then break down? The change from open world to enclosed capsule might be too great to endure.

But Moon colonists would already have gone part of the way toward outermost space. They will already be in a capsule, within a giant enclosed spaceship called the Moon. They will already be living in a tightly cycled society, and under certain mitigating circumstances. Earth would still be there in the Moon's sky. Radio contact would still exist. There would even be the chance of returning to Earth if absolutely necessary. Life would not be quite as bad on the Moon, with perhaps thousands of companions, as on a spaceship with perhaps only half a dozen.

Then, once the Moon had been established as a home, its colonists could more easily cut the last connections to Earth. Next, Moonmen could, with relative ease, shift into a slightly more isolated capsule than they were used to, and explore the solar system to its furthest edge, where Earthmen themselves could not travel.

But more than that is at stake—and still more . . .

The Moon colony will be a completely new kind of society, facing completely new kinds of problems and finding completely new kinds of answers. Men will be living close together on the Moon; they will be isolated from other species of life; they will be in thrall to a controlled environment with little room for error. They will have to meet that brutal challenge in a way that might well be infinitely illuminating to the billions who will watch the process from Earth.

Just as the greatest consequence of Columbus' discovery of America was the kind of society described in Lincoln's Gettysburg Address, so the greatest consequence of Project Apollo may eventually be the kind of society that will finally answer the problems raised by man's overwhelming development of technology.

And just as the greatest export of the New World was what we might call the "American idea," so it may well be that the greatest export of the Moon will be the "Lunar idea," whatever that may prove to be!

The answer to "After Apollo, what?" may just possibly be "After Apollo, everything!"

AFTERWORD (1972)

This article was written in 1967, over two years before the first landing on the Moon. Although no trace of water has been found on the Moon's surface, there may be water, at least in small quantities, several feet beneath the surface. That has not yet been investigated, directly.

There has been one report of water vapor being detected by an instrument left behind by the astronauts. Perhaps it issued from some nearby crack.

If there is no water anywhere on the Moon, then a lunar colony may be unfeasible. If water is present in enough quantity to be useful, then I still stand by everything I said in this article.

NO SPACE FOR WOMEN?

In one respect, and in one only, has the United States been willing to allow a Soviet space first stand unchallenged.

Did the Soviets launch the first satellite, and the second, too? As soon as we could, we were launching them higher, better, and more often.

Did the Soviets send the first man into space, and the second, too? We were right on their heels, and sent more men into space for longer intervals. Did they take pictures of the other side of the Moon first? Did they space-walk first? Did they make an unmanned soft landing on the Moon first? Quite all right! We ended by taking better pictures, making longer space-walks, and bringing about softer and more sophisticated landings.

Then, on July 20, 1969, we capped the sundae with the beautiful cherry of the first lunar landing. The men who walked the Moon were Americans and the Soviets were nowhere in sight.

Which leaves the one exception:

On June 16, 1963, a Soviet woman, Valentina V. Tereshkova, was launched into orbit and remained there for forty-eight orbits over a period of seventy and a half hours. She performed well in her solo flight, brought back her vessel, emerged in top shape and went on to marry a male cosmonaut, Andrian G. Nikolayev, who had been in space for sixty-four orbits in August 1962. Now she has a perfectly normal baby—the first and only child, so far, to have had both parents in space.

The Soviet Union has never repeated the feat; no other Soviet woman has risen above the atmosphere; but of

SOURCE: "No Space for Women?" appeared in *The Ladies Home Journal*, March 1971.

about a hundred cosmonauts now in training, five are female.

The American space effort was unruffled by this Soviet first; and by *only* this Soviet first. NASA never budged. No American woman was accepted for training as an astronaut then, or during the next year, or the next, or now. Of the fifty-nine astronauts-in-fact-or-in-training in the United States, not one is a woman.

Why is this so? Are women unfit for space? Obviously not, in view of the Soviet experiment. Are American women too shy to make the effort, too ladylike in some Victorian sense, too cowardly? Surely, no one can maintain this with a straight face. American women have volunteered for space in numbers, and since women have done well in any athletic event opened to them, there is no reason to think that nowhere in this 200,000,000-individual nation are there any women who would qualify.

It is just that they are not wanted. Period.

Yet they should be. In rocket vessels, compactness of contents is essential. Every extra pound that must be lifted into orbit or to the Moon must be paid for with additional capacity of the rocket engines, additional hundredweights of fuel. For that reason, none of the astronauts are giants among men. They are of medium height and medium weight. Of two men of equal ability, the smaller is preferable for space flight.

And yet women are, on the average, distinctly smaller and lighter than men. If a woman could be found who qualified as an astronaut, the mere fact that she was a woman would probably make her more suitable than a man—at least in terms of size.

Furthermore, women are biologically sounder than men. They are more resistant to stress and are less subject to a variety of metabolic diseases, including (in particular) coronary thrombosis, strokes, and other circulatory disorders. (Valentina Tereshkova, who should know if anyone does, pointed out in an article published in the spring of 1970 that women had endured silence and isolation as well as men, and that they had adapted themselves to weightlessness more quickly.) The ultimate proof of women's biological fitness is that, when protected from the dangers inherent in childbirth, women live anywhere from three to seven years longer than men.

Are women, then, intellectually inferior to men and inherently incapable of piloting a spacecraft? Considering that women in our society have, from early childhood on, been assiduously trained to avoid displaying high intelligence and to bend submissively to captious male desires (as the surest way of "getting a man") it is not surprising that most men think women are intellectually inferior and that most women accept that judgment.

But not all women do. Despite everything that custom and pressure can do, there are a number of women who are as intelligent as any man, admit and maintain the fact, and prove it by making their way through a hostile male world to achieve positions of responsibility and success. Can it be believed, then, that no woman can qualify as an astronaut? Is there no use even in making the search for one?

Or is it that they are emotionally inferior? It is sometimes asked with respect to the possibility of women serving in risk-laden positions such as that of jet plane pilots, whether anyone would be willing to chance a hundred lives or more on the judgment of a person subject to the erratic effects on her emotions of inevitable hormonal changes.

The implication is that all women become ill-adjusted neurotics now and then in connection with the menstrual cycle. Perhaps some do. Who dares say all do?

And how well would men stand up under close examination for possible emotional changes from time to time? How do men react when they've had a drink or two—not enough to be visibly affected? How do they react when they haven't had a drink but desperately wish they had one? How do men react when they've just had sex and feel somnolent? Or when they badly desire sex and feel frustrated?

If women might conceivably have their touchy moments, so do men, and to use the fact against women only is merely to disguise male chauvinism with a specious veneer. Indeed, one might argue that women's hormonal variations are usually fairly regular, so that each individual can allow for them (or even repress them altogether by appropriate medication), whereas men vary much more unpredictably, with masculine mystique often refusing to permit them to acknowledge the variation.

Yet though one could argue endlessly, the brutal fact remains that there seems to be no room for women astronauts in the American space program, either now or in the foreseeable future. If we are to talk about American ladies in space, then, we must be satisfied with a mixture of 100 per cent fancy and 0 per cent fact.

But the fancy is worth it, for there is only one way in which even the most hidebound functionary in the space agency can avoid permitting women into the rocket ships, and that is to freeze the space program at its present level or dismantle it altogether. Barring that, space exploration cannot remain an exclusively male preserve for much longer.

It is all very well to send middle-aged married men into space when they need spend only a week or two out there before returning home. For the short period involved, they can remain isolated, and leave their demure wives at home to be photographed as they sit there with hands folded, waiting for their men to return.

But what about the trip to Mars?

Do we really plan to send men to Mars? If we do, there are, at the moment, no short cuts. The trip out there will take nine months; the trip back will take nine months; and there will be a period of unavoidable waiting on the planet for the proper time to make that return. Our astronauts, in heading out for Mars, will have to reconcile themselves to being away from home for some two years.

Do we ask one man to go into solitary confinement for two years; a kind of solitary confinement that not even Coleridge's "Ancient Mariner" knew? Do we send two men to be company for each other? Do we send three? Do we send how many?

Never mind how many for a moment. Do we send only men?

Exploration is traditionally a male venture. There were no women on Columbus' ships—but his crew spent only two months at sea, and when they landed there were women available. And don't think Columbus' men didn't know what to do with those women, even though their costumes, customs, and complexions were most un-Spanish.

This was true of all the great explorations in the past. No vessel stayed very long at sea at one time and there was always the promise of relief when land was reached. In one well-known case, that of the British vessel the *Bounty*, so successful was the relief that the crew mutinied when they put out to sea again and returned to the women.

Our astronauts going to Mars will be making a voyage longer, more isolated, and far more fearsome than any made by man before. And there will be no women waiting on Mars to console them; only the prospect of a hostile environment dozens of millions of miles from home, with the further prospect of a homeward voyage no shorter than the outer one. (Nor is this to be compared with long tours of duty in Antarctica or anywhere else on Earth, where there is at least the psychological advantage of knowing that any emergency can lead to a quick return to civilization.)

Certainly there will be men to face the Martian voyage even so, but are we to be so thin-lipped in our attitude as to fail to recognize that sending astronauts to Mars in bisexual couples might lessen a totally unnecessary part of the strain.

Are there objections? What happens if a woman gets pregnant? Let's not be naïve. These days no woman need get pregnant if she doesn't want to. What happens if there is a lovers' quarrel and efficiency suffers? Nothing worse than if two male astronauts quarrel, we can be sure.

Will the possibility of sex on board ship offend the moral bulk of America's population? Is there the thought that a crew made up of three men and three women (for instance) might engage in "orgies"? Would anyone care to think what might very conceivably happen if six men (and no women) were cooped up for two years? Would that be better?

It seems very likely, then, that if we are to have manned exploration of Mars at all, men and women will both have to be included. And if so, ought not women be trained for the task of astronaut? And why not begin now so that we can work the bugs out of the system, learn what special conditions need be evolved (if any) in the training of women, and what special problems, if any, will arise?

It is possible, though, that our sexual hangups, or our untouchable assumptions of male superiority, may bar the thought of lady astronauts at any price. In that case, we may decide to cross Mars off the list, with a grunt of grumpy masculinity. Perhaps we can argue ourselves into believing that unmanned probes to Mars and beyond will give us all the information we will need.

In that case, for the manned exploration of space, we will have to concentrate on the Moon, for that is the only object which will require rocket trips that will take weeks, rather than months or years. Only the Moon can be reached and explored in celibate austerity without undue strain.

But that depends. Might we not want to colonize the Moon? It could be very convenient to have individuals assigned to the Moon for long periods; or actually to establish an area upon the Moon that is engineered for human occupancy and made self-sufficient.

Quite apart from the chances of using the Moon as an astronomical and geological observatory, and as a physical and chemical laboratory, a lunar colony could be an unprecedented and uniquely important sociological experiment. For the first time in history, a human society would be organized within a totally engineered environment, with a totally managed ecology, and with a totally organized turnover of food, air, and water.

If such a colony worked at all, it would afford a sample of what we are coming to on Earth, where, on a much larger scale, we must learn to administer the relationship of man to the other living members of the ecology and to the inanimate environment that supports it. Failure to do so will mean utter disaster for mankind and, perhaps, for all the higher life-forms. We might (let us hope) muddle through in reasonable safety over the next half-century, and then the example set us by the lunar colony might guide our efforts to improve the muddle.

The colony would be of maximum use to us, of course,

if it were a true society, with men, women, and children living on the Moon more or less permanently from generation to generation. This means that emigration to the Moon must include women. The situation will not be like the all-male crew on Columbus' ships, but rather like the families of the American nineteenth century, trekking westward in their covered wagons.

And if the Moon is to have its colony, when are we to begin training women for space flight? Why not now?

But perhaps even this is too much for NASA's sturdy masculinity. They might abandon the possibility of a colony on the Moon—at least of the kind that will feature family life. Instead, there will continue to be all-male trips, but, as technology improves and experience allows, there will be longer and longer stays on our satellite. Eventually, a party of men will remain for months, perhaps, until the next ship takes them off and replaces them.

While on the Moon, these men may not form a true colony, but they can set up an astronomical observatory, or conduct chemical experiments, or explore the features of our satellite in detail. NASA may feel, with great satisfaction, that there is much useful work to be done even without a true colony.

But then we must ask ourselves: Are there no women scientists? Are women (members of Earth's largest and most consistently discriminated against minority) even now to be forbidden a share in the great adventure? Is the accident of sex alone to deny a human being, otherwise qualified, from contributing to man's outward thrust from home?

Indeed, remember that women *do* make scientists, and many more would if the social climate were more favorable. There is no intention of arguing that woman's role in space is entirely that of sexual partner and surrogate mother, serving the men who do the real work. Under other conditions, it might well have been women—smaller, more dexterous, more resistant to stress—who would be the primary workers in space, and then it would be right to argue that men should also be sent for the comfort to be derived from their company by the women.

Neither sex alone; both sexes together! It is only because

in actual reality it is men astronauts who are doing the work that the argument must stress women as the solace-bringers.

And returning to that view, if men are to remain on the Moon for months at a time, for whatever purpose, are they to be forced to be celibate? Or homosexual? It may well be that the lunar explorers may *choose* to be celibate, that they may be too fascinated by their task to worry about sex. The question is, though: Are we to make it an absolute requirement?

If not, then, when do we plan to begin training women for tasks in space? Why not now?

Retreat again! Suppose we see to it that men never stay on the Moon for extended periods. Let them go there, when necessary, stay for a short period, and return—a matter of a couple of weeks at most.

But is that all? If the space effort is to be a repeat, in endless installments, of the first Apollo ventures, the whole thing cannot survive. The lack of excitement and glamour will pall right where it will hurt the most—in the public pocketbook.

In that case, a still further retreat might be necessary.

After all (we might argue) who needs the Moon except for a very occasional venture to study its actual crust? For everything else, a large space station might be just as good; in many respects, even better.

The space around a station that is hovering several thousand miles above Earth's surface would be as airless as the surface of the Moon. An astronomical observatory would see outward just as freely and as easily. The Sun could be studied in as great detail, the planetary surfaces viewed with as great clarity, the stars studied with as great precision.

Experiments taking advantage of the short-wave radiation of the Sun, or of the hard vacuum of space, or of the cold temperatures attained in an airless space shielded from the Sun, could be performed on the space station with something of the same ease that they might be performed on the Moon.

And think of the advantages. The Earth and its atmosphere could be studied in far greater detail from a space station than from the Moon. The space station could be reached far more safely and economically than the Moon could; a virtual ferry service could see to it that men were replaced whenever necessary, reducing the strain of isolation and, therefore, the pressure to have women present.

With less money spent (after the initial investment) there would be less likelihood of public ire at the lack of periodic "spectaculars."

Most of all, a space station would afford the chance to indulge in a variety of experiments involving the gravitational field. For hundreds of millions of years, land life on Earth has flourished under the constant pull of the planet's gravity, which has never varied significantly. What would happen if gravitational fields were altered in intensity?

The field can be altered very slightly by going to the top of a mountain, but the changes due to alterations in temperature and air pressure would drown out any gravitational effect. The field can be reduced to almost zero by total immersion in water, but there would be side effects because water is much more viscous than air and restricts movement. The field can be reduced to zero in a space vessel in orbit, but in ordinary vessels the astronaut is virtually immobilized and is under unnatural constraint.

On the surface of the Moon, an astronaut would be free to move at will, but he would be hampered by a space suit. If he were in a large domed area within which he could move freely without such a suit, he would be subject to a gravitational field only one sixth the intensity of that of the Earth, it is true, but it, too, would be of unvarying strength.

On a space station, set in rotation, there would be a centrifugal effect that would mimic the gravitational field in many important respects, and that would vary in intensity with one's position within the station. Men (or other life-forms), moving and exercising freely, could remain at zero gravity at the hub of the station or at increasing intensities of gravity to whatever maximum would be experienced at the outer rim of the station.

Gravitational experiments on living creatures could, conceivably, yield a great deal of valuable information on the nature of life, information that might not easily be available by any other means. It might even have direct medical benefits. (Could a man with a weak heart survive more comfortably in low-gravity fields? Could certain delicate operations be more safely performed there?)

But surely we cannot reasonably eliminate the study of low-gravity effects on women, who in some important physiological ways are interestingly different from men.

What would be the effect of low gravity on the physiologic mechanics of conception? On the development of an embryo? On the birth of a baby? On the maturation of an infant?

Is there no knowledge we can expect to gain from such studies? Can we safely trust the knowledge we gain from rats, dogs, or even chimpanzees to apply to human beings?

And if we want to study women as well as men in low-intensity gravitational fields, when are we going to begin training women for tasks in space? And if some day, why not now?

Or do we retreat yet again and, even on a space station, limit our experiments, limit the knowledge gained, limit our horizons to whatever is necessary to exclude women.

And if we do that, then we are really down to a contemptible minimum. With all the vastness of the Universe beckoning us, we will have throttled ourselves down to the region just beyond the atmosphere and to a march toward knowledge at half-speed or less; all in order to preserve space as a masculine domain.

If so, it isn't worth the money, the effort, the dreams.

Call it off; call it *all* off—or open it to the human race; the *whole* human race.

FUTURE FUN

There's the story (and if you've heard it, you can't stop me) of the Brooklyn traveler who returned from a glamour-filled trip to Paris, and who gathered his cronies about him in order to tell them of his experiences.

He gave them, in particular, the story of what had happened to him in the city's fanciest house of joy. While his friends listened, popeyed, our traveler went through every second of preliminary maneuver in careful and loving detail. Then, at the crucial moment, he stopped.

"Go on," cried out his audience. "What came after that?"

The traveler shrugged. "After that," he said, "it was the same as in Brooklyn."

—And so it will be with recreation in the future to a large extent. Some of it will be very much as it is in Brooklyn today or, for that matter, as it was in Babylon three thousand years ago.

Fun is where you find it and it is always to be found in feasting and laughing and loving and roughhousing and gambling and hiking and noisemaking and yelling and moving chessmen and chasing rubber balls and sleeping in the sun and dancing and swimming and watching entertainers and risking one's neck for foolish reasons. There are even some fortunates who find their fun in their work —as does your humble servant.

If we are to look into the future, then, and try to see what kind of recreation we are likely to have, let us agree to eliminate from consideration the kinds of recreation we already have. Much of this will continue unchanged and if some of it is to undergo modification, the alterations will not be essential. So television might go three-dimensional or movies might be piped directly into the home or a new dance may be invented—such things are trivial.

Let us instead ask ourselves, what recreations may become common in the future that are barely possible today or perhaps completely impossible? What entirely new sources of delight may we expect to be bestowed upon us (or upon our descendants) by the inexorable advance of science and technology.

To begin with, man's environment is on the point of being greatly broadened, and with that will come an accompanying expansion of recreational potential.

This has happened once before. Man was a tropical animal originally, confined to such areas as central Africa and to Indonesia (where the great apes of today are still confined); but then he discovered fire and all the realm of winter was open to him. Not only did the colder regions offer new lands, new foods, and new dangers, but (eventually) a new world of fun, too, from snowball fights to skating and skiing.

The consequences of this long-past conquest of winter have about run their course. All the world now belongs to man and settlements can be established with reasonable comfort even in Greenland and Antarctica. For now, those polar establishments are intended for scientists and soldiers, but the tourists will eventually follow, and people now alive may yet see the establishment of the Hilton-Antarctica and the Sheraton-Greenland.

But by this opening of "all the world" to human occupancy, we mean dry land, of course. —What about the sea and, in particular, the continental shelves?

If man can solve his social problems; if he can restrain his itch to set nuclear fire to himself, or breed himself into starvation, surely he will soon step back into the sea from which he sprung and the spires of his towers will begin to shine dimly beneath the waves.

Consider the dwellings of man-in-the-sea. Inside his watertight sea buildings, or perhaps under the watertight dome that will enclose an entire settlement, he will live in air and have his usual fun. But outside the dome, there will be a world of water at his disposal. That same world is at our landlubbing disposal, but we must travel to it; we are not used to it; it is a novelty to us.

To the sea-dwellers, water will be an ever constant fact of life. Children will learn to swim as they learn to walk, and scuba diving will be as common to them as hiking is to us. The sea will fill with flippered humanity hunting barracuda and exploring the drowned bottoms.

And how friendly will the new aquanauts become with sea creatures? Will boys have their pet salmons, so to speak, who will follow them about in the water?

I suspect not. Fish are not very brainy. Yet there are seabirds and sea mammals that offer a far more hopeful prospect. There are penguins and seals and, in particular, dolphins, which are intelligent and friendly.

Even landlubbing men get along with dolphins—but when men enter the sea, the friendship ought to get closer still. Dolphins are more intelligent than dogs (some suspect they may be more intelligent than men) and it may be that for the first time in history two species of intelligent creatures may meet on roughly equal terms.

And fun? Dolphin-riding ought to be a sensation that cannot possibly be duplicated on land, and I am certain that dolphins will instantly get into the spirit of the thing.

In all ordinary sea sports, even for the sea-dwellers, humans must remain air-breathing. The buildings and settlements themselves will be air-immersed and a man who ventures into the sea will do so with oxygen cylinders strapped to himself.

But will that *always* be necessary? Successful experiments have already been conducted with water that has been oxygenated under pressure. (After all, it is not the water that drowns you, but the oxygen lack.) Enough oxygen can be forced into solution in water to support an air-breathing animal. Dogs can breathe such water and their lungs can scrabble enough oxygen out of it to support life. Dogs have remained under water for extended periods and emerged none the worse for the ordeal.

Naturally, we can't oxygenate the entire ocean, but surely we can oxygenate indoor pools under pressure. Within those pools, men can swim as water-breathing creatures and, with no equipment at all, stay immersed for hours at a time. How it would feel, I can't possibly imagine, but I suspect that it would introduce a new kind of freedom and a new sort of sensation that would be completely exciting to many.

Theoretically, we don't need a sea environment to make this form of recreation possible. (Let's call it "sub-water and breathing," or "swab," for short.) We can construct "swab" pools in Rockefeller Center if we wish and do so right now. However, persuading land-dwellers to immerse themselves in water and breathe may be most difficult. It would be far less difficult to persuade sea-dwellers—used to the friendly ocean—to do so. "Swab" may be the recreation of sea-dwellers only, however much it may be possible on land.

Then, of course, we have the Moon. Men should be standing on the Moon soon, and in one more generation, we ought to have a colony on the Moon. This, at first, will consist only of specialists, scientists, technicians, and explorers, remaining for short watches upon our satellite. Give us still another generation, however, and commercial flights to the Moon will be possible.

That might give us an answer, for the while, to the problem of "But where can one go that's really exciting?"

Just being on the Moon will certainly be fun and excitement enough for tourists. The scenery will be novel, and the sky overhead, in particular, will have the beauty of the never seen. Imagine a black sky in which there are more and brighter stars than ever we see on Earth (because there is no atmosphere on the Moon to dim them). Imagine too the Earth, as it hangs almost motionless in the sky, going through its phases like a vast and brilliant Moon.

The Earth in the Moon's sky will be four times the width of the Moon as we see it from Earth. When the Earth is full it will be seventy times as bright as our full Moon. The Earth's globe will be bluish-white and its cloud pattern will paint it in interesting spirals. Faint washes of green and brown may indicate the continents at times but I doubt that their outlines will ever be made out clearly.

There will be dangers on the Moon, of course, for without a protecting atmosphere, tiny meteorites can do harm, and so can the Sun's ultraviolet radiation. The Moon's surface can grow very hot in the sunlight and very cold during its long night. Underground, however, none of these dangers and extremes will exist and the Moon will be very comfortable.

Nor need the underground be viewed as nothing more than forever imprisoning caves. Through television receivers, views of the outside and even (properly filtered) of the Sun itself can be shown. And men will be able to emerge comfortably in the early night when the Sun is below the horizon and when the cold is not yet at its worst.

Undoubtedly, the greatest sight of all, bar none—whether seen directly or by closed-circuit television within the underground—will be those occasions when the Sun slips behind the Earth. We see such occasions from the Earth as an "eclipse of the Moon."

Once the Sun is behind the Earth, the globe of our planet will be entirely black (we will be seeing its night side) but the atmosphere all about will blaze orange-red with the slanting rays of the Sun. It will be as though we were watching a sunset scene through all Earth's atmosphere at once. And around that large bright orange circle in the sky will be the pearly streamers of the Sun's corona, visible far more brightly and clearly than ever it is on Earth. Beyond the corona, will be the hard brilliance of the stars.

Passage to the Moon will surely be at a premium in the weeks before an eclipse of the Moon is due.

But the Moon will be more than a sight-seeing paradise. It will offer active sport to Earthmen, too, thanks to its gravity. Anyone on the Moon will be pulled downward with a force only one sixth that which is experienced on the Earth. A man who weighs 180 pounds on the Earth will weigh only thirty pounds on the Moon. This will give rise to a whole new range of sensations and offer the pleasure of mastering a whole new range of skills.

Any physical activity from walking to playing football will require bodily maneuvering that will be perfected only after considerable practice. This is so, particularly, since although weight decreases, the mass of an object (the amount of matter it contains—which determines the difficulty of setting it into motion and getting it to stop) isn't changed. A medicine ball may weigh no more on the

Moon than a football does on the Earth, but the medicine ball there will not at all be manipulated as easily as a football here. Its great mass will make the medicine ball just as hard to throw on the Moon as on the Earth.

Eventually, games of "Moon-ball" will have their own practitioners and their own expertise, their own rules and strategies and excitements. The "World Series on the Moon" between teams from underground stations at Tycho and Copernicus may well be followed avidly on Earth.

There will be mountain climbing on the Moon, too, less dangerous and difficult—and therefore more nearly a mass sport in potentiality—than on the Earth. This is not a paradox. The mountain slopes on the Moon are gentle and the weak gravity is easy to overcome in the upward climb. Nor do the conditions on the mountaintops grow difficult. They are airless but so are the valleys.

On the other hand, if the mountain slopes are sandy enough, the weak gravity will make them quite slippery (the smaller the force pulling you down against the surface, the less the friction). Men, using flat-bottomed canes for support and balance, may go sliding down a mountain slope for miles with all the effect of skiing, and do so (despite the necessity for space suits and oxygen cylinders) in greater safety than on Earth.

Lunar skiing may yet be the Moon's most popular sport in its early history as a human settlement.

But what about a world of no gravity at all? What about artificial space stations built in orbit about the Earth?

The purposes of such space stations will surely be purely scientific and astronautic at first, but by the time the Moon has become a tourists' paradise (and perhaps a little "spoiled") surely some space station will be hanging in Earth's sky that will have been built primarily for recreation.

It will have to be built outside the main regions of the Van Allen belts and once placed in a nearly circular orbit out there, it will remain indefinitely circling Earth—for millions of years, if it is not struck by a sizable meteor.

Such a pleasure-satellite might have many of the ordinary pleasures of Earth and wine-women-and-song there may be essentially the same as that trio down here. (It occurs to me to wonder what novelties might be introduced into amorous techniques under conditions of little or no gravity—but let's not go into that now.)

It will also have pleasures that cannot possibly be duplicated on Earth—or even on the Moon. For instance, what about space-walking? For people who like the "wide, open spaces," what can possibly be more wide and more open than space itself? One could have a small reaction motor for maneuvering and one would have to be careful to remain in the satellite's shadow (or, preferably, to choose space-walking time when the satellite was in the Earth's shadow).

Then, for those who like it, there may be nothing quite like a few hours spent in the awful emptiness and silence of the void, when a man can really be alone with his thoughts and when he can look at the Earth's swollen body, at the Moon's more distant shape, and at the quiet stars.

You might imagine that our space walker can indulge in acrobatics, but if he does he will not be conscious of them. It will be the rest of the Universe that will seem to jump about and he himself may merely become dizzy.

For acrobatics, I suggest another recreation that can probably be found only on our space station. Why not a large empty cavernous room somewhere in the station, filled with air—possibly under pressure, to make it denser.

A man's arms can then be outfitted with "wings" for maneuvering and he can launch himself into space. The sensation of air about him will give him the feeling of movement he could not have had in empty space, and his wings will give him a personal control of his maneuvering far more delicate than would be possible by means of a reaction motor.

In short, he would be flying under his own power and, with sufficient practice, he could gain the proficiency of a bird on Earth. There would be others using the "fly-room" at the same time and a whole new spectrum of fun and games would become possible.

How about three-dimensional square dancing? Why not

have two couples do-si-do-ing at right angles to each other —one couple does it right-to-left-to-right; the other, up-to-down-to-up.

Would this not be "cube dancing"?

But is nothing left for us Earth-lubbers down here? Are the new excitements to be found only in sea and space?

Not at all! The greatest new world of all lies within ourselves. There are mental recreations as well as physical ones.

Consider chess—an endlessly fascinating game which involves not the muscles but the mind. It is at present of limited interest because only a few people have the temperament and ability to make worthwhile chess players.

That can also be said about baseball, yet baseball is popular because millions who could not play except in the most amateurish fashion are willing to spend hours upon hours in watching professionals. I understand there are people in the Soviet Union and elsewhere who will similarly stand and watch large chessboards on which the moves of grand master tournaments are displayed, but this can never grow as popular a spectator sport as such games as baseball or soccer.

The trouble is that where ballgames are fast and simple, chess is slow and subtle. —But computers can play chess, too. Even as I write, a computer at Stanford University is playing another at the Institute of Experimental and Theoretical Physics in Moscow.

Computers are pretty poor chess players at present, but they will improve. Perhaps the day will come when computers will play chess at great speed and men will watch large reproductions of the swiftly changing patterns on chessboards with interest and absorption. Great games can be repeated in "slow motion" and analyzed. We could become a nation of "chess watchers."

And why just chess? New games can be invented—deliberately complicated ones with tantalizing rules that would be far too difficult to serve as efficient recreation for men, but which could tickle the fancies of computers. —Three-dimensional chess, for one thing.

To be sure, computers can't play by themselves. They

have to be "programmed" by men: the rules of the game must be fed into them together with a description of desirable courses of action. Computers may start as fifth-rate players indeed, but if they are programmed to modify their play in accord with experience, they can improve just as human beings do. Computers may even become more proficient than any human being at some game in which they are designed to specialize.

We may eventually have a whole family of computer games to serve mankind.

You might ask if this is indeed the sort of thing to which one ought to apply computers and programmers, and the answer is a clear and loud, "Yes!" In the first place, what is wrong with entertaining human beings? Man must be amused as well as fed or in what way is he different from an ox?

Then, too, computer games will serve a purpose. We call them "games" but any decent game has an underlying order and pattern which, when properly studied, can serve as contributions to mathematics. To program a computer to play chess is a way of testing mathematical techniques that can then be applied to more "serious" problems. And programmers who whet their mathematical fangs on chess will find them all the sharper in other directions.

Horse racing "improves the breed," they say. Well, game programming will improve the breed of computer and programmers alike.

But even the computer is an artifact. What about man's mind itself?

Already, we are playing games with the mind (not altogether safe games) that would have been unthinkable a generation ago. The psychedelic drugs offer us a means to a new direct form of entertainment, *if* they can ever become safe enough to use, and if we can learn enough to use them with full control.

Why read of events in a book, or listen to them on radio, or watch them on television, when we can *live* them in the mind? The time may come when a man may live a complete hallucination to order; live another life far more colorful and exciting than the one of every day; live a fantasy, designed and created to order, one that is guaranteed to be as risky and dangerous as might be desired, but to end safely at last.

Many, it may well be, will prefer such dream lives to reality; dream lives in which they are much more capable and fortunate than they really are, and in which other people are much better-looking and agreeable than they really are, and in which all really happens for the best in the long run. They may prefer to remain in the fantasy more or less permanently.

Is this a horrible eventuality? I don't think so. In the automated world of the future, in which there will be, in any case, a superfluity of human hands no longer needed for daily work, why shouldn't some retire into permanent fantasy if they wish?

It may even be that the actual powers of the human mind itself will be intensified (with or without enhancement by mechanical device) so that men may finally learn to be telepaths. —Some more so than others, of course.

Who can imagine what fun it might be to think to one another rather than to talk? What wonders of the human spirit may emerge when each individual is no longer imprisoned by a wall of flesh, but can commune directly with others?

It may be, in fact, that this is the ultimate pleasure and recreation, the purpose toward which all of intelligent life has been tending since the beginning. The delight of direct communion may be such as to sink all other pleasures to nothing.

It may even be that, just as I sit here now trying to imagine the pleasures of the future, some centuries hence another man may sit and try to reconstruct, in sorrow and sympathy, the miseries of a past in which billions of human beings wandered lonely, seeking in the wildest physical and mental activities that pleasure which could only be obtained through the touch of the mental tendrils of a loved one.

AFTERWORD

When one writes as much as I do, and in as many different fields, there is bound to be interesting cross-fertilization at times. Four years after I wrote this article I wrote a science fiction novel, *The Gods Themselves* (Doubleday, 1972). In the last section, the scene was set on the Moon and if you will read it you will see that I did not forget what I had written (without any thought of fiction in mind) in "Future Fun."

2 · ON EARTH

PERSONAL FLIGHT

Air flight has become so common nowadays that it is a rare person who doesn't fly for even the most trifling reasons. Yet at the same time, flight is becoming less and less personal. As planes grow larger and more elaborate, the very sensation of being in the air diminishes.

One can get into a plane as large and as crowded as a movie theater, fitted out with the screens and motion pictures that go with the simile; with a dozen smiling hostesses and with luxury food and drink. The earth sinks down, moves backward, and comes up. It is the earth, somehow, that has shifted, while the movie theater one has inhabited has remained motionless.

But the very success of the luxury is enslaving. The traveler must go only at a time when hundreds of other people want to go. He must travel to a place where there is enough room and enough elaboration of facilities to make it possible for an object the size of an ocean liner to rise into the air. He must descend finally in another such place. He is far from home when he starts his flight and far from his destination when he ends it. It may well be that battling his way from starting point to airport and from airport to end point takes far more time than the flight itself.

Short flights increasingly lose their time-saving advantage.

Is there no way in which one man can go where and when he pleases? Can he not start from a point of his own choosing and land in another point of his own choosing?

Is there no flying automobile?

In science fiction we have taken up the problem for a couple of generations now and one romantic answer was to eliminate all the trappings and frills of flight and reduce it to the very minimum required to move a man—a reaction engine strapped to his back.

The man riding the jet blast rises, travels at will, and descends. He would be the lineal descendant of wing-flapping Icarus in the Greek myth or the man in the soaring glider of the late nineteenth century.

But though the jet-propelled man is a practical possibility, he is the aeronautical equivalent of the motorcyclist, who has reduced the equipment of a multi-passenger bus to a pair of wheels and an internal-combustion engine.

Individual jet propulsion might be suitable as a sport, and valued by the young for the cachet of danger it carries with it, but it probably can never be a suitable form of mass short-distance transportation. The human body riding the individual jet, like the human body riding the individual wheels on the motorcycle, is insufficiently protected, and the opportunities for luggage, or for a fellow-passenger, are limited.

We need not the air equivalent of the motorcycle, but the air equivalent of the automobile.

Would that not be the small one-man airplane? Yes, but for the difficulties of the takeoff and landing. If enough room is to be allowed for taxi-ing into the air and then for taxi-ing to a stop, the whole thing becomes impractical in just those areas where such transportation is most required but where there is no room.

Helicopters, then? Perhaps, but they are slow and vulnerable, the equivalent of the Model T Ford. Their one advantage—the ability to take off and land vertically—will be the property of properly designed conventional planes.

Once the VTOL ("Vertical Take-off and Landing") plane is ready for mass use, we will then finally have the equivalent of the automobile in the sky. We can expect to see a world in which it will be common for the commuter to rise out of his backyard and land in a VTOL parking spot—or in a friend's backyard.

Undoubtedly both take off and landing spots will have to be specially designed to withstand the shock of departure and arrival, and not any place will do, but it may be taken for granted that any important advance in technology requires the spin-off of subsidiary improvements. The use of the automobile meant the arrival of garages, paved driveways, and service stations.

The advantages of commuting by air, rather than by land, are considerable. The air is a three-dimensional medium, without (given enough height) physical obstruction at any point. The room available in the air is therefore, to begin with, much greater than on the ground.

This means that at the start, at least, the VTOL commuter will have a great sense of freedom and will be able to make a beeline for his destination.

Yet that will represent a transitional period only, for as VTOL travel becomes more common and the airways become thicker with the flying automobiles, the crowding will become serious, three dimensions and all. There will then have to be roadways through the air, as there are along the ground.

The air is a more elusive medium than the ground and the roadways will have to be correspondingly more abstract. They will consist of radio beacons. Each commuter will have to fly his radio beacon to the point of destination and each will have to make sure it is clear first.

As time goes on, there will cease to be the necessity of the commuter's choosing and clearing his own beacon. We can look forward to the computerization of the process. The one- or two-man VTOL will become, in a sense, a flying robot. Each commuter, having dialed (or otherwise indicated) his destination, will be informed of the exact time his beacon will be free.

In advance of that time, he will get into his VTOL, adjust its controls for proper receipt of the signal, and open his book or newspaper, or just prepare to stare thoughtfully or sleepily at the scenery. At the appropriate time, the VTOL will rise into the air, make its way along the beacon, and sink to its destination.

If the commuting is at a fixed daily time, a particular VTOL may have its regular run reserved. If an emergency trip must be made, there may well have to be a wait, longer or shorter, for an appropriate beacon to become available and our friend may then indulge in the favorite occupation of commuters everywhere—that of muttering remarks concerning the inefficiency of the system.

The effect of VTOL would have enormous effects on ground travel, too. The latter would not disappear, of course, since it would still offer the most economic method for transporting goods and heavy freight. In fact, the decline in the number of automobiles on the highways and, particularly, within the cities, would make the transport of goods so much more efficient as, in itself, to pay back many-fold the investment in mass VTOL.

By draining off those who would travel personally, and sending them into the air, it would be easier to develop and expand facilities for mass transportation for those who, for any reason, wish to travel by land, so that a healthy equilibrium between land and air travel may be set up which will shift back and forth slightly in accordance with the season of the year and the condition of the weather.

Still further, the coming of the VTOL would encourage a vast decentralization of mankind.

Let us suppose, to begin with, that when the twenty-first century opens, mankind has achieved population stability and firmly recognizes the fact that Earth's population must be allowed, humanely, to decline to some optimum level. (Without such an enlightened population policy, it is impossible to look into the future and see anything but catastrophe.) Let us suppose, further, that the gathering intensifications of the problems facing us today have brought about the equivalent of world government.

The next step, then, would be somehow to untie the vast knots of mankind that have coagulated into unwieldy and decaying metropolitan centers. (These centers are already visibly breaking down and will be in even more serious case a generation from now.)

In an earlier period, the automobile had made possible a step toward decentralization. It had built up the suburbs and drawn men away from the centers of cities. This influence, useful and beneficial in itself, was overtaken by population increase generally, so that the cities grew faster than their populations could escape and the suburbs, one by one, were steadily engulfed by the problems of the metropolis.

The coming of the VTOL, *combined with a sane population policy*, gives us another chance. Men, traveling more quickly and more conveniently, can base themselves farther from their business. They can be farther from centers of amusement and culture without feeling uncomfortably isolated. The city will begin to spread out.

So, for that matter, will centers of amusement, culture, and business. When it becomes easy to travel several hundred miles, and child's play to hop several dozen, a dozen moderately sized cities, well spread out, will serve the same purpose as a single monstrous metropolitan center. In a sense, the city will disappear and nothing but suburbs will remain. Or, to put it another way, the suburbs, knit together by VTOL, will *be* the city, with all its advantages and few or none of its disadvantages.

The developing computerization will even tend to reduce the absolute need for VTOL travel for business reasons. More and more it will be information that is sent back and forth electronically, while human bodies are allowed to stay put. There will be less necessity for a dozen men to gather physically, when their images can do so by closed-circuit television (thanks to communications satellites). There will be less necessity for blue collars, white collars, and gray flannels to gather at an industrial plant when its machinery is fully automated and it can be controlled by electronic monitoring from a distance.

Does this mean that transportation will cease altogether?

Not at all. It means that *imposed* transportation will diminish, but people don't travel for business only, surely. They will still travel for pleasure, whether to see the sights, or each other, and do so in greater comfort thanks to the unclogging of the airways that the diminishing of business travel will bring about.

With information spreading the world over by radio-borne facsimile and with people borne all over by radio-guided VTOL planes, the world will be small indeed.

It will be small enough for its inhabitants to come to know each other intimately; small enough for its population to grow to know all Earth's corners and learn to love all of it and not just their own region; small enough for the land to become a "global village" and learn to live in peace; small enough for its ecology to be grasped as a whole, to be understood and cherished; small enough to form a unified base from which men can reach out and explore the solar system and the wide Universe beyond, not out of national pride and fear, but out of the calm pride of a species who, having organized their own planet, at last, in peace and harmony, seek new frontiers against which to sharpen their wits and stretch their abilities.

AFTERWORD

In my capacity as writer I am completely different from myself in my capacity as myself. In real life, for instance, I am coarse and ribald; as a writer, I am pure and refined. In real life, I can't bear the sight of blood and turn queasy at the description of any ailment or accident, however mild. As a writer, however, I can discuss the most ferocious physiological misadventures without turning a hair.

Well then, in real life, I won't go on planes out of nothing more than sheer cowardice, but as a writer, I can turn out the foregoing article with ease. So for those of you who happen to know I won't fly, don't bother to ask me how I can sound so enthusiastic about all those futuristic aeronautical devices when I know I'll never use them. —No contradiction! It's Asimov the Writer who did the article, not Asimov the Me.

I admit I wasn't honest enough to tell the editor of *Private Pilot* that I didn't fly, when he asked me to do the article; but I'm telling *you*, am I not?

FREEDOM AT LAST

A baby girl, born today (1969), will be a young lady of twenty-one in 1990—and she may well be free in a sense we can scarcely grasp now.

How can we know that? By deciding on what will inevitably come to pass by 1990 and attempting to judge the sure consequences.

Some things we cannot know of the future and cannot, in good conscience, pretend to predict. We have no way of knowing who will be Pope in 1990 or who will be President of the United States or even who will win the World Series.

Some things *may* have happened by 1990. We *might* have had an all-out nuclear war by then; there *might* be peace in the Middle East; there *might* be a permanent colony on the Moon. We can only hope or shrug in such cases.

An all-out nuclear war may reduce mankind to scattered groups of degenerating survivors and what will happen then can scarcely be predicted now. We can only cross our fingers and work to prevent such a dreadful possibility.

Peace in the Middle East or a permanent colony on the Moon might be most interesting and desirable, on the other hand, but neither might immediately affect everyday life in the United States, even if it came to pass.

We must ask ourselves what events of great consequence will be *sure* to happen in the United States and in the world, barring unforeseen and unwanted worldwide catastrophes?

One thing, of course, comes to mind instantly—a further

SOURCE: "Freedom at Last" appeared in *Newsday* as "You've Come a Long Way, Baby . . .", March 14, 1970.

increase in population. The huge strain placed on society by the result of that further increase imposed upon an already overpopulated world will have shocking consequences and it ought to be possible, perhaps, to see how those might affect Miss Twenty-One of 1990.

We are 3.5 billion strong on Earth today. There will be 4.7 billion of us on Earth in 1990. The population of the United States will stand at 300 million, nearly a third of a billion. There will be twice as many Americans in 1990 as there were human beings on all the Earth in the time of Julius Caesar.

We can be quite certain, then, that by 1990, the debate over the desirability of birth control will be over. The question of its morality will have become quite academic. The necessity for halting the population upswing will be denied by no important government figure, nor, for that matter, by any notable religious leader, either.

India and Indonesia, and perhaps other sections of the world as well, will have supplied the necessary object lesson. The great and grisly famines of the 1980s will be fresh in every mind and will have settled the matter.

The old biblical injunction of "Be fruitful, and multiply, and replenish the earth" will no longer be applied to conditions so radically different from the times in which the Book of Genesis was written.

Mankind *has* been fruitful, he *has* multiplied, he *has* replenished and over-replenished the Earth. He can go no farther without utter disaster. It is not just numbers alone, but what those numbers will do; the strain on the food supply and on the very fertility of a soil turned more and more desperately to a single-minded absorption in the growth of food crops; the swallowing of the resources of the world; the outpouring of pollution and poison; most of all, the vanishing of the dignity and comfort that comes with space and privacy.

Clearly, age-old assumptions and attitudes will have to change, despite all protests—particularly in those areas of the world where a large part of the population is kept intimately aware of world problems. It will be in urban America where changes will be most rapid and radical.

Large families in 1990 will seem anti-social. Motherhood will be an uncomfortable, rather than an idolized, condition, and every child will seem a threat. Unpalatable? Of course! But with the actuality of famine staring every person in the face it will be necessary to turn to the unpalatable because the alternative will be even less palatable.

The impact of all this on the young lady of 1990 is clear enough. The age-old feeling that a girl's chief role in life must be that of an eventual wife and mother will have been lifted. She may be a wife, if she chooses to be; and a mother (within careful limits) if she chooses to be. But she may also be neither, if she chooses that, and society (for the first time in history) will not sneer at her. There will be no pressure on her to breed, by way of the superior status societies almost invariably place on the mother as compared to the non-mother and on the wife as compared to the non-wife.

This freedom to be a non-wife and non-mother, if she chooses, will lift a tremendous burden from her shoulders, one that crushes down upon every woman now and goes unnoticed only because it has been there for dozens of centuries.

Once motherhood no longer comes to represent the highest and noblest status to which women can aspire, there will be a readjustment of many mother-related outlooks.

Sex will no longer be a quasi-holy sacrament because it involves the potentiality of motherhood; or a base and wicked act under those conditions where it threatens the security of motherhood. It will be neither, but will become one more variety of pleasure to be discussed freely and experimented with joyously. There must be the proper forewarning of the possible dangers of disease or pregnancy but that is not earth-shaking. The pleasures of the table are enjoyed despite the forewarning of the possible dangers of food poisoning and obesity.

Through many centuries, our culture has made every effort to restrict the sexual activity of women to single partners, at least partly because of woman's role as a potential mother. A father would naturally wish to be sure that the son who inherits his property is really his and once there is this economic reason for pre-empting the sex life of a particular woman, it becomes intertwined with masculine self-respect as well. Once the economic factor is diminished, the occasion for jealousy will diminish as well.

There will be greater variety to the sex act as well. In the world in which our traditions were formed, child mortality was always high and it took maximum sexual effort to bring enough children into the world to supply the eventual peasants, artisans, and soldiers to keep the society going.

In such a case, sex had to be channeled toward childbearing specifically. Those methods of achieving sexual satisfaction which had no chance of leading to conception were branded immoral and illegal. Masturbation, homosexuality and oral-genital contacts were, for instance, labeled unnatural and perverse not because they were really unnatural (they were all too natural, or it would not prove so impossible to stamp them out even with all the rigor of the law and all the threat of hellfire) but because they are effective birth control methods.

Once motherhood is de-emphasized, birth control becomes easier. Instead of requiring abstinence (a lost cause) or some sort of "rhythm" method (very risky), or using some sort of mechanical or chemical device (always costly, always troublesome), there would be the added method of merely encouraging what is, in any case, a natural impulse.

Practices previously considered perverse because they do not lead to conception, will become tolerable and even praiseworthy for exactly the same reason. (Naturally, those "perverse" acts which involve physiological harm, notably sado-masochistic practices, will continue to be subjected to cultural disapproval.)

The young lady of 1990, then, sexually unforced and unchanneled, will undoubtedly have been experimenting with sex for years, will know exactly what she enjoys and wants, and will have no hesitation in asking for it.

Nor need we look forward, necessarily, to a 1990 that will consist of a perpetual sexual orgy, or expect that the young lady will be exhausting herself in search of sexual novelty.

The contrary is much more likely. With the taint of the

follow the intricacies of politics, made faint by the necessity of understanding science. Indeed, they have trained themselves to be proud of their incompetence at anything intellectual.

The reward for all this is the privilege of being thought "cute" and of having a man patronizingly reward them with such nonsense services as the removal of a hat in the elevator, the offer of an arm at the curb, the holding of a door, and the kissing of a hand. All this in exchange for abandoning the intellectual role that is the highest and proudest mark of a human being and for being condemned to a lifetime of degrading service.

The punishment for the woman who does not choose to cooperate is quite marked, and is visible even today. The "career woman" is harassed at her work by resentful men who consider her a menace to the security of their own position. They are harassed to an even further extent by other women who suspect careerists of being unwomanly and of dismissing their "proper" role as wife and mother—but who perhaps are really resentful at being made to feel the degradation of their own position.

But the young lady of 1990 will be free of condemnation to such degradation. With motherhood no longer an insistent goal, she will be encouraged to find other goals. With brains increasingly at a premium as the years of the future pass, there will be less and less readiness to dismiss half the human race. Half-speed ahead will just not be enough.

And again we can ask, Will women meet the intellectual challenge? Why not, once she is no longer brainwashed into imbecility as the price of catching a man?

Not so long ago, for instance, bank tellers were almost always men and we were all convinced that that was only reasonable since women could scarcely be expected to add up columns of figures and get correct answers. But the employment spectrum of today is such that it is hard to get men to work as tellers, women are hired, and—surprise, surprise—they can apparently handle columns of figures perfectly well.

The two freedoms—economic and sexual—will reinforce each other. The young lady of 1990 will not need to sell herself to any man because that is the only legal and respectable way of having sex and children; or because that is the only socially acceptable way of achieving economic security.

She need only give herself to a man if she wants to and only for as long as she wants to; and all she requires in return is that he give himself to her on the same terms.

This does not necessarily mean the end of the family as an institution. It does mean the end of the family as a prison.

Men and women can still form an association that may prove loving and life-long; but will not be forced to form an association that is life-long even after it ceases to be loving and therefore becomes hating.

The chances of a happy marriage will very likely increase and the number of *successful* families grow larger once the element of force is removed. Nor need a marriage begin for reasons of desperation and panic. As long as marriage is not necessary for status and as long as casual contacts are available for sexual needs and work for economic independence, our young lady need not end up with a man who is merely the best of a bad lot, or merely the only one who asked.

Nor need children (and there will be children even in 1990, for an average of two per couple will allow for the necessary slow decline in population—considering the fact that some will always die before puberty) be subjected to the insecurity of a forced and hate-filled marriage. It is generally agreed that this is worse for the child than a broken marriage and in a society where women are economically independent and where lack of a husband is no bar to either status or respectability, the man can go.

Where freedom stands in greatest danger of being lost is in the anonymity, the cipherism that may easily mark the individual in a super-crowded society. To prevent that and to retain the joy of life, every form of self-expression should and would be encouraged.

Take clothes, for instance—

There is a wide difference in the traditional clothing of men and women in most cultures today and in the past, because the two sexes play such different roles in society that it is necessary for some visible distinguishing badge to be insisted upon. You don't want to mistake a man for a woman for the same reason that you don't want to mistake a chairman of the board for a janitor.

A young woman must (in our culture particularly) advertise her womanhood because of the never ending competition to trap or hold a husband. And so we find our advertisements featuring clothes that are relatively tight, brief, and sheer, designed to show off the smooth curve of the buttocks; lift, separate, and (if necessary) pad the breasts; outline and redden the lips, and so on. It is the eye-catching exterior designed to attract the attention of men at as great a distance as possible.

But where women can find fulfillment in a role other than that of wife and mother, where a man need not be lured into a total, permanent arrangement, but allowed to enter a casual, temporary one, the advertisement need be less strident.

Again it is a matter of freedom. The young lady of 1990 may, if she chooses, dress in the acme of what we would today consider femininity, but she need not. She is not bound in the prison of sexual advertisement and may therefore use her clothing as an expression of individuality. (This will be true of men, too, of course.)

The range of variation in clothing and other adornment, both in color and styling, will be much greater than it now is from person to person, and, for a given person, from time to time. Clothing will probably be valued for its versatility and flexibility and Miss 1990 will be prouder of the creativity and ingenuity with which she can bend the dress to fit her mood than of the dress itself. (With added leisure there will, in any case, be considerable pressure to develop creativity in all ways, for the good of society as well as that of the individual. If a novel adornment is perhaps less exalted than a new symphony, it will still have its satisfying place in the scheme of things.)

The enhanced individuality may well be sexually useful, too. What Miss 1990 advertises is not herself as a generalized female, a role she may fit rather poorly on closer examination. She will instead proclaim herself as an individual. This may attract fewer moths to her flame but those who come (unconditioned to expect only certain standards of clothes and makeup) will be reaching for the genuine article and will be more worth having.

Naturally, with bizarre and individual costumes tolerated for both sexes, it will become less easy "to tell the boys from the girls." The more conservative members of our present society are already disturbed about this and yet one wonders why. Why does it disturb anyone that he cannot tell whether a stranger a block away is a boy or a girl? What does he have in mind?

Such distinctions, in a world of increasing economic and social equality of the sexes, would be of interest chiefly for immediate sexual reasons. Undoubtedly it will always be possible for a young man to recognize a young lady (or another young man if he happens to be in a homosexual mood), and for uninterested strangers the distinction is really irrelevant.

In the world of 1990, the colleges and universities should have become citadels of individuality. With more leisure than ever and with less formal work, it is more important to encourage creativity than to insist on drilling irrelevant and identical knowledge into all heads, of whatever intellectual shape they may be.

The necessary courses to fit the ordinary person for a place in a computerized and automated society may be brief and there will be (we can hope) enough who will, of their own accord and for their own delight, wish to undertake the extensive and intensive educational program that will lead to qualification as scientists and as other specialists. This will free the others for doing *their* thing.

For all, the important matter is to learn to live as an individual and to know how to express one's self in such a way as to delight the ego and, if possible, delight other egos in the neighborhood as well.

Miss 1990, in her college, will not be there in order to attend set courses, but in order to find an environment which will best encourage her to be in the learning mood —for whatever she chooses to learn. It may be knitting rather than Latin, or it may be anthropology rather than television repair—that's her business.

And the true passing grade will mark not the successful parrot, but the successfully happy person.

A thoroughly controlled birth rate then (and without one, all, *all* is lost) ought to mean freedom for the young lady of 1990; freedom beyond our present dreams; freedom not to be a wife and mother; freedom not to be a sexual chattel sold for economic security; freedom to be an individual in sex, in work, and in play; freedom, in short, to be the one unique human being one is, and no one else.

THE AGE OF THE COMPUTER

We live in a privileged age, for today, as never before, we have a choice of dooms for every taste. We can look into the future and see the planet poisoned by pollution; or rent by racial conflict; or suffocated by overpopulation; or devastated by nuclear warfare.

All these cruel visions of the future are horrible enough and, alas, possible enough, to warrant the strongest efforts to avoid them. And, for my own part, I see one possible highway to safety.

We live in the beginning of the age of the computers and, barring violent catastrophe, the age is sure to grow and intensify. There will be more computers each year, doing more tasks more intensively, and requiring ever less interference from mankind.

To some people, this seems like one more variety of doom. The computers seem to them to be cold, hard, and impersonal; they are mechanical minds without warmth, sheer mentality without sympathy, absolute justice without mercy.

But is this necessarily so? Certainly, not so far.

As yet, the computer is primarily a tool for solving mathematical equations by the rapid manipulation of electric currents. We have had tools to aid our thinking before this. A slide rule is a simple example of such a tool. Pencil and paper is a still simpler one, whenever we use them to multiply two large numbers that we cannot multiply in our head.

In fact, the very notion of mathematics is the basic tool of this sort. In the early days of civilization, the Egyptian architects made careful measurements in order

SOURCE: "The Age of the Computer" appeared in *Newsday* as "Who's Afraid of Computers?", January 20, 1968.

to direct the placing of the layers of huge rocks that were eventually to form the pyramids.

I can see some ancient Egyptian philosopher worrying that mankind was entering "The Age of Stretched Rope," an age in which architects would no longer be guided by their good sense and artistic intuition, but by the dictates of lengths of stretched rope, counted off impersonally from point to point.

Well, if the architect looks at a distance he must span and judges it to be 500 feet and then measures it with his stretched rope of fixed length and finds it to be 483 feet, had he better believe the judgment of his own magnificent brain, or the statement of the brainless piece of stretched rope?

Perhaps, when the notion of mechanical measurement was new, there might have been some hesitation, but nowadays there wouldn't be. We see at once that the stretched rope, mindless as it is, would be perfectly adapted to the task of measuring lengths and should be accepted for the purpose. It is the task of the human brain to guide the placing of the stretched rope, and to build an artistic structure based on the information received from it. But should the mind replace the rope? Never! The task of the stretched rope is so mechanical and primitive that it is beneath the dignity of the human brain to try to substitute for it.

Now, put "computer" in place of "stretched rope" and you have it.

We give a computer a problem to solve and program it; that is, tell the computer exactly what to do to solve the problem. We could solve the problem ourselves by following our own instructions exactly, but our mind and fingers don't work as quickly, as automatically, or in as error-free a manner, as do the tiny electric currents in the computer.

It is not that the computer can do what we cannot do; it's just that it does in a hundred seconds what would take us a hundred years.

Thus, back in 1609, the German astronomer Johann Kepler worked out generalizations that described the orbits of the planets traveling about the Sun. For the first time in history, the solar system was correctly described.

But in order to work out those laws Kepler had to

begin with many hundreds of observations of the exact position of the planet Mars at different times. He then had to spend years of calculation in an attempt to find out how to relate all those observations.

A couple of years ago, a modern mathematician took all Kepler's raw data and fed it into a computer. It took him several days to gather the data and prepare a program for it, of course, but once the computer received data and program, it worked out Kepler's laws in exactly *eight minutes!*

Does that mean we wouldn't have needed Kepler if we had only had a computer? Not at all. We would still have had to gather the original data concerning Mars (though photography would have meant much greater speed and accuracy) and we would still have had to figure out what to do with the data. No computer existing today could have done that.

But once Kepler decided what data he wanted, and exactly what he wanted to do with it, the actual mathematical somersaults could have been done by anybody. Kepler could easily have allowed an assistant to do it, if he had had one, and he would gladly have allowed a computer to do it, if he had had that. The actual mathematical manipulation, once Kepler had had his creative inspiration, was nothing more than intellectual thumb-twiddling.

It is tragic that Kepler had to waste years on such stultifying labors. With a modern computer, he could have done the dull part in eight minutes and spent the saved years trying to work out additional creative thoughts.

The computer frees mankind from slavery to dull mental hackwork, as power machinery frees him from slavery to the pick and shovel.

But what will become of the men and women who are "freed" from their routine jobs? Are they freed into misery and starvation?

In any changing society, there are bound to be dislocations, and in those dislocations lies the potential of much human misery. But it is precisely in a computerized society that such misery stands the best chance of being minimized.

Not only can computers do today's mental scut-work

faster and better than humans can; they can do so much problem solving that tasks impossible now will become possible, and jobs inconceivable now will become practical.

For instance, one of the difficulties of modern life (perhaps the essential and basic difficulty) is just this: Society has grown so complex that no human mind, indeed no combination of freely communicating human minds, can, with the tools at hand, analyze social problems and work out solutions quickly enough to prevent disaster.

How do we handle overpopulation? How do we best and most economically bring about the development of underdeveloped nations? How do we prevent a runaway nuclear proliferation? What measures are best suited to reduce racial tension? How are our limited resources best and most usefully exploited? What measures must be taken to minimize pollution? How organize the giant cities of today in order to keep them from becoming unlivable?

The problems are many and there isn't one—not one!—that is being efficiently solved today; or even sufficiently quickly solved (however inefficiently) to stave off disaster within the century.

If computers could be built complex enough to take in the data, organize it, and perhaps even help devise methods for handling it, they could offer solutions in time. A computerized society would give us our opportunity at the first truly rational way of life in man's history.

The creative human tasks in such a society would be many and perhaps unimaginable in detail today. But there would be no lack of work for human beings to do; interesting and important work. In place of the poor jobs that vanish in the process of computerization, good jobs would appear.

To be sure, particular individuals might not make the transition. There are more automobile repairmen now than there were blacksmiths fifty years ago, but not every blacksmith could become an automobile repairman. Yet it is precisely in a rational society that the methods for handling the displaced will be worked out in a manner that will best conserve his sense of dignity and ours of decency.

Yet is "rational" always the thing we want? Suppose a "soul-less" computer tells us that the best way of combatting over-population in India is to pick out the one hundred million poorest, oldest, and sickest (calculated by a complicated formula) and gas them to death, then use their bodies for fertilizer.

There might be some "rationality" to this, but it bitterly offends our moral sense. Can a machine have a moral sense?

A computer can, if we instruct it properly. If we program it to accept only solutions that do not involve deliberate killing, it will do so, and give us the best that does not.

As a matter of fact, computers are much more likely to stop killing than to encourage it, for indiscriminate killing as a solution to problems is a feature of human history. From riots to wars, the cry of "Kill!" has rung consistently in men's ears.

At the present time, for instance, the war in Vietnam solves some problems for us. It keeps the wheels of industry turning and unemployment down to a minimum. It gives generals a feeling of importance and some of us a sense of national purpose. It saves many rural Congressmen from having to spend money on the cities by allowing them to cover a hard heart with the mantle of patriotism.

It is a rotten solution, for it is succeeding in creating problems that will almost certainly end by being worse than those it seems to solve. It is to be hoped that a computerized society will work out better solutions.

But can we really rely on computers? I began by saying they are just tools to do a lot of mechanical arithmetic. If that is so, would we not quickly reach the limits of their usefulness? If they only do what we tell them to do, what happens when we can no longer think of what to tell them to do?

I doubt that we will so easily or quickly run out of computer programs, but never mind that. Is the computer "just" a tool?

If it is just a tool, it is at least no less a tool (potentially) than the human brain.

The basic difference between a computer and the brain can be expressed in a single word: complexity.

The human brain contains ten billion neurons and ninety billion smaller cells. These many billions of cells are interconnected in a vastly complicated network that we can't begin to unravel as yet.

Even the most complicated computer man has yet built can't compare in intricacy to the brain. Computer switches and components number in the thousands rather than in the billions. What's more, the computer switch is just an on-off device, whereas the brain cell is itself possessed of a tremendously complex inner structure.

But need we quail before the simplicity of the computer and the complexity of the brain? The computer is perhaps not as simple as it seems, or the brain as complex.

The computer may be simple now, but it is gaining in complexity in giant strides and there are no limits, visible, to the complexity that may yet be gained.

Nor is the goal of the brain so unattainable, for the brain is not so very different from a computer. We have the illusion that unlike the computer, which must be told what to do, we can think freely and on our own.

Not so. We, too, are programmed—by the genes we inherit. And although the program in the genes is tremendously more complex than any we can feed into a computer, it does represent a limit even to the brain.

Someone might find the brain unlimited in its creativity and ask triumphantly, "But can a computer compose a great symphony?" It must be admitted that present computers cannot, but then neither can most present brains, so this does not really differentiate computers and brains—only computers and a very few highly talented brains.

Yet if we took a brain that could compose a great symphony and duplicated its complexity exactly, we would produce a computer that could produce a great symphony and, almost undoubtedly, do so in far less time and with far greater assurance.

But can the brain's complexity be duplicated? Eventually, why not?

Even if I am being overoptimistic here, it would still pay to try first to unravel and then duplicate the complexity of the human brain. If ultimate success were to evade us, the gains on the way would still be incalculable.

After all, the human brain is the most magnificently organized piece of matter in the Universe. What can be more pleasurable and exciting than to take up the task of working out its intricacy; what problem would be at once so fascinating and so important?

Then, even if we understand the brain's working just a little bit better than before, we might make use of that knowledge to improve the organization of the computer's wiring. An improved computer would better help us tackle the problem of the brain, which would give us new advances that would be reflected in better computers, which would— And so on.

In fact, the attempt to improve computers would, almost inevitably, it seems to me, guide us to a better understanding of ourselves. It would help us wipe out mental disease, help us find methods for improving and extending our own intelligence—*and* help us build computers with human or near-human intelligence.

But that may rouse a new fear. As computers approach the human brain in intelligence, will they not compete with us? Might they not destroy us?

Those who think in this fashion might perhaps think of the manner in which we have grown dependent on our more ordinary machinery even though it fails and kills us —the way in which we depend upon the automobile even though it places fifty thousand of us in the grave each year and mangles many more; the way in which we depend upon electric devices even though we risk disaster in a "great blackout."

The cases, though, are fundamentally different. We are helpless in the grip of our own machines because they are guided by our own inadequate brains.

The computers will supply us with additional brainpower to guide that machinery, and to guide themselves as well.

We will have allies. We and the computers *together* can guide human society and its products, *including* the computers, and even, very probably, *including ourselves*.

Nor need we think of ourselves and the computers falling out. As far as we know now, there are no varieties of intelligence. There may be different techniques of thinking and differences in estimating the importance of various goals, but we have no trouble recognizing intelligence when we see it.

And even if there were different varieties of intelligence, still, since we design the computers with our own type of intelligence in mind, the computers would end up our-kind-of-intelligent.

If that is so, there will form a bond between man and computer that will effectively block any storybook fantasy about "robots destroying their creators." There would much more likely be sympathy and companionship between equal intelligences that would rise above a mere difference in form.

But what if computers grew more intelligent still?

Suppose one imagined a computer capable of designing and assembling another computer just like itself. That is not inconceivable. Suppose a computer could design and assemble another computer slightly more complex than itself. That, too, is not inconceivable.

But then, the more complex computer formed by the first computer would be even more capable of designing a still more complex computer. Each computer would design another in larger jumps of complexity and in a very short period of time, computer intelligence would have risen beyond the human level; probably far beyond.

And then what? Will the Supercomputers wipe us out?

Why should they? Do we wipe out dogs just because they are less intelligent than we are?

Would the Supercomputers, with part of their vast potential, take care of us as we take care of dogs, and with the rest of their mind go about their own business in a fashion that would be beyond our comprehension?

If so, is that frightening? Would mankind resent the existence of a greater intelligence and find his own life, as second best, meaningless?

Why should he? Throughout history, mankind has consistently and willingly assumed a second-best position, considering himself to be at the capricious mercy of a wide variety of gods and demons populating a supernatural world of awesome power.

Now he would have a new kind of "god" that would be beneficent or, at worst, impersonal. And if the new "god" were basically his own creation, should that not be a source of pride rather than humiliation?

What counts, after all, is Intelligence.

Suppose that in the entire history of the Universe, no intelligent life-form had ever developed anywhere. The magnificent pattern of stars and galaxies would play itself out for trillions of years but without Intelligence to witness it, what would be its significance?

It seems obvious to me that the Universe can have meaning only insofar as its incredible intricacies can be sensed, interpreted, and analyzed by Intelligence.

It is the task of Intelligence to wrest as much meaning from the Universe as possible, assert as much control over the Universe as possible, and bend the Universe to its own will as much as possible. The human Intelligence has been at work in this way ever since the first crude tool was taken in hand and the first spark of fire was blown into life.

If a form of Intelligence superior to our own appears on the scene, ought it not automatically, and by right, inherit the game? Is it not proper to allow a better Champion to face the Universe as we cheerfully allow better baseball players than ourselves to represent our city in the race for the pennant?

After all, if Intelligence, in any form, makes great progress toward winning the game, then its victories may well be great enough to benefit all intelligent beings—even those as primitive and unworthy as ourselves.

THE END

Among other things, I am a prophet by profession. That is, I predict the future and get paid for doing so.

There is a catch, of course. I don't cheat, so there is a sharp limit to my usefulness. Since I make no passes over a crystal ball, lack the services of a henchman in the spirit world, have no talent for receiving revelation, and am utterly free of mystic intuition, I can't tell anyone which horse will win the Derby, or whether his wife is cheating on him, or how long he will live.

All I can do is look at the world as steadily as possible (a difficult enough task these days), try to estimate what is happening, and then make the basic assumption that whatever is happening will continue to happen. Once that is done, I can make very limited predictions. I can tell you, for instance, about when the Derby will no longer be run at all; about when it will cease to matter whether anyone's wife is cheating on him, and, most of all, how long all of us (with perhaps inconsiderable exceptions) are going to live.

For instance, I look at the world today and I see people, lots of them. Concerning these people, there are two things to say: (1) there are more people now than there have ever before existed at any one time, and (2) these people are increasing in numbers at a faster rate now than ever before in history.

Just as an example—

In the time of Julius Caesar, the total number of people on Earth was probably something like 150,000,000 and the world population was increasing at the rate of perhaps 0.07 per cent per year; or 100,000 per year.

Nowadays, the population is (at latest estimates) 3,650,-

000,000, or twenty-four times what it was in old Julius' time, and is increasing at a rate of nearly 2 per cent per year, thirty times the ancient percentage rate. The Earth is now gaining people at a rate of 70,000,000 a year, so that it takes us only two years to add to the population a number equal to all those who lived on the planet in the palmy days of Rome.

The question is: What does this mean for the future?

The doom-criers, of whom I am one, cry, "Doom!". The optimists, on the other hand, talk about modern science and the utilization of hybrid grain and fertilizers. They talk of distilling the ocean for fresh water, of fusion energy, and of the colonization of other planets.

Well, why not? Let's grant everything the optimists want and take a look at some figures.

If we accept 3,650,000,000 as the population of the Earth today and allow an average of 100 pounds per person (some are small, some are children), then the total mass of human flesh and blood is equal, at present, to about 180,000,000 tons.

It is also estimated that the number of people on Earth (and therefore the mass of human flesh and blood) is presently increasing at a rate that will cause it to double in thirty-five years.

(Actually, the time it has taken for the population of Earth to double has been decreasing rather steadily through history. In Roman times, the rate of natural increase was doubling the Earth's population only after 900 years. Presumably, we ought to suppose that as time goes on the Earth will continue to double its population in shorter and shorter intervals. However, I will be conservative and suppose that thirty-five years will remain the period of doubling throughout the future.)

Let me then introduce a mathematical equation not because any of you absolutely need it but because, without it, I will be accused of pulling figures out of a hat. The equation is:

$$(180{,}000{,}000)\ 2^{x/35} = y \qquad \text{(Equation 1)}$$

This equation will tell us the number of years, x, it will take to reach a mass of human flesh and blood equal to *y*, if we start with Earth's present population and double it every thirty-five years. To make the equation easier to handle we can solve for *x* and we get:

$$x = 115 (\log y - 8.25) \qquad \text{(Equation 2)}$$

Using this equation, we might ask ourselves the following question, for instance: How many years will it take to increase our numbers to the point where the total mass of humanity equals the total mass of the Universe?

I introduce this question because I assume that no optimist will ever dream of arguing that man can possibly reach this point, so that it will represent an ultimate limit beyond cavil. It may be, of course, that the time it will take to achieve this fantastic end is so long (trillions of years, do you suppose?) that there is no point in discussing it. Well, let's see—

The Universe consists (as a rough estimate) of a hundred billion galaxies, each one containing a hundred billion stars about the size of our own Sun, on the average. The mass of the Sun is about 2.2 billion billion billion tons, so the mass of the known Universe in tons (throwing in some extra mass to allow for planets, interstellar dust and so on) is perhaps the figure 3 followed by fifty zeros (or 3×10^{50} in mathematical lingo.) If we set this equal to *y* in Equation 2, then log *y* is equal to 50.48. Subtract 8.25 from this and multiply the difference by 115 and we find that *x* is equal to 4,846.

What this means, in turn, is that at the present rate of increase in human population, the mass of humanity will equal the mass of the known Universe in 4,856 years, so that by A.D. 6826 we reach absolute dead end.

A period of 4,856 years is long, certainly, in comparison to an individual life, but if it takes only that much time to run out of Universe (rather than the trillions of years that might have been suspected), then there has to be the queasy feeling that the actual limit will come much sooner. After all, even the most starry-eyed idealist wouldn't think we could colonize all the planets of all the stars of all the galaxies—let alone convert the stars themselves into food —all in the next few thousand years.

Actually, during that period of time, we are almost certain to be confined to the planet Earth. Even if we colonize the rest of the solar system, it is beyond hope that we can actually transfer sizable portions of the human population to such forbidding worlds as the Moon and Mars.

So suppose we ask ourselves how long it will take (at the present rate of human increase) for mankind to attain a mass equal to no more than that of the single planet Earth. The Earth's mass is 6,600 billion billion tons, and if that is taken as *y*, then log *y* is 21.82. Throwing that into the equation, we find that *x* equals 1,560.

In 1,560 years, at the present rate of increase; that is, by A.D. 3530, the mass of humanity will be equal to the mass of the Earth. Will any optimist in the audience raise his hand if he thinks that mankind can possibly achieve this under any circumstances?

Let's search for a more realistic limit, then. The total mass of living tissue on Earth today is estimated to be something like twenty million million tons, and this cannot really increase as long as the basic energy source for life is sunlight. Only so much sunlight reaches Earth; only so much of that sunlight can be used in photosynthesis; and therefore only so much new living plant tissue can be built up each year. This amount built up is balanced by the amount that is destroyed each year, either through spontaneous death or through consumption by animal life.

Animal life may be roughly estimated as one tenth the mass of plant life or about two million million tons the world over. This cannot increase either, for if, for any reason, the total mass of animal life were to increase significantly, the mass of plants would be consumed faster than it could be replaced, as long as sunlight is only what it is. The food supply would decrease drastically and animals would die of starvation in sufficient numbers to reduce them to their proper level.

To be sure, the total mass of *human* life has been increasing throughout history, but only at the expense of other forms of animal life. Every additional ton of humanity has meant, as a matter of absolute necessity, one less ton of non-human animal life.

Not only that, but the greater the number of human beings, the greater the mass of plants that must be grown for human consumption as food (either directly, or indirectly by feeding animals destined for the butcher) or for other reasons. The greater the mass of grains, fruits, vegetables, and fibers grown, the smaller the mass of other plants on the face of the Earth.

Suppose we ask, then, how many years it will take for mankind to increase in numbers to the point where the mass of humanity is equal to the present mass of all animal life? Remember that when that happens there will be no other animals left—no elephants or lions, no cattle or horses, no cats or dogs, no rats or mice, no trout or crabs, no flies or fleas.

Furthermore, to feed that mass of humanity, all the present mass of plant life must be in a form edible to man; which means no shade trees, no grass, no roses. We couldn't afford fruits or nuts because the rest of the tree would be inedible. Even grain would be uneconomic, for what would we do with the stalks? We would most likely be forced to feed on the only plants that are totally nutritious and that require only sunlight and inorganic matter for rapid growth—the one-celled plants called algae.

Well then, if the total mass of animal life is two million million tons, log y equals 12.30 and x works out to 466. This means that by A.D. 2436 the last animal (other than man) will have died, and the last plant (other than algae) will also have died.

By A.D. 2436 the number of human beings on Earth will be forty trillion or over eight thousand times the present number. The total surface of the Earth is equal to about 200,000,000 square miles, which means that by A.D. 2436 the average density of the human population will be 200,000 per square mile.

Compare this with the present density of Manhattan at noon—which is 100,000 per square mile. By A.D. 2436, even if mankind is spread out evenly over every part of the Earth—Greenland, the Himalayas, the Sahara, the Antarctic—the density of population will be twice as high *everywhere* as it is in Manhattan now.

We might imagine a huge, world-girdling complex of highrise apartments (over both land *and* sea) for housing, for offices, for industry. The roof of this complex will be given over entirely to algae tanks containing an ocean of water, literally, and twenty million million tons of algae. At periodic intervals there will be conduits down which water and algae will pour, to be separated, with the algae dried, treated, and prepared for food, while the water is returned to the tanks above. Other conduits, leading upward, will bring up the raw minerals needed for algae growth, consisting of (what else?) human wastes and finely chopped up human corpses.

Even this limit, quite modest compared to the earlier suggestions of allowing the human race to multiply till its mass equaled that of the Universe or merely that of the Earth, is quite unbearable. Where would we find any optimist so dead to reality as actually to believe that in a space of four and a half centuries, we can build a planetary city twice as densely populated as Manhattan.

To be sure, all this is based on the assumption that the increase in human population will continue at its present rate indefinitely. Clearly, it won't. Something will happen to slow that growth, bring it to an utter halt, even reverse it and allow the human race to decrease in numbers once more. The only question is what that "something" will be.

To any sane person it would surely seem that the safest way of bringing this about is a worldwide program for the voluntary limitation of births; with the enthusiastic participation of humanity as a whole . . .

Failing this, the same result will inevitably be brought about by an increase in the death rate—through famine, for instance.

The question is: How much time do we have to persuade the people of Earth to limit their births?

Anyone, however optimistic, can see that global birth control will not be achieved easily. There are stumbling blocks. There are important religious bodies who object strongly to the utilization of sex for pleasure rather than for progeny. There are long-standing sociological traditions that equate many children with strong national defense, with help around the farm and home, with security in parental old age. There are long-standing psychological factors which equate many children with a demonstration of masculine virility and wifely duty. There are new nationalist factors which cause minority groups to view birth control as a device to limit *their* numbers in particular, and to view unlimited births as a method for outbreeding the establishment and "taking over."

So how much time do we have to counter all this?

If it were a matter of population alone, we might argue that even if things went on exactly as they are, science would keep us going for 466 years anyway, till man was the only form of animal life left on Earth.

Unfortunately, it isn't a matter of population alone. There are factors in our technological society which are multiplying at a more rapid rate than population is and which introduce further complications.

There is the matter of energy, for instance. Mankind has been using energy at a greater and greater rate throughout his existence. Partly this reflects the steady increase in his numbers; but partly this also reflects the advance in the level of human technology. The discovery of fire, the development of metallurgy, the invention of the steam engine, of the internal-combustion engine, the electric generator, all meant sharp increases in the rate of energy utilization beyond what could be accounted for by the increase in man's numbers alone.

At the present moment, the total rate of energy utilization by mankind is doubling every fifteen years, and we might reasonably ask how long that can continue.

Mankind is currently using energy, it is estimated, at the rate of 20,000,000,000,000,000,000 (20 billion billion) calories per year. To avoid dealing with too many zeros, we can define this quantity as one "annual energy unit" and abbreviate that as AEU. In other words, we will say that mankind is using energy, now, at the rate of 1 AEU a year. Allowing a doubling every fifteen years and using an equation similar to that of Equation 2 (which I will not plague you with, for by now you have the idea), you can calculate the rate of energy utilization in any given year and the total utilization up to that year.

Right now, the major portion of our energy comes from the burning of fossil fuels (coal, oil, and gas), which have been gradually formed over hundreds of millions of years. There is a fixed quantity of these and they cannot be re-formed in any reasonable time.

The total quantity of fossil fuels thought to be stored in

the Earth's crust will liberate about 7500 AEU when burned. Not all that quantity of fuel can be dug or drilled out of the Earth. Some of it is so deep or so widely dispersed that more energy must be expended to get it than would be obtained from it. We might estimate the energy of the recoverable fossil fuels to be about 1000 AEU.

If that 1000 AEU of fossil fuels is all we will have as an energy source, then, at the present increase of energy utilization, we will have used it up completely in 135 years; that is, by A.D. 2105. If we suppose that those reserves of fossil fuel which seem unrecoverable now will become recoverable in the next century or so, then that will give us about forty-five years more at the ever increasing rate and we will have till A.D. 2150.

Of course, it is not fossil fuels only that we can work with. There is energy to be derived from nuclear fission of uranium and thorium. The total energy from recoverable fission fuel is uncertain, but it may be a hundred times as great as that from fossil fuels, and that will give us 135 years more and carry us to A.D. 2285.

In other words, in 315 years, or a century and a half *before* we have reached the ridiculous population limit of having mankind the only form of animal life, we will have utterly run out of the major energy sources we use today—assuming things continue as they are going.

Are there other sources? There is sunlight, which brings Earth 60,000 AEU per year, but we'll need that for the algae tanks.

There is fusion power, the energy derived from the conversion of the heavy hydrogen atoms (deuterium) of the oceans to helium. If all the deuterium of the ocean were fused, the energy released would be equal to 500,000,000,000 AEU, enough to keep us going comfortably, even at an endlessly accelerating rate, to a time well past the population limit of the planetary double-Manhattan. (It will bring about a problem as to what to do with all the heat that will be developed—thermal pollution—but there are earlier worries.)

Energy will not be the real limit of mankind, *if* we can harness controlled fusion in massive quantities. We haven't done it yet, but we're on the trail and presumably will do it eventually. The question now is: How much time do we have to make fusion possible, practical, and massive?

We ought to do it before our supply of fossil and fission fuels gives out, obviously, and that means we will have 315 years at most (unless we manage to limit population and energy utilization before then).

That sounds like time enough, but wait. The utilization of energy is inevitably accompanied by pollution, and the deterioration of the environment through a rate of pollution that will double every fifteen years may bring a limit much sooner than that imposed by the disappearance of energy sources.

But we want to deal only with the inevitable. Suppose we bring pollution under control. Suppose we block the effluent of chemical industries, control smoke, eliminate the sulfur in smoke and the lead in gasoline, make use of degradable plastics, convert garbage into fertilizer and mines for raw materials. What then? Is there any pollution that cannot possibly be controlled?

Well, as long as we burn fossil fuels (and only so can we get energy out of them) we must produce carbon dioxide. At the moment, we are adding about 8 billion tons of carbon dioxide to the atmosphere each year by burning fossil fuels. This doesn't seem like much when you consider that the total amount of carbon dioxide in the atmosphere is about 2,280 billion tons or nearly 300 times the quantity we are adding per year.

However, by the time all our fossil fuel is gone, in A.D. 2150, we will have added a total of 60,000 billion tons of carbon dioxide to the atmosphere or better than twenty-five times the total quantity now present in the air. A little of this added supply might be dissolved in the oceans, absorbed by chemicals in the soil, taken up by a faster-growing plant life. Most, however, would remain in the atmosphere.

By A.D. 2150, then, the percentage of carbon dioxide in the air would rise from the present 0.04 per cent to somewhere in the neighborhood of 1 per cent. (The oxygen content, five hundred times the carbon dioxide, would be scarcely affected by this change alone.)

This higher percentage of carbon dioxide would not be enough to asphyxiate us, but it wouldn't have to.

Carbon dioxide is responsible for what is called the

"greenhouse effect." It is transparent to the short waves of sunlight, but is relatively opaque to the longer waves of infrared. Sunlight passes through the atmosphere, reaches the surface of the Earth and heats it. At night, the Earth re-radiates heat as infrared and this has trouble getting past the carbon dioxide. The Earth therefore remains warmer than it would be if there were no carbon dioxide at all in the atmosphere.

If the present carbon dioxide content of the atmosphere were merely to double, the average temperature of the Earth would increase by 3.6° C. We might be able to stand the warmer summers and the milder winters but what of the ice caps on Greenland and Antarctica?

At the higher temperatures, the ice caps would lose more ice in the summer than they would regain in the winter. They would begin to melt year by year at an accelerating pace and the sea level would inexorably rise. By the time all the ice caps were melted, the sea level would be at least 200 feet higher than it is and the ocean, at low tide, would lap about the twentieth floor of the Empire State Building. All the lowlands of Earth, containing its most desirable farmland and its densest load of population, would be covered by the rolling waters.

At the rate at which fossil fuels are being increasingly used now, the ice caps will be melting rapidly about a century from now. To prevent this, we might make every effort to switch from fossil fuel to fission fuel, but in doing that, we would be producing radioactive ash in enormous quantities and that would present an even greater and more dangerous problem than carbon dioxide would.

The outside limit of safety, thanks to pollution, no matter *what* we do (short of limiting population and energy consumption) is only a hundred years from now. Unless we develop massive fusion power by 2070, the face of the Earth will be irremediably changed, with enormous damage to mankind.

But do we even have that century in which to maneuver if we don't limit population?

It is not just that population is increasing, but that it is growing ever more unbalanced. It is the cities, the metropolitan agglomerates, that are increasing their loads of humanity, while the rural areas are, if anything, actually decreasing in population. This is most marked in the industrialized and "advanced" areas of the world, but it is making itself felt everywhere, with increasing force, as the decades slip by.

It is estimated that the urban population of the Earth is doubling not every thirty-five years, but every *eleven* years. By A.D. 2005, when the Earth's total population will have doubled, the metropolitan population will have increased over ninefold.

This is serious. We are already witnessing a breakdown in the social structure; a breakdown that is concentrated most strongly in just those advanced nations where urbanization is most apparent. Within those nations, it is concentrated most in the cities, and, in particular, in the most crowded portions of those cities.

There is no question but that when living beings are crowded beyond a certain point, many forms of pathological behavior become manifest. This has been found to be true in laboratory experiments on rats, and the newspaper and our own experience should convince us that this is true for human beings, also.

Population has been increasing as long as the human race has existed, but never at the present rate, and never under conditions of such fullness-of-Earth. In past generations, when a man could not stand the crowds, he could run away to sea, emigrate to America or Australia, move toward the frontier. But now the Earth is filled up and one can only remain festering in the crowds, which grow ever worse.

And does social disintegration increase merely as the population increases, or as the level of urbanization increases? Will its level double only every thirty-five years or even only every eleven years? Somehow, I think not.

I suspect that what counts in creating the kind of troubles we see about us—the hostilities, angers, rebellions, withdrawals—is not just the number of people swarming about each individual, but the number of interactions possible between an individual and the people swarming about him.

For instance: if A and B are in close proximity, they may possibly quarrel; but an A–B quarrel is all that is possible. If A, B, and C are all in close proximity, then A may quarrel with B or with C; or B may quarrel with C. Where two individuals may have only one two-way quarrel, three individuals may have three different quarrels of this sort, and four individuals, six different quarrels.

In short, the number of possible interactions increases much more rapidly than the mere number of people crowded together does. If the metropolitan areas increase ninefold in population by the year 2000 then I suspect that the level of social disorder and disintegration will increase (at a guess) fiftyfold, and I feel pretty sure that society will not be able to bear the load.

I conclude, then, that we have only the space of the next generation to stop the population increase and reorganize our cities to prevent the pathological crowding that now occurs. We have thirty years—till A.D. 2000—to do it in and that estimate is rather on the optimistic side, if anything.

Unfortunately, I don't think that mankind can fundamentally alter its ways of thinking and acting within thirty years, even under the most favorable conditions; and the conditions are far from favorable. As it happens, those who dominate human society are, generally, old men in comfortable circumstances, who are frozen in the thought patterns of a past generation, and who cling suicidally to the way of life to which they are accustomed.

It seems to me, then, that by A.D. 2000 or possibly earlier, man's social structure will have utterly collapsed, and that in the chaos that will result as many as three billion people will die.

Nor is there likely to be a chance of recovery thereafter, for in the chaos, the nuclear buttons are only too apt to be pushed and those who survive will then face an Earth which will probably be poisoned by radiation for an indefinite period into the future.

And as far as human civilization is concerned, that will be

THE END

AFTERWORD

Articles like the foregoing qualify me for the title of "doom-crier." That word is usually used in a derogatory sense, but I accept it cheerfully. When I foresee doom, I intend to cry it. The doom won't be averted by looking the other way, I assure you; it will, rather, be hastened.

Sometimes people ask why doom-criers don't make constructive suggestions. Well, they do; or at least, I do. All you have to do is look at the next article, which, by the chances of the game, hit the newsstands at the same time as the foregoing (although in a different magazine).

THE END, UNLESS . . .

We all know, or at least we have been told often enough through every medium of information, that the world is dangerously overpopulated, and that the pressure of numbers is rising daily. In thirty years, the world population, if matters continue as they are now, will have nearly doubled, to six billion or so. The concentration of population in metropolitan areas, the rape of resources, the level of pollution will all have increased to far more than double.

Under the stress of famine and poison, as numbers increase and the environment grows less livable, the unrest we can plainly see and experience now, the social alienation, the escape to violence out of sheer frustration, will rise to the explosion point. Even if we escape an actual nuclear war, our technological civilization, precariously enough balanced now, will topple, and the world we know will come to a bloody, catastrophic end.

The year 2000 is the bimillennium and by then, it seems to me, the growth of present pressures will have burst our fragile balloon and our world will be in fragments.

But is this inevitable? Is there any way we can prevent this happening?

Perhaps—If we can alter our way of thinking.

There are certain deeply ingrained habits of thought that date back to the world as it has always been till now and that were once useful.

Now, however, the world is as it has never been before; it is an utterly different world; it is a world dying of irrelevant thinking.

If we want to survive into the twenty-first century, then,

SOURCE: "The End, Unless . . ." appeared in *True* as "Can Man Survive the Year 2000?" in January 1971.

here are some of the changes in thinking that it seems to me we must make—

I

Our religions must no longer be other-world centered. Through all the ages during which the nature of the Universe was completely uncomprehended, it was fair enough to speak of "God's will" as a conventional phrase meaning "I don't know what's going on." In an age when the Earth was sturdy, and indifferent to any damage that mankind with its small numbers and feeble powers could do, refuge in fantasy-security was psychologically comfortable and could do little harm.

Nowadays, such fantasies would kill us all. It is so easy to face the apparently insoluble problem of population and pollution and murmur about having faith in God. We need not then be inconvenienced by the kind of hard decisions that must be made for the world to survive. It is so comforting to hear of the possible destruction of the world yet think that after all Earth is but the anteroom to the real and much better world in heaven, and that even a thermonuclear war might simply be the prelude to the good Lord's Judgement Day.

To do this is simply to surrender.

In some cases, it is a particularly cowardly surrender, for I suspect that those most likely to abandon the Earth, to the tune of pious mouthings, are those who feel no sense of personal danger. I feel it is the old, rather than the young, who are most likely to express themselves as resigned to the will of heaven—perhaps because even if the world lasts only thirty years more, it will yet last their time.

I feel, too, it is those inclined to conservatism who are more likely to adopt this particular cop-out, for they are generally satisfied with the world as it is (or as they imagine it would be if troublemakers would just stop unsettling things) and see no reason to change it.

And yet who really feels resigned to God's will when their immediate safety is threatened?

Where are those profound trusters in a Fundamentalist version of God who are willing to ask the United States to disband its army, destroy its nuclear weapons and its missiles, call back its ships—thus saving uncounted billions of dollars for use in more constructive ways—in the clear assurance that the good Lord will serve God-fearing America as a shield against its vicious enemies?

Or, for that matter, who advocates the disbanding of all the police forces of the nation on the ground that trust in the Divine is enough to protect the virtuous, who will, in any case, sleep that night in Paradise, if mugged hard enough?

Is it that the elderly and comfortable of the world feel the need of immediate protection against the hoodlum within and the soldier outside but are willing to trust in God in matters where their own welfare is not directly at stake?

But in doing so, they sap the will of the world generally, and soothe its fears just long enough to make it all too late when it is finally forced to snap to attention.

If we are to escape world destruction, our beliefs, our aspirations, our ideals, must all be centered upon this world exclusively, and we must all be very sure that, just as it is man alone that is destroying the world, so it must be man alone—*alone*—who must save the world.

II

Once we make up our mind to deal with the world like men and not like puppets waiting for the string-puller, we must next tackle the matter of motherhood.

It is quite clear to anyone who has studied the situation that the Earth is seriously overpopulated *now* and that it is sure to become still more overpopulated in the next few decades.

Before anything else can be done, then, the population growth must be met squarely. Measures must be taken to bring it to a standstill and eventually into a decline. We may manage to make it through that six-billion population figure in A.D. 2000 if all goes well but even if we do, we can't maintain it and shouldn't want to. We ought to allow for a controlled and humane downward slide to an eventual figure of, say, one billion. One billion well-fed, creative human beings are a far happier and more worthwhile load for our good planet than six billion starving, half-mad wretches.

But how is this to be done? We can use all the mechanical and chemical devices we want to in order to prevent conception. We can pass laws; we can educate; we can persuade; we can threaten. All will be useless if we don't change some of our myths.

Through all of history, down to almost this very day, life expectancy has been low; child mortality has been high. Women have had to be baby-making machines to keep the population from declining and whole tribes from withering away. Yet baby making, through all those generations, has been dangerous, agonizing, and, remarkably often, fatal.

To keep up enthusiasm for the process, it is not surprising, then, that the myth therefore arose and was sedulously spread that there was something sacred and beautiful about motherhood; that no woman could possibly be fulfilled unless she became a wife and mother; that to be childless was a dreadful misery and a punishment by God for one's sins; and that to have many children was a blessing.

But now we live in a world where we are being murdered by numbers, where life expectancy is (for the moment) long and child mortality low, and the global population increases by 70 million each year. Can we still preach those old tales about the glories of motherhood?

Must we not make the turnaround and accept the fact that in our present world, excessive motherhood is an evil and, indeed, genocide? For a woman to have more than two children nowadays is evidence of a frightening and callous disregard (or, possibly, ignorance) of the nature of the greatest crisis ever to have faced man. It is the woman who deliberately decides to limit her child-bearing capacity who is now the worthwhile and noble citizen of the planet.

In short, we must stop mouthing clichés about motherhood and put an end to the slobbering "Mother's Day" aspects of society. Motherhood must be viewed as a privilege to be doled out carefully and parsimoniously and not as a free-for-all litter-producing device.

III

Once we are freed of our superstitions concerning motherhood and make up our mind to treat it as something that must and will be regulated for the good of mankind as a whole we will next have to make up our mind to alter our thinking with regard to sex.

A vast number of myths concerning sex have arisen as a result of its connection with childbirth and, sometimes, with the necessity of a clear line of inheritance.

Sex can be considered holy and as a quasi-sacrament, and therefore not to be used for casual pleasure but only for the sacred purpose of having children. Based on this myth, birth control devices become wicked, for they subvert the child-bearing aspect of sex and leave only the fun.

Or sex can be considered dirty and evil, something that is altogether unpleasantly animal, which men may indulge in perhaps, but which no well-brought-up woman would consider doing for a moment except (as an unpleasant duty) to please her husband. This may serve the purpose of keeping a wife from straying, in a society where the use of eunuchs as guardians of a one-woman harem is frowned upon. It also makes it impossible to teach children anything about sex (how broach so filthy and horrible a subject?), so that they grow up in ignorance or, worse, in distorted knowledge.

There is the myth that having many children is a sign of sexual virility on the part of a man, or a sign of heavenly favor, with results as destructive to the possibility of birth control as the myth of the holiness of sex.

There is the myth that indulging in sexual practices that have no chance of leading to conception (masturbation, homosexuality, etc.) is perverse and unnatural, so that the uncounted millions who continue to practice these "perversions" do so only under the blanket of guilt and danger of punishment, and many are forced into chancing conception when they might have had their fun while avoiding it.

It is clear that in a world of limited births, where something short of forcible sterilization is used to bring it about, we will have to eliminate all these myths and learn to look at sex as a phenomenon which, except on relatively rare occasions, is utterly divorced from the matter of childbirth. Sex will have to be looked on as essentially a way of amusing one's self and one's partner, and as neither holy nor dirty. Personal preferences in sex, between consenting adults, where no physiological harm is involved, will be no more a matter of public concern than personal preferences in food and drink.

Under those circumstances, birth control will no longer be a matter of morals, or of offense to virility, and may actually come to pass.

IV

The adoption of new attitudes toward motherhood and sex clearly cannot succeed on a piecemeal basis, or in one country alone, so the death of the modern variety of nationalism is also required.

The problems mankind now faces are planetary in nature. Overpopulation, the overconsumption of natural resources, the overdestruction of the ecological fabric, the overpoisoning of the environment, are now going on everywhere. To alter social attitudes in order to stop such a trend in one nation only, even the strongest, such as the United States, or the largest, such as the Soviet Union, or the most populous, such as China, is insufficient.

No one nation, no matter how it stabilizes population within its own borders, no matter how it rationalizes the use of its resources and the conservation of its environment, can possibly succeed if the rest of the world continues in its rabbit multiplication and its free-will poisoning. Even if every nation sincerely takes measures, independently one of another, to correct the situation, those solutions that one nation finds may conflict with the needs of its neighbor, and all might fail.

To put it bluntly, planetary problems require a planetary attack and a planetary solution, and that means co-operation among nations; *real* co-operation.

To put it still more bluntly, we need a world government that can come to logical and humane decisions and can then enforce them.

But before such a world government can come into existence, the whole myth of nationality will have to go.

Yes, we can have special pride in our country, but it has to be the impractical pride we have in our baseball team or our college—a pride that cannot be backed by force of arms.

We cannot, under any circumstances, translate this pride

into that form of patriotism that allows us to place the good of a small part of mankind above the good of the whole, or persuades us that any means whatever are justifiable in the pursuit of the security of a small part of mankind.

Parochial pride is attractive and gives meaning to lives that might otherwise be empty, but it also leads to the emotional feeling that if my group (name any group) can't have its rights, then it is reasonable to tear down the whole world in revenge. Given that attitude, the whole world *will* be torn down, for at the present moment, there is needed only one good push and it will all go.

Of what odds are parochial values anyway? The Middle East is a jungle of emotions but, if we continue as we are going now, there will in thirty years be no Israel worth preserving, no Palestine worth regaining. There will be no black rights, or white rights either, worth fighting for. What's more, all of us, Red or non-Red, Free or non-Free, Privileged or Under-privileged, will either be dead or wishing we were.

All the patriotic slogans men shout these days and paint on signs, all the stirring songs they sing, all the exciting legends with which they regale themselves, are fun and will remain fun, but must nevermore be anything other than fun. We can't live by them any more; we can only die by them.

V

And if regional, sectional, and ethnic values must give way to a consideration of mankind as a single political, economic, and sociological entity, that same surrender must work its way down to the private level as well.

Until the mid-twentieth century, the Earth was, to all intents and purposes, infinite. Not all the harm man was capable of doing could seriously or permanently damage it. For that reason it was logical to develop the notion of infinite freedom; of doing as one liked.

With the invention of the nuclear bomb and with the steadily accelerating intensification and extensification of technology, a boundary line was passed about 1950. We can now destroy a world grown finite in any of several ways. We can radiate it to death, explode it to death, crowd it to death, strip it to death, starve it to death, poison it to death.

In order to do none of those things, we have to restrain ourselves and recognize life on Earth to be a single rather fragile fabric. No one can any longer think of himself as Man the Individual, or even as Men the Nation. We can think of ourselves only as Mankind the Ecological Unit.

Each of us is not only his brother's keeper; he is the keeper of his animal and plant brother as well; the keeper of the air he breathes, the water he drinks, and the soil he stands on. We are all planet keepers, and in all the Universe we have only this one planet to keep.

Private freedom in the sense that we can do as we please is impossible if we are to survive; property in the sense that we can do what we like with our own is impossible, too. We are part of a greater whole and it is the interests of the whole that are paramount, if we are to have any individual interests at all. We are going to have to recognize ourselves as guests on a finite Earth, limited by the code of good manners to what, as guests, we can do.

The grand law will be: Recycle!

Nothing can be discarded that cannot be reused. If technology is described as a complex device for converting resources into garbage, it will have to do so only at the expense of working out methods for reconverting garbage into resources at equal speed. It is only when that is taken care of that within the areas that remain (and *only* within the areas that remain) human freedoms can exist.

VI

But these changes are negative ones, in a sense. They are designed to force men *not* to evade their problems by refuge in the supernatural, to force men *not* to overpopulate, *not* to pollute, *not* to destroy each other in the name of patriotism.

And when that is done, what then? Is a world carefully kept in balance worth living in just because it is in balance? If we do nothing more than keep the cycle going, do we not still have the kind of alienation and frustration that arises from a lack of worthwhile values, aggravated, perhaps, by the loss of other-world ideals and of the pleasure of private do-as-you-please?

Consider, though, that there is another change overtaking the world that will be all the more prominent if the evil effects of population growth, regional hatreds, and ecological destruction are brought to an end. There is the continuing elaboration of the machine.

The era of computerization and automation is upon us and if we survive the next generation, it could well eliminate more and more kinds of non-creative work, both physical and mental. Leisure time, which exists already in greater quantities than would have seemed possible a century ago, will exist in still greater quantities in the future.

And the devil *does* find mischief still for idle hands to do. Or if not the devil, then our own boredoms.

All through man's history it has been necessary for all, save an extremely thin layer on top, to work incessantly for bare survival. To make this palatable, we have worked up numerous myths concerning the desirability of industry and hard work, and we have finally established an educational system supposedly designed to make men better fit to do their work.

In the name of educating for work, boys and girls are put through years of schooling in which they are taught by rote an uninspired potpourri of subjects that are expected to fit, unmodified, into minds of all shapes and sizes.

And we are still doing it in an age when jobs in the old sense are growing fewer and requiring less time. We still educate for work when what men and women are coming to have most of is leisure. And what are we having them do with leasure? We leave them nothing but to watch in dull stupefaction the posturings on a TV screen, or to invent for themselves the fun of drugs and vandalism.

Useful education nowadays must involve educating for leisure. Men and women must be taught to use their leisure constructively, each in his or her own way. There is fun in doing when what you are doing is your own thing.

Almost everyone has in himself some potential for creativity. It ought to be searched for and found and the philosophy of education will have to organize itself about this search and discovery. It will have to develop methods for helping each person discover the sound of his own drummer and then how best to march to that drumming.

And whatever it is, so that it fulfills the doer and does not harm his neighbor, it will be important. The man who gets his fun out of programming computers and the man who gets his fun out of building model skyscrapers out of toothpicks—are both having fun. And, for the sheer fun of it, there will be enough men and women and to spare, to run the serious work of the world.

VII

There you have it, then.

Do you think that we can learn to abandon the world after death, the sacredness of motherhood, the holiness of sex, the intoxication of national patriotism, the itch for infinite freedom, and the respect for industry, in favor of man-centered population restriction involving sex for fun and implying world government, managed ecology, and education for leisure?—And do it all before the twentieth century has run out?

We don't have to, you know.

It's just that if we don't, our civilization will be destroyed in thirty years, that's all.

THE FOURTH REVOLUTION

That which distinguishes men from animals is the ability to communicate abstractions; the ability to do more than signal "Help!" or "Food!"

At some time during the history of the early hominids there developed, somehow, a code of sounds flexible enough to make at least a beginning at transferring thoughts from one mind to another. Speech was invented.

When and where that happened, we haven't the faintest idea. Obviously, though, it did happen, and that was mankind's first communications revolution. We might argue that it was this revolution that made man man, for it was through speech that a society could develop traditions that would stretch across generations; through speech that discoveries could be made to accumulate instead of having to be devised anew by each man in his lifetime.

The nature of the actual changes imposed on human society by the development of speech is unknown and can only be guessed, but we have a somewhat clearer view of the second revolution—the development of writing.

Writing was developed in ancient Sumeria not long before 3000 B.C. It came to an urbanized culture based on a highly developed agricultural technology that was already what we call civilization.

Civilization can develop without writing. The Inca civilization of fifteenth-century Peru did not have it. We might suspect, though, that without writing, civilization would advance only slowly and reach a dead end at a certain comparatively low level of complexity simply because, with its slowness, evanescence, and uncertainty, speech will not, of itself, suffice to support any higher

SOURCE: "The Fourth Revolution" appeared in *Saturday Review*, October 24, 1970.

level of civilization. The Inca world may well be as high as we can get in the days of the first revolution, then.

With speech frozen in writing, with technical instructions and legal codes made permanently available and placed beyond distortion because of the fallibility of memory, the complexity of man's technology and sociology could be carried to new heights—and was.

Nevertheless, writing in itself, still had its elements of fragility. The reproduction of books was a slow and expensive process and few books (by present standards) ever existed in the world at one time for nearly five millennia after writing was invented. Because books were as precious as jewels, literacy remained the monopoly of the priests and aristocrats. The common man had no use for reading and writing.

Again, because books were so few, the entire heritage of a civilization could be destroyed by barbarian inroads; and more than once was. Successive waves of tribal invasions wiped out the great libraries accumulated by the Graeco-Roman world and by A.D. 1204, the only place left in which the complete corpus of ancient learning and culture was preserved was in Constantinople, the fading metropolis of the remnants of the Byzantine Empire.

In that year, Western Crusaders took the city and destroyed it, burning and looting what they suspected to be heretical or despised as being worthless. The main body of what the ancients had gathered was lost forever. Out of the more than a hundred plays that Sophocles had written, we have preserved exactly seven. Of the writings of such great thinkers as Democritus, Aristarchus, and Epicurus, there remains nothing but vague references in some few books that have been preserved.

Writing, then, can in itself serve only to support a civilization as complex as that of the Roman Empire rather precariously, and Rome may be as high as we can get in the days of the second revolution.

But then there came the third revolution in the fifteenth century—brought on by a device for reproducing the written word mechanically, over a brief period of time, and in an indefinite number of copies. In short, the printing press was invented.

By the standards of the times, the technique of printing spread like wildfire—a good measure of its value and of the need it fulfilled. Once again, human civilization, placed on a firmer foundation, could advance to new levels of complexity.

It is easy to argue that printing was a necessary (if, of course, not sufficient) condition for the development of modern science. The findings of one man could be rapidly issued in a form that would make the matter available to other men across the length and breadth of Europe. A "community of science" was formed that could not have existed before the invention of printing. It became large enough and compact enough to make its power felt, too, so that Copernican views, for instance, could not be crushed by the disapproval of Churchmen.

As books grew in number and waned in expense, it became much more worthwhile to know how to read and write. From 1500 on, there was a steady increase in literacy, a growing broadening of the base of education. The possibility of scholarship was opened to larger percentages of the European population so that more could contribute to the developing technology. And each development, as it came, was broadcast more rapidly and more thoroughly, serving to stimulate other developments—until by 1800 the Industrial Revolution was in full swing in Great Britain and the Low Countries.

We have now advanced about as far as we can, perhaps, in the world of the third revolution. Indeed, signs of breakdown are everywhere, for the problems introduced by our contemporary level of technology seem insuperable.

Not only is the population too great, but worse still, they have crowded themselves unbearably into metropolitan centers. After all, as civilization grows more complex, greater numbers are required to run its nerve centers; and since it is at those nerve centers that the advantages of its culture and technology are greatest, still more people flood inward to take advantage of that. —Until we arrive at giant cities that are sociologically diseased, technologically polluted, culturally decadent, and dying from the center outward. Nowhere is this more true than in the United States, where the world of the third revolution has advanced furthest.

A fourth revolution is needed, and the first signs of its

coming were to be noted in the mid-nineteenth century. Within the Industrial Revolution, there has been a subsidiary Electrical-Electronic one. The human voice was extended by the telegraph, the telephone, and the radio, until it could reach all around the globe in a fraction of a second. It became possible to stimulate the human eye as well across space and time. Photography was invented; photographs could be transmitted by wire; then made to move; then, by way of television, made to move concurrently with events.

For a century, however, this fourth revolution has remained limited in scope and powerless to exert anything but fringe effects. The equipment was intricate and expensive and could be used but sparingly. There were sharp limitations; cables could carry only so many messages; radio only so many wavelengths; television only so many channels; and all suffered from static and "noise" of one sort or another.

This is not to say that the fringe effects were not important even so. To conduct business without a telephone became unthinkable; to conduct social contacts without one equally unthinkable. To raise children without a television set is becoming unthinkable.

In areas of the world where the third revolution has not yet established itself, where books and newspapers are few, and illiteracy widespread, the leap to the transistor radio has brought an enormous change. The new nationalism of the Arab countries and of Black Africa would be impossible without the binding power of the spoken word through those tiny speech-boxes that were strewn through the population.

Yet all these changes, notable enough though they may be, are insufficient to alter the fact that civilization rests on the printed word.

The fourth revolution in its present stage has some of the characteristics that writing once had. It is too restricted, too fragile. As writing was once kept under the control of local priestly castes, so electronic communications remain under the control of local industries and local governments.

What is needed is an electronic change analogous to that from writing to printing. Electronic communications must become so widespread that there must be a kind of "electronic literacy" established, with every man owning his own electronic outlet, as now every man can own his own library. Only then can the fourth revolution really be established; only then can it make its effect felt and, very possibly, lift civilization to a new level of complexity and effectiveness and correct the evils of a technology grown beyond the limits its base makes optimal.

The full establishment of the fourth revolution after the fashion just described is upon us now. What was needed to make this possible was first predicted in the October 1945 issue of *Wireless World* by science fiction writer Arthur C. Clarke.

He pointed out that a truly efficient relay designed to carry electronic communications over global distances without significant interference by static would have to be located in space. A relay station, placed 22,000 miles over some point on Earth's equator, would revolve about Earth in twenty-four hours, just the time it takes Earth to rotate in space, and would thus seem fixed in the sky to observers on Earth's surface. Relative to Earth, it would be a stationary relay. As few as three such relays, properly placed, would suffice to blanket the Earth and to make it possible to establish communications from any one point to any other.

Furthermore, the use of outer-space relays would make available a vast number of simultaneous TV channels and an even vaster number of wavelengths for mere voice communications.

In 1945, what Clarke presented was only a dream, but the disciplined dream of an intelligent and far-sighted thinker. Within twenty years, it was something that was actually within man's grasp.

In 1965, "Early Bird," the first commercial communications satellite, was launched. Its relay made available 240 voice circuits and one TV channel. Within six years, there was "Intelsat IV," with a capacity for 6,000 voice circuits and twelve TV channels.

Mankind is on its way and is moving rapidly. The race is on between the coming of the true fourth revolution, and the death of civilization that will otherwise inevitably occur through growth past the limits of the third.

Suppose the fourth revolution is established before civilization breaks down, what may we expect it to accomplish?

For one thing, the day of the individual television station (of which hundreds are needed today merely to cover the United States with their limited short-range beams) will be over. Signals can be bounced off the space relays direct to the home set. Indeed, person-to-person communication on a scale of massive freedom becomes thinkable.

With an unlimited number of voice and picture channels available, every man could have his portable phone, and dial any number on Earth. No one with such a phone need ever be lost; for if he is, an emergency button can send out a signal that can be traced from anywhere else on Earth.

The printed word will be capable of being transmitted easily and widely, in a computerized space-relay world, so that facsimile mail can be transmitted from point to point in a fraction of a second (with traditional methods available, for cases where privacy is essential.) Facsimile newspapers, magazines, books can be readily available at the press of a button. Perhaps eventually, a single world-computer will hold in its vitals the library of mankind, any part of which will be available to any man at any time.

(Does this mean man's knowledge becomes vulnerable once more as was the single body of Greek lore at Constantinople in 1204? What happens to copyrights and publishers? —The fourth revolution will generate its problems, too, but at the moment it is the third revolution problems that are a matter of mass life and mass death.)

And the consequences of personalized mass communication? What will make it revolutionary and not merely a further extension of a world in which there is already a kind of world-communication?

The new extension will be so much more massive, so much more individualized, so much more widespread, as to pass beyond a matter of degree and become different in kind.

The Earth, for the first time, will be knit together on a personal level and not on a governmental level. There will be the kind of immediacy possible over all the world as has hitherto existed only at the level of the village. In fact, we will have what has been called the "global village."

To know all your neighbors on the global level does not mean that you will automatically love them all; it does not, in and of itself, introduce a reign of peace and brotherhood. But to be potentially in touch with everybody at least makes fighting more uncomfortable. It becomes easier to argue instead.

What is more, the concept of national boundaries will become even more ridiculous than it now is (and it is ridiculous enough already, Heaven knows), once all men are equally distant from you in point of communication time. This will be all the more so since, with global communications on the personal level and with the simultaneous advance of computerization, business will become truly international.

There are no boundaries in a global village. All problems will become so intimate as to be one's own. No problem can arise at one point without affecting all points immediately and emotionally, and world government will become a fact even if no one particularly wants it (thanks to past prejudices) and perhaps even if no one is particularly aware that it is taking place. We will just all wake up one morning and realize that for some time the world has been acting in reasonable unison.

Contributing to this will be the fact that with global, personalized civilization a fact, the differences among men, differences that go so far to create suspicion and hostility, will lessen.

There will be a great need, for instance, for some common language, if all men are to talk directly to all men. This does not mean that anyone will have to abandon his own language altogether or that the multiplicity of tongues will have to vanish from the Earth with all the splendid variety of thought and culture to which it gives rise. It does mean, though, that everyone will find it a great advantage to speak some global language in addition to his own.

To invent one would be too difficult a task in the time available but that is not necessary. English is almost there already. It is the first language of more people than any other language but Chinese, and the second language of more people than any other language including Chinese. The global village of the fourth revolution, then, will have English as its "lingua franca."

The world will tend toward homogeneity in other respects, too, and this need not frighten anybody. Homogeneity may not be a good in itself, to be sure, for there is wonder and vitality in variations and in differences. But remember that homogeneity is not an evil in itself, either. Where heterogeneity means that some parts of the world are distinctly more malnourished than others; distinctly more uneducated; distinctly more diseased; distinctly less comfortable—we have a right to hope for less heterogeneity and greater homogeneity, toward the favorable side, in those cases.

And it is precisely for that kind of greater homogeneity that we can hope in the new age of the fourth revolution. By the use of the new techniques of mass communications, we can expect an enormous revolution in education. For one thing, American and European children can do much of their learning at home under individualized conditions with an electronic tutor geared to their own needs and paced to the beat of their own drummer. That is a comparatively minor improvement of an educational system which is savage and insensitive now, but which does work after a fashion.

What is much more important is that regions of the world which, except possibly for a very small governing caste, do not receive any education at all that would fit them even for the world of the third revolution, can leapfrog directly into the fourth. With mass electronics, the Indian, the Pakistani, the Indonesian, the Black African can, essentially for the first time, get the information he needs—information the whole world needs to make sure he gets.

The population of the submerged nations can grow up learning about modern agricultural methods, the proper use of fertilizers and pesticides (as opposed to non-use or improper use). It can learn about techniques for birth control and the desirability of limiting population. It can be brought into intimate contact with the rest of the world and be made a part of it.

This is not a dream; we have seen it happen before. The early limited stages of the fourth revolution have already shown the way. The coming of movies, radio, and television has done much to eliminate the dichotomy between city and country in the United States. Homogenization is not complete and perhaps never will be (or ought to be) but the mass media are shared by all, so that the day of the "backwoods" is gone.

In the full stretch of the fourth revolution that will be repeated on a global scale. The man on the shores of the Congo River will have as much of human knowledge available to him as the man on the shores of the Hudson River.

And what else? —Decentralization!

The centralization that has been the keyword of human development for the ten thousand years since the invention of agriculture has so far only once showed signs of being reversed without a Dark Age. That tentative step came in connection with transportation.

The mechanization of transportation, with one exception, was institutionalized. Whether it was stagecoaches, steamships, railroads (or even jet planes), men could travel more easily, but only at the times and places controlled by the commercial units who owned the devices. The time and place of departure and arrival were fixed.

Only with the automobile were things different. The automobile was personal; it meant door-to-door; it meant come-and-go-at-will; it meant suit-your-own-convenience. (Yes, there were barriers, involving traffic density, parking difficulties, and so on, but these represented a different class of limitations.)

As a result of the automobile, it was no longer necessary for the worker and executive to cluster so tightly around the factory and office. Men could spread out; the cities broadened; the suburbs came into existence; for the first time a movement toward decentralization arose.

This partial decentralization was swallowed up. The city and its problems expanded faster than the suburbanites could escape.

The fourth revolution will do much better. Even the early stages showed that it wasn't necessary to transmit material objects for no other reason than to transport the information they contained. We have had foretastes of this. The telephone has supplanted the personal visit and, to a certain extent, the mail—but it only transfers sound and only under limited conditions.

With every man possessing his own television outlet, men can both hear and see each other at global distances. Conferences can be held where individual men are seated in a dozen different nations, yet where their images are all together. Documents can be facsimilized and brought from one point to any other at the speed of light; information can be supplied from a central computer to any point.

No one would need to be at any one particular spot to control affairs and businessmen need not congregate in offices. Nor, with the advance of automation, need workingmen congregate in factories. Men can locate themselves at will and shift that location only when they wish to travel for fun.

Which means that the cities will spread out and disappear. They won't even have to exist for cultural reasons in a day when a play acted anywhere can be reproduced electronically at any point on Earth, and a symphony, and an important news event, and any book in a library.

Every place on Earth will be "where it's at."

The world of the fourth revolution will be a "global village" in actuality and not merely metaphorically speaking.

The benefits will be enormous. The greatest problems of the world of the third revolution arise, after all, from the fact of overconcentration, which many times multiplies the basic fact of overpopulation. It is the great cities that are the chief source of pollution, and the chief deprivers of dignity. Let the same billions be spread out and the condition will already be not so acute.

Further, let the same billions be educated into birth control and let their numbers slowly decrease; let the same billions learn to contact each other, know each other, and even understand each other; let the same billions come to live under a world government—and our present problems will no longer be insoluble.

That there will be problems inseparable from the world of the fourth revolution will be certain, but they can be handled in their turn by the generations who must face them—provided we first handle ours.

So the race is on, and by 2000 at the latest it will be decided: Either the world of the fourth revolution will be in full swing or it will not be; and in the latter case the world of the third revolution (and all mankind with it, probably) will be in its death throes.

3 · *IN SCIENCE FICTION*

THE PERFECT MACHINE

A science fiction writer, like myself, is privileged by virtue of his profession to anticipate in concept (if not in detail) some of the great achievements of human ingenuity.

Indeed, when something is longed for intensely, the anticipation is likely to precede the realization by thousands of years. The dream of flight through the air is a case in point.

Another is the fantasy of the perfect machine: the machine that surpasses everything on Earth, even its erratic lord, Man.

Surely the thought of something that lacks all men's weaknesses, yet possesses all man's strengths in superabundant measure, is a terribly attractive one. Imagine a device that can walk and talk, do what it is asked to do with perfect efficiency and without ever growing tired, depressed, or rebellious.

The earliest mention of such a thing in literature is in Homer's *Iliad*, where mechanical girls, made of gold, help the smith-god Hephaistos.

Since then there have been many artificial men of one sort or another in literature and fancy. There have been Roger Bacon's legendary talking head, Rabbi Löw's golem, and Mary Shelley's tale of the monster built by Frankenstein.

In 1920, the Czech playwright Karel Capek, wrote *R.U.R.*, dealing with the manufacture of mechanical men (the initials stand for "Rossum's Universal Robots"). The word "robot" merely means "worker" in the Czech language, but in English it lost that mundane connotation

SOURCE: "The Perfect Machine" appeared in *Science Journal*, October 1968.

and now gives rise to thoughts of metallic beings, vaguely man-shaped, somber, single-minded—and dangerous.

The science fiction writers who followed Capek could not rid themselves of the notion that the manufacture of robots involved forbidden knowledge, a wicked aspiration on the part of man to abilities reserved for God. The attempt to create artificial life was an example of *hubris* and demanded punishment. In story after story, with grim inevitability, the robot destroyed its creator before being itself destroyed.

There were exceptions, to be sure, occasional tales in which robots were sympathetic or even virtuous, but it was not until 1939 that, for the first time as far as I know, a science fiction writer approached the robots from a systematic engineering standpoint.

Without further coyness, I will state that that science fiction writer was myself. In the course of my career I have written two novels and some two dozen short stories in which robots were treated as machines, created by human beings to fulfill human purposes. There was no hint of "forbidden knowledge," only rational engineering.

Those robot stories of mine killed the Frankenstein motif in respectable science fiction as dead as ever *Don Quixote* killed knight-errantry.

To me, the applied science of manufacturing robots, of designing them, of studying them, was "robotics." I used this word because it seemed the obvious analog of physics, mechanics, hydraulics, and a hundred other terms. In fact, I was sure it was an existing word. Recently, however, it was pointed out to me that "robotics" doesn't appear in any edition of Webster's Unabridged Dictionary, so I suppose I invented the word.

Let us assume, to begin with then, that we can build a machine, more or less in the shape of a man, a machine that will be sufficiently complicated to receive the various sense impressions men receive, interpret them in a man-like way at least as rapidly as man, and respond to them in a way a man would consider appropriate.

This implies that the robot must possess an organizing center that is roughly as complicated and as compact as a man's brain. Such a man-made device is as yet beyond the scientific horizon but it is necessary to assume it if a robot is to be manlike in size and shape.

I assumed such an artificial object and even gave it a name. I called it a "positronic brain" and imagined it made of platinum-iridium sponge. There were no details, of course, but I deliberately gave the vague impression that streams of positrons were created each moment, flashing here and there in the millionth of a second before they were destroyed, and simulating by their varying paths, the complexities of human thought. Where the energy of positron formation was to come from, or the energy of annihilation was to go to, I never said.

Of course, is it truly necessary for a robot to be shaped like a man? Is that not merely an anthropocentric fetish on our part? Do not machines mimic human actions every day in homes, fields, and factories, and yet do so without looking anything like men? A thermostat turns a furnace on and off to keep a house comfortably and uniformly warm, doing it more tirelessly and efficiently than a man could. Would its work improve if it were a man-shaped metal object manually turning a furnace on and off?

As long as we concern ourselves with a machine that performs a single function we can indeed specialize. We can adapt it to that one function and care nothing for the rest. But this is not what we are after; we want the perfect machine; and for now, we will define a perfect machine as one that can do everything man can do and do it better.

If a machine is to do all that man can do, it had better be shaped like a man. Not only does the human body possess its present shape because it is adapted to its environment, but the technological environment man has superimposed upon the natural one is adapted to himself. A chair is constructed as it is because it is then just the right height to greet the buttocks when the knees bend. Tools have handles to be gripped by human hands and fingers; knobs and switches are placed where they can be reached by limbs and joints that move and bend just as our limbs and joints do.

In short, a robot shaped like a man fits the world that has made us and that we have made. He is therefore that much more nearly perfect.

A second point is that a robot in the shape of a human being would be more pleasing to us. We could identify better with it. We would, in other words, like a machine in the shape of a man better than any other kind.

I don't always follow my own logic, of course. In my story "Sally," published in 1953, I deal with an automobile that is outfitted with a brain sufficiently complex to allow it to operate itself without human interference. —But then, men have grown to like automobiles and we are even told that there is much phallic symbolism deliberately built into cars.

Interestingly enough, Dr. John McCarthy, at Stanford University, is currently engaged in trying to design a self-driving car—a very simple one, of course.

Given then a robot, similar to man in size, shape, and intelligence, what would be required next? Clearly, there must be safeguards built into the original design. A robot has great potentialities and must use them to the benefit of its creator and not to his harm. The one thing a robot must be designed *not* to do is the very thing that earlier science fiction writers had been constantly making it do—destroy its creator.

Surely, the thought of such safeguards is not new or startling. Sharp knives have blunt handles, swords have hilts, and electric circuits have fuses. Why should robots be different?

Eventually, I formulated my safeguards in the shape of what I called "The Three Laws of Robotics." These were first specifically stated in my story "Runaround," which was published in 1942. They are:

> 1. *A robot may not injure a human being, or, through inaction, allow a human being to come to harm.*
> 2. *A robot must obey the orders given it by human beings except where such orders would conflict with the First Law.*
> 3. *A robot must protect its own existence except where such protection would conflict with the First or Second Law.*

Presumably, the brains of my positronic robots were so designed as to make all their responses consistent with those laws. How such designs were prepared I never (of course) stated specifically.

Since these laws possess their ambiguities (Is a five-year-old child a human being in the meaning of the Second Law? Must a robot prevent a surgeon from operating because the initial incision seems to damage the patient?), I have been able to write numbers of stories in which these laws create crises to be resolved.

Rather to my surprise, it has turned out that these laws, which I meant to apply only to robots, can be interpreted as applying to tools generally. Professor John Wade of Tuskegee Institute in his article "An Architecture of Purpose" (*AIA Journal*, October 1967) rewords the Three Laws to make them refer to "today's nonanimate and nonconscious tools," regarding which, he says:

> 1. *Each must maintain and, where possible, positively support human life.*
> 2. *Each must serve the human purposes for which it is designed unless doing so conflicts with the first criterion.*
> 3. *Each must maintain itself ready for use, unless doing so conflicts with the first or second criterion.*

"These," Professor Wade goes on to say, "form a simple sequence: Maintain the existence of man, the purposer; maintain his purposes; maintain the tool as the means to the accomplishment of the purposes."

Clearly, if a manlike machine approaches perfection the more nearly as it becomes more manlike, its metallicity is a major stumbling block. It would automatically become better if it were constructed out of fibrous material that more nearly approximated human flesh—at least as far as its outer covering was concerned.

It would then become, in science fiction terminology, an android rather than a robot.

An early attempt of mine to use such an android was in the story "Satisfaction Guaranteed," published in 1951. In this story an android named Tony, darkly handsome and perfect in every way, was placed in the house of one of the employees of the robot company for testing "under field conditions."

It had to be withdrawn, not because of any failing of its own as a servant, but because it was entirely too successful. The lady of the house fell in love with it.

Unexpectedly, I received an unusual outpouring of mail from readers, all of whom were interested in Tony, and all of whom were female.

Later in the 1950s I wrote two novels that involved an android, *The Caves of Steel* and *The Naked Sun.*

These novels were science fiction murder mysteries in which the detective team consisted of an Earthman, Elijah Baley, and an android, R. Daneel Olivaw (the R. standing for "Robot").

The Earthman is middle-aged, neurotic, emotional, and weak in many ways, but he has a flexible and intuitive mind. R. Daneel is strong, perfectly balanced, purely intellectual, unemotional—but he is bound by the Three Laws of Robotics and his mind is a literal one. In each case, it is Elijah Baley who solves the crime.

And in each case, there came a new outpouring of letters, again from girls (without exception) and again interested exclusively in R. Daneel. It is quite apparent that if a mechanical man is made sufficiently like man, only better, the appeal to women becomes irresistible.

Further evidence of that may be found in connection with the television show "Star Trek," which reached the television screen a decade and more after my own Elijah Baley novels. In "Star Trek" there is a character, Mr. Spock, who, in some ways, is rather like my own R. Daneel. Mr. Spock is not an android, but he is a member of an extraterrestrial race which is strong, perfectly balanced, purely intellectual, and utterly unemotional—and Mr. Spock proved extremely popular with the lady viewers.

Here then is the ideal we approach in connection with manlike machines.

And yet is this the best we can do? Can "perfection" boil down to "manlike but better"?

I suspect that I myself wasn't satisfied with this interpretation, for in my robot stories I set the robots trivial tasks for the most part.

In "Robbie," my very first robot story (with robots not yet advanced to the point of being able to talk), the robot was used as a nursemaid. In most of the other stories, robots were used in more or less unskilled labor on other planets.

In a later story, "Galley Slave," published in 1957, I did use a robot in a more intellectual endeavor. Reflecting my own needs, I had the robot in that story skilled at proofreading galleys and in the making of minor literary corrections. (Ah, me!)

Even my androids were used trivially. Tony was a household servant; R. Daneel, a detective's assistant. (To be sure, in "Evidence," published in 1946, I had an android who was elected to a post equivalent to that of president of a world government, but that was exceptional.)

Something more is needed: a new look, perhaps, at the adjective "manlike."

If a machine is manlike, must that indeed necessarily imply that the likeness is primarily physical? Might it not be mental?

Is it man's body that makes him all that is essentially man? Or is it his mind? If a machine can think as well as a man, or better, does it matter what it looks like? Would the machine not be accepted as human if it thinks, without demanding anything more of it?

In other words, having taken the robot into the android stage and brought him as far as R. Daneel, I would like now to consider the computer, rather than the robot, and see if the perfect machine is more satisfyingly groped for in that direction.

Among my early robot stories, there was indeed one entitled "Escape," published in 1945, in which the robot was merely an isolated and specialized brain. (It was even called "Brain.") It was an advanced computer that could talk and had personality—the personality of a child.

In a later story, "The Evitable Conflict," published in 1950, a later generation of Brains were running the economy of the world, purportedly at the command of human leaders. It was only slowly that men came to realize that the computers were in charge, following their own devices, but—under the dictates of the Three Laws—doing so for the good of humanity and performing the job far better than men ever had or could.

Actually, though, my real interest in computers began with my story "Franchise," published in 1955, which came in the aftermath of the 1952 presidential election, when "Univac" had predicted the outcome of the election with almost the first votes, and had done so accurately.

"Univac" is an acronym for "Universal Analog Computer," but I chose to consider it "Uni-vac" ("one vacuum tube") and invented my own favorite computer, "Multivac."

In "Franchise," I had Multivac select (by methods best known to itself) one American, whom it could consider typical for that year. It asked the American a series of questions (selected, again, by certain methods it alone knew), recorded the answers, the intonations, the various accompanying physical manifestations such as blood pressure, heartbeat, perspiration activity, and so on, and was then able to announce, at once, the winners of all the elections of that year, national, state, and local.

Satire, yes, but the point was that I accepted Multivac as Supermind, just as R. Daneel was Superbody.

In "Jokester," published in 1956, I visualized a level of human development at such a computerized height that further knowledge could only be gained by questions too clever for any but a few to ask. Those few who could, intuitively, still ask meaningful questions were the Grand Masters.

One of them was asking Multivac who invented the jokes people told. Why should this question be meaningful? Ah—that's what the story is about.

In "The Feeling of Power," published in 1957, I went even farther. The world of the future had been so computerized that men had forgotten how to work out the simplest arithmetical sum without a computer. A computer technologist rediscovered pencil-and-paper mathematics and revolutionized the planet.

And in "All the Troubles of the World," published in 1958, I go in greater detail into the sociology of a completely computerized world. Multivac is the repository, in this one, of all the statistics in the world: all the vital data, the medical data, the day-to-day data; all the most intimate private matters involving every person in the world.

By constantly weighing all this data, Multivac can predict the probabilities of individual illness, crime, and unhappiness. Mankind, with Multivac's help, turns to the prevention of the undesirable before the fact, rather than to its punishment afterward. But it is at a price, for Multivac must, within its vitals, bear all the troubles of the world, and its reaction to that is an unexpected and distressing one.

It was, however, in my story "The Last Question," published in 1956, that I explored, specifically, the question of the creation of the perfect machine.

The result was rather unexpected in a way. No other story has elicited so great a response of one particular type. Numerous people have asked me to identify and help them locate that story. They remember the plot but don't recall the title or where they saw it. Apparently, the story impressed them profoundly, yet disturbed them so much that they could no longer remember how to locate it without help. Nothing of this sort has happened with any other story of mine and you can judge the reasons for yourself, for I will now describe the story in some detail.

"The Last Question," in seven brief scenes taking up less than 5,000 words all told, traces trillions of years of history beginning in 2061, when, with the aid of Multivac (now spread out over many square miles), all the power-utilizing machinery of Earth has been hooked up directly to the Sun. All power is free as long as the Sun lasts. And now, for greater clarity, I will number the scenes.

1. Two of Multivac's technicians, half-drunk, are disturbed that energy will be available only as long as the Sun lasts. They ask Multivac if there is any way of turning the Sun back on once it runs down: that is, if there is any way of massively decreasing the entropy of the Universe. Multivac replies, "Insufficient Data for Meaningful Answer."

2. Centuries later, interstellar travel is a reality and the expanding population of humanity is spreading rapidly to planets on other stars. Each planet has a huge "Planetary AC" which guides its economy and solves its problems. On

each ship is a "Microvac," a much-miniaturized computer that is, in itself, far more advanced than the ancient Multivac with which the story opened.

One family on an interstellar spaceship asks the same question of Microvac and gets the same answer, "Insufficient Data for Meaningful Answer." Over and over that question is going to be asked, with the same answer.

3. Millions of years later, mankind has spread throughout the Milky Way Galaxy. Men are now immortal and are looking outward to the colonization of other galaxies.

There is now a single "Galactic AC" for all mankind. It is on a world of its own, and each man can reach it through an "AC-contact" he owns. The Galactic AC has long since passed beyond any human control, however indirect. Each generation of computers is capable of spending vast periods of time painstakingly designing a computer better than itself, of gathering the raw materials through robots it controls, and of building the better computer to replace itself. And the better computer promptly undertakes the long task of designing a still better one.

But even Galactic AC can not explain how entropy might be massively decreased.

4. Hundreds of millions of years later, mankind has spread through all the galaxies and no longer has physical bodies. Men consist of radiating energy which somehow represents their identity and personality. The "Universal AC" is a two-foot globe, difficult to see. Much of it does not exist in space at all, but in a multi-dimensional "hyperspace."

The influence of the Universal AC spreads out everywhere and no physical device of any kind is needed to reach it. It intercepts the personal energies of all mankind and answers all questions wherever the individual questioner may be located. Even the speed of light is no barrier, for in "hyperspace" (whatever that is) the rigidities of relativistic space-time do not apply.

And even so, it can not answer the question.

5. Billions of additional years pass, and mankind has lost all individual identity. It is a single personality, the fusion of trillions of trillions of human beings, all of which it feels within itself. This fusion of Man fills the Universe

from end to end, but nevertheless it still depends upon the gradually thinning energy supplies of dying stars.

The computer has now become "Cosmic AC" and none of it is in ordinary space. It is entirely in hyperspace, which means that it is nowhere, yet everywhere, for hyperspace touches space at every point.

And with the stars dying, Man still asks if entropy might be decreased and there is still no answer.

6. Trillions of years later, the last stars are fading out and the ultimate heat death is coming upon the Universe. Little by little Man fuses with the computer, which is now simply AC—changeless, eternal, omnipresent, and omniscient.

—Yet not quite omniscient, for as the last bit of Man is about to fuse with AC, it asks once more that old, old question and even now AC can not answer.

7. And then comes the last scene of all, which goes like this:

> *Matter and energy had ended and with it space and time. Even AC existed only for the sake of the one last question that it had never answered from the time a half-drunken technician ten trillion years before had asked it of a computer that was to AC far less than was a man to Man.*
>
> *All other questions had been answered, and until this last question was answered also, AC might not release his consciousness.*
>
> *All collected data had come to a final end. Nothing was left to be collected.*
>
> *But all collected data had yet to be completely correlated and put together in all possible relationships.*
>
> *A timeless interval was spent in doing that.*
>
> *And it came to pass that AC learned, at last, how to reverse the direction of entropy flow.*
>
> *But there was now no man to whom AC might give the answer of the last question. No matter. The answer—by demonstration—would take care of that, too.*
>
> *For another timeless interval, AC thought how best to do this. Carefully, AC organized the program.*

The consciousness of AC encompassed all of what had once been a Universe and brooded over what was now Chaos. Step by step, it must be done.

And AC said, "LET THERE BE LIGHT!"

And there was light—

And yet—did I really have to go through all this to point out the obvious? We want a perfect machine and surely perfection is perfection, and nothing (we are so often told) can be Perfect, but God.

AFTERWORD

I sometimes have it pointed out to me that I talk about myself an awful lot in my essays, and it is even hinted that I do so with a lack of becoming modesty.

If this occurred to any reader as he went through the foregoing, let me make my defense now and save on correspondence.

There is nothing as becoming as modesty and nothing as disgusting as false modesty (or as obvious). I long ago discovered I could only manage the false variety and that was that. If I have to choose between immodesty and hypocrisy, I must take the former.

PREDICTION AS A SIDE EFFECT

It is not really the business of science fiction writers to predict the future. It is particularly not our business to predict trivia. If we could foresee, with accuracy, the minor details of tomorrow and tomorrow and tomorrow, we wouldn't waste our time in that most insecure of all occupations—free-lance writing. We would play the stock market and the horses, instead, and grow rich.

The fact is that the science fiction writer's first aim is to tell an interesting and exciting story that will amuse the reader. His own particular type of story involves events and attitudes that are not common, and perhaps are not even possible, in his own society, and therefore his tale has the value of novelty.

If he is a conscientious science fiction writer, he will try to build up his unusual events and attitudes in a way that will make them seem plausible to the reader, however strange they may be.

This is not absolutely necessary, of course. The storytellers of the Orient could have flying carpets, invisible demons and a thousand fantasies, and the listeners would be fascinated. We are still fascinated by such things today.

The ancient Greek tradition, from which our modern intellectual attitudes stem, was one of rationalism, however. It produced a Universe that went only as far as the senses could observe and reason could deduce. It is in that direction that science fiction (as opposed to fantasy) turns.

And yet observation and deduction, if ingenious enough, can produce almost anything that fantasy can.

Greek engineers, for instance, had built numerous clever mechanical devices, driven by steam or compressed air. These were mostly useless novelties, but they showed what

SOURCE: "Prediction as a Side Effect" appeared in Boston Review of Arts, July 1972.

could be done. Might not some such device, more elaborate than any actually built, make it possible for a man to fly?

Again, Greek astronomers had accurately determined the size of the Moon. It was a globe two thousand miles across. It was a world; a world smaller than the Earth, but still sizable.

There was no indication in ancient times that the atmosphere did not continue all the way to the Moon, so why might it not be possible for a man to use a mechanical device with which to fly to the Moon, and then have adventures there? Or if he would grow tired during the long journey, why might he not hitch large birds to a chariot and go to the Moon in that fashion?

So it came about that tales of Moon voyages were written in ancient times without any vestige of magic and with the down-to-earthness of something that might possibly be.

In the 1650s, the French duelist, poet, and science fiction writer Cyrano de Bergerac (yes, he really lived, nose and all) was writing a tale of a trip to the Moon. In it, his hero thought of various ways of reaching the Moon, each logical after a fashion. One way, for instance, was to strap vials of dew about his waist. The dew rose when the day grew warm and turned it to vapor. Might it not draw the man up as well, once it rose? (The idea was wrong, but it had the germ of the balloon in it.)

Another of Cyrano's notions was that his hero might stand on an iron plate and throw a magnet up into the air. The magnet would draw the iron plate upward, together with the man upon it. When the iron plate reached the magnet, both would tend to fall down again, but before that could happen, the voyager would quickly seize the magnet and throw it up again, drawing the plate still higher, and so on. (Quite impossible, of course, but it sounds so plausible.)

And a third idea was to use rockets.

It so happens that now, three centuries after the time of Cyrano, we do use rockets to reach the Moon. It is the *only* method by which we can reach the Moon, at least so far and for the foreseeable future.

The first man to show that this was so in the scientific sense was Isaac Newton in the 1680s, and we still use his equations to guide our astronauts in their flight to the Moon. However, as it turns out, the first to consider the use of rockets was not Newton, but the science fiction writer Cyrano, thirty years *before* Newton.

Did Cyrano have some weird spyglass into the future?

Not at all! Rockets had been introduced into Europe over three centuries before Cyrano's time. They were only toys, but they rose in the air. Why shouldn't large ones reach the Moon?

It seems to be a general rule that the science fiction writer does not invent his ideas. He simply explores the ideas others invent.

Science fiction writers wrote about the atomic bomb, for instance, long before it existed, but *not* before the scientific basis for it had been established.

The first mention of an atomic bomb was in a story written by H. G. Wells in 1901. He even called it an atomic bomb. Did he have a crystal ball?

Again, not at all. Radioactivity was discovered in 1896 and within a couple of years it turned out that there was a vast store of energy within the atom that scientists had never previously known or suspected to exist. Once it was known to be there, why not a bomb making use of it? And since the energy within the atom was so much greater than the energy within dynamite, the atomic bomb would be a more dangerous explosive than anything that had previously existed.

Wells, of course, hadn't the foggiest notions of the detailed workings of an atomic bomb. Forty years later, however, Cleve Cartmill wrote a story, "Deadline" (*Astounding Science Fiction*, March 1944), that described some of the engineering details of the atomic bomb so accurately that the government began an investigation into the matter. After all, World War II was still on and atomic bomb research was super-secret.

Cartmill was not a magician. The fact of uranium fission had been announced in 1939 and enough details were published, before secrecy was clamped down, to make it possible for Cartmill to write his story.

Does that mean that science fiction writers do nothing remarkable at all?

We needn't go that far. If it weren't remarkable, then

anyone could do it. Sherlock Holmes, in Conan Doyle's famous stories, was forever astounding Dr. Watson with his accurate analyses. When Watson begged for an explanation and Holmes gave it, Watson would say, "Oh, yes, I see how you did that. That was very simple, actually." To which Holmes would reply, "Of course, it's very simple—*after I explain it.*"

Then, too, the really important predictions that science fiction writers make are not the technological advances—which are trivial—but the consequences of those advances.

For instance, in 1880, it wouldn't have been in the least difficult to foresee a practical automobile. Stories might well have been written about such things, on the lines of "Dick Daring and his Horseless Carriage." All the excitement would lie in whether young Dick Daring would make it work; whether the villainous stagecoach interests would thwart him; whether he would rescue the pretty heroine by driving his new machine to the far place where she was imprisoned, and so on.

Trivia! All trivia!

The competent science fiction writer today would deal, not with the horseless carriage, but with its consequences. Won't the automobile mean the decentralization of the city and the growth of suburbs? Won't it mean a network of paved highways? Won't it mean traffic policemen and parking problems? Won't it mean air pollution?

Actually, there were no science fiction stories that predicted these consequences of the automobile, which is a pity. If some clever writer had written a sufficiently popular story about parking problems and air pollution, it might have driven governmental leaders to think about such things before we were overwhelmed by them.

But some rather amazing predictions of consequences *were* made. The most astonishing, in my opinion, appeared in "Solution Unsatisfactory" by Robert A. Heinlein under the pseudonym Anson Macdonald (*Astounding Science Fiction*, May 1941).

The story was written before Pearl Harbor but Heinlein did not predict American involvement in World War II. In the story, he *did* predict, however, the establishment of the Manhattan Project, and the development of a nuclear weapon. He was wrong in his details, but he was right in essence. Even more amazing, he went on to predict the nuclear stalemate that would exist after World War II, and got that quite correct.

If world leaders had foreseen the stalemate as clearly as Heinlein, postwar history might possibly have been considerably different.

In another story by Heinlein, "Blowups Happen" (*Astounding Science Fiction*, September 1940), there was an astonishingly vivid description of a nuclear power plant and the nerve-racking attempts to keep it from destroying or polluting the environment. Again Heinlein was wrong in his details, but correct in essence—two years before the first nuclear reactor was made to work.

Similarly correct in essence, similarly sound in science, was another treatment of the theme of danger in a nuclear power station—"Nerves" by Lester del Rey (*Astounding Science Fiction*, September 1942).

There is also the curious prediction of certain consequences of space exploration.

Through all the tales of trips to the Moon, it was always assumed that mankind would be enthusiastic. Every exciting new space feat in fiction had mankind cheering; there was never any question of opposition.

In the July 1939 issue of *Astounding Science Fiction*, however, there was a story called "Trends" in which the focus was upon popular opposition to space exploration. All the details were wrong, but for the first time in the history of mankind (as far as I know) it was suggested that many people would not be interested in reaching the Moon, but would prefer mankind to tend to its business on Earth.

The story, as it happens, was written by a nineteen-year-old science fiction novice named Isaac Asimov.

Was I, then, so much smarter than anyone else? Not at all! That year I was helping a sociology professor track down references for a book he was writing in social resistance to technological innovations. It occurred to me that if there were people who objected to every single technological advance in man's history, from the introduction of metal and of writing, to the development of the airplane, why shouldn't there be people who opposed space exploration?

Absurdly simple, as Dr. Watson would say—once I put it on paper.

Some predictions are forced by the exigencies of plotting and no one is more surprised than the science fiction writer when it turns out that he has hold of something.

For instance, once Einstein showed that the speed of light was as fast as anything material could possibly travel, a terrible handicap was placed on the science fiction writer. Light travels at 186,282 miles per second, which is enormous by earthly standards, but is a mere crawl on the cosmic scale. It would take so long to reach even fairly near stars that tales on a galactic scale become hopelessly complicated.

To get away from our dull solar system, in which only Earth is truly fit for human habitation and where the existence of any other intelligent beings is in the highest degree unlikely, we have to get round Einstein's speed limit. The usual device is to imagine some other universe where the speed limit does not hold. We then travel to a distant star by way of the other universe—through "hyperspace."

Then, in the 1960s, theoretical physicists pointed out that it was thoroughly consistent with Einstein's theory to suppose there might be particles that *always* traveled faster than the speed of light up to any speed at all, but which could never travel *slower* than light. These particles were called "tachyons" and the concept of a tachyon-universe arose that was quite like the science-fictional hyperspace, to the delight of us all.

Again, it is possible to make predictions which have not yet come true, but which seem so plausible and logical that quite serious scientists accept them as reasonably likely to come true some day.

Consider robots! The notion of mechanical men stretches back to ancient Greece, and probably to prehistoric times, too. Usually, such robots are pictured as threatening; as without human souls or emotions; as driven by a need to destroy.

The modern science fiction writer, however, is less apt to take such a melodramatic attitude. A mechanical man is no more intrinsically threatening than any other mechanical device. After all, any machine can kill. A man can trip and accidentally fall on a knife he may be holding. The automobile kills 50,000 Americans each year.

It is necessary, therefore, to build safety devices. A knife has a handle and a scabbard; an automobile has bumpers, safety glass, and seat belts.

Why not, then, build robots with safety devices? Why not design their pseudo-human intelligence in such a way as to fill it with love. Early tales of gentle and lovable robots were "Helen O'Loy" by Lester del Rey (*Astounding Science Fiction*, December 1938) and "I, Robot" by Eando Binder (*Amazing Stories*, January 1939).

In 1939, however, I myself, went into greater detail. For the first time in history (as far as I know) the prospective behavior of robots was expressed in simple and explicit "laws," as follows:

> 1. *A robot may not injure a human being, or, through inaction, allow a human being to come to harm.*
> 2. *A robot must obey the orders given it by human beings except where such orders would conflict with the First Law.*
> 3. *A robot must protect its own existence except where such protection would conflict with the First or Second Law.*

I wrote a number of short stories and novels based on these laws of "robotics" (a term I invented) and these proved quite popular (see the previous article).

Now, robots in the science fictional sense do not yet exist, but almost everyone admits they can and may someday exist. Once we have a computer that is as compact as the human brain and has a respectable fraction of its capacity and versatility, an intelligent robot is at once possible. And when it is (I am told by people who work in the field) something like my Three Laws of Robotics will surely be involved.

It is rather odd to think that in centuries to come, I may be remembered (if I am remembered at all) only for having laid the conceptual groundwonk for a science which in my own time was non-existent.

But at that, my fate would not be as queer as that of

the British science fiction writer Arthur C. Clarke. Back in 1948, he wrote a scientific article (not a science fiction story) in which he described how satellites could be placed in orbit about the Earth in such a way as to serve as efficient communications relays.

Although he wrote a decade before the first satellite was placed in orbit, his analysis was completely accurate. Communications satellites now exist, placed precisely as he advised. He has frequently sighed over his short-sightedness in not trying to patent some of his notions.

It is also Arthur C. Clarke who is responsible for the motion picture *2001*. While the details of the space station and the lunar base shown in that picture have not yet come true, there is little doubt that they will, provided mankind does not abandon space exploration altogether. What's more, when the real thing is established, and real photographs are made of the result, I doubt if they will be as clear, as beautiful, and as authentic in appearance, as those in the motion picture.

Naturally, predictions are most successful in the more elementary sciences: astronomy and physics. There one deals with bodies that can be treated as simple structures following simple laws that have been completely worked out.

Chemistry is harder to work with and biology still harder. Even so, science fiction has scored some successes there.

It doesn't take much, for instance, to realize that the population is increasing, and has been throughout history. As far back as 1798, Malthus predicted some of the dire consequences thereof. It is only in the last decade, however, that people have truly become aware of the threat to the quality of the environment that is posed by unrestricted population growth.

Yet well before the current understanding of the ecological crisis, a powerful and dramatic picture of an overcrowded planet was drawn in "Gravy Planet" by Frederik Pohl and Cyril Kornbluth (*Galaxy*, June, July, and August 1952).

Medical advances also have been predicted. I wrote a story about a heart transplant before one had been carried through, but by the time it appeared, Christian

Barnard had made it fact. Brain transplants had also been dealt with and those have not yet come to pass, really.

Cyril Kornbluth is responsible for two medical s.f. stories that live in memory. In "The Marching Morons" (*Galaxy*, April 1951) he pictured a world in which medical advances had succeeded in keeping so many people alive, whom unrestricted competition would have killed off, that the human race had degenerated in intelligence. A tiny proportion of intelligent people was desperately trying to keep society working.

On a smaller scale, "The Little Black Bag" (*Astounding Science Fiction*, July 1950) pictured doctors as morons, thanks to the developing use in medicine of computers and "miracle drugs." In their little black bags, doctors used small computers that analyzed symptoms and directed the use of this hypodermic or that, each filled with an appropriate drug.

But I repeat, now, in closing, that all these predictions, however accurate and amazing they may be, are not our business. They are merely the side effects of our efforts to tell interesting and plausible stories outside the background of the humdrum world of every day.

And when our ideas will only work if we make use of the scientifically impossible that, as far as we know, can never come true—such as time travel and anti-gravity—why, believe me, we do that, too, and without the tiniest compunction or remorse, provided only that we make it *sound* plausible.

THE SERIOUS SIDE OF SCIENCE FICTION

When I was a young man, fresh into my teens, I discovered I had a serious disease that earned me a great deal of opprobrium. I was a science fiction addict, and that meant I was an escapist.

This wasn't the only way of escaping by way of trashy reading. There were detective stories, and western stories, and horror stories, and spy stories, and war stories, and even (for those strange creatures called girls) love stories. But of all the varieties of cheap fiction, the escapiest of all, and therefore the most to be condemned by hard-headed realists, was science fiction.

Where science fiction was concerned, one escaped, in a pretty literal sense, right out of this world. Other pulp fiction trash dealt with subjects that were at least partly connected with reality. The Shadow dealt with crime, for instance, while G-8 (and his Battle Aces) were involved in World War I.

But Mars? And death rays? Come *on*.

So I huddled close to other teen-agers like myself and felt trapped in an alien and unsympathetic world.

Now I am no longer a teen-ager and when I look back over the time lapse of a generation, I can only laugh—with maybe a trace of bitterness.

Would you like to know how we escaped? Well, when all the non-science-fiction-reading youngsters were facing the hard realities of baseball and the first cigarette, and all the adults were grimly betting on the horses and yelling at each other, we were reading stories about rocket trips to the Moon, about space stations and overpopula-

SOURCE: "The Serious Side of Science Fiction" appeared in *Smithsonian* as "Science fiction, an aid to science, forsees the future," May 1970.

tion, about guided missiles and computers, about nuclear bombs and ruined planets.

Our "escape" consisted of having to worry about the problems and conditions of 1970 ever since 1930. You can call that escape if you want to, but, personally, I feel terribly cheated.

Our world is now future-oriented, you see, in the sense that the rate of change has become so rapid that we can no longer wait until a problem is upon us to work out the solution. If we do, then there is no real solution, for by the time one has been worked out and applied, change has progressed still further and our solution no longer makes sense at all. The change must be anticipated *before* it happens.

The trouble is that though the world is future-oriented, people aren't. For uncounted generations change has been so slow in the things that really counted, that preparation in advance was not necessary. A whole library of aphorisms can be quoted *against* the condition of future-orientation—

"Don't count your chickens until they're hatched."

"Don't cross the bridge until you come to it."

"Never trouble trouble till trouble troubles you."

And, of course, most prestigious of all is "Take therefore no thought for the morrow: for the morrow shall take thought for the things of itself. Sufficient unto the day is the evil thereof." That is from the Sermon on the Mount (Matthew 6:34).

So because we have never, as a species, taken thought for the morrow, we find ourselves now with a population we do not support, which is increasing with explosive force to a population we can not support. We find ourselves with nuclear war hanging forever over our head and with the more insidious death by pollution closing in upon us.

We are, in short, in the middle of a deepening nightmare. Since we have so long thought that sufficient unto the day is the evil thereof, the evil of *this* day *now* is more than we can bear.

There have, of course, always been individuals who have looked into the future with varying degrees of dread and hope and have tried to warn their fellowmen. Their efforts usually failed, and both legend and history are littered with the tales of prophets whose reward was mocking laughter—from Noah and Cassandra right down to Winston Churchill.

As far as I know, though, there has never been in all of world history until today, the concept of professional futurism as a way of life. And this arose first not among professional scientists or economists or historians (except for occasional individuals) but in the field of literature. The twentieth century saw the development of a flourishing subsection of literature devoted entirely to conjuring up visions of the future.

It was the world's misfortune that it did not take the idea of science fiction seriously. So strong was the non-seriousness that even science fiction writers themselves dared not be too serious about what they were saying.

Back in 1939, I published a story that dealt with the first flight around the Moon and back, an event I placed in 1973. I didn't *really* believe it would happen by then—let alone four years earlier.

Yet even though science fiction was not taken seriously by the general public, or very seriously by most of its readers and writers, it had its effect. Trips to the Moon and beyond were the chief staple of science fiction all through the 1920s and afterward and this was important. We accomplished something with all our talk of spaceships.

We were laughed at, of course, by all the serious non-escapist practical men of the world, but the notion penetrated. Buck Rogers and Flash Gordon, plus assorted lesser comic strips, presented the notion to the very young. Cheap movies presented it to those who couldn't or didn't read. The very sneers evoked by the suggestion of space travel was an announcement that the suggestion existed.

Thus, when the notion of flights to the Moon was brought before the public seriously, it turned out to be something that people had heard of. It had been laughed at, yes, but it had been heard of. And something ridiculous, but familiar, is far more easily accepted than something utterly unheard of.

The proof of the acceptance is dramatic, for not only is there an appreciation of the fact that we have walked on the Moon, but a readiness to consider the matter still farther.

There was once a time when I wrote of colonies on the Moon, and the only place I could have such outlandish nonsense published was in science fiction magazines. Now I write of colonies on the Moon in very much the same way—and the articles are published by the New York *Times.*

My science fiction comrades and I haven't changed, but the rest of the world has; and we have helped bring about that change.

It's a pity we couldn't do it faster and better but alas for the inertia of humanity, it takes the lever of Archimedes to move mankind.

All the plagues that threaten us with doom today; from the arsenals of horror bombs and nightmare germs, to the pollution that is poisoning our air and water; from the stripping of earth's resources to the loss of human dignity; from the tensions of packing crowds to the lunacies of human prejudice; all, all, all have been treated at length and over and over from every aspect in science fiction, at a time when all other varieties of fiction dealt with trivia only, by comparison.

And *we* are escapists?

But that part of our job is done. We didn't do it well enough. We didn't do it quickly enough. The task was too great; the human population was too numerous, too set in its ways, too determined on its folly, too stubbornly intent on avoiding the uncomfortable, too obstinate in finding sufficient unto the day the evil thereof.

—Yet, never mind. Too little and too late, but what we could do, we have done.

The meeting of the American Association for the Advancement of Science, held in Boston on December 26–31, 1969, had as its theme, iterated over and over and over, the need of science to face the gathering doom of the future. I was at the meeting and on several of the panels and repeatedly we agonized over the population problem, over the coming starvation, over the collecting poisons, over the pending bombs.

Good heavens, I never heard anything sound so much like a science fiction fan gathering of the 1930s.

Very well, men of science, take over. We have roused *you* at least; now see if you can rouse the rest of the world before the first tolling strokes of the midnight of disaster wake them to the unmistakable horror.

And what can science fiction do to help in this, now that we are respectable and that we are recognized as the harbingers of change? Are there any concrete and specific ways in which we can help bring about the necessary change?

There are, indeed, in my opinion, several ways in which science fiction can contribute—on the assumption that what is basically needed is more intelligent science and more foresighted scientists.

I consider that assumption an inevitably correct one. To be sure, it is the misuse of science and the unseeing enthusiasm of scientists that have brought us to our present plight. Undoubtedly, but for the advances in medical science, from antitoxins to insecticides, from anesthesia to antibiotics, the death rate would be as high as it ever was and population would be that much less a problem. Undoubtedly, but for the mechanization of agriculture, industry, and transportation, we would still have our famines to cull the population further, and oil and coal would stay in the ground so that the pollution that accompanies their burning would not be here.

But do we really want to go back? The price of going back is the death of nine tenths of ourselves and the loss of ten tenths of our technology. Anyone for the Stone Age?

To cure our ills, while keeping what we have, requires more science and more intelligent science. You may wish that a wave of the wand would restore Earth to some never-never pastoral paradise, but wishing will not make it so, despite Disney. You will have to try science.

And to have more and better science, we need more and better scientists, for science is a creation of scientists and has no independent existence.

How do we go about recruiting scientists? How can we persuade youngsters to take up science? A science education isn't easy and neither is a scientific career. To those who are born enthusiasts, this doesn't matter, but, unfortunately, there aren't enough born enthusiasts to supply us with all the scientists we are going to need. We must tap the much larger supply of youngsters who, *properly stimulated*, will become enthusiastic scientists but who, without proper stimulation, will become, perhaps, advertising copywriters instead.

Isn't science fiction a natural stimulant? I have never counted the letters I have received from young readers who have told me that as a result of reading my science fiction they plan to become scientists someday—but they have been many. I am sure that every other science fiction writer of note has received a similar set of letters. I am sure that for every youngster who begins to yearn for science as a result of reading science fiction and writes a letter to say so, there are ten who yearn, but *don't* write to us to say so.

It works the other way around, too. I have estimated that only one American in 400 has ever read any of my science fiction, but in the scientific circles I frequent at least half have. It would seem, then, that the habit of science fiction reading is perhaps two hundred times as common among scientists as among the general public. It is unavoidable, then, that a number of those scientists may have been encouraged to enter the field through their reading. (Actually, I know specific cases where this is so, but the gentlemen involved may not care to have it publicized, so I will content myself with one safe example—science fiction stimulated *me* to enter science.)

Aside from a generalized stimulation, science fiction can serve as a definite educational device. Good science fiction generally has some scientific theme which may be handled with great rigor, or with varying degrees of elasticity. Ideally, the theme should be handled rigorously, but even the violation of a natural law in a science fiction story can be useful, if it is handled by a writer who knows science.

Consider, for instance, the Second Law of Thermodynamics. It insists on the inevitable and inexorable increase in disorder with time. This pessimistic law is a hard one to grasp in all its aspects and even scientists stumble over it. Yet so fundamental is it that C. P. Snow has stated that an understanding of the Second Law is to science what an understanding of the plays of Shakespeare is to the humanities.

In that case, ought we not teach Second Law in junior high school at the same time that we begin to acquaint youngsters with Shakespeare? And how can we do that?

One way might be to get him to read a story by Walter S. Tevis, entitled "The Big Bounce," which appeared in the February 1958 issue of *Galaxy Science Fiction.* It dealt with an object made of a substance so elastic that when it bounced it rose higher than the height from which it had fallen. Then it would fall from the new higher height and would bounce still higher and so on and so on.

Naturally, it was necessary to keep it from bouncing at all, for even an initial quiver might lead to disastrous results. It did; the bouncing object got away from its constraint and began to bounce. Eventually it was bouncing a mile high and was striking the ground with bulletlike force.

But the energy of the bounce had to come from somewhere and it came from the internal heat of the material. As it bounced, the temperature of the object dropped until it froze hard enough to become brittle. At a final collision with the earth, it broke into a million pieces.

Very well. The fact that the energy of motion of the bouncing ball was derived from its heat content is in agreement with the law of conservation of energy, which happens to be the First Law of Thermodynamics. Nevertheless, the conversion of heat into motion in the manner described violates the Second Law.

A junior high school student in general science set to reading this story couldn't help wondering whether a rubber ball might possibly be so constructed as to bounce higher and higher. If not, why not? The story is just the sort of thing that will make the student *want* to know about the Second Law and no amount of external pounding can duplicate the effect of a stimulated internal yearning.

Properly used science fiction is an educational resource that is just beginning to be tapped in our school systems. If teachers will rid themselves of the notion that science fiction is nothing more than "escape literature," the tapping can be made more efficient to the benefit of all.

But science fiction can serve others than youngsters. It is not students only that ought to know about science these days. Every intelligent, concerned layman ought to take science seriously.

After all, the dangers that face the world can, every one of them, be traced back to science. The salvations that may save the world will, every one of them, be traced back to science. The non-scientist, then, must look to science for either destruction or safety, and he has every right, every *duty*, to understand as much about science as possible so that he might understand the potentialities for both destruction and safety and lend his personal weight in the direction of safety.

I might further point out that the scientific techniques that will lead to safety will cost money—lots of it—more money than can possibly be justified by anything but the fact that the alternative is holocaust. The layman ought to want to understand what his money is being spent on so that he might lend his personal weight toward its use in the most efficient manner.

Then, too, consider the scientist himself. Unfortunately, science has grown so large and so all-embracing that it is absolutely impossible for any one scientist to grasp it all in sufficient depth to lead the way to further advances in every direction. He is doing well if he knows enough about one ultranarrow segment of science to do constructive research in it alone; and even then, so intense must be his concentration in that field that he may well end by knowing very little of any other field.

This can hamper research, for it often happens that advances in one field can be encouraged in unexpected and useful directions by knowledge of other seemingly unrelated fields.

It would seem to me, then, that scientists and laymen both need to learn about science under present-day conditions. I don't suggest science fiction for the purpose (though they are welcome to read it), because I should hope that concerned adults, whether in science or not, will not need the sugar coating of fiction. Whether they read science fiction or not, they should welcome, in addition, the greater information density of the straightforward exposition of science.

But how are we to get good science exposition? Of all the branches of literature, surely science exposition is the trickiest.

One essential requirement for anyone hoping to write effectively on science for the general public is, obviously, a keen and thorough grasp of at least the basics of the various branches of science. That usually cannot be done without an extensive education (either in school or outside) in the field.

Another essential requirement, just as obviously, is the ability to write well and the capacity to explain subtle difficulties in a clear and lucid fashion without loss of accuracy. And that is a talent one doesn't pick up at every street corner, either.

The trouble is that the two requirements rarely overlap. A scientist does not necessarily have a talent for good and clear writing. Such a talent would be helpful to him but it is not essential, and the fact is that few scientists can write well, or even easily. Many a scientist who can conduct the most elegant experiments without a false move is driven to drink at the thought of having to write up those experiments in even the most stilted English.

Then, on the other hand, a naturally talented writer is likely to concentrate on writing and it is not at all probable that he will just happen to gain a thorough scientific education.

Where, then, are we going to get the science writers we need in a world where the translation of science from one scientist to another and from all scientists to laymen will be essential? There is always the possibility that a newspaper will order its music critic to bone up on science —and get a first-class science writer as a result. Yet we are sure to want a more certain source of supply.

May I point out, then, that the field of science fiction is the *only* field that has the same two essential requirements that science writing does.

The science fiction writer has to be able to write well if he is to be published at all; and he has to have a feeling for science, a love of its essence, and an understanding of many of its details, if he is going to write *good* science fiction.

It is not surprising, then, that a number of science fiction writers have, under the stress of contemporary facts of life, switched to straight science writing and done well at it. (My none-too-humble self is an example.)

I hope, then, that science fiction will continue to be a recruting ground for science writers, and for scientists, too, and even for scientific concepts for which the rest of the world is not quite ready. Then, someday in the future, when the world looks back upon its narrow escape (I earnestly trust) from doom, some of the credit may fall upon that ridiculous escapist field of literature—science fiction.

A LITERATURE OF IDEAS

It is odd to be asked whether science fiction is a literature of ideas. Far from doubting that it is, I would like to suggest that it is the *only* literature of relevant ideas, since it is the only literature that, at its best, is firmly based on scientific thought.

Of the products of the human intellect, the scientific method is unique. This is not because it ought to be considered the only path to Truth; it isn't. In fact, it firmly admits it isn't. It doesn't even pretend to define what Truth (with a capital *T*) is, or whether the word has meaning. In this it parts company with the self-assured thinkers of various religious, philosophical and mystical persuasions who have drowned the world in sorrow and blood through the conviction that they and they alone own Truth.

The uniqueness of Science comes in this: the scientific method offers a way of determining the False. Science is the only gateway to proven error. There have been Homeric disputes in the history of science, and while it could not be maintained that either party was wholly right or had the key to Truth, it could be shown that the views of at least one of the sides were at variance with what seemed to be the facts available to us through observation.

Pasteur maintained alcholic fermentation to be the product of living cells; Liebig said, No. Liebig, in the mid-nineteenth century context of observation, was proved wrong; his views were abandoned. Newton advanced a brilliantly successful picture of the Universe, but it failed in certain apparently minor respects. Einstein advanced

SOURCE: "A Literature of Ideas" appeared in *Intellectual Digest* as "When Aristotle Fails, Try Science Fiction," December 1971. Copyright © 1971 by Communications/Research/Machines, Inc.

another picture that did not fail in those respects. Whether Einstein's view is True is still argued, and may be argued for an indefinite time to come, but Newton's view is False. There is no argument about the latter.

Compare this with other fields in which intellectuals amuse themselves. Who has ever proved a school of philosophy to be False? When has one religion triumphed over another by debate, experiment, and observation? What rules of criticism can settle matters in such a way that all critics will agree on a particular work of art or literature?

A man without chemical training can speak learnedly of chemistry, making use of a large vocabulary and a stately oratorical style—and he will be caught out almost at once by any bright teen-ager who has studied chemistry in high school.

The same man, without training in art, can speak learnedly of art in the same way, and while his ignorance may be evident to some real expert in the field, no one else would venture to dispute him with any real hope of success.

There is an accepted consensus in science, and to be a plausible fake in science (before any audience not utterly ignorant in the field) one must learn that consensus thoroughly. Having learned it, however, there is no need to be a plausible fake.

In other fields of intellectual endeavor there is, however, no accepted consensus. The different schools argue endlessly, moving in circles about each other as fad succeeds fashion over the centuries. Though individuals may be unbelievably eloquent and sincere, there is, short of the rack and the stake, no decision ever. Consequently, to be a plausible fake in religion, art, politics, mysticism, or even any of the "soft" sciences such as sociology (to anyone not utterly expert in the field) one need only learn the vocabulary and develop a certain self-assurance.

It is not surprising, then, that so many young intellectuals avoid the study of science and so many old intellectuals are proud of their ignorance of science. Science has a bad habit of puncturing pretension for all to see. Those who value their pretension to intellect and are insecure over it are particularly well advised to avoid science.

To be sure, when a scientist ventures outside his field and pontificates elsewhere, he is as likely to speak nonsense as anyone else. (And there may be those unkind enough to say I am demonstrating this fact in this very article.) However, since nonsense outside science is difficult or impossible to demonstrate, the scientist is at least no worse than anyone else in this respect.

If we consider Literature (with a capital *L*) as a vehicle of ideas, we can only conclude that, by and large, the ideas with which it is concerned, are the same ideas that Homer and Aeschylus struggled with. They are well worth discussing, I am sure; even fun. There is enough there to keep an infinite number of minds busy for an infinite amount of time, but they weren't settled and aren't settled.

It is these "eternal verities" that are precisely what science fiction doesn't deal with. Science fiction deals with change. It deals with the possible advance in science and with the potential changes—even in those damned eternal verities—this may bring about in society.

As it happens, we are living in a society in which all the enormous changes—the *only* enormous changes—are being brought about by science, and its application to everyday life. Count up the changes introduced by the automobile, by the television set, by the jet plane. Ask yourself what might happen to the world of tomorrow if there is complete automation, if robots become practical, if the disease of old age is cured, if hydrogen fusion is made a workable source of energy.

The fact is that no previous generation has had to face the possibility and the potentialities of such enormous and such rapid change. No generation has had to face the appalling certainty that if the advance of science isn't judged accurately, if the problems of tomorrow aren't solved before they are upon us, then that advance and those problems will overwhelm us.

This generation, then, is the first that can't take as its primary concern the age-old questions that have agitated all deep thinkers since civilization began. Those questions are still interesting, but they are no longer of first importance, and any literature that deals with them (that is, any literature but science fiction) is increasingly irrelevant.

If this thought seems too large to swallow, consider a rather simple analogy: The faster an automobile is moving, the less the driver can concern himself with the eternal beauties of the scenery and the more he must involve himself with the trivial obstacles in the road ahead.

And that is where science fiction comes in.

Not all science fiction, of course. Theodore Sturgeon, one of the outstanding practitioners in the field, once said to a group of fans, "Nine tenths of science fiction is crud." There was a startled gasp from the audience and he went on, "But why not? Nine tenths of everything is crud." Including mainstream literature, of course.

It must be understood, then, that I am talking of the one tenth (or possibly less) of science fiction that is not crud.

This means you will have to take my word for what follows if you are not yourself an experienced science fiction fan. The non-fan or even the mild fan with occasional experiences in the field is almost certain to have been exposed only to the crud, which is, alas, of high visibility. He sees the comic strips, the monster movies, the pale TV fantasies. He never sees the better magazines and paperbacks where the science fiction writers of greatest repute are to be found.

So let's see—

In 1940, there was endless talk about Fascism, Communism, and Democracy; talk that must have varied little in actual content concerning the conflicts of freedom and authority, of race, religion, and patriotism, from analogous discussions carried on in fifth- and fourth-century B.C. Greece. In 1940, when the Nazis were everywhere victorious, such talk might well have been considered important. It might plausibly have been argued that these discussions dealt with the great issues of the century.

And what was science fiction talking about? Well, in the May 1941 issue of *Astounding Science Fiction*, there appeared a story (written in 1940) called "Solution Unsatisfactory" by Anson Macdonald (real name, Robert A. Heinlein) which suggested that the United States might put together a huge scientific project designed to work out a nuclear weapon that would end World War II. It then went on, carefully and thoughtfully, to consider the nuclear stalemate into which the world would consequently be thrown. At about the same time, John W. Campbell, Jr., editor of the magazine, was saying, in print, that the apparent issues of the war were, in a sense, trivial, since nuclear energy was on the point of being tamed, and that this would so change the world that what then seemed life-and-death differences in philosophy would prove unimportant.

Well, who were the thinkers who, in 1940, were considering the nuclear stalemate? What generals were planning for a world in which each major power had nuclear bombs? What political scientists were thinking of a situation in which no matter how hot the rhetoric between competing great powers, any war between them would have to stay cold—not through consideration of fine points of economics or morals, but over the brutal fact that a nuclear stalemate cannot be broken, short of world suicide?

These thoughts, which were, after all, the truly relevant ideas on 1940's horizon, were reserved to science fiction writers.

Nowadays, articles on the ecology are in great demand, and it is quite fashionable to talk of population and pollution, and of all the vast changes they may bring about. It is easy to do so now. Rachel Carson started it, most people would say, with her *Silent Spring*. But did anyone precede her?

Well, in the June, July, and August 1952 issues of *Galaxy*, there appeared a three-part serial, "Gravy Planet," by Frederik Pohl and Cyril Kornbluth, which is a detailed picture of an enormously overpopulated world from almost every possible aspect. In the February 1956 issue of *Fantasy and Science Fiction*, there appeared "Census Takers" by Frederik Pohl, in which it is (ironically) suggested that the time will come when one of the chief duties of census takers would be to shoot down every tenth (or fourteenth, or eighth, depending on the population increase in the past decade) person they count, as the only means of keeping the population under control.

What sociologist (not now, but twenty years ago) was clamoring in print, over the overwhelming effect of population increase? What government functionary (not now, but twenty years ago) was getting it clearly through his head that there existed no social problem that didn't depend for its cure, *first of all*, on a cessation of population growth? (Surely not President Eisenhower, who piously stated that if there was one problem in which the government must not interfere, it was the matter of birth control. He changed his mind later; I'll give him credit for that.) What psychologist or philosopher (not now, but twenty years ago) was pointing out that if population continued to increase, there was no hope for human freedom or dignity under any circumstances.

Such thoughts were pretty largely reserved, twenty years ago, to science fiction writers.

There are many people (invariably those who know nothing about science fiction) who think that because men have reached the Moon, science has caught up with science fiction and that science fiction writers now have "nothing to write about."

They would be surprised to know that the mere act of reaching the Moon was outdated in science fiction in the 1920s and that no reputable science fiction writer has been excited by such a little thing in nearly half a century.

In the July 1939 issue of *Astounding Science Fiction*, there appeared a story called "Trends," written by myself while I was still a teen-ager. It did indeed deal with the first flights to the Moon, which I put in the period between 1973 and 1978. (I underestimated the push that would be given rocket research by World War II.) My predictions on the details of the beginnings of space exploration were ludicrously wrong at every point, but none of that represented the point of the story, anyway.

What made the story publishable was the social background I presented for the rocket flights. In my story, I pictured strong popular opposition to the notion of space travel.

Many years later it was pointed out to me that in all the voluminous literature about space travel, either fictional or non-fictional, no such suggestion had ever before been broached. The world was always pictured as wildly and unanimously enthusiastic.

Well, where, in 1939, was there the engineer or the industrialist who was taking into serious account the necessity of justifying the expense and risk of space exploration? Where was the engineer or the industrialist who was soberly considering the possibility of space exploration?

Such thoughts were largely reserved for the science fiction writer and for a few engineers, who in almost every case, were science fiction fans—Willy Ley and Wernher von Braun, to name a couple.

And where does science fiction stand today?

It is more popular than ever and has gained a new respectability. Dozens of courses in it are being given in dozens of colleges. Literary figures have grown interested in it as a branch of the art. And, of course, the very growth in popularity tends to dilute and weaken it.

It has grown sufficiently popular and respectable, since the days of Sputnik, for people to wish to enter it as a purely literary field. And once that becomes a motive, the writers don't need to know science any more. To write purely literary science fiction, one returns to the "eternal verities" but surrounds them with some of the verbiage of science fiction, together with a bit of the stylistic experimentation one comes across in the mainstream, and with some of the explicit sex which is now in fashion.

And this is what some people in science fiction call the "new wave."

To me, it seems that the new wave merely attempts to reduce real science fiction to the tasteless pap of the mainstream.

New wave science fiction can be interesting, daring, even fascinating, if it is written well enough, but if the author knows no science, the product is no more valuable for its content of relevant ideas than is the writing outside science fiction.

Fortunately, the real science fiction—those stories that deal with scientific ideas and their impact on the future as written by someone knowledgeable in science—still exists and will undoubtedly continue to exist as long as mankind does (which, alas, may not be long).

This does not mean that every science fiction story is good prediction or is necessarily intended to be a prediction at all, in the first place; or that very good science fiction stories might not deal with futures that cannot reasonably be expected ever to come to pass.

That does not matter. The point is that the habit of looking sensibly toward the future, the habit of assuming change and trying to penetrate beyond the mere fact of change to its effect and to the new problems it will introduce, the habit of accepting change as now more important to mankind than those dreary eternal verities—is to be found only in science fiction, or in those serious nonfictional discussions of the future by people who, almost always, are or have been deeply interested in science fiction.

For instance, while ordinary literature deals merry-go-round-wise with the white-black racial dilemma in the United States, I await the science fiction story which will seriously consider the kind of society America might be attempting to rebuild *after* the infinitely costly racial war we are facing—a war which may destroy our world influence and our internal affluence. Perhaps such a story, sufficiently well thought out and well written, may force those who read it into a contemplation of the problem from a new and utterly relevant angle.

To see what I mean, ask yourself how many of those, North and South, who blithely talked abolition and secession in the 1850s in terms of pure rhetoric, might not have utterly changed their attitudes and gotten down to sober realities if they could have foreseen the exact nature of the Civil War and of the Reconstruction that followed, and have understood that none of the torture of the 1860s and 1870s would in the least solve the problem of white-and-black after all.

So read this magazine [*Intellectual Digest*] and others of the sort by all means, and follow the clash of stock ideas as an amusing intellectual game. Or read Plato or Sophocles and follow the same clash in more readable prose. But if you want the real ideas, the ideas that count today and may even count tomorrow, the ideas for which Aristotle offers little real help, nor Senator X nor Commissar Y either, then read science fiction.

AFTERWORD

One of the great values of being a writer is the automatic barrier you have against ulcers and frustrations. When

Intellectual Digest phoned and asked for an article, I begged off because I was loaded with a sizable backlog. Nevertheless, I suggested they write me and tell me what they had in mind and I would consider—

They wrote, and the gist of the letter was editorial wonder as to whether science fiction had any real ideas in it or if it was just a load of junk.

Naturally, I fired up and, under ordinary circumstances, would have fumed and made myself miserable.

No need, however. I simply swept everything off my desk and sat down to write the above article at a sitting with a little overlapping of earlier articles I had written. As you can see for yourself, it sounds considerably more angry than my other articles on the subject.

(Hmm, I wonder if *Intellectual Digest* counted on that reaction when they asked the question?)

THREE

AND...

THE SCIENTISTS' RESPONSIBILITY

(I am choosing the following as the last item in this collection of essays, partly because of its novelty. It is the only serious editorial I ever wrote addressed to the world outside science fiction. It was at the request of the editor of *Chemical and Engineering News.* I was entirely free to choose a subject of my choice and after some thought I decided to write something I felt most deeply—even desperately. And that, too, is why I want to end with it.)

I think it may be reasonably maintained that neither the United States nor any other nation can, by itself, solve the important problems that plague the world today. The problems that count today—the steady population increase, the diminishing of our resources, the multiplication of our wastes, the damage to the environment, the decay of the cities, the declining quality of life—are all interdependent and are all global in nature.

No nation, be it as wealthy as the United States, as large as the Soviet Union, or as populous as China, can correct these problems without reference to the rest of the world. Though the United States, for instance, brought its population to a firm plateau, cleaned its soil, purified its water, filtered its air, swept up its waste, and cycled its resources, all would avail it nothing as long as the rest of the world did none of these things.

These problems, left unsolved, will weigh us down under a steady acceleration of increasing misery with each passing year; yet to solve them requires us to think above the level of nationalism. No amount of local pride anywhere in the world; no amount of patriotic ardor on a

SOURCE: "The Scientists' Responsibility" appeared in *Chemical and Engineering News,* April 19, 1971.

less-than-all-mankind scale; no amount of flag waving; no prejudice in favor of some specific regional culture and tradition; no conviction of personal or ethnic superiority, can prevail against the cold equations. The nations of the world must co-operate to seek the possibility of mutual life, or remain separately hostile to face the certainty of mutual death.

Nor can the co-operation be the peevish agreement of haughty equals: each quick to resent slurs, eager to snuff out injustice to itself, and ready to profit at the expense of others. So little time is left and so high have become the stakes, that there no longer remains any profitable way of haggling over details, maneuvering for position, or threatening at every moment to pick up our local marbles and go home.

The international co-operation must take the form of a world government sufficiently effective to make and enforce the necessary decisions, and against which the individual nations would have neither the right nor the power to take up arms.

Tyranny? Yes, of course. Just about the tyranny of Washington over Albany; Albany over New York City; and New York City over me. Though we are each of us personally harried by the financial demands and plagued by the endless orders of the officialdom of three different levels of government, we accept it all, more or less stoically, under the firm conviction that life would be worse otherwise. To accept a fourth level would be a cheap price to pay for keeping our planet viable.

But who on Earth best realizes the serious nature of the problems that beset us? As a class, the scientists, I should think. They can weigh, most accurately and most judiciously, the drain on the world's resources, the effect of global pollution, the dangers to a fragmenting ecology.

And who on Earth might most realistically bear a considerable share of responsibility for the problems that beset us? As a class, the scientists, I should think. Since they gladly accept the credit for lowering the death rate and for industrializing the world, they might with some grace accept a good share of the responsibility for the less than desirable side effects that have accompanied those victories.

And who on Earth might be expected to lead the way in finding solutions to the problems that beset us? As a class, the scientists, I should think. On whom else can we depend for the elaboration of humane systems for limiting population, effective ways of preventing or reversing pollution, elegant methods of cycling resources? All this will clearly depend on steadily increasing scientific knowledge and on steadily increasing the wisdom with which this knowledge is applied.

And who on Earth is most likely to rise above the limitations of national and ethnic prejudice and speak in the name of mankind as a whole? As a class, the scientists, I should think. The nations of the world are divided in culture: in language, in religion, in tastes, in philosophy, in heritage—but wherever science exists at all, it is the same science; and scientists from anywhere and everywhere speak the same language, professionally, and accept the same mode of thought.

Is it not, then, as a class, to the scientists that we must turn to find leaders in the fight for world government?